A Tear of Love

A Tear of Love

Alene Roberts

Bonneville Books
Springville, Utah

ISBN: 1-55517-850-2
v. 1

Published by Bonneville Books,
an imprint of Cedar Fort, Inc.
925 N. Main Springville, Utah, 84663
www.cedarfort.com

Distributed by:

Cover design by Nicole Williams
Cover design © 2005 by Lyle Mortimer

Printed in the United States of America
10 9 8 7 6 5 4 3 2 1

Printed on acid-free paper

*d*edication
To Shirene

Other Books by Alene Roberts

Fragrance of Lilacs
A Rescued Heart
A Butterfly in Winter
It's Bliss
Pipit's Song
Heart of the Rose
Gustavia Browne

*a*cknowledgments

I want to thank my granddaughter Eliza Maria Laurizten for lending me her beautiful face for Casey.

Special thanks to Shirene, who read the manuscript for content and accuracy. Her suggestions and insights helped immensely. But more than anything, her enthusiasm for the book was invaluable.

I thank the outstanding and well-known writer Lee Nelson for reading the manuscript so quickly and giving me a written response that was both interesting and complimentary. Coming from a writer of such stature, the compliments are extra special to me.

I appreciate Michael Morris, managing editor of Cedar Fort, for the understanding and help he has given me on the editing of the manuscript. A big thanks also goes to everyone else at Cedar Fort. I appreciate their kindness, forthrightness, and professionalism.

Chapter One

*A lie once believed precludes all
evidence to the contrary.*
—Elliot D. Roberts

Jacob Seely Jacobson's long fingers curled into fists as he stared out the window at his beautiful daughter, Casey, limping painfully to her car. Gone were the tennis matches, the dancing, and the hiking she loved, leaving only weakness and pain.

Swiveling his large study chair around, he leaned forward, placed his elbows on the desk, and pressed his fingers into his temples, trying to ease the persistent headache. The disturbing conversation he'd just had with Casey brought back the nightmare and Casey's severely burned and mangled right leg. It felt as though his heart was being ripped out of his chest.

Anger boiled up in his throat like bile, but the object of his anger had moved beyond his reach. Her husband, Nick Carter, who had purposely caused the accident, had been killed.

The fact that Nick had been burned to death wasn't enough for Jacob. He wanted Nick to suffer as Casey had suffered during the long three years of their marriage. He wanted him to feel the agony Casey had felt from the burns that ran from her thigh to inches above her ankle—burns that were complicated by the deep gashes on her thigh and through muscles and tendons near her broken shinbone. He wanted Nick to feel the pain of the infections, the operations, the skin grafting, the painful therapy, and the two and a half years in and out of hospitals.

Instead, Nick continued to reach out from the grave,

causing even greater suffering. Though it had been three years since the accident, the authorities hadn't closed the investigation. Because Casey had been driving, the possibility that she could be indicted for negligent homicide hung like a black cloud over her head. What neither Jacob nor Casey could understand was why the delay? Why hadn't something been resolved by now? Before he could take a breath, his chest tightened with another spasm of anxiety. Were the results of this man's cruelty never to end?

All this had to have had a psychological effect upon Casey, but she had insisted she was all right. Many times he had watched her carefully, but the only clues he had were few and far between—a haunted expression, a passing look of fear when she didn't know he was watching. He had broached the subject of psychotherapy to her several times, but she adamantly insisted she was fine. Still, in his mind, she needed help and needed to talk to someone.

Casey had finally been able to go back to work six months ago. Hartner and Hart, an advertising agency in Scottsdale, which had always given her the bulk of her contracts, had allowed her to adjust slowly, starting with in-house photography until she had the strength to do a little outdoor work—her specialty. She had this period to adjust somewhat to normal life. Physically she was improving, but Jacob felt it was time for some emotional therapy. Impulsively, he decided to call Belle before he left town, make an appointment for Casey, and hope for the best.

His mind swept over the conversation with Casey and what she had come to talk to him about.

"How are you, Dad?" was her first question upon finding him in the study paying bills. She went around the desk, hugged him, and then studied his face. "I can see in your eyes that you have a headache."

He smiled at her intuitiveness and motioned for her to sit down. "The question is, how are *you*, Casey?"

She pulled a chair around close to his. "I'm doing okay, considering." She smiled, her large Dresden-blue eyes, so much like his mother's, were exceptionally expressive.

"How's the pain?"

"Day by day it's getting less."

"I'm going to the cabin for a few days. How about coming with me?"

"I wish I could, but I have some pressing work. Right now, I'm headed out to the desert to shoot some pictures." At his look of concern, she added, "Don't worry, Dad. I'll be all right. I can walk greater distances each time I go out. Just you wait, one of these days we'll go to the cabin and hike the hills like we used to." Then with an impish smile, she added, "And you'd better keep in shape, or I'll leave you in the dust."

"Oh yeah?" he said in the competitive banter they used to engage in before the accident.

"Yeah. But since you're forty-nine and practically decrepit, I might take pity on you and let you catch up once in a while."

He smiled tenderly at his daughter. "Thanks. That's mighty big of you. Now, what is it you wanted to talk with me about?"

"Oh, uh . . . I just wanted to see you—see how you were."

"Casey, what is it? You didn't come here just to ask me that. Has something happened?" His eyes sharpened and sudden lines of worry creased his face.

"Oh no, I'm fine." She impulsively reached out, touching his arm in a reassuring gesture. "It's not about me . . . at least not directly. Uh . . . would you believe it," she smiled ruefully, "now that I'm here, I'm not sure I'm ready to talk about it."

"Talk about what?" he asked, his voice more insistent. "Come on, Casey, give."

"It's . . .uh, about my friend, Tiffany. You remember her, don't you? I had lunch with her last week and again today." She took a deep breath before continuing. "Dad, she's in a situation so much like mine, an abusive marriage that seems to be getting worse. She's frightened and confused, and doesn't know what to do. I was wondering—"

Casey stopped in midthought. She opened her mouth as

though to continue but then closed it.

"Go on." Jacob studied his daughter's face and saw the grim backwash of memory in her eyes. He waited with growing uneasiness at what was coming next.

"Dad," she said at last, "I've had a lot of time to think about my marriage. Because of your example I recognized Nick's abusiveness and what it was doing to me. As you know, I kept hoping that I could fix it somehow, that he'd agree to go to marriage counseling with me. But what I didn't fully see and understand soon enough were the *weaknesses* that were *behind* the abuse. If I'd understood sooner, I think I could have used that understanding to safely get out of the marriage—before the accident."

"In my mind, Casey, Nick had a lot of weaknesses. Which ones are you referring to?"

"Well . . . after trying unsuccessfully to make my marriage work, I began watching Nick closely. Then about ten months before the accident, it came to me—almost like a revelation—his dominant weaknesses. He had a pathological need to appear perfect and in control at all times—a sick kind of pride. When this came to me, I began thinking, fantasizing ways I could use this against him—to disable him emotionally so he couldn't come after me if I left." She grimaced. "You'd be surprised at the crazy things I came up with, but . . ." She sighed. "I wasn't able to do anything about it before Nick acted."

She eyed her father apprehensively. "I wanted to discuss some of the ideas I had come up with. Maybe we could use some of them on Tiffany's husband. You know, to help Tiffany," she added in a small voice.

"Casey! This is not the time for you to become involved with someone else's spousal abuse problems. You're still healing yourself."

"I know. I'm not going to impulsively rush into anything, Dad."

"I don't want you to even crawl into anything. How can you possibly do more than you're already doing?"

"You know, maybe I'd better think it over some more before I discuss it with you in detail."

Jacob pushed his chair back abruptly, stood up and stared out the window, his hand furiously jingling the keys in his pocket. His back to her, he asked warily, "What do you mean by 'disable emotionally'? It sounds like wishful thinking. You can't be serious about this."

"I *am* serious, Dad, but I'd better think it over thoroughly first. I always tend to run to you with whatever's on my mind, no matter how impulsive the thought or how improbable, or how silly. I'm twenty-eight. It's about time I grew up a little isn't it?"

Jacob turned around smiling. "You've been grown up since you were a child. But what bothers me about this strange idea of yours is that you've always been an independent thinker to the point of being a little too daring—a rebel of sorts."

Casey put on an innocent face. "I can't imagine what you're talking about."

"For starters, even in high school, you were always a non-conformist."

Casey laughed. "How you do exaggerate. But to ease your worry, Dad, I'm not as brave as I used to be. I'd definitely need your support if I tried to help Tiffany."

Jacob exhaled with relief. "Well, good. Let me know when you've worked through this, and then come and pass it by me." He scrutinized her and then pointed a finger. "Don't do *anything* until you talk to me. Okay?"

"You don't trust me?" she teased. "I assure you, Dad, this is something I wouldn't think of doing without consulting you first. When are you leaving for Sedona?"

"Tomorrow morning I guess. If you can rearrange your work and come with me, give me a call."

"I will, Dad. I love you. See you soon."

Jacob sighed. It had been too short a visit. He stood up and stretched, debating whether to take something for his headache.

Aimlessly, he walked into the kitchen and then into the family room. The house, which was much too large for him now that he was alone, held wonderful memories of his years with Casey growing up, as well as memories of his wife, Silvia.

Silvia had pushed Casey's relationship with Nick, but she died a year after Casey and Nick were married. *Trust Sil to escape all the suffering!* he thought bitterly.

When he allowed himself to think about it, Silvia's death was still a shock. She was in New York playing the lead in Verdi's *La Traviata.* As the opera was ending and her voice was reaching a crescendo, filling the hall with heart-wrenching beauty, she suddenly collapsed. At first the audience thought it was part of the act, but he knew differently. He jumped up and quickly eased himself past people's knees, ran down the aisle and onto the stage.

In the ambulance he tried to talk to her, but there was no response. Eight hours later she died from a brain aneurysm. The doctors said that she probably had the weakness for many years—a time bomb waiting to go off. High blood pressure, exacerbated by singing operatic arias, had put stress on the artery.

Casey had planned to go with him to New York, but, as usual, Nick found a reason to prevent it, and she missed the last time her mother would ever perform. Casey was devastated. Silvia's demanding career as a renowned opera star took her away from home much of Casey's life and because of this, Casey needed her all the more.

On the other hand, Jacob's loneliness didn't feel much different with Silvia gone since she had been something like a ghost, wafting in and out of their lives. He'd had to be both mother and father to Casey all her growing up years. Besides, his feeling of helplessness to relieve Casey's pain and ease her fear of a possible indictment far surpassed his personal loneliness.

Walking slowly down the driveway of her father's home, Casey automatically rubbed her thigh. The damaged nerves stung with penetrating pain. After the last operation, the doctor said that nerve injuries are the slowest to heal. Day by day her leg was getting better, but the pain seemed to be increasing since her luncheon date with Tiffany.

Was she physically and emotionally ready to help someone else going through abuse? It seemed to bring back all the fear and tension she had experienced while living with Nick. Apparently stress affected the weakest part of the body—her leg—causing more pain. She could bear it though. After the racking torture she had endured in the burn center, this pain seemed mild.

Driving away, she headed toward the outlying Arizona desert to take some photographs for future ads to put in her file. Her mind hovered unwillingly over the day she met Nick at the country club. A friend of hers had introduced them, feeling they would have a lot in common. Nick was president of a local bank in Scottsdale, Arizona, and she had done the photography for one of their ad campaigns.

She was immediately drawn to Nick. He was six feet tall, blond, handsome, and charismatic. He was also smart and had a dry wit. She had dated many young men and none of them could hold a candle to the father she adored. Nick seemed to come closest.

She had been trying to forget the past and now Tiffany's problem was bringing it all back. Painfully, she recalled how her father had disliked Nick from the start. Nick had sensed his feelings and had convinced her that it was because she was "Daddy's little girl" and that her father simply didn't want to let her go. Thinking about it now, Nick had been so convincing it was frightening. In addition, her mother was enamored with Nick and pushed the relationship. Sadly, this had caused some arguments between her parents.

But Nick still haunted her. It wasn't over. She had recurring nightmares where she relived the last moments before his death—Nick grabbing the wheel and turning it over the embankment, sending the car careening down the slope into a couple of large trees that stopped the descent. She didn't remember the crash, the burning car, or being pulled out of it. Her father had related everything the police had told him. Apparently, though half-conscious and in a state of shock, she kept screaming over and over, "Nick kidnapped me! He had a gun! He forced me to drive!"

Because her rescuers had told the police of her accusations, the officers examined the tire tracks and saw no signs of braking, just tire tracks veering off the shoulder and down the hill. This corroborated Casey's hysterical accusations and the testimony of the witnesses, who happened to be coming from the opposite direction in time to see the car turn suddenly and go over the side of the road.

The two men called for help immediately and then went down, half running, half sliding, and managed to pull her out and far enough away from the car before it exploded. By then the flames had already engulfed her right pant leg, leaving it a mass of burned flesh. The men had applied a makeshift tourniquet to stem the flow of blood from the wounds. It wasn't long before she was airlifted to the nearest hospital.

Her father verified the kidnapping story, explaining that his daughter would never have left town without letting him know. Unknown to her, Nick had become a suspect when authorities found that someone had embezzled large sums of money from the bank. Because of this, the investigation of the accident and Nick's death came under the jurisdiction of the FBI. Casey shivered as she thought about the FBI finding and bagging Nick's charred remains. However, in all their searching they never found the gun.

Once Casey was out of intensive care, the FBI agents repeatedly questioned her, forcing her to relive the nightmare over and over. Because of the lack of evidence and her insistence that Nick had grabbed the wheel, she wasn't charged, but neither did the FBI close the case. She felt as though something dark and foreboding loomed just around the corner.

In spite of it all, she was simply glad to be alive. Nick had done her a favor. She didn't have to go to the police and try to get a restraining order when she left him, and she didn't have to live in fear that he would come after her.

She was determined to enjoy each moment and each hour of her freedom from Nick and from the hospital. At last she could really start living, going out into nature once again, photographing its beauty and basking in its serenity.

Turning off McDowell Road onto Ellsworth Road she entered Usery Mountain Park, located at the western end of the Goldfield Mountains. Finding a trailhead, she parked the car and put on her backpack, which carried the light reflectors, film, a variety of lenses, and the camera. She was too weak to carry a tripod, but since her hands were steady she didn't always need one.

Casey followed the sandy, foot-worn path, which curved gently around paloverde trees, saguaros, and bushes, stopping to take a picture here and there. The light was perfect. Only a few cottony strands of clouds drifted across the clear blue sky. As usual in the Phoenix area, April weather was delightful. The desert plants, trees, and grasses were green. The purple wolfberry, the orange fetid marigold, and the flat-topped pink buckwheat were blooming. Spring birds were breeding and calling to each other. A black-tailed gnatcatcher clinging to a limb sang its rapid series of *jee* notes on one pitch followed by a raspy *cheeh*. From somewhere close another one called back.

A pleasant breeze whipped by, blowing her loose silky pants—her "uniform" as she called them. Silk and nylon were the only fabrics that didn't rub on her scars. She paid to have several pants made of different colors so she could wear them everyday. Though her pants were not the "in thing," she wore the latest trend in tops, sometimes with light batiste overblouses that matched the pants.

She took several deep breaths of the clear fresh air, feeling grateful that she was able to walk well enough to be out in nature once again doing what she loved. She didn't even notice the growing fatigue in her leg. Finishing off the last of her film, she put the camera in the backpack and walked back down the trail toward her car.

Startled, she paused. About a hundred yards away, a man stood slightly concealed behind a creosote bush. Fear prickled down her spine. She hadn't seen any hikers along the path today. As far as she knew she was alone, except for the man who seemed to be furtively watching her.

She drew in a sharp breath and walked toward her car as quickly as she could. Feeling the man's eyes upon her, she was keenly aware of her limp. What was the matter with her? She should be used to people staring at her clumsy gait. Nervously she turned to look at him once more. He was too far away to recognize but close enough to see that there was nothing familiar about him. He had a head of dark hair and was wearing jeans and a blue shirt.

Relieved to get inside the car, she quickly locked the doors, not waiting for the automatic lock. Shoving the key into the ignition, she wheeled around and drove out the way she had come, scanning the rearview mirror, afraid that the man was following her. She shook her head. "I'm getting as paranoid as Nick was. The man was just curious, that's all," she muttered to herself. She drove north on Pima Freeway until she reached Scottsdale.

Arriving at the old concrete block building where she rented a two-room space she called her studio, she drove around back, braked with her left foot and turned off the motor. Learning to brake with her left foot had taken time, but now it had become natural.

She limped tiredly to the entrance feeling grateful that she had found this place. It was next door to the new multi-storied building that housed Hartner and Hart Advertising, one of the largest firms in the Southwest. Unlocking the door, she stepped in. Without turning on the light she navigated the clutter of props—tripods, rear-projection equipment, and assorted odds and ends used in the in-house photo sessions—to the small darkroom. She removed the film from her camera and then retrieved the developed pictures from a previous assignment and placed them in a manila envelope to take to the graphics director.

A four-foot wall between the two buildings forced her to walk along the driveway and around to the sidewalk that led her to the entrance of Hartner and Hart. Although they did all kinds of advertising, magazines, corporate identity, and logos were their specialty. Companies from all over the United States paid them hundreds of thousands of dollars for one logo. Casey felt fortunate that they considered her photography good enough to do contract work for them.

She entered the building and rode the elevator to the third floor. Reaching Vicky's desk, she handed her the manila envelope. "Hi, Vicky, these need to be put on Sy's desk first thing in the morning."

"You could hand them to him yourself right now," Vicky said grinning. "He wants to see you. He's meeting with some one, but he'll be through shortly."

"Oh. All right. Thanks." Casey seated herself in a chair nearby.

Vicky was the graphic director's secretary. She was an empty nester who had worked at the agency for years. Thin and bony with permed, shoulder-length, dyed brown hair, she always wore a big smile and oversize brown-rimmed glasses. Vicky was the only one on the third floor who hadn't acted differently toward her when she returned to work. She was her same warm, friendly self. The rest appeared to be affected by what they had read in the newspapers about her and her case. It was nothing overt—a subtle shift in the sibilant noise of normal conversation and a corresponding increase in activity whenever she entered an area.

Still tense over her fright in the desert, Casey wasn't looking forward to meeting with Syrus Tucker, the new graphics director. The previous director, Mr. Waukman, had been much easier to work with. From the first day she and Syrus Tucker had worked together, they were like flint and steel, igniting sparks. She had tried to figure out why. They were in total agreement when it came to work and they seemed to have the same sense of art, style, and composition. One thing she was aware of—she was annoyed over his insistence that everyone call him by a contraction of his first name, yet his private life was a mystery to everyone. The conjecture or gossip at Hartner and Hart was that he was single and preferred it that way.

She frowned, thinking. Maybe their friction stemmed from the questions he asked her. They tended to be too direct, bordering on the personal. When she had answered testily several times, his reactions had surprised her.

She thought of the first time Syrus Tucker walked past the cluster of desks toward his office to take over as graphics director. It was only ten days ago, and Casey just happened to be there. Mr. Waukman was also totally different in appearance and manner—short, somewhat overweight, and rather formal. Syrus, on the other hand, was tall, long legged, and lanky. He dressed casually, even wearing jeans, knit shirts, and cowboy boots at times.

His manner was also casual, putting everyone at ease. *His facial features, however, certainly contradicted his manner,* she mused. Black brows hovered over eyes that often seemed to brood on something other than the present. At first she thought his eyes were black, but they were actually brown— charcoal brown. Hollow cheeks emphasized a Roman nose, soaring cheek bones, and a strong contoured jaw, giving his appearance a craggy look.

It was his eyes that both fascinated and disconcerted Casey. At times they were terribly intense as if at any moment they could spew lightening. In contrast, his smile, like the sun bursting through clouds, changed his demeanor dramatically.

A man exited Syrus' office. Casey got up and moved down

the aisle a few feet to the open door. Syrus was studying something intently.

"You wanted to see me, Sy?"

He looked up, a strand of his dark unruly hair had fallen onto his forehead. His eyes lit up when he saw her, and a slow grin followed. "You look tired." His voice matched the grin—a mild, lazy drawl.

In no mood to discuss her physical state, she ignored the comment. Then, unexpectedly, an unsettling thought eased its way into her consciousness. Syrus Tucker had dark hair and he was wearing a blue shirt and jeans like the man that had been watching her in the desert. *Ridiculous*, she thought. *Syrus was already here at the agency meeting with someone when I arrived.*

Syrus noted her uneasy expression come and go. "Something the matter, Casey? What's on your mind?"

"Uh," she stammered, "I think you wanted to see me, right?"

He studied her intently. "You didn't answer my question."

She lifted her chin in an obstinate gesture. "My mind is on whatever you want to see me about."

He raised his brows. "I see. I wanted to show you the graphics for the business ad we're working on. I'm going to turn it in tomorrow morning if you're satisfied with the way I placed your photos."

"You're the boss. You don't have to have my approval."

"But I don't want to get on the bad side of an artist," he said, half teasing.

"Artist? I'm just a photographer. You're the artist."

"I call your photography art, Casey."

Surprised and pleased, she replied, "Thank you, Mr. Tucker—I mean, Sy. Sorry. I can't get used to calling you Sy."

"It seems everyone in the office pool is having a hard time with it. Guess they'll have to get used to it because I'm uncomfortable with formality, and I do have some authority—so it says on my door." He grinned.

Casey gave him a small smile and turned her attention to

the layout. She could feel his eyes on her as she studied it. Curious, she glanced up at him and caught an expression in his eyes that puzzled her. It flickered in their depths and he quickly looked down at the layout.

When he looked up again, it was gone. "Well? What do you think?"

"It looks good. Go ahead if you're pleased with it."

"All right. Go home and rest, Casey."

"Thank you, I will. Here are the pictures for the real estate company," she said placing them on the desk.

Casey turned into the subdivision called The Cottages. Her father had purchased a small home here for her. It was a community where the yards were maintained, and there was a swimming pool and an exercise room. He had originally wanted her to live with him or let him build a small home for her with a private swimming pool. She had turned down both offers. Since Nick had subtly but effectively destroyed all the relationships she had established at the country club and at church, she wanted ordinary neighbors who weren't concerned about their social status and who hadn't known Nick. Because all the cottages were small, they drew in empty nesters or senior citizens, and some of them hobbled as badly as she did.

She waved at her neighbor, Betty Middleton, who was out puttering in a flower bed. Betty waved back and smiled just before Casey drove into the single car garage.

Sighing, she entered her small kitchen, glad to be home. She flipped on the diminutive stereo hooked under one of the kitchen cabinets, put in a CD of soothing music, and went into the bedroom to rest for a while.

She closed her eyes and tried to relax, but the image of the man in the desert played over and over in her mind. Why wasn't she able to get rid of the deep underlying fear inside? It had been some time since the fear had surfaced and she was certain that the catalyst was her visit with Tiffany.

Could she help Tiffany? To answer these questions she needed to think back over her marriage to Nick again.

Months before the accident, she began to feel certain that Nick would not change, that she had to take drastic steps—despite her dad's example. He had made a difficult marriage work. No. It had never worked. He simply made the best of a painful situation. Her Grandpa Jacobson had once mentioned that her parents were "unevenly yoked." It had always seemed an appropriate expression.

She had gone into marriage with wonderful dreams, goals, and expectations, seeds of which she had planted deep inside herself years ago—sometime around age fourteen. Changed and revised in high school, they grew and flowered into a burning desire in college.

Determined not to repeat the heartaches caused by the mistakes of her parents, she committed to be the kind of wife her mother never was. She would love and serve her husband as her father had his wife. But after the wedding the real Nick began to emerge. Subtle criticism of little things she would do and say increased steadily to outright verbal abuse and bouts of frightening anger. Though this type of abuse was not physical, it was just as destructive. It was as if maintaining his perfect public image was too much. His real nature had to be released at home behind closed doors.

In the beginning she thought that it was her fault, that somehow, like her mother, she was failing. Still, nothing she did or said made the slightest difference. Begging him to get help made him angrier. Her insistence that they have marriage counseling was met with cutting ridicule, and he blamed her for everything. But as bad as the abuse was, her independent nature rebelled at his efforts to control.

During the third year of their marriage, her expectations ceased when at last she allowed herself to fully recognize Nick's true nature—his diabolical disposition. Giving up her dreams and goals of a good marriage after such a short time brought her deep grief, but she decided that a future with Nick was impossible.

After much anguish, she reached toward a higher source and finally regained faith in her future, a future which did not include Nick.

It had been eerie how Nick seemed to sense her thoughts long before she had actually made the decision to leave him. Unknown to her, and in order to put himself in a good light, he had for some time been cleverly and carefully poisoning everyone's minds against her. He turned the minister of their church against her simply by acting concerned for her. She learned of this when the minister called her into his office one day. He told her that Nick had come to him worried that she was developing some mental problems similar to those of her mother. She recalled how she had tried to explain her mother's real problem, feeling she could trust Reverend Staley's fairness and understanding.

"Reverend Staley, I don't know why Nick would tell you that. As Mother became well known and popular she was in greater demand, as you're well aware. The operas lasted for weeks. In the beginning, when she came home for a rest, she would sleep for a couple of days because she was so exhausted. But the last seven or eight years, she would come home from a production with terrible headaches and backaches. The operas running the length of time they did began to take their toll. The doctor gave her mild pain medication which helped in the beginning. But by the time I married, she had to have more painkillers and stronger ones."

Reverend Staley listened thoughtfully as Casey continued. "The strange thing about one particular pain medication, which seemed to be her favorite, was it made her want to go out and socialize. No amount of Dad's persuasion would change her mind, so he took her. Nick and I went to the club with Mom and Dad on several occasions and I was so embarrassed, I quit going when she was taking that medication. It made her extremely talkative, and sometimes she would slur her words and say things that didn't make sense. When the medication wore off, she was fine. She wasn't addicted, Reverend, because she never took medication when she was preparing for a production and none during the length of its run.

"So you see, Reverend Staley, she didn't have mental problems. It was only the medication she had to take once in a great while."

The minister was quiet for a few moments, a look of concern on his face. "But Casey, naturally you wouldn't want to think that your mother was delusional—"

"What? Delusional? Mother wasn't even delusional when she was on the medication."

Casey pulled herself back from that painful meeting with the minister. His expression and his replies indicated that she hadn't changed his thinking in the least. Instead of trying to be neutral with his flock, he preferred to make a judgment without thoroughly looking into both sides, without even discussing it with her father. And he chose to believe Nick's lies, apparently without praying about it or investigating further. Nick was so articulate and sounded so credible that not only did the minister believe him but also those members of his congregation who had been their friends at the country club. All accepted Nick's lies as fact. Because they thought they had seen evidence of it in her mother's behavior it wasn't difficult for Nick to convince them that his wife was becoming as "unstable and delusional" as her mother. And many of these people, of course, were questioned by the police.

Casey sat up with a start. Going over her own nightmare hadn't proven helpful at all. She hadn't found an answer to Tiffany's situation. How could she compare her marriage to someone else's? Yes, there were similarities, but in the end she would simply have to pray about Tiffany's particular circumstance and hope the ideas she had could possibly help her.

She wanted to give in and rest, but she had to do water therapy every day. Changing into her swimming suit, she threw on a cover-up and slipped into flip-flops, grateful that the burn ended a few inches above the ankle, saving her foot. Glancing into the long mirror on the outside of her closet door, she opened the cover-up and studied her appearance. Because she had to swim everyday, she wore her hair very short, something Nick would have hated. Her dad said the hairstyle made her look like a "pixie fairy-child," but all she saw was sun-bleached blonde hair, tired blue eyes, and a golden tan. That was one thing she had going for her—she tanned nicely except for the scarred leg. She had to keep suntan lotion on it. So she had one tan leg and one pale, scarred, atrophied one. She shrugged her shoulders in resignation and spoke aloud to her image. "At least most of the residents here don't look any better in a swimming suit than I do."

Chapter Two

*Who that has a heart fails to recognize
the silent presence of another?*
—Charles Dickens

The log cabin, situated on the Mogollon Plateau, afforded an escape from the burgeoning city of Phoenix. It was April and still chilly, but to Nan Hunter, who sat on the back porch hugging her knees and shivering, it was therapeutic to smell the pungent odor of pine. It felt good to get away and for a while leave everything behind.

She and Chet had built this log cabin in the pines of Sedona, a hundred miles north of Phoenix. Though constructed with wider doors and a ramp, along with all the other conveniences needed to accommodate Chet's wheelchair, they came only twice. After that, he had refused to come again. Now she was glad. There weren't memories here.

Even as her soul was filled with the beauty of the ponderosa pines against the red hills, the ever present ache remained deep inside. It had been with her for so many years, she didn't know when it began. She hoped that coming here would somehow lessen it. She smiled cynically. "That's a useless hope." At age forty-four it was too late.

Getting up, she stepped off the porch allowing herself a wider view of the scenery. The neighboring cabin on the left some distance away was empty. The major exodus from Phoenix and surrounding areas didn't start until June. She was grateful for the solitude. Strange as it seemed, she could face the loneliness easier when she was totally alone.

She sighed and went inside, fixed herself a cup of hot

chocolate, and moved to the seating area in the next room. The padded bleached oak furniture was large and uncomfortable. It had been Chet's idea. She didn't care for it, but it fit Chet's big frame and his comfort had been more important.

She curled up in one of the chairs and began reading an old out-of-print book she had found in the secondhand book store, a tattered copy of Agnes Sligh Turnbull's *The Golden Journey*. It had been a long time since she had been able sit down and leisurely read, yet try as she would, she found herself unable to focus.

Her thoughts returned to Chet, his last days in the hospital as he clung to life, and then to the wrenching moment when he let go. Few people outside relatives attended his funeral. His illness had been so consuming there had been no time or room left for friends for either of them.

Since his death, her mind had returned over and over to their life together during his long illness. She desperately tried to recall the good memories, the occasional golden moments which held her together. *Had she done everything she could have?* She couldn't answer to her satisfaction. Chet needed all her attention and time. To find strength for both of them, she daily read to him out of her grandmother's Bible. How much it helped Chet, she didn't know; however, it was her salvation.

As he got weaker their reading time was severely shortened and at times had to be put aside. She could no longer assist him alone and had to hire a male nurse to come in once a day to bathe and dress him. Later she had to have him stay for longer periods of time. Chet accepted his presence but insisted she be there with him except at bath time. It was during this respite she ran short errands to the grocery store or pharmacy.

When the daily burden became too great, she tried several times to hire a woman to take her place so she could get out of the house once in a while. Each time, Chet would pressure her, insisting he needed her constant cheerful presence to make it from one moment to the next. She had shed many tears for Chet as she witnessed his anguish over his big and strong body becoming weaker and more dependent upon her.

Only during the last six weeks of his life, spent in the hospital, did she have any time to herself, but by then she didn't know what to do with it. She felt as though she had withered inside—an empty shell covered with familiar skin and bones.

Now the tears that blurred her vision were for herself, for what might have been, for the life she wasn't able to have—the old ache—a life full of children and laughter.

Jacob drove into the driveway of the log cabin, already feeling more peaceful. Many years ago his parents bought this acreage and built the cabin. The three of them had come up often in the heat of the summer. He stepped out of the car and looked around, feeling the cool breeze on his face and listening to the whisper of pine needles. He gazed up at the trees, standing solid, straight, and secure, much the same as when he last saw them, except taller and more expansive, growing within themselves toward heaven, unlike his own static life. Through the pines he could see the colorful rock formations that comprised much of the Sedona landscape. The area had provided the backdrop for many of Hollywood's westerns.

Unlocking the front door, he carried his suitcase in and immediately went around the cabin, opening all the windows. A gentle breeze blew in, replacing the stale, closed-in smell with fresh air.

Glancing around the room, everything reminded him of his parents, who, even in old age, had always been there for him. When Silvia died, they immediately sold their home and moved in with him. They were aware of his loneliness and were especially concerned over how Nick was trying to isolate Casey from all of them. They had been his salvation during most of it, helping him endure each day.

Like a safety net, a series of unconnected thoughts took him back thirty-nine years to his mother's kitchen. Their home was situated on a large citrus farm. He was ten years old.

"Mama, why did you make Seely my middle name?"

"You know that was my name before I married your father. We wanted you to remember that you're a Seely as well as a Jacobson."

"But, Mom, you know everybody calls me Jake and . . ."

"Thought you liked that nickname," she grunted as she bent down to wipe up a spot off the floor.

"I do. I like it almost as much as I like the name Jacob, but when you . . ."

His mother scurried into the pantry.

Jake followed. "Mama! You never talk to me except on the dead run."

"There's a lot of work to be done here on the farm. You know that, Jake," she said as she skimmed the thick yellow cream off the top of the pan of milk and dropped it into a bowl.

"Mom, listen! This is serious."

His mother's loving blue eyes focused on her son's anxious face for the first time since he arrived home from school. "Come and let's sit down at the kitchen table and you tell me what's troubling you. The work can wait."

An expression of relief brightened his face. "Well," he said, taking a deep breath, "in English today, we were supposed to be writing sentences and some of us guys were goofin' off by writing each other's names. I wrote Joey Johnson's name; then I wrote Joey's 'john.' So he wrote Jake S. Jacobson, then just Jake S. He got a funny look on his face and started whispering it to himself over and over. Then he started to laugh. He whispered it to the other guys and they all laughed so hard that Miss Hilliard had to threaten them with the ruler to stop the noise. I didn't know why they were laughing until after school they all teased me by calling me Jake S. over and over."

His mother was perplexed. Then the confusion was replaced by an indignant reply. "It's a sorry soul that will twist a person's name like that!"

"Well, all my friends are sorry souls then."

"But didn't you twist Joey's name too?"

"Yeah but only on paper. I never said it out loud. What I'm worried about is that they'll call me Jake S. for the rest of my life."

His father, who had been standing just outside the screen door and had heard all the conversation, entered. "Jake S. Now that *is* funny!" He laughed. "Jake S., Jake S.," he repeated annoyingly. "The important thing isn't that they call you Jake S., but that you don't act like a Jake S." Then he doubled over with laughter.

Jake sulked for a moment, shocked that his dad would laugh at something so serious. Then, in spite of himself, he began laughing with him. Mama had turned away, busying herself so she could hide her own amusement at such uncouthness.

Afterward, his dad sat down at the kitchen table with him and taught him three things. One: Don't take yourself too seriously. Two: If you laugh *with* the boys, they can't laugh *at* you. Three: If you can laugh at yourself, it will untie all the knots in your stomach and help you get through life.

Because he took his dad's advice, the crisis blew over and his buddies began calling him Jake again and sometimes affectionately "Jake-us" in place of Jake S.

Jacob came back to the present with a jolt. Why had this episode come into his mind? He certainly needed a sense of humor right now, but as he had when a boy, the thought that "this is too serious" crowded out everything else. Until the authorities closed the investigation of Casey's accident, he couldn't be himself, he couldn't be happy, and he certainly couldn't see humor in anything and everything like he used to. He wished his parents were living. His loneliness had taken on a new and disturbing dimension. He needed his parents' wisdom, their understanding, and their love. They weren't able to have children until later in their lives; then he came along. By the time he was in his forties, they were in their eighties. His mother died first and then not too long after, his dad followed. He missed them terribly. So did Casey. She was closer to his mother than to her own.

The cabin was a place where he hoped he could put aside his concerns and ground himself before going back to work and back to life with all its uncertainties.

He went to the back door and admired the scenery. Before he could take a deep breath his legs were taking him into the pines and Arizona cypress.

He had only covered fifty yards when he glimpsed a lilac shirt and jeans through the foliage coming toward him. He stopped and muttered, "The last thing I want is company!" The neighboring cabins were usually vacant this time of year.

Quickly veering right, he continued walking up the hill and promptly bumped into the lilac shirt.

The woman let out a small frightened scream.

Jacob backed up, his hands in the air. "Sorry. I didn't see you. I'm harmless. I promise. If anything, I'm more frightened than you are."

"I doubt it," the woman said, scrutinizing his face. "You're a lot bigger than I am."

He chuckled. "Yeah, guess I am. But I'm really a coward, you see. I'm afraid of women—any shape or size."

The woman laughed. "Where did you come from? I didn't know anyone was around."

"That cabin back down there," he said pointing.

"No one was there yesterday."

"I just arrived. Where did you say your cabin was?"

"The one just east of you."

"Oh. I guess I've been here when you haven't. Never saw anyone there."

"We've only used it a couple of times."

"You and your husband?" he asked hesitantly, glancing at her ringless left hand.

"Yes. You might have noticed the ramp. He suffered from muscular dystrophy and was in a wheelchair for most of our life together."

"Was?"

"He died two months ago of cardiopulmonary complications."

He noted her tired eyes and the dark circles beneath them. "You must have gone through a terrible ordeal before he died—and much since. I'm sorry."

She didn't respond for a moment, curious at his understanding. "Thank you." An awkward silence followed. A little flustered, she blurted out, "Uh, since we're neighbors why don't you come over for a soft drink when you're through hiking?" Nan regretted the offer the moment the words came out and was suddenly afraid he might accept it.

Jacob was silent. That was the last thing he wanted to do. His purpose in coming here was to be alone. It was obvious the woman was more flustered after the invitation.

His silence unnerved Nan. "I'm sorry, you must have family with you and have a lot of things planned."

"No. I'm alone." He forced a smile. "Sure, I'd like to have a soft drink. How about right now?" he said, wanting to get it over with.

"All right," she said, putting on an answering smile and trying not to sound nervous. "Let's go."

Jacob followed her, noting her willowy figure moving gracefully around the clumps of fallen wood, weeds, and bushes. Her dark brown hair, pulled back into an eight-shaped bun, glistened reddish in the sunlight. *This isn't the kind of a neighbor I need right now.* His loneliness created a bottomless pit of vulnerability to women, but his heart was hard and unwilling.

Arriving at the woman's porch, Jacob held out his hand. "My name's Jake, Jake Jacobson. And yours?" Her slim hand was firm in his.

"Nan Hunter. Glad to meet you, Jake. Have a seat here on the porch and I'll bring out the only kind of drink I have—sparkling cider, my favorite."

"Sounds good."

She was back quickly with glasses of cool cider. Handing

him one, she seated herself opposite him across a small green plastic table. They sipped their drinks in uncomfortable silence.

"Are you up here for a relaxing break from work?" she asked, finally.

"Well, it's a break of some kind. Not sure if it will work since I need to keep busy. But if I look, I'm sure I can find some repairs to take care of in the cabin. I imagine you're here for other reasons?"

"I guess I'm trying to adjust to my new title of widow. I'm like you—I don't know if my trip up here will work. I'm not used to having free time on my hands."

Jacob only half-heard what she said because he was studying her arresting features. Her dark hair pulled back tightly emphasized prominent cheekbones and beautiful large gray eyes framed by long dark lashes. Her full lips gave one the impression she was about to pout then instead quirked in amusement. While Jacob studied these uniquely shaped lips, they spread into the warm and captivating smile he had first seen when they ran into each other.

Nan cocked her head quizzically, still smiling. "Hello?"

"Oh, excuse me," he said, embarrassed at his gawking. "Uh . . . that's an interesting knit shirt you have on there."

"You're probably referring to the Indian designs on it. A friend of mine painted this shirt for me. She's Navajo." Noting Jacob's puzzled look she said, "My grandparents owned a trading post in Moenkopi near Tuba City."

Jacob's brows rose. "An Indian trading post. Interesting. Did they do well with it?"

"It supported us. Tourists passing through the reservation stopped in since it was near Highway 160 on the way to Kayenta and Monument Valley."

"What did you sell?

"We purchased Indian rugs, baskets, sand paintings, and jewelry from the Navajos and Utes and then resold them to the tourists. We also sold gas, groceries, and some dry goods to the residents, both Indians and biligaanas."

"Biligaanas?"

"That's the name the Indians called us. I suppose nowadays it isn't politically correct to say Indian but rather Native American."

Jacob smiled ruefully. "I've heard many white people, or biligaanas, say with pride, 'I have Indian blood in me,' so I don't know what the furor is about."

"I don't either."

Jacob swallowed the last of the cider. "Well," he said, standing up, "I think I'd better go find a grocery store somewhere and get some food in the house. It was nice to meet you." He moved to the end of the porch and then turned back to her. "Thank you for the cider and the visit."

It was obvious to Nan that he was anxious to leave. "You're welcome. Feel free to drop over any time."

He smiled. "Thank you."

Nan watched him step off the porch, his long legs striding quickly toward his cabin. He left her feeling lonelier. Why? Probably because he left before she could ask questions about him. Did he have a family, a wife, children? She did notice that he wasn't wearing a wedding band, but then a lot of men didn't—much to her frustration. "But wives are expected to wear one," she said aloud. "When a man chooses not to wear a wedding band, it simply says he's available—whether he intends it or not." *Why am I going on like this?* she asked herself. Feeling restless, she got up and went inside.

She hadn't felt at ease while visiting with Jake Jacobson. Talking with a man without Chet there didn't feel right. She missed Chet terribly, but she was happy for his sake that he didn't have to endure years more of the frightening experience of his illness. This had taken the edge off her grief. But she felt lost and awkward about reentering the world of people and normal living.

She admitted, with some disquiet, that there was another reason she didn't feel at ease visiting with Jake—his looks. He was a tall, attractive man with an olive complexion and eyes the color of a ripe chestnut, sprinkled with green. His thick brown hair, parted on the side, stayed nicely in place. Above brown brows, a lofty forehead gave his oval face length and the appearance of great intelligence. His eyes reflected seasoned understanding and wisdom.

But something in his eyes troubled her. She frowned, thinking, and then came up with the only way she could describe it. *Haunted*. His eyes looked haunted. Though his smile caught her breath when she first met him, the laugh lines at the corners of his eyes hadn't deepened, nor did the smile reach his eyes. Only later on the porch did she get a glimpse of how expressive his eyes could be.

She plopped down on the couch, surprised at her total awareness of his appearance. When Chet passed away she told herself she was too worn out to ever consider remarrying. She still felt that way, but for some reason Jake Jacobson had aroused her curiosity. Even though he probably had a wife and children, her desire to know why he was unhappy was greater than it should be—and she felt rather puzzled by it, even a little concerned. Had her life been so centered around caring for someone night and day that it had become habitual? Did she need to be needed?

She shook the thought away. Although she had also worried over and helped her grandparents, deep down she knew she could be a very independent woman. She picked up her book, determined to lose herself in it.

Chapter Three

Only time shall show us whither
each traveler is bound.
—Charles Dickens

Syrus Tucker and Casey were taking a break after reviewing the final layout of the present advertising project. This wasn't the first time Casey had been uncomfortable with him. She had felt him looking her several times while she studied the layouts. When she caught him, he wasn't embarrassed nor was he apologetic.

When they were through, his intense eyes were upon her. "So Sil Jacobson was your mother?"

Surprised by the question, she didn't reply right away. "Yes. Why do you ask?"

"Because I heard her sing. She had a marvelous voice."

"Yes . . . she did."

"Do you sing?"

"I can sing, but I've never wanted to take lessons."

"Why?"

"Why do you want to know?" she asked, unnerved that the conversation was turning personal.

A lazy grin spread across his face. "Because I've always wanted to sing and if I, like you, had any singing talent, stampeding horses couldn't stop me from taking voice lessons."

"Oh. Well, frankly, I resented my mother putting her singing—her performing—before my father, before me. There. Now you know."

He nodded. "I can understand that." He nodded again. "I hear you lost your husband in the accident that burned and tore up your leg. I'm sorry."

Her lips tight, she replied. "That was three years ago."

Syrus' dark brows rose in surprise. "Doesn't sound like you're very grieved over it."

"I'm sorry, Mr. Tucker, but that is none of your . . . that's my private business."

"Whoa! I guess I just stepped in some horse manure. Didn't mean to upset you. You know, rumors go around, rumors about your mental state at the time of the accident and so forth. As one of my more valuable colleagues, I want to know you a little better."

"Thank you, but if we're through, Mr. Tucker, I need to get back to my studio."

"Sy."

"Mr. Tucker."

Syrus' gaze turned cold. "As I said, I prefer to be called Sy." He got up, stepped around the desk and closed the door. Reseating himself, he said, "I'm serious about rumors going around. That's why I'm asking probing questions. Since I'm new on the job, I need to know what's going on."

"Why? Mr. Waukman didn't find the rumors a problem."

"It's in the best interest of the company, that's why. I've learned that it's possible the authorities might indict you for negligent homicide. Is that right?"

Casey wilted inside. This was the first time it had been brought up openly at work.

"Why don't I take you out to lunch at some quiet place and you can tell me your side. I'd like to put the rumors to rest."

"It's been in the papers. Why would anyone at work still be talking about it?"

"You know how sensationalism affects people, Casey."

Her thoughts were explosive. *And I know how easy it is for people to believe lies from a handsome, articulate man like Nick!* She stood up and tried to walk around a little to ease the tension rising within her.

"Come on," he said, getting up and taking her arm. "It's a

little early for lunch, but how about we find an out-of-the-way booth in an out-of-the-way hole in the wall and talk?"

Casey stiffened, refusing to be led. "Why is it necessary to talk?"

"Because your work is being affected."

"I beg your pardon?"

"That's a good enough excuse for now, Mrs. Carter."

"Please don't call me Mrs. Carter."

"Sorry. Shall we go?"

"Unwillingly, yes."

Out in the parking lot, Syrus stopped before an old blue pickup, unlocked it, and opened the door for Casey.

Casey studied the step up to the running board, which wasn't as high as the new trucks. She stepped up with her good left leg, and then with her right hand gripping the top of the open door, she slowly and with great effort lifted her right leg, turned, and sat on the seat, relieved that Syrus hadn't offered help.

"Good job," was all he said and went around to his side.

When he turned on the motor, Casey was surprised that it hummed like a new one. "I expected this old rattletrap to sputter and stop a few times."

Syrus grinned. "Nope. This is my baby. I take good care of her."

What an odd man, thought Casey. *He's supposed to be a genius in advertising, but he acts more like a cowboy!*

After turning off a major street, Syrus drove down a couple of back roads and pulled into the small parking lot of a run-down place called Rosarita's.

When Syrus opened the door for her, she said, "You really aren't going to take me in there are you?"

"Yeah, I am. It's my favorite Mexican food restaurant."

If he weren't her boss she wouldn't be here. Refusing his hand, she got herself down and limped beside him.

When they entered, a buxom, dark-haired woman greeted him with a big smile and a warm welcome in Spanish. He answered her in Spanish and then ambled toward the back booth and waited until Casey scooted in.

"I'm impressed. You know the help and you speak Spanish," she stated sarcastically, still chafing over Syrus probing into her personal life.

"Rosarita is the owner."

"Oh," she said with peaked inflection. "I'm really impressed now."

"You know, you're not speaking very respectfully to your boss. I'm surprised you're relationship with the company has lasted this long, especially if you spoke to Waukman in that manner."

"He didn't invade my privacy."

"Well, get off your attitude, Casey, or else," he stated sharply.

Casey's eyes widened. "I didn't know my easygoin' cowhand boss could be so quick tempered."

"You know how you're acting?"

Her chin rose defiantly. "How?"

"Like a spoiled brat."

The remark unstrung her. The only one who ever called her that was Nick and it struck a frightening note. She looked down at the table. "My husband called me that too. Maybe I am. I'll have to give that some serious thought. I believed *him*—at first, anyway."

Surprised at the sudden candidness, Syrus studied her in silence, thinking about the pain she must have gone through with her burns and injuries. Mentally he stepped back. He couldn't be drawn in emotionally. Emotionalism was an abyss he couldn't afford to approach. He had a job to do

With regained objectivity, he examined her features. Her eyes were lowered so he couldn't see them, but they were the one thing that had struck him the first time he saw her. Large and bright, they were a brilliant blue. The effect was so startling that initially he had wondered if she wore colored contacts. At that first meeting, she had gazed into his eyes with such open directness he was momentarily flustered. They were eyes that were aware, interested, and intelligent. His gaze slid over to her well-defined cheek bones and then down to the ever-so-slight dimple in her blunt chin that almost looked pointed in the wide jaw which fanned out to her ears. Her nose was straight and slightly upturned. She had a cheerful mouth, both upper and lower lips equally full. She looked up just as he was examining her hair.

Surprised at his change of mood, she asked, "Why are you smiling?"

"Not many girls can get away with such short hair. On you it looks great."

"I don't really care how it looks," she snapped. "It's practical for my daily water therapy." She knew she was acting overly defensive and prickly.

"So it is." His eyes turned hard. "Let's get right down to heating the branding iron. Were you responsible for the accident?"

Casey glared at him. She could feel the heat rising in her cheeks. "Surely, you've read the papers. You know what I've said about that."

"I did, as a matter of fact. One particular boss has a collection of them. He had me read them."

"He did?" she asked, disturbed.

"Yes. Sorry," he stated in a matter-of-fact tone. "I don't care what the papers reported you saying. I would like to hear the answer from your own lips."

Casey clamped her teeth tightly and rubbed the throbbing pain in her temples. Covering her face, she murmured, "I'd rather not." Removing her hands, she saw his usual determined expression, the one that tended to bring out the worst in her. "I'd rather not because I don't know you, or anything about you."

"It's not your business to know anything about me. I'm not obligated to give you any information about me or my life." He paused. When he continued, the edge in his voice was gone.

"But, I'll tell you this much. You can trust me."

"And I know you so well I can believe your word?" She saw Syrus' displeasure at the further sarcasm. She ground her teeth. *Is keeping my relationship with Hartner and Hart worth this?* She answered herself quickly. *Yes. I have to keep myself busy.* Besides, where could she go that people wouldn't know of her and stare and wonder? "All right," she replied through tight lips. "I'll give you an abbreviated version." He said nothing, merely waited.

She tried to suppress the burgeoning knot of resentment inside her chest over having to retell the painful story to a virtual stranger. She was unsuccessful. All she could do was mask it the best she could. Clenching her hands, she began. "Almost immediately after we were married, Nick began in small ways, insignificant ways, to belittle me. To make the long three-year story short, it escalated to severe verbal abuse. Two years into the marriage, I realized I couldn't go on like that. I was beginning to be afraid of him. He never hit me, but I felt he could be violent. As it turned out, he was."

"Did you tell him you were planning to leave him?"

"No. Instead, I stayed with him another year, but during that time I went to the library and researched spousal abuse, all the while hoping that somehow he would consent to get help and that we could go to counseling together. He vehemently rejected both suggestions. Though he didn't say so, he seemed to sense that I wouldn't go on as we were and began to act strangely. One Friday he left and was gone for two days without explanation. He'd done that before, so that wasn't unusual. When I asked him to tell me where he'd been, he refused. Several days later, with no warning at all, he pointed a gun at me and told me to go get into the car. I was shocked. I asked him why the gun. He wouldn't answer—just said, 'Get into the car and drive. I'll tell you where to go.' I cried, I begged, but nothing moved him."

Casey rubbed her tense shoulder and let out a weary breath. "I planned on causing a minor accident to stop it, but he was too clever. It was as though he could read my mind. He said, 'If you do anything to try and stop this little trip, I'll see to it that your father doesn't live much longer than your mother.'" She shivered. "He seemed to know exactly where we were going. He made me drive out of Scottsdale up Highway 87 toward Payson. Once in the mountains, he suddenly leaned forward as I drove up a hill and turned a bend. The last thing I heard him say was, 'This is it!' Then he grabbed the wheel and we went off the road and down the hill."

Syrus' eyes were more brooding than usual. "Did he, by any chance, say, 'If I can't have you, no one can?'"

"No. Why would he? What made you ask that?"

Syrus ignored the questions. "Do you think he was trying to commit suicide?"

Her brows creased in troubled thought. Slowly she shook her head. "I know it sounds unreasonable considering the circumstances, but no. He wasn't the type. He was too selfish, too self-absorbed and narcissistic to hurt himself. To this day, I can't figure it out. It doesn't make sense. I wouldn't believe it if they hadn't found his remains."

"Did he tell you anything about his work at Central Arizona Bank?"

"I often asked him about it, but he said he didn't want to talk about it, that he needed to leave work at work."

"Were there signs of being apprehensive? Was he secretive, as though he were hiding something?"

Casey frowned and fell silent, thinking. "The FBI has asked me those very questions. Why would *you* have to know that?"

"It would help me understand why your husband would want to hurt you—in other words, it would make you look more innocent. I suppose that's why the FBI asked you. Were they satisfied with your answers?"

"Why would I want to help them? They said they might have to indict me." Casey hoped this would end the questions, but Syrus' silence outlasted hers. "I don't suppose they were satisfied for two reasons. One, while I was in the burn center, a policeman interrogated me as though I were guilty. The FBI men were more careful, but I assumed they too thought I was guilty, so I really didn't try to remember."

"You didn't try?" Syrus asked. "That seems a little self-defeating to me."

She evaded his question. "It's painful to think about it. Besides, since the accident my memory has been sketchy." Syrus remained silent, and during the stillness, for some cryptic reason, her mind began probing for answers. "Wait! There was one incident that should have warned me he was hiding something."

"Did you report it to the FBI?"

"No. I didn't remember it until this very moment." Casey's eyes glazed over in thought. "I think it was about a month before the accident. Nick brought home a medium-sized manila envelope. I believe he . . . took it in the study then immediately locked the door, as he always did. I think he stayed there most of the evening." She paused, wondering if she should be telling Syrus this, but the pressure of the newly remembered incident needed an outlet.

She stared past Syrus. "Let me think. Oh yes. The details are coming back. The next morning right after he left for work, I noticed the same envelope on the entryway table. I wondered if it was important enough for me to go out of my way and take it to his office. I remember barely getting the contents out of the envelope, preparing to look at them when he burst through the door. Seeing the papers in my hand, he became furious, yelling at me, wanting to know if I had read them." She rubbed her forehead, troubled. "Nothing I said would convince him I hadn't. Then . . . then he started accusing me of spying on him. He grabbed my wrist and twisted it."

Casey's voice faltered as she recalled the emotional storm. "I jerked free and stumbled backward. I remember falling against the wall, trying to make sense out of what was happening. The look on my face must have finally convinced him. The change was like turning on a light switch. One minute he seemed angry enough to kill me, and then suddenly he was blaming problems and people at work, asking—almost pleading with me—to forget about what happened."

Syrus gazed intently at Casey. "What happened then?"

Her expression hardened as she remembered. "He tried to put his arms around me, and when I resisted, he turned around, shoved the papers into the envelope and left without another word, not even *good-bye.*"

Syrus' brows wrenched in thought as he gazed down at the table. When he looked up at Casey, he made no effort to conceal his feelings. "That whole episode—his volatility, then his sudden affection—must have been difficult."

Syrus seemed so genuinely empathetic, for a ridiculous moment Casey thought she might start crying. Her eyes misted and she was embarrassed that Syrus had seen her vulnerability.

"Look, Casey, you must know that there's a lot of speculation going on. The fact that the authorities have left this whole thing up in the air leaves room for people to talk. For what it's worth, I want you to know I believe you."

She gazed at him, feeling emotionally wasted. "I'm glad you believe me, but who knows what your boss will believe? It's so easy to suspect." *And so easy to believe lies,* she added to herself.

"How about ordering some of Rosie's delicious Mexican food now?"

She nodded, opened her purse, and pulled out a couple of aspirin.

Chapter Four

Humor—a light-saber, parting the clouds

*T*he phone jarred Casey awake. She blinked with bleary eyes at the red numbers on the digital alarm clock. It was six in the morning! Who could be calling at this hour? The ringing was insistent. Her arm reached out and picked up the phone. "Hello?"

"Did I wake you?" her father's voice asked, surprised.

"Dad? Where are you calling from?"

"The cabin."

"That's right. You went there yesterday morning, didn't you?"

"You're usually up by now. It sounds like I woke you."

"Yes. I didn't sleep very well last night."

"Why's that, honey?"

"It's nothing serious, Dad. The new graphics director, Syrus Tucker, took me out to lunch and interrogated me about the accident. Apparently, he was a little concerned about my part in it. I guess I went to bed thinking about it."

"I'm sorry, Casey. What was the outcome?"

"It was amazing, Dad. While talking with Syrus, I remembered something." She related it.

"Casey, you've got to call the FBI and tell them." He heard her sigh with impatience. "Casey? Remember, you told me you wouldn't stubborn up against them anymore. They really are trying to help you."

"All right. I'll call Mr. Welles this morning. Syrus believed me, at least he said he did, but I don't know him well enough to believe him or not. You know what they say when the boss says, 'I'm behind you one thousand percent;' you better start looking for another job. Anyway, Syrus told me he'd pass what I told him on to the big wheels."

Jacob let out a silent breath of relief. "Good. You've got to learn to trust, Casey, generally speaking of course. This brings me to the reason for my call. I've made an appointment with a psychotherapist for you this afternoon at four." Jacob held his breath for the explosion. When there was only silence, he quickly went on. "I should have talked to you about it when you came over, but that headache I had—you know."

"You can't fool me, Dad. You purposely waited until you were at the cabin to tell me. Right?"

"I refuse to answer on the grounds that it may incriminate me."

"It's not funny, Dad," she said gently. "You know how I feel about going to a therapist. We've had this discussion over and over. I'm not a child anymore. You can't just make appointments for me and tell me to go."

"I know, Casey. On the surface, it seems you're handling everything very well, but I also know that you don't want to burden me with anything—so burden Belle."

"Belle who?"

"Belle Levine. She's a survivor of spousal abuse herself and an excellent therapist. I've used her before in counseling several of my employees. Though she's a bit unconventional, she helped them tremendously."

"Dad, you're great to do this for me, but I don't need a therapist," she reiterated, trying to be patient. Her voice rose in spite of her efforts. "I just need to have the case closed!"

Ignoring her protest, he went on. "Belle's office is near Sixteenth Street and McDowell. I've forgotten the address, but she's in the Yellow Pages—Belle Levine. It's not in a fancy office. She couldn't care less about appearances, and she turns down more women than she accepts. She interviews them first to see if they're ready to help themselves. She's doing me a favor by interviewing you. That's all it is, Casey, an interview."

Casey liked Belle already, but she felt railroaded. She closed her eyes, and took a deep breath, feeling herself stiffen—her usual resistance when pushed. Then her heart softened. Her dad had suffered so much because of her. She decided to keep the appointment but only go through the motions. "All right, Dad. I'll go be interviewed."

Jacob was silent.

"Dad?"

"Please don't sabotage the interview, Casey."

Casey laughed. That was exactly what she had intended to do.

Jacob smiled, but he didn't respond and she said nothing, each playing the waiting game.

Casey remembered her dad saying that in a business negotiation, the first one to break the silence was the loser. Begrudgingly, she spoke. "I guess I'm the loser." They both laughed. "I promise I won't *try* to sabotage the interview, but I seem to be good at it without even trying. I'll just be my old lovable self, so don't be disappointed when she doesn't accept me."

Jacob laughed. Without knowing it, Casey had cheered him.

It was four o'clock and Jacob felt good. He'd put a new washer in the kitchen faucet, fixed the screen door, swept, vacuumed, and cleaned the bathroom. He had just returned from a hike in the refreshing mountain air and was ready to fix a hamburger. Debating about how many hamburgers he could eat, he surprised himself by wondering if he should invite Nan Hunter over.

Now the real debate was on. He thought of the pros and cons. He would probably feel as uncomfortable as he did before. And it was obvious she wasn't relaxed either—so it was possible she wouldn't accept his invitation.

One reason to invite her was that he disliked eating alone, even if he were reading the morning newspaper. Maybe she felt the same way. Finally, he admitted to himself the main reason he was even considering it—a subtle aura of mystery surrounded her, which aroused his curiosity.

The pros won. He walked over to her cabin, puzzled at himself. He had been so sure he wanted to be alone. Knocking on her back door, he waited and waited. Disappointed, he had turned to leave when he saw her walking toward him.

"Hi," he said, "you've been hiking?"

"I have," she said breathlessly, stepping up on the porch. She smiled. "You're better today, I see."

"How do you know?" he asked surprised.

"I can see it in your eyes."

"Hmm. I came over to invite you to have a hamburger sandwich with me. I think I got carried away and bought too much of everything."

"That sounds good, but—uh, I think I acted a little impulsively yesterday. I probably should have found out something more about you before I invited you to my place. For all I know you could be an escaped convict."

Jacob chuckled. "What do you want to know?"

"For starters, are you married?"

"Oh. I'm sorry. I should have told you. My wife died five years ago."

"I'm sorry."

"Thank you. You'll join me then?"

"I would love to. I'm starved. What can I bring?"

"I won't know until we start cooking. I probably forgot something. What say we just go ahead and start? We can take it from there."

In the kitchen Jacob put the meat patties in the frying pan to cook while Nan began washing the lettuce and tomatoes. "How long have you had this cabin, Jake?"

"Since I was a boy. My father and mother brought me up here as often as they could." Jacob smiled as he turned the heat down on the meat. "Even when my parents were in their eighties we'd come up, and darned if they couldn't almost outhike me."

"Amazing. You're an only child then?"

"Yes," he said, turning the meat over.

Nan opened several drawers until she found a knife. "How old are you, Jake?" she asked, slicing a large tomato.

"Forty-nine. How old are you?"

Nan sighed. "Forty-four."

"Why the big sigh?" Jake asked, shaking salt and pepper on the meat.

"I wasn't aware I sighed. I suppose you want this onion sliced?"

"You bet." He went to the cupboard and pulled out two plates and two glasses. "What's a hamburger without onions?"

"Ah . . . a man with good taste."

"Great. You like them too. At least my breath won't make you uncomfortable," he said, throwing a bag of potato chips on the table.

Nan laughed.

When they were finally seated at the table ready to eat, they smiled at each other.

"At last, we got it together," Jacob said, chuckling. "I've done a lot of cooking at home, but I haven't worked in this kitchen for some time."

They prepared their sandwiches and ate in silence for a while.

"I can't remember when a hamburger tasted so good," Jacob said. "That says something about hiking in the fresh mountain air."

"Definitely. But for me it's not only the exercise, it's the company."

"Thank you. I can say the same. You seem to have uh—how do I say it—a calming effect upon me."

"I do?" Nan asked surprised. No one's ever told me that before."

"I can't imagine that your husband didn't feel that way," he said and then took another big bite of the hamburger.

Chewing slowly, she thought about it. "I guess he did, though he never used those words. He didn't want me out of his sight for a minute."

Jacob gulped a drink of water. "Literally?"

"I'm afraid so. Muscular dystrophy is a terrible and frightening illness, especially to a man as physically active as Chet was."

Jacob stopped eating, a look of concern on his face. "Did you or he have any family around to help you out once in a while?"

"No. Chet had an older brother and sister who lived out of state. His father died about ten years ago. His mother, who lived near, came to see him often, but she wasn't strong enough to help. Her health wasn't good."

"Did you have family, other than your grandparents, who could give you a break?"

"No. My parents were killed in a car accident when I was two years old. I was raised by my maternal grandparents who, as I told you, lived on the Indian reservation and owned a trading post. After my grandfather died, leaving my grandmother alone to run the business, I tried to convince her to sell out and come to live with us. Eventually she did, but . . ." she hesitated; a troubled frown creased her brow. "Unfortunately, it didn't work out as I had hoped."

"I'm sorry." Jacob leaned back in the chair and stared past her for a moment. "I know about things not working out as hoped. I have a daughter, Casey, my only child. She's twenty-eight now. She was married for three years and during that time, her husband began isolating her from her mother, from me, and from her friends. He wanted total control over everything she did."

"That's terrible, Jake."

Jacob didn't hear her. His thoughts now on Casey, he wondered how she had fared with Belle Levine.

Nan fidgeted with her glass, not certain whether he had heard her. "I'm sorry about your daughter, Jacob," she repeated.

"What? Oh. Thank you."

When they were through eating, Nan began helping Jacob clean up, expecting at least to enjoy a little light banter, as they had while fixing dinner, but Jacob seemed far away.

Jacob was immersed in an argument with himself about whether or not he should call Casey and find out if she even went to see Belle. If she didn't, what then?

"Did you and your wife come up here often?"

No answer. Nan repeated the question.

"What? No, but my daughter and I came up here as often as we could."

Nan was curious at to why his wife didn't go with them, but it was obvious Jake didn't want to talk about it—or anything else. She gave up trying to keep the conversation going by herself. When she quit trying, they worked in silence. The longer the silence lasted the more irritated Nan got.

The memory of how her grandfather often disregarded her grandmother's presence by his preoccupation aroused Nan's ire. No matter what Jacob's problems were, she wasn't about to put up with unexplained silences from him.

She wiped off the kitchen table. "There, we're through. I need to get back to the cabin now, Jake," she said, heading for the back door. "Thank you for inviting me over."

"You're leaving so soon?" he asked, surprised.

"Yes."

"I'll walk you over."

"No thank you. If it were dark, I'd take you up on it."

Frowning at Nan's abruptness, Jacob watched her until she reached the cabin. He felt like kicking himself. It was clear as the Arizona sky that he had run her off with his self-absorption.

Casey found the address and parked in front of the old run-down building that housed Belle Levine's office, dreading the encounter. Opening the door to a long hallway carpeted in old brown tweed commercial carpet, she quickly located the suite number and knocked.

"It's open!" a voice yelled.

Casey opened it slightly and peered in.

"I won't bite, kid, come on in."

There was no receptionist. Behind a small desk in the left corner of the room sat a woman who was obviously Belle, writing something. Casey stepped in, closed the door, and waited.

Belle got up and went over to her, holding out her hand. Casey responded and they shook hands. "I'm Belle, and you're Casey?"

"Yes."

"Go over and have a seat, Casey," Belle said, locking the door.

Moving over to the conversational grouping of furniture on the right, Casey noted one couch and three upholstered chairs with a small table in the middle. The table was empty except for a box of tissues. The furniture was upholstered in cheery blues and yellows. A beautiful painting of a peaceful garden with trees and flowers hung on the wall behind the couch. The floor was covered in a soft gray-blue carpet.

Across the room, lining the wall at the side of the desk was a large bookcase filled with books. There were two doors. One was behind the desk, and through it Casey glimpsed some filing cabinets. The other door was near the furniture, with Restroom printed on it. She sat down in one of the yellow and blue print chairs, and Belle sat on a chair facing her.

The room itself relaxed Casey. And Belle herself was certainly not what she expected. She had dark blonde naturally curly hair, cut just below the ear. She was about five foot three, slightly overweight, and probably around fifty. Her floral print dress wasn't slimming by any standard, but her warm hazel eyes fit perfectly with her freckled face and arms. Her smile was wide, welcoming, and to Casey's surprise, disarming.

"So you're Jake's girl. You're small like your mother, but where did you get that face of yours? You don't look like either of your parents."

"My Grandma Jacobson," Casey said, smiling at the friendly woman.

"Oh, of course. I met your grandmother once."

"You seem to know my family. How come I've never met you?"

"Because you've never needed a therapist, I guess."

"They all needed a therapist?"

"No. Just met them. Now, kid, you're here for an interview I understand."

"Under duress, yes."

"You don't want therapy?"

"No."

"Hmm. You don't think you need it?"

"All I need is to get the case closed," Casey said, hoping Belle knew about the accident so she didn't have to go over it.

"Don't blame you a bit! Damnable situation that man brought upon you."

"Then you believe me?"

"Of course. Jake's kid wouldn't lie."

Casey sighed in relief. "Thank you."

"Okay. Why did you marry that loser in the first place?"

Taken aback by the blunt question, she had to gather her thoughts. "Because I never met anyone that could come close to Dad. Then, when I met Nick, who was so charismatic, convincing, clever, I thought he—"

"Yeah. When did you discover differently?"

"Now that I've looked back on it, I saw signs of a controlling nature before I married him, but I didn't recognize them. My mother was intrigued with him, and I was so infatuated I justified the few things about Nick that bothered me. I can't believe I really loved him." She shivered. "How could it have been love?"

"It was love. You loved and trusted the picture he painted for you."

"That's exactly right. I loved an illusion. I feel like such a fool."

"Of course you do. Who wouldn't?"

Casey blinked in surprise. She had a preconceived notion that therapists didn't act so personable and human. She found herself wanting to say more. "After we were married, I gradually became aware that Nick's constant digs and criticisms were making me lose confidence in myself. I thought it was the usual marriage adjustment, so I tried hard to make it work." She stopped, unsure if she should continue.

Belle nodded in understanding. "Soon you found yourself spending all your time trying to find ways to please him, to keep him from criticizing—right?"

Casey's eyes widened in surprise. "Yes . . . how did you know?"

"There's something you should know right now, Casey. "You're experience isn't unusual; in fact, I'm sorry to say, it's getting to be more common as time goes on. I've seen the same thing hundreds of times. Don't burden yourself with guilt, feeling that somehow *you* failed."

"Thanks. I guess I needed someone besides Dad to tell me that. I can see now that Nick was using my desire to please, to avoid conflict, as a way to control me. Anyway, no matter what I did, it only got worse. He even kept me from going to New York with Dad to see my mother perform—her last performance." Angry tears surfaced. "Dad had quit going to many of Mother's performances, so when he invited me to go along to this one, I thought it was a wonderful opportunity."

"How did Nick keep you from going?"

"He told me he had arranged an important meeting with a major depositor. He said it was very important to have his wife there since the man was bringing his wife. When I insisted that I was going to New York, he promised he would take me himself the very next week to hear her. I gave in. Knowing what I know now, even if mother hadn't died, I know he would have found another excuse not to take me."

"Does the name slime-bucket come to mind?"

Casey laughed. "Thanks! It does. Anyway, after my mother's funeral, my grandparents sold their home and moved in with Dad. Whenever I could, I would go over and visit them. I had learned early on that Nick didn't even want me to see my family. I was very upset and hurt over that, but my feelings didn't change his attitude at all. At last, in order to keep peace, I began to keep the visits to my family secret, but Nick seemed to have a sixth sense. Somehow he always found out or cleverly got it out of me, after which he became more unkind and controlling.

"We only saw his friends, not mine. It was obvious that this was terribly wrong and it finally sent me to the library to look up abuse. I had read about many spousal abuse cases in the newspapers and had learned about them from TV shows. I didn't want to believe it was happening to *me*, but I knew it was."

"You did?" Belle asked, totally surprised. "You recognized it as abuse so early in your marriage?"

"Early in my marriage? Two years doesn't seem early to me."

"Believe me, it is. Most abused women don't really realize what's happening to them for much longer than that."

"Well, I guess I had an advantage. My father and I were close. He was so kind, so considerate to me. I watched how he treated my mother—even when she seemed unaware of his needs. He was strong but patient and long-suffering. I couldn't help but compare Nick with my dad."

"Interesting. In most cases, the wife excuses and excuses her husband's unkind or cruel behavior, and then she begins to think it's all her fault. If she did this better, or looked better and so on, he wouldn't get so angry."

"I did that at first. I was determined to make my marriage work. Well, as time went on and the more I studied abuse, I began to feel that Nick would never change, any more than my mother did. The difference was, I began to feel frightened that the abuse might turn into physical violence. Though my father would never divorce my mother for her neglect, for abandoning me, I began trying to figure out how to get out of *my* marriage—safely. I began to watch Nick, listen to him carefully, study his habits, his ways, and I discovered something interesting—his Achilles' heel."

"I'm on the edge of my seat, Casey, but your time is up. I have another client coming in fifteen minutes."

Casey looked at her watch. "Amazing. Did I pass the interview?"

"That wasn't an interview. It was short, but it was a session."

"It was? I don't understand. I thought . . . "

"Nick isn't the only one with a sixth sense. I knew the minute I looked into your eyes that you were approachable and honest. When you opened your mouth you confirmed it."

Casey's brows rose in surprise. "I did?"

Belle nodded and smiled. "Here's my card. Call me if you want to talk with me again. You have to leave through the door behind my desk and through the filing room. Follow the short hall to the other side and go out the back entrance."

Casey's brows rose questioningly.

Belle grinned. "I know. It's odd, but as you see, I don't have a reception room and this is one way I try to keep other patients from knowing who I'm seeing."

"Oh. Thank you, Belle," Casey said smiling. "I'll be calling you. I guess I do need to talk to someone after all."

Chapter Five

*Gratitude unexpressed is
akin to ingratitude.*
—Nan's grandmother

The next evening, just before sundown, Nan sat at the small kitchen table holding her face in her hands, feeling a wave of despondency wash over her. To avoid thinking she had kept herself busy going into town, cleaning, and reading. It was all in vain. Though still impatient over Jacob's behavior the night before, she was afraid she had effectively ruined a possible friendship with him. Had she been too quick to take offense? After all, they were just friends, weren't they? Or to be more accurate, just acquaintances. She probably should have been more understanding. Was she acting like Chet, demanding attention?

Thinking about Chet's actions brought back painful memories of her grandmother's last days. What she had allowed to happen to her. Tears streamed down her cheeks. *How can I ever forgive myself?* She laid her head on her arms, exhausted, trying to think what she could have done differently.

Something awakened Nan. How long she had dozed at the table she didn't know. It was an insistent knock. The unexpected darkness inside and out frightened her. Quickly moving to the door, she locked it and then turned on the porch light. It was Jake. Her spirits rose and she wondered why, when she had felt so ill at ease in his presence earlier. Fumbling with the lock, she got the door open.

"I'm sorry. I frightened you," Jacob said. "I'm glad you're careful."

"Come in, Jake," she said, flipping on the light. "I didn't sleep well last night, and I must have fallen asleep at the table. I was a little disoriented when I heard the knock and saw that it was dark inside and out." She looked at her watch and smiled. "My goodness, it's eight forty five. Let's go in where it's more comfortable."

Jake noticed her swollen eyes but made no comment. When they were seated, he wondered why he felt compelled to come over and make things right. He probably wouldn't see her again when he went home. Nevertheless, he said, "I came over to apologize for last night. I didn't realize till after you left how thoughtless I'd been."

Nan was silent, wanting and expecting more.

When Jacob could see Nan wasn't going to respond, he tried to explain. "I know it appeared as though I was ignoring you. I'm afraid my concern for my daughter makes me a boring and inconsiderate person to be around. You see, it isn't over yet."

Relieved that Jacob recognized what he had done, she asked, "What do you mean, it's not over?"

"My daughter and I have been close all her life and now she won't let me help her. No. That's not quite true. She doesn't want to burden me, but my mind is never off her. I worry about her." He cleared his throat. "I was rude last night. I'm sorry."

"You have no idea how much I appreciate you coming over and apologizing. And I apologize for being so abrupt. I have a problem too. Retreating from people became a habit while caring for Chet. It's something I need to work on."

"Well, join the leaky boat. There's quite a crowd. In or out of marriage we compensate the best we can. So," he grinned, "what shall we talk about?"

She laughed nervously. "I don't know." She concentrated on pushing a cuticle back on her left forefinger.

"For starters, tell me how you met your husband," Jacob asked, knowing women usually liked to talk about this, while at the same time surprised at his eagerness to make her feel comfortable.

Nan smiled at his efforts to get the conversation going, and allowed herself to relax. "I'd graduated from college and was home for the summer to help my grandparents when Chet passed through the reservation on a sightseeing tour. He stopped in at our trading post. He was a tall, strong, good-looking man. To look at him, you would never suspect he would ever become seriously ill. He was full of personality."

"And he swept you off your feet."

"You might say that."

Determined to mend his ways and be more considerate, Jacob was aware that the bereaved usually need to talk about those they've lost. "Tell me more about Chet."

Nan's thoughts turned inward. Then a tender smile graced her features. "He had a never-ending ability to feel gratitude. He sincerely thanked me almost every day for staying with him and helping him, for putting up with him—sometimes with tears."

Jake nodded. He understood this well through caring for Casey. "When someone is grateful for what you've done or what you're doing and actually *expresses* that gratitude, some-how the task becomes easier—and even makes you want to do more for them."

"How true! My grandmother used to say, 'Gratitude unex-pressed is akin to ingratitude.'"

"That's quite profound. I'm going to remember that."

She smiled. "I always like to share that with people."

"Did Chet go to college?"

"Yes. But he dropped out and became a salesman. He was good at it, but when he mastered one job and became success-ful he got bored and quit. Then he went to the next job." She smiled. "With his personality and brains, he could always get another job and make a success of it. We were actually quite well-off when he became ill."

"That was fortunate."

"It was. With our savings, investments, and insurance, I could stay home and care for him."

A warm, appreciative expression appeared on Jacob's face. "Even in the short time I've known you, Nan, it's obvious that you're a selfless, serving woman."

"Why, thank you, Jacob."

He smiled and nodded; then it was as if he disappeared while gazing at her. His eyes turned expressionless. He got up and walked around restlessly. "Here I go again. My mind is back on my daughter. I'm sorry, Nan, but she's lovely and kind, like you. I've asked myself a hundred times. How could Casey have married that man?"

Moving over to the window he looked out, seeing only his own miserable reflection. Silently he remembered asking himself many times why he had married the woman he did as he watched Silvia abandon her daughter and forget about him for the sake of her musical career. *What was my excuse?* he asked his reflection. *I had wonderful parents who raised me right. I knew what I wanted in a wife. I dated a lot of nice girls.* He felt like a total failure in his marriage, a total failure as a father, a father who hadn't been able to stop his daughter from marrying a con artist—even a murderer who had tried to kill her! His breathing turned rapid.

Nan waited, watching him curiously. She would like to have comforted him, but she didn't know how at the moment. She didn't know him well enough. They were both silent for a few moments, and then Nan finally asked, "What are you thinking, Jake?" He turned a troubled face to her but didn't answer. "What's the matter?" she pressed.

He laughed bitterly, thinking. *What gives me the right to question my daughter when I couldn't help myself, my wife, or my daughter?* Remembering Nan's question, he replied. "It's such a long, complicated story. I'm afraid I'm in no frame of mind to tell it."

"Sometimes it helps to get someone else's perspective. You're so close to the picture, Jake."

"I know you're right, but I'm not used to talking to anyone about it, and it's a little difficult right now. It seems like I'm always saying I'm sorry, Nan, but I am. I guess I'm still not fit company. I'd better leave."

This time Nan wasn't concerned with Jacob's preoccupation. He had explained it. It helped to understand. "You don't need to leave, Jake. I wish you felt comfortable confiding in me, but since you don't, feel free to stay anyway. At least you'll have company while you fret."

Jacob laughed. "Thanks for the magnanimous offer, but I'd rather not afflict you with my moodiness." He turned and walked back into the kitchen.

Nan followed him to the door.

Jacob turned back to her and smiled. "I hope you're able to sleep better tonight."

"Thank you, Jake."

He opened the door and stepped out quickly, shutting the door behind him.

The early morning light is perfect, Casey thought as she drove toward a home with a wonderfully landscaped three-acre backyard. The owners, whose home she had previously featured in an ad, had graciously given her permission to videotape the acreage for her own special project. She didn't have to hand in her latest assignment to Syrus until eleven, so she took this time to work on the project—a video of beautiful gardens and nature in various settings with special emphasis on the walking paths through them, to which she intended to add a background of music. She hoped to eventually donate the videos to hospitals for burn patients. For now, this served only as a trial run, a rough example. When it was finished she intended to test it on some burn patients and see if it soothed them, helping to take their minds off the pain. She also hoped that it might momentarily ease the depression that so often accompanied the recognition of newly altered appearance and limitations. If it did, she would have to have more professional help and equipment in order to do the project right, and that would mean finding a source of funding.

The seed of this idea came to her when she was in the burn unit suffering the excruciating pain that only burns can generate. The pain of the burns overrode the pain from the deep cuts and broken bone. Her father had brought some of her favorite CDs. The gentle music flowing through her mind allowed her imagination to take her out of the hospital to a place where she mentally moved through winding paths where golden sunlight cascaded through leafless paloverdes and dappled the ground through feathery-leafed trees and desert willows, each scene new with different foliage and trees.

She wanted to do a second video like the first but with a voice-over—her father reading poetry and Psalms in his deep, rich baritone, as he had done for her. This had significantly helped her emotions and the healing progress during the long, dark days, and she hoped it would do the same for others.

Arriving at her destination, she parked on the road, picked up her video camera, and walked a short distance to the wide wrought iron gates guarding the estate. She punched in the code she had been given to open the gates, and walked up the driveway, past the magnificent house, and into the huge backyard. She was delighted to find tree-lined paths canopied by leafy branches and a path that traveled over an old bridge crossing a running stream. Everywhere seemed to speak to her of peace and the eternal promise of renewal. She lost track of time recording all the paths both going and coming. She needed many more scenes before she could assemble them and add background music, but these, along with those from the desert wilderness, were a good start.

She glanced at her watch and realized if she didn't hurry she would be late for her appointment. Limping tiredly back toward the gated entry, she was within sixty feet when she saw through the bars what looked like the same man who had been watching her in the desert. He was leaning against a tree across the street, looking at her! This time not only did she feel fear, she felt something ominous. He had on a beige shirt and jeans. When he realized she had noticed him, he ducked behind the tree. Swallowing her fear, she decided to confront him. By the time she reached the slowly opening gate and walked to her car, he had disappeared. If he had come in a car, that was gone too. She took in a tremulous breath, wondering why this had to happen after such a peaceful and delightful morning.

Upon reaching work, she parked and grabbed her purse and video. The raw nerve endings in her leg were signaling their painful message as she stepped out of the car. Starting toward the entrance of her studio, she saw Syrus Tucker exit a black sedan in the next lot just before the car drove away. He was wearing beige shirt and jeans. Her heart began to pound; her breath came out in short gasps.

He saw her and waved.

"Who *are* you?" she yelled. "Where have you been?"

"What?" he asked, seemingly shocked at her emotional outburst.

She almost screamed at him. "Are you following me and watching me?"

"I can't hear you. What are you talking about, Casey?" he asked, his long legs quickly reaching the low wall separating the two buildings. He stepped over it easily and moved toward her.

"I think you know what I'm talking about," she said, backing up, her nervousness obvious.

"Let me carry your camera in for you."

"No thank you. I can take it in."

"All right. Suit yourself, but we need to talk."

"I'll be up to your office shortly." She went into her studio, shut the door, and quickly locked it. Putting the camera away, she picked up the pictures she had ready for him and went back out.

She found Syrus waiting for her. Startled, she asked "Why are you still here?"

"You have an appointment with me at eleven, remember?"

"Of course. I was headed to your office with these pictures."

"Let's get in my truck and go somewhere and talk."

"I . . . I'm not going anywhere with you."

He studied her for a moment, measuring her state of mind. "Okay then, let's go up to my office and you can show me these," he said, reaching for the manila envelope in her hand.

"All right," she said with relief.

When she sat down in front of Syrus' desk, she was still shaking.

Setting the envelope on the desk, he pulled his chair around closer to her.

"Okay, what's eating you, Casey?"

"When I was out in the desert the other day, a man was watching me from some distance away. He was standing behind a creosote bush. It gave me the shivers and I was frightened." She glared at him. "He had dark hair and wore a blue shirt and jeans. When I got back to the office, that is exactly what *you* had on. I was videotaping scenes this morning, and as I was coming back toward the gate, a man was across the street beside a tree watching me. When he noticed that I saw him he ducked behind the tree." Casey watched Syrus' expression carefully, but he revealed nothing.

"He was wearing exactly what you're wearing today, Syrus. A beige shirt and jeans."

"Well, I'll be darned. Quite a coincidence isn't it?"

"Don't patronize me, Syrus."

His expression was enigmatic. "As beautiful as you are, Casey, I'm afraid I have better things to do than to follow you around and watch you—even though I might like to," he added with an unsettling gleam in his eyes.

"That isn't an answer," she said, her voice low with distrust. "Yes or no."

"No. I wasn't following you. There, do you believe me any more than before?"

"I don't know." She got up and left his office, not satisfied.

Syrus went over and locked the door. Returning to his desk he picked up the phone and dialed. A moment later he spoke tersely into the mouthpiece. "Casey Carter is getting suspicious."

$\mathcal{C}$hapter $\mathcal{S}$ix

To teach and never be weary is love.
—Anonymous

$\mathcal{N}$an walked into the kitchen, feeling drugged and lethargic from the sleeping pill. After Chet's death, her sleep had been sporadic and fitful. The doctor had given her a prescription, which she had used only once. She hated the feeling it gave her the next morning, but after Jake left the night before, she knew she wouldn't be able to turn her mind off his contradictory actions. They left her feeling more lost and lonely. Being groggy in the morning was worth it, she had decided—so she took a pill and slept heavily.

She fixed herself a cup of strong coffee, sat down, and sipped it. She had to face life without Chet, let him go, and allow time ease her grief and loneliness. The problem was how to get on with life. What could she do with the rest of the years ahead of her?"

As she swallowed the last drop of coffee, the groggy feeling left. Grateful as she was that the coffee had done the job, she knew she would pay for it later with jittery nerves. She had decided that as soon as she was more adjusted to her new freedom, she would quit drinking coffee entirely.

A gentle tap on the door broke the silence. Could it be Jake this early? She couldn't let him see her like this! Opening the door two inches, she peeked out. "Jake! Hi."

"Good morning, Nan. I came to say good-bye."

Numb at this disclosure, she asked through the narrow opening, "Why are you leaving so soon?"

Jake had asked himself that question and couldn't answer it

satisfactorily. "Uh, could I come in for a minute and talk to you?"

"I'm not dressed, as you can see."

"You're thoroughly covered aren't you?" he asked, smiling.

"Yes, but my hair . . . it's a mess and—"

"From what I can see, it looks great. Please, I won't stay long."

Why did she care how she looked? She opened the door wide and stepped aside for him to enter. "I was just having some coffee. Would you like some?"

"No thank you."

"Have a seat and tell me why you're leaving so soon."

He sat down and looked across the table at her, feeling a little breathless at her appearance. Her long dark hair was rumpled. Thick shiny strands rippled loosely over the shoulders of the soft white robe, enhancing their darkness. Her ivory complexion was free of any makeup, revealing long dark lashes that needed no mascara. "You look beautiful, Nan," he heard himself saying. He noted that her tired-looking gray eyes brightened, and her cheeks flushed a rosy hue.

It had been so many years since Chet had even really looked at her, let alone said anything like that, that Nan hardly knew how to answer but managed a flustered, "Thank you." A nervous smile teased her lips.

The silence that followed was fraught with self-consciousness on both their parts.

Jake knew it was his place to speak first, but his mind was blank for a moment. "I, uh . . . want to apologize again. I imagine you were as puzzled as I was over my actions last night. I'd like to reiterate that it was simply frustration over . . . several things . . . things beyond my control."

"It's all right, Jake. We're both trying to work through unhappy situations. She smiled. "Why are you leaving?"

He couldn't explain the exact reason. One unsettling fact was confirmed this morning. He was attracted to Nan Hunter, but it didn't matter; he knew he couldn't marry again. In fact, everything inside him revolted at the thought of it. He had experienced too many years of hell in his marriage. Selfishly, he would like to have Nan's companionship, but it wouldn't be fair to her. She deserved to find happiness with some nice man who wanted to be married. After all the years she had given to her invalid husband, she deserved it.

Nan smiled. "Your silence says what?"

He was startled that his mind had traveled so far afield. "What? Oh, I think I'm too restless to relax right now."

Nan nodded with understanding. "And I think that I'm rather lost with time on my hands, so I may be leaving too. I need to find something worthwhile to do with the rest of my life."

"Are you all right financially?"

"Yes. My parents were professional people, both attorneys. By the time I came along, which was later in their lives, they had already made investments that made them wealthy. Gram turned it over to me before she died. I had to use some of it for expenses that began piling up. I was able to pay off our debts and still have enough to carry me for a while—hopefully until I decide what to do."

"Good. I'm glad to hear that." He stood. "Well, I think I'd better be on my way. I have a lot of work waiting for me." He hesitated and then went to the door.

Nan realized they probably wouldn't see each other again. She followed him. "It's been very nice getting acquainted with you, Jake—different but nice."

Jacob noted the same beautiful warm smile she had given him when they first met. He felt a flush of pleasure wash over him. Returning her smile, he muttered a thanks. She walked out with him and watched him move away. He stopped, turned around, shrugged his shoulders, and walked back to her. "You know, Nan, I think I'd like to have your address and phone number. I don't know why. I'm carrying around too much baggage to be a friend to anyone, but—"

"I'll go write it down on a piece of paper for you," she said quickly. She was back before he had time to berate himself. "It would be nice to hear from you sometime," she said casually, handing it to him. "And I'm carrying around some baggage of my own. It's apparent we're both rather self-absorbed with our respective burdens at the present, but in the future," she smiled, "who knows?"

"Yeah," he said nodding, "who knows."

Casey waited uneasily at the restaurant for Tiffany, almost hoping she wouldn't show up. It was a small Mexican food place in Phoenix that she and her mother had liked. Tiffany had called, very agitated, telling her that she needed to talk, then adding that it would probably be the last time she could see her. This might be the only time Casey could get the information she needed if she were to possibly help her. Feeling emotionally fragile, Casey had hoped to put it off until she was stronger and until Tiffany was more knowledgeable about her situation.

She and Tiffany went back a long way. Tiffany was one of her best friends in grade school when they lived in the Encanto Park area of Phoenix. When Casey's mother insisted they build a beautiful home in Paradise Valley in Scottsdale, they lost contact until they were in college. Tiffany was a beautiful, slender girl with brown shoulder-length hair, chocolate brown eyes, and a creamy complexion. After college they continued to keep in contact by phone every once in a while, learning of each other's marriages. When Tiffany read about her tragic accident and the disturbing aftermath in the papers, she had sent her get well cards. Then two and a half weeks ago, she had called and suggested they meet for lunch.

Casey had always felt sorry for Tiffany. Her family life wasn't good. Her father drank a lot and she seemed to be afraid of him. She never wanted to have friends come to her house, preferring to play at theirs.

Her first luncheon date with Tiffany had aroused Casey's suspicion that her husband, Russ, was abusive. Though Tiffany had tried to hide it, she was nervous and kept looking over her shoulder and around the restaurant. It was confirmed during the second luncheon date. Casey, knowing just how she felt, candidly asked if Russ was good to her. Tiffany was terrified to discuss it until Casey revealed her own experience with an abusive husband. After Tiffany had confided in her, she was even more afraid, more fearful that Russ would find out she was talking to someone about it.

Tiffany and Russ had only been married two years. It was possible they could get some help. Casey hoped to convince Tiffany to get marriage counseling for her and Russ.

With a mixture of relief and uneasiness Casey saw Tiffany enter, nervously looking behind her, checking out the restaurant. Casey stood up and waved her over to the back booth.

"Hi," Tiffany said, scooting in. "I'm glad you chose a small place. This way, I can see everyone and be sure that Russ hasn't followed me here. He checks my car mileage and knows when I've been somewhere besides the office."

"Is there somewhere you can shop or buy something out this way?"

"I'll find something, but he doesn't like me to spend money."

"Do you know how much he makes?"

"No. He keeps me on edge by saying he might lose his job or how tight we are."

"I know how difficult this is—I've been there. But why is this the last time we can see each other?"

"I didn't tell Russ about seeing you, of course, but he seemed aware of something different and questioned me relentlessly, especially after our last luncheon date. He knows about you and that we've been friends for years. He doesn't like me to have friends, so I've quit seeing or calling all of them except you. I guess I seemed a little more independent or something after visiting with you and it made him suspicious. I'm afraid

I'm not a very good actress or a very good liar."

"I know what you mean." Casey smiled and tried to lighten her friend's spirits. "The food is good here. Let's enjoy it as much as we can." She waved over a waitress.

After they ordered Casey got right down to business. "Tell me where Russ works and what he does."

Tiffany looked frightened. "Why?"

"Oh, no special reason," she hedged. "I was just wondering why he was so tight with money."

"He works for a large investment company called Global Investments. They have offices in most major cities. Russ' office is on Central near Indian School Road. Besides Phoenix, Russ is over the offices in Salt Lake, Denver, and Albuquerque."

"It sounds like he should be making a good salary."

"I know, but he says everything is tied up in long term investments. He told me I have to be patient, that eventually it will pay off. I don't know what he invests in, what he does with the money. He won't tell me. If I press it he gets angry and accuses me of not trusting him."

"Don't you handle the money *you* make?"

"No. He insists that it be put into our mutual bank account. When I wanted my own account, he accused me again of not trusting him and wouldn't speak to me for a couple of days. I ended up apologizing and doing what he wanted."

The waitress brought them their food and they ate for a while. "This is the best food I've tasted in a long time, Casey. I haven't had much of an appetite."

"My mother and I came here once in a while when she was in town. Tell me about Russ' clothes and shoes."

"Why are you asking me all this?"

"Tiffany, you know my husband was abusive. I'm trying to get a handle on your situation. I would like to know if it's anything like mine. If it's similar I'll tell you what you can do to help yourself as best I can in the short time we have."

Tiffany gave her a pathetic smile. "Thank you, Casey. I've

always appreciated your friendship and it's all I have to hang on to at the moment. My parents live back East and I can't trust anyone but you. To answer your question, Russ has his own closet. It's huge. I haven't counted, but it's filled with at least eleven or twelve suits and lots of shoes, slacks, and shirts—all purchased from the best department stores. He's very particular about his appearance. He has to appear in the best light at work, at the country club, at church, and to the neighbors."

"Do you have a big closet full of clothes?"

"My closet is small, comparatively. When I want to buy clothes, he says we can't afford it. When I pointed out to him what he spends on his clothes, he got angry and said that in his position at work and in the community, he has to appear well-dressed, that it's a necessity. I end up shopping at the thrift store most of the time. Actually, I'm getting quite good at finding stylish clothes there. I'm wearing a suit I purchased from one."

Casey, amazed, studied the pale green suit and colorful scarf. "It looks lovely with your brown hair and eyes. I never would have known it wasn't new. What kind of a neighborhood do you live in, Tiff?"

"It's an elite neighborhood. We have a beautiful home. Again, appearances in that area are important to Russ."

"Is Russ good with words, does he express himself well?"

"Oh, he's so polished and self-assured, he exudes self-confidence."

"Does he always sound credible when talking with other people?"

"Oh yes! Everyone believes everything he says. I sometimes wonder what he says about me to other people. Whatever he says, I'm sure they'd believe it."

Casey shuddered. Tiffany might as well have been talking about Nick. She had read books on verbal abuse and found that most or all abusive men used the same methods, talked the same, used the same words and the same subtleties to control. It was almost as if they all belonged to a secret and sinister club.

Casey took a deep breath to calm herself. "Are there other ways he isolates you besides not letting you associate with your friends?"

Tiffany thought a minute and shook her head in confusion.

"Does he call you disloyal when you try to visit with friends at parties, instead of staying right by him?"

"Yes!"

"Did he find fault with your friends, the ones you finally had to quit seeing? Does he find fault with anyone you like?"

"How could you know this, Casey?"

"I want you to go to the library and look up books and articles on verbal abuse. You'll find a lot. Read them at the library, and then go home and do your best to act as natural as possible so he won't have any reason to know what you're doing. If you pray for help, eventually you can start putting into practice what the books and articles tell you to do."

Tiffany's face brightened with a flicker of hope. "What a good idea. I never would have thought about doing that, Casey. Thank you."

"Also, don't call me on your home or cell phone anymore. Call me only on the library phone or from your work phone. Since you're afraid to see me anymore, I want you to call regularly and tell me how things are."

"Oh, I will, Casey. I can't thank you enough for helping me realize what Russ is really doing. He has belittled me and blamed me for everything, called me crazy, told me I imagine things and—Oh! I can hardly think for myself anymore."

"I don't know how it's going to work out for you, Tiff, but I'll be praying that you'll find a way out."

"A way out of my marriage?" she asked fearfully.

"I didn't mean that exactly, I—"

"I want to leave Russ, Casey, but I'm terrified to try. I said something one day that gave him the impression I might leave. His eyes turned frighteningly hateful. He said, 'No woman leaves me, Tiffany.' I asked him what he meant by that. He said, 'Leave me and you'll find out.'"

Casey's breath turned shallow. "Have you suggested to Russ that you and he need to have marriage counseling?"

"Yes, but he was furious. He said that it was me that was causing the problems. And maybe I am, Casey. If I were thinner, if I were more careful about what I said to him, if—"

"Tiffany! Stop it. You are not to blame for his cruelty. I know you well. Please, don't blame yourself. I did that myself for a while before I realized that nothing I said or didn't say, nothing I did or didn't do would make any difference."

"I'll try to believe that. But he said I was crazy and . . ." She covered her face.

"I don't know for sure, of course, but it sounds like you can't help this man or your marriage, Tiffany. If you find out you can't, you might have to get out before the abuse gets worse."

"I have no idea what I could possibly do. I feel trapped."

"Let me give it some thought, Tiffany. As I said, call me and keep me informed, will you?"

"Oh, I will, Casey. I have no one but you to call. The police wouldn't believe me unless I had bruises, a black eye, and a broken rib or two."

"The system isn't perfect, Tiff, but from what I've heard and read, the authorities are beginning to accept and recognize emotional battery as well as physical."

Chapter Seven

Defeat isn't bitter if you don't swallow it.
—Anonymous

Shaken up after talking with Tiffany, Casey's heart pounded heavily as she drove toward her studio. She had a nagging worry. Was she being too suspicious of Russ because of her own experience, too skeptical that their marriage couldn't work? Not all abusive men turn violent. What made her think there was no hope for Russ? In her studies she had read the story of a man who remorsefully realized his abusive ways, sought therapy, and saved his marriage.

A troubled thought slipped into her consciousness. *Could Nick have changed?* Immediately she remembered—Nick had tried to kill her! *But, have I been too precipitous in thinking that Tiffany and Russ' marriage isn't salvageable?* she asked herself uneasily. "No!" she stated adamantly. She had watched Tiffany carefully as she answered her questions and when she saw the fear on her face, a grinding knot churned inside her stomach. She simply had to prayerfully trust that her feelings were correct.

Miserably she continued to argue with herself. *But how can I possibly consider this—especially at this time in my life? I don't feel physically or emotionally strong enough!* As if in answer, the words of Grandmother Jacobson came to mind, *When someone needs our help, it never comes at a fitting time. If it's handy and easy, it's probably not true service.* Casey sighed. Grandma was right.

She wished she had met Tiffany's husband, Russ Eden, but she had been in no condition to attend their reception. She was at least glad she had a picture of him. When she and Tiffany first had lunch together, Tiffany gave her a picture of the two of them standing together, proud to show her friend what a handsome man she had married.

Now she needed to talk with her dad.

Syrus Tucker parked his truck in the Hartner and Hart parking lot. It was then that he saw Casey Carter parking in the same lot instead of behind her studio. He watched her move slowly toward the back entrance, her limp more pronounced. His heart felt compressed. The girl had guts!

Walking rapidly, he arrived at the entrance at the same time. He opened the door for her. She hadn't noticed him coming and looked up at him in surprise.

"Syrus, where did you come from?"

"I'm coming back from lunch. Have you been out doing your video shooting again?"

"No. I've just come back from lunch too."

"Eating gives me more energy. Why not you? You seem tired. What's up?"

Irritated at the personal question, she spoke with brusqueness. "Nothing." They stepped into the elevator. "Sorry. I shouldn't act like a spoiled brat now, should I?" she added tartly.

Syrus' jaw clenched. "You know, if anyone else talked to me like you do, I wouldn't give him or her any more work."

Distressed at her prickliness, Casey looked up into his face, trying to be pleasant.

"How tall are you, anyway? I'm getting a crick in my neck. The rumor is six foot three."

"It's not a rumor. It's a fact. As I was saying . . ."

"I'm so tired, Sy, I wouldn't mind if you didn't give me one more assignment."

His chest felt tight. "How tall are you, sprite?"

"Five feet five inches." She answered before she realized

what he had called her. "Sprite?"

Surprised at the word himself, Syrus gave her a small grin, shrugged his shoulders, and immediately changed the subject. He looked her up and down. "I've never seen you wear anything but silky looking pants. Is that because they won't rub on your scars?"

She threw him a puzzled glance. "You ask the most unusual questions."

They stepped out of the elevator and Syrus looked at his watch. "You're a little early for our appointment, but I'm free, so come on into my office."

She followed his long strides and plopped into a chair in front of his desk while he closed the door. He sat behind the desk and scrutinized her. "Are you going to answer my question about your pants, slacks, whatever they are?"

"You're very astute. That's exactly why I wear silk pants. I can wear longer dresses or skirts, but I have to be careful. My leg is a sight. What is it you want to see me about?"

Syrus accepted Casey's shift in the conversation. "I have another assignment for you. It's a big account—a big chain. It will require taking photos of people in certain settings inside homes. Your specialty is scenery, but I've seen your work with people and it's good." He handed her a copy of the company instructions and the addresses and phone numbers of the homes where the shoots would be held.

"Thank you, Syrus. I think I'll go look at the homes before I call the talent agency and tell them who I want for models. Is that all?"

"No. I get the feeling that you still don't trust me, Casey. Why?"

"Does it matter what I feel? We can work well together professionally, regardless."

"Why don't you trust me?" he said in a tone that demanded an answer.

"First of all, the last questions you asked me at Rosarita's seemed far beyond what the company needed to know. I'm a freelancer and as long as I perform my assignment in an acceptable manner, I can't see any reason why this company should know what you asked."

"No fooling you, I see."

"No. I've already been fooled and it's made me rather distrusting and skeptical. Why did you ask those last questions?"

"You're right. They weren't questions the company needed to know. I personally wanted to know those things."

"Why?" she asked. Her eyes gazed unflinchingly into his.

"You don't need to know that," he returned quietly.

"I do need to know. That was an intrusion of my privacy, using your status as my liaison and de facto boss in the company."

"Forget it, Casey."

Casey glared at him for a moment and then stood. "Is that all, Mr. Tucker?"

Syrus gazed at her for a moment, a bemused expression on his face. "Not until you call me Sy."

Casey gazed back at him, refusing.

He tilted his head to one side, a tight-lipped smile on his face. "It's a little hard to believe your story about an abusive husband, Casey. You're such a strong-willed little spitfire. How did he get away with it, anyway?"

Casey crumpled back into the chair and covered her face to hide the sudden angry tears.

He couldn't let himself be drawn in by her tears. He had a job to do. Shoving his chair back, he stood at the window, his back to Casey, trying to harden his resolve. When he turned around, she was hastily wiping her eyes with her fingers.

"When I feel extreme anger, I cry."

Appearing unmoved, Syrus asked, "Anger at me or your husband?"

She refused to answer.

"Surely, you didn't allow him to manipulate you."

"I've already told you about it!" Taking a deep breath to

calm herself, her eyes focused unblinkingly on his. "Why are you baiting me?" she asked quietly.

"Since you won't let it go, I'd better tell you." He sat back down. "Because one man over me has been skeptical about your role in the accident. I've been asked to find out what I can. Hartner and Hart is a well respected company and they don't want to be caught up in any kind of scandal."

"I don't have to tell them about my private life. I could sue them for harassment."

"Casey," he began, his eyes resuming their lightening glint, "a possible indictment is hanging over your head. I doubt you could sue and I doubt you'll be able to find another company who'll work with you as we have—in case you're thinking of trying. But if you are, be my guest . . . there's the door."

Casey set her teeth and for a moment, her body language was that of one who was about to get up. Leaning forward, her hand on the arm of the chair to hoist herself—then she wilted and sat back. Her eyes downcast, she said in almost a whisper, "It feels as though Nick is reaching out from the grave, still trying to control me. I wonder when my life will ever be my own."

Syrus studied her for a moment as he tried to resolve his own inner conflict. "I'm sure the police are still working on it."

"No. It's in the jurisdiction of the FBI for reasons I can't tell you since I'm not sure the FBI divulged that to the paper."

"Have you tried to find out how far along they are on the case?"

"Yes and so has my father, over and over. All they tell us is they're working on it."

"It seems to be taking a long time."

"Since it was already leaked to the papers, I can tell you that it's because they never found the gun, and therefore, my story is suspect." She thought for a moment and then spoke quietly, as if to herself. "But I can't imagine what they could be working on—unless . . . unless it has something to do with his work at Arizona Central Bank." Looking directly at Syrus, she said, "When the FBI asked me about it before, I didn't remember the incident of the manila folder I told you about."

Syrus saw a look of concern suddenly appear on her face. "What is it, Casey?"

"The FBI wouldn't be happy at all that I told you. I'm supposed to only talk about the case with the FBI agent who's working directly with me."

"You don't need to mention you told me. As I said, you can trust me. The information is safe with me."

"I hope I can trust you, Syrus. At the moment I'm afraid I have some doubts."

"That's your problem, Casey. And, I don't like the name Syrus. That's why I've asked everyone to call me Sy."

She rolled her eyes over his annoying request and then reasserted herself. "I happen to like the name Syrus, so when I'm not in the mood to call you Sy, I'm going to call you Syrus." With that announcement, she got up and left the room.

Syrus leaned back in his chair and smiled.

After a soothing bath, Casey put on her nightgown and went into her small family room off the kitchen, propped up her leg on the soft footstool, and turned on the television. She looked at her watch and saw that it was eight. She wished her dad were home. Restlessly she turned off the television, got up, and moved to the phone. Back in the chair she dialed his cell phone in Sedona. It had been turned off. She tried his home number and was rewarded with the pleasant timbre of his voice, the voice that had, day after day, soothed her through the pain in the burn center, the voice that had comforted her hundreds of times during the ups and downs of her life. When she cried with loneliness for her mother, it was his voice that made the years bearable.

"Dad! I'm so glad you're home."

"To be honest, I'm glad to be home. I wasn't able to relax like I thought I would. I found I couldn't run away from myself and my thoughts." He chuckled. "What's up, Case?"

"I've had kind of a grueling day. I don't suppose you could come over for a little while?"

"I sure can. Besides, I was feeling a little lonely."

"Thanks, Dad. I love you."

Fifteen minutes later, Casey's doorbell rang. She eagerly opened the door and threw her arms around her dad. "It's good to see you," she murmured against his chest.

When they were settled in the family room, the first thing Jacob asked was how her interview with Belle Levine went.

Casey smiled slyly. "I didn't have an interview."

Disappointment creased his brows. "Why?"

"She liked me so well, we had a short session instead."

Jacob eyed her accusingly. "You little tease, you had me going for a second. What do you think of her?"

"I like her." She got up and kissed him on the cheek. "Thank you, Dad. You're wiser than I am. Talking with her made me realize I really do need some therapy. I made another appointment with her."

"Good girl! That relieves my mind."

"You don't need to worry anymore, I'm in good hands."

He smiled and nodded. "Now tell me about your grueling day."

Not wanting to worry him unnecessarily, she didn't mention her concern with the man she caught watching her. Briefly as she could, she told him about her luncheon date with Tiffany, what she had learned from her, and then her conversation with Syrus.

Jacob looked grim. "Two things, Casey. First, I'm sorry about Hartner and Hart being concerned about your part in the accident. It will end soon. We have to believe that. And secondly, I don't think you should try to carry Tiffany's burden. You're still recovering yourself."

"I know, Dad, and I had just about decided that I wasn't

able to help her when Grandma's favorite statement on service came into my mind. So I knew I had to."

Jacob sighed and shook his head. "My mother is still managing things, I see."

"Dad, you know when I told you I needed to think over something concerning Tiffany before talking to you about it? I've given it a lot of thought and I want to discuss it tonight."

Jacob hid his disappointment that she hadn't given up on the idea. "All right, go ahead."

"Remember I said I wanted to play on Nick's weaknesses, something that would put him off-balance to such a extent he wouldn't be able to come after me?" Casey saw her dad's jaw tighten, followed by a slight nod. She took a deep breath. "What I didn't tell you is I had actually gotten to the planning stage. But that's as far as I got before he tried to kill me. Well . . . uh, I'd like to try this plan on Tiffany's husband, Russ Eden. I don't know how we'll accomplish it or even if it will work, but I'd like to try."

Jacob rubbed his temples wearily. "Casey, Casey, even if it were possible to do what you want to do, it's too much for you right now. Please wait until you're a little stronger."

"I would like to, Dad, believe me. I'm not looking forward to the project at all. But Russ Eden sounds so much like Nick that I'm frightened for Tiffany."

"Didn't you tell me that most abusers exercise control in the same ways, use the same words and phrases, use the same techniques?"

"Yes."

"But not all of them are violent or murderous like Nick."

"I know, Dad. I've told myself that, but for some reason, I . . . I think I need to try and help Tiffany. Besides, she has no one. I had you."

Jacob was silent for a few moments. "If this man is anything like Nick, what you do may turn him violent. You may do more harm than good."

"Believe me, I've thought of that. Whatever is done or

however we do it, it has to be in a way that Russ couldn't possibly know who's doing it."

"That doesn't do much to lessen my concern, Casey. You're being so vague. Tell me what you're planning to do. I need to know."

"It's vague in my mind, too. I can't explain it intelligently yet. I need to go over it with someone, bat it around a little so I can make you understand. I promise I'll tell you when the plan becomes clear."

Jacob was frustrated. "What do you want me to do?"

"Are you willing to fund it?"

Jacob knew that Casey couldn't even try to put this alarming idea into practice without his financial help. He was sorely tempted to refuse. "I can't imagine any plan working. I would have to feel that it was all right, and not dangerous for you and that it stood a good chance of being successful, and of helping your friend."

"Fair enough. After I get all the details worked out, if you feel we can't pull it off or if it's too dangerous, I'll drop the idea. For now, I need somebody to work with me—somebody who will listen to my ideas, someone with whom I can go over the pros and cons."

"And you don't want that somebody to be me?"

Casey smiled. "I would love it to be you, Dad, if you could be objective."

"Well, I guess that lets me out. Have you mentioned this plan to Tiffany?"

"Oh no. I don't want her to know anything about it. This way, Russ can't suspect her because most of the time he can tell when she's evading the truth. I told her to only call from the library phone or work phone and not use her cell phone anymore when she calls me. She said we couldn't meet anymore because Russ could see a difference in her after our previous visits and he became worse."

Jacob's apprehension grew. "I wish you'd give this up, Casey." His eyes locked on those of his daughter's. "But I see you're determined. Let me think. Who could we ask to help you?"

They were both silent, thinking.

Casey smiled bitterly. "After Nick poisoned everyone we knew with his vicious rumors, I doubt if we have any real friends left. But let's try to come up with someone anyway."

The minutes ticked away and finally, Casey said, "I can't think of one person."

Jacob's face turned grim. "I can't either. You know what, honey?"

"What?"

"We both need to sleep on this, even think about it for a week or two, then—"

"Dad, I know what you're trying to do. You're hoping I'll forget about it or chicken out after a few weeks."

He looked at her, trying to come up with an answer. She nodded and smiled knowingly. "You know me too well," Jacob said, shaking his head.

"Let's both sleep on it tonight, Dad. Then I'll take you to lunch at our favorite restaurant, La Madeliene's, tomorrow."

He tried once more. "How about a week from now?"

"Tomorrow I have time. I don't know if I'll have time a week from now."

"All right. You win, but it doesn't mean I'll approve of it any more tomorrow than I do today, or that we'll be able to come up with a name."

"I know, Dad, but let's give it a try. I'll pick you up at your office at noon."

Lunch at La Madeliene's was a treat for Casey, but as she took the last bite of dessert she sighed over their failure to think of anyone to help her. She simply couldn't plan it alone. They both tried their best, but each time someone mentioned a name, one or the other promptly vetoed it.

"I'm sorry, Casey. I know how badly you want to help Tiffany."

"I guess it was a bizarre idea anyway."

"You said it, I didn't." Jacob smiled. "Though you didn't tell me the details, it does sound a little bizarre."

"Jake, hello," came a voice above them.

They looked up. "Nan!" Jacob exclaimed. Scooting his chair back, he quickly stood. "What a surprise."

"Yes, isn't it. We just walked in and I saw you immediately." Her eyes fastened on Casey. "Is this your daughter?"

"Yes it is. Casey, I want you to meet Nan Hunter."

Nan smiled. "I'm so happy to meet you. Your father has told me about you and I've very much wanted to meet you."

Casey looked puzzled. "I . . . I'm happy to meet you."

Nan laughed. "I see your father hasn't mentioned me."

"Can you join us?" Jacob asked uncomfortably.

"Thank you, but I'm with a friend and besides, I see you've already finished your meal."

Jacob glanced over at the man waiting for Nan. A sliver of annoyance went through him. "You're dating, I see."

"Dating's an uncomfortable word for me, Jake. He's just a good friend I haven't seen for years. And I better get back to him. It was wonderful running into you both."

Casey's wide eyes watched Nan Hunter walk back to her friend. Never had she seen such a stunning woman. She stood up. "Shall we go, Dad? . . . Dad?"

"Uh, yes," he said, pulling his eyes away from Nan and her friend.

Casey slid behind the wheel. Turning on the motor, she gave him a "why didn't you tell me about Nan Hunter?" look.

"All right," she said, "you know what I want to hear." Pulling out onto Camelback Road, she asked, "How or when did you meet Nan Hunter?"

"You know that cabin east of us?"

"Yes."

"As you know, we've never seen it in use when we've been

there. Well, this time someone was there. It was Nan. She's a widow of two months. Her husband had muscular dystrophy, and after he died she wanted to get away for a while. After taking him to the cabin only twice, he refused to go anymore. That's why we've never seen anyone there."

"It didn't take you long to get acquainted with her."

He smiled. "No it didn't. But it was strictly accidental. The first hour I was there, I went out hiking and we nearly bumped into each other. Scared us both to death since we didn't think anyone else was around and we were each pretty deep in our own thoughts. She invited me to have a soda with her. Then the next night, I bought too much food and invited her over to have a hamburger with me."

Casey's eyes widened. "You did?"

Jacob smiled. "Yes. So you see, I'm not as antisocial as you've accused me of being. However, as it turned out, we were both too absorbed in our own problems and felt a little awkward. I did find out, though, that she has taken care of her husband for so many years she's having a hard time trying to adjust to normal living."

Casey was silent, thinking. When Nan Hunter smiled at her, a feeling of warmth spread through her. She liked her immediately. "She seems very nice."

"She is. She reminds me of you a little."

"How?" Casey asked surprised.

"She's a very selfless and giving person."

"Why thank you, Dad. You know, I wish we knew her well enough. She's the kind of person I'd like to try out my ideas on."

"Uh, I don't know about that, Case. She's at a rather vulnerable place in her life right now."

"It looks like she's getting on with life just fine." She glanced at her dad and saw his eyes narrow. "Does it bother you that she was out with a man?" she asked, watching him as closely as she could and still keep her eyes on the road.

"Of course not."

It seemed to Casey that it did—perhaps more than he himself was aware. "Do you know how to get in touch with her?"

"Yes. I got her address and phone number."

"Wow! Good for you. Would you just feel her out about helping me?"

"I'd rather not, Casey."

"It might help take her mind off her grief," she suggested, trying to interpret his expression.

Jacob rubbed his brow. "The last thing she needs is to get into what appears is going to be a ticklish situation."

"Please, Dad, just feel her out. You might get an ally. If you and she feel I shouldn't try to implement my ideas, I'll give up the whole thing."

Jacob sucked in a deep breath and let it out, wishing this would all go away.

"Dad, these crazy ideas I have floating around in my head may not even be feasible. Nan seems like the kind of person who could be discerning and objective." She entered the parking lot of his office building and parked.

"All right," he agreed uneasily. "I'll call her and ask her out to lunch. But only if you agree to let it go if she's also concerned about it."

"Gotcha," she grinned. She leaned over and kissed him on the cheek. "You know, I feel better. If we all decide that this might work I think it will be cathartic for me." She grinned impishly. "It will almost be as if I were doing it to Nick."

Chapter Eight

When the artist's life also inspires us,
we're doubly blessed.

Jacob was already seated when he saw the restaurant hostess lead Nan Hunter toward the table. The sight of her almost took his breath away. She was dressed in a green skirt and matching long-sleeved blouse, belted in with a silver concho belt. The color was outstanding with her dark hair, which was pulled tightly back the same way she had worn it up at the cabin. He found it a very flattering style for her face. He stood up and smiled. When he had seated her, he sat opposite.

"Thank you for coming."

Her eyes sparkled. "You sounded rather mysterious when you mentioned you might want me to help your daughter with something a little offbeat." She gave him her wide, warm smile. "Sounds like something right up my alley."

Jacob laughed, more out of nervousness than humor. "This is a side of you I didn't see up at the cabin. Shall we look at the menus and get that out of the way before we talk?"

"By all means, I'm starved. I didn't eat breakfast this morning."

They studied the menus, closed them, and placed them on the table almost at the same time. Their eyes met and the action brought a smile to each. After the waitress took their orders and left, Nan spoke. "All right, Jake, tell me why you wanted to see me. I'm on pins and needles."

"I can only tell you a little. I don't know exactly what my daughter has in mind and frankly, I'm more than a little concerned about it. She's such a maverick at times. For now, she needs to have a partner, a woman with whom she can bat her ideas around. It has something to do with helping a friend."

"Hmm. So far, it sounds interesting. I'm glad I got to meet her. She's even more lovely than I expected. After what you told me at the cabin, I've given her a lot of thought, wondering what it was that she has gone through."

"Well . . . as much as I dislike talking about it, I'm afraid I have to tell you a little about it so you can understand why she wants to help a friend who is in a similar situation." As briefly as possible, he began telling the whole ghastly story of his daughter and Nick Carter. He looked at the table most of the time, but when he glanced up at her intermittently, he saw expressions of shock and deep empathy.

When the food arrived, Nan looked at it. "It looks good, but your story has dampened my appetite."

"I'm sorry. Since it's never off my mind, my eating much of the time is automatic, just to give me energy to keep going. However, I did have a better appetite up at the cabin when we ate hamburgers together." He smiled at her.

"They did taste good, didn't they?"

They ate in silence for a few minutes before Nan asked. "I'm afraid I'm confused, Jake. You want me to meet with Casey so she can bounce her ideas off me? Is that all?"

"I'm afraid there's more to it. Casey won't tell me until she talks with someone. After meeting you yesterday, she requested that someone be you."

"I consider that quite a compliment. I'd like to help, but considering the emotional state I'm in right now, I'm not sure how much value my help will be."

"If you find that it's too much to even consider it right now, I'll certainly understand."

"May I talk with Casey before I make up my mind?"

"Yes. But whatever she tells you, it has to be kept confidential. A young girl's happiness may depend on it—maybe even her life."

"Casey's?" Nan asked, concerned.

"No, her friend's."

"When do you want me to talk with her?"

"I'll check with Casey and see if tonight is convenient with her. If it is, and if it's convenient for you, can you come over to my home tonight around seven?"

"Yes. Give me your address and phone number."

"I'll call and let you know for sure," he said writing the information down and handing it to her. "Thank you, Nan."

At four-thirty, Casey, feeling exhausted, entered the building that housed Belle Levine's office. Before she left work, her dad had called with the news that he'd had lunch with Nan Hunter, who was willing to meet with them at seven tonight at the house if they were available. She thanked him and said she would see him then. At the moment, the task she had set out for herself looked overwhelming. Reaching Belle's door, she knocked.

Belle opened the door. She was wearing a different dress today, another flowered print. Her smile was warm. "You look beat, kid. Come on in and sit down."

"Thank you, Belle. I am tired—emotionally and physically."

"What's up? Something's hit you hard today."

Casey gave a brief account of Tiffany. Then told her of the ad agency's reaction about her own situation.

"That comes with the territory, Casey. Got to expect it. People are automatically polarized when they hear or read about something as controversial as your case. And from now on, you'll be very aware of those who are being abused. It will come to your attention as it never has before. Are you ready to deal with it?"

"No."

"Of course not. And you never will be. It's always painful.

Do you have any friends or a friend you can do something fun with once in a while?"

"No. Nick took care of that long before the accident. He poisoned everyone's mind."

"Then they weren't friends, were they?"

"No. But what hurts is the way he maligned my mother. She brought some of it upon herself, of course, but he told lies about her and he knew differently."

"Do you want to tell me about it?"

"Yes. I don't think I've dealt with that yet. I don't want to talk to my father about it because it's too painful for him." Casey told Belle in detail of her mother's increasing popularity, the headaches and backaches, the painkillers and how she had acted in public when she was on one of them. "What was amazing is she never took that medication while she was in a production. Nevertheless, Nick told everyone she was mentally ill and delusional and that I was becoming delusional like her."

"Why do you suppose he called you delusional?"

"I've given that a lot of thought. Maybe it was because it was part of his plan to isolate me from everyone but him."

Belle nodded. "Could be."

"Or maybe it was because he found he couldn't control me like he wanted to. It was eerie, Belle. I think he could tell that I wasn't going to stay with him, that I was planning to do something. Either I'm a terrible actress or he had a sixth sense or something."

"You're right. Abusers seem to have the amazing ability to tune in on anything. They don't trust anyone and they're always on guard and watching."

"It seems as though that would take an inordinate amount of energy."

"I'm sure it does, but it has actually become a way of life with them—almost as necessary as breathing."

"It's incredible that someone would find a reward in controlling someone else."

"It is. Do you have any idea why Nick was like that?"

"No. I tried to find out what made him like he was. He wouldn't talk about his parents much. I wanted to get to know them better, but since they live in Florida, we didn't see them very often. His father is a successful businessman. He and his wife socialize with wealthy people, which impressed my mother."

Casey gazed, unseeing, at the picture on the wall. "After we were married and our relationship began to deteriorate I was desperate to find out why. I began listening and watching Nick carefully. Remember last time I told you I thought I found Nick's Achilles' heel?"

"Oh yes. I was going to ask you about that."

"It was like an epiphany. One day it just came to me. I knew that *fear* ruled Nick. Fear of being put in a bad light, fear of not looking perfect and in control at all times while in public, fear of his inadequacies being found out, fear of not having a lot of money, fear of being unsuccessful in anything, and I'm certain there were other things I wasn't aware of."

Belle shook her head. "You're one astute young woman. It usually takes years of marriage for women to recognize those things. Did you have any support from friends?"

"No. After the accident none of them came to see me, or Dad—not even our minister. Now, if I happen to run into any of them, Dad's friends or mine, and I use that term loosely, they snub me or in some cases actually seem frightened of me. I can tell by the way they look at me that they believe that my alleged mental state caused the accident."

"Through the years, Casey, I've come to realize two things. First, it takes less thought and energy to believe the negative. Being objective and fair takes a lot of thought, consideration, and care. It takes effort to seek more knowledge before allowing oneself to believe one way or another. Secondly, I find that people who easily believe the unkind, the negative, the gossip, are people who are deficient spiritually or are, themselves, battling some guilt of their own."

"I've never thought of it like that, Belle." Considering it a moment, Casey added, "I'm sure that at one time or another I've been guilty of believing something too readily, but after going through what Dad and I have, I've tried to be very careful what I believe about someone. It's difficult though, because I've become so distrusting."

"That should pass in time. Do you feel that your mother pursuing her career to the extent she did had an effect on you?"

"I'm not sure to what extent it affected me. My dad and I were so close, and I was close to Grandma Jacobson before she died."

"When your mother was alive and came home between productions, did she fill your needs?"

Casey brooded over the question. "'I'm sure you've heard the old adage, "the theater is a very demanding mistress"? It's true. I never felt she could give me or Dad her thoughts. When she came home, she was exhausted and had to rest for days. When she was feeling better and I tried to talk to her, it was difficult for her to understand my daily life, my frustrations and problems. She tried, but her efforts were only superficial and unsatisfying."

"Do you think that your mother-deprived state made it easier to be deceived by Nick?"

Anxiety furrowed Casey's brow and a look of pain crossed her face. "As Mother became more and more involved in these productions, her language changed, her values changed. I talked with Dad about it, and he said, 'It appears that the entertainment world coarsens many people—even in the opera.' He said, 'Many artists add richness to our lives by their talent only, others enrich us by their talent *and* their lives.' He didn't say which description fit Mother, but I knew. I know he was remorseful for encouraging her, but I'm positive she would have done it without his encouragement." A tight knot in her chest prevented her from continuing.

Belle waited patiently.

"I remember feeling so proud of her, but . . ." Casey was shocked at the flood of tears that suddenly burst from her. "I'm sorry." One hand fluttered in the air as though to banish the pain.

"Cry, Casey. Let it all out. That's a good kid. Good, let it all out."

A few minutes later, Casey grabbed several more tissues and wiped her eyes and nose. "I had no idea all that was inside me."

"There are more tears inside you, Casey. Don't hold them in anymore."

She nodded and more tears surfaced. She promptly blinked them back. "At the moment, I feel like I could cry for days." She smiled. "But I think I'll cry on my own time, not yours. It's less expensive."

Belled laughed. "Good thinking. What were you feeling?"

"I'm not sure. I guess I was grieving over losing my mother—not when she died, but when she seriously started her career. I found myself hanging on to every bit of attention Mother could give me. She had a delightful personality and she loved life." She paused, her face distorted with grief that hadn't yet found the easing path of tears.

"When I met Nick," she began slowly, "she gave me more attention than I'd ever had from her. She wanted to hear everything about him, what we did on our dates, what we talked about and so on. It was a double whammy—my infatuation with him and her attention. Besides that, she gave me what I wanted—enthusiastic approval of Nick. I'm afraid I didn't take into account her change of values. Why didn't I think of that, Belle?"

"Because you're human, Casey."

Chapter Nine

*The person who misses all the fun is
one who says, "It can't be done."*
—Anonymous

Jacob's doorbell rang promptly at seven. "Will you get
the door, Case, I have to get out of this suit," he yelled
from the bedroom.

"All right," she said, starting for the door. Her leg felt leaden
with each step. *Can I go through with this?* she asked herself.
After all, it's only an offbeat idea rolling around in my head. Now
that another person might get involved, it loomed in her mind
as terribly unrealistic.

Her thoughts came to a sudden halt when she opened the
door. She couldn't speak for a moment. She could only stare
at Nan's appearance. She was wearing the same vivid green
blouse and skirt she had worn at lunch with Jacob except for a
sash of green and earthy colors accented with designs of desert
and Indian folklore. She had thrown it across her shoulder with
a dramatic flair and draped it diagonally across her bosom.

Poor Dad, Casey thought, remembering his adamant and
negative reaction to her suggestion one day he should date and
consider remarrying.

Nan smiled. "Hello, Casey."

"Oh, I'm sorry, Nan. I'm afraid I was a little speechless, you
look so glamorous."

"Why thank you. I was thinking the same thing about
you."

"Glamorous in this?" she asked, surprised, looking down
at her usual silk pants. "That's nice to hear. I haven't put much

thought into what I wear since the accident. Please come in."

"Thank you."

"Dad is changing from his suit into something more comfortable. He'll be right out. We'll be meeting in the family room," she said.

"This is a beautiful home," Nan said, glancing around at the spacious marble-floored entryway. Against the wall on the right stood a red lacquered Louis XV table with a parcel-gilt finish. Above it was a fascinating picture. Nan was enthralled. It was a painting of two cement steps with two large red vases overflowing with flowers. Next to them was a path that traveled under an arbor of vines and flowers.

"My mother bought that when she and Dad were on a trip to Italy many years ago. It's a fresco. It was painted by an Italian artisan who uses a special method handed down from ancient times."

"It's beautiful."

"I like it too," Casey said, taking a couple of steps and then stopping as her guest paused.

Nan admired the center rug, an Aubusson with an ornate and elegant weave of red, yellow, and black. On her left was a spacious living room. It was a sea of yellow fabrics, ceramics, and a custom Portuguese needlepoint rug. Touches of red on the wood arms of the Regency-style lounge chairs pulled in the red from the entryway. The black chinoiserie tray table and coffee table were as startling to Nan as the red wood trim. A large ivory-colored grand piano graced one corner. The windows were covered with white sheers, letting light fill the room.

Nan was drawn to it in one way but repelled in another.

Casey studied Nan curiously. "People usually love this room or they hate it."

Nan smiled. "Somehow it doesn't beckon me in at the moment. But it's lovely and very different."

"So was mother . . . lovely and different. Let's go on into the family room."

They passed an elegant dining room on the right. Turning

right a few steps, Casey stopped in front of two lead glass doors on the left. Opening them, they entered a large family room that was much more inviting. The couches and chairs looked comfortable and the colors were light green, yellow, and light tan. Large windows and green plants added to the surroundings.

"Let's sit down and get acquainted while we wait for Dad."

Before they could do so, Jacob walked in.

Jacob greeted his guest with a broad smile. "Hello, Nan. Thanks for coming."

"It's a pleasure, I assure you. As I said before, your daughter is lovely."

"I think so," he said, winking at Casey. "Shall we all be seated? Nan, you sit in that chair and Casey and I will sit here on the couch."

Jacob couldn't take his eyes off Nan. "You look nice, Nan."

"Thank you, Jake," she said, removing the sash. It was Nan's favorite clothing style in part because it reflected her love of Arizona and the Native Americans she grew up with.

Jacob smiled. "Now," he said turning to Casey, "where do we start? I've already told Nan briefly about your married life and the accident. You take it from there."

"Do you want to stay, Dad?"

"I want to know what you have in mind, of course. But would you like to talk it over with Nan alone first, get her feedback, and then tell me afterward?"

"Yes, I think I would. This is more of a woman thing anyway, and I don't want to hear any shocked outbursts from you, if you don't mind." She smiled.

Jacob eyed his daughter, a shadow of a smile on his lips. He turned to Nan and announced, "You can see why I've enlisted your help."

Nan laughed. "See you later, Jake."

He rose and eyed Casey again. "You'll tell me all about it later. Everything, right?"

"Right."

Casey watched him leave and then turned to Nan and saw the smile still on her face.

"You have a great relationship with your father."

"I do. You're a good sport to come and listen to the hare-brained ideas I have," she said, giving Nan a small apologetic smile.

"Don't give me too much credit yet, Casey. I may not be able to help. I have to be frank with you. My emotions are still rather close to the surface."

"Dad told me you've just lost your husband. I'm sorry. If you don't feel you can get involved, I'll understand. I'm not sure I can, myself."

"Wanting to help a friend so soon after your terrible ordeal is rather brave of you. I'm amazed you even have the strength to try. Tell me what you have in mind."

Casey's hands were rigid in her lap. "I'll try to be brief." She began Tiffany's story and was surprised that, in the process of telling it, the tension left and her strength expanded, both physically and emotionally. When she finished, she tried to discern how it had affected Nan. "Those are the facts as I know them. It's heavy stuff."

"I know of one that's worse. It's about a friend of mine I was close to before my husband became so ill and needed all my attention."

"Can you tell me about it?"

"Yes. I'll be brief because it's such a tragic story. I became acquainted with Sue at college, and we became good friends. She got married, had two daughters, and fell into deep depression, which she learned later came from emotional and sexual abuse by her father. As often happens, she married an abusive man. Her husband ended up having several affairs; then he turned her daughters against her, as well as neighbors and friends. He snowed the court-appointed therapists and the judge and got custody. Sue's now living alone and grieving over her daughters. So you see, Casey, I understand more than I care to. And I've only told you the tip of the iceberg."

Casey shuddered. "I'm grateful I didn't have children and that Tiffany doesn't yet. I don't know how you feel, Nan, but Tiffany's story has made me angry and I want to bring her husband, Russ, down to where he's groveling on his knees, begging for help. Of course, much of that anger is directed at Nick and all men like him."

"Angry? I get livid whenever I think of Sue. I would give anything if her ex could get what's coming to him."

"Then maybe you'll understand what I would like to do. I'm not sure how it can be done or even if my idea will work."

"I'm anxious to hear it. Tell me."

"From what I've learned, most abusers have the same weaknesses. They have to control, to appear perfect to the world. To be otherwise is their worst nightmare. The whole concept is to work on Russ' weaknesses until he becomes a blithering idiot."

Nan laughed. "Delicious! What are some of your ideas?"

Leaving his study door open, Jacob tried to read. When that didn't work, he tried to watch the small television that was perched on the corner of his desk. Flipping to his usual stations, he found he couldn't concentrate on anything. He drummed his fingers on the desk waiting impatiently.

Some time later, he was about to go find out how much longer he would be banished when he heard laughter. "Hmm? That's strange," he muttered to himself. He waited. More laughter, and more excited talk, whereas until then their conversation had been subdued. More laughter. "What is going on?"

The phone rang. It was the manager of one of his apartment buildings. When he finally hung up, he decided it was time Casey let him in on what she wanted to do.

When he entered, Casey and Nan were laughing again. They looked up at him, their cheeks flushed, their eyes bright with something he couldn't discern. "How can you expect me to remain in my office while listening to all the hilarity coming from out here?" They looked at each other and laughed again.

"Do I dare tell him, Nan?"

"Do you have any choice?"

"No." Jacob answered for her, seating himself. "Go on."

Casey took a deep breath. "All right. But don't say a word until I'm through explaining some of the things Nan and I have come up with."

"Good enough." He placed his forearms on his knees and leaned toward her.

Casey began telling him the plan and the possible implementations of it. Jacob sat back in his seat, his mouth ajar. Instead of laughing as they had, he shook his head in disbelief. When she was through telling him what they had come up with so far, he said, "You can't be serious about all this."

"I'm dead serious, Dad."

"How are you going to pull it off?"

"With difficulty." She and Nan laughed.

"It's impossible."

"Not with your money it isn't."

Jacob laughed. "You really think I'd put money toward these bizarre capers?"

"Of course. Haven't you told me you wished you could do something to Nick?" Her father didn't respond. "Just pretend it's Nick we're doing it to."

Jacob's eyes were suspicious slits. "This is a female thing! I told you my daughter was a maverick, Nan. How do you feel about all of it, as if I had to ask."

"I'm ready and willing to help, Jake."

"Why?"

"Because it will give me great satisfaction on several levels. I'll let Casey fill you in after I leave."

"But you said that in your emotional state you might not be able to help," he said, sounding a little desperate. "How can you possibly help with this outlandish—"

"All of a sudden," she interrupted, smiling, "I feel like I could wrestle a lion."

Jacob was surprised at Nan's sudden burst of strength. He had been counting on her finding it too difficult. He heaved a sigh of frustration. "All right, you two, just how do you propose to put this into action without getting caught?"

"Nan and I have decided that we'll have to hire people to implement it who don't know us or Russ. However, before we can do anything we'll have to hire a private detective to follow Russ and find out his habits and the places he goes and what he does."

"My minor in college was theater," Nan said. "I'm a pretty good actress, which might come in handy."

Jacob let out a heavy breath, rubbed his chin, and stared into space, wondering how Casey had come up with such ideas, and how Nan, of all people, would champion them. "The things you want to do to Russ seem harmless, Casey, even humorous in theory. I know you wouldn't think of doing anything harmful to his person or property, but apparently Russ Eden is an unpredictable man. We don't know how he'll react to these things and how safe Tiffany will be."

"I know, Dad. If I didn't know Nick so well, I might be more frightened. I know that if any one of these things were done to him in public, he would mainly concentrate on keeping his cool and how he was appearing to others. Oh, he'd get suspicious of me and everyone else and want revenge, but his greatest attention would be on keeping up the facade he'd created for the world."

Jacob didn't reply. His brows furrowed, he remained silent for some time. Finally, he looked from one to the other. "I'd like this to be successful. I haven't as yet been able to forgive Nick, so it would satisfy some of the feelings I have in my heart. However, I'm very skeptical about you pulling it off."

"So am I, Dad. But oh—how I'd like to try." She smiled at Nan. "Especially since I have complete support from Nan. Thank you for asking her to come and talk with me."

"You're welcome—I think."

"Then I have your financial support?"

He nodded, a grim expression on his face.

Nan stood up. "Well, I'd better leave so you two can discuss it further. Let me know when you want to meet again, Casey."

"I will. And thank you."

"I'll walk you to your car, Nan," Jake said quickly.

Outside, they sauntered slowly down the circular driveway, closer to the street where Nan had parked. The evening was pleasant. A slight breeze carried the fragrance of orange blossoms from his backyard and neighboring lots. The season had begun a month and a half ago and this was the first time he had been aware of it.

Reaching the car, Jake leaned against it, wanting to talk with her. He gazed at the clear canopy of sky full of glistening stars half a world wide. "I like Sedona and its mountains and hills, but I prefer the wide open spaces. I like to see the whole sky from side to side."

Nan's eyes traveled the sky. "I do too. I suppose it's because we've grown so accustomed to this spectacular view that when we're surrounded by hills, mountains, and tall trees we feel a little closed in."

"Exactly," he said turning his gaze on her. He noticed her dark hair glistening in the moonlight, her face and eyes strikingly mysterious. "Are you real, Nan? Or are you just an ethereal spirit conjured up by some Navajo ceremonial to come and haunt us with promises, only to disappear into the mist?" He smiled. "At least that's the way it feels as I look at you in the evening light."

Surprised, Nan studied Jacob's face and saw that he was partially serious. Silence stretched out before she reached up and caressed his cheek. "I have to go, Jake," she said softly, "but I won't disappear. I'll be back."

He moved away from the car and opened the door for her. "Thank you."

Chapter Ten

Perseverance when once applied,
if interrupted, is quickly revived.

$\mathcal{I}$t had taken Casey an afternoon to check out the homes for the next photo assignment. She was moving down the front walk of the third home when her attention was drawn to a man sitting in a black car. It was parked against the curb a couple of doors down. She stopped and stared at him. It looked as though he was wearing a suit, white shirt, and tie, but his face was shadowed. A prickly uneasiness crept over her. Was he the man from the desert? The man she had seen watching her twice before? She was suddenly seized by an unreasoning fear. Her breathing grew ragged and her heart rate accelerated. Was she letting her imagination run wild? Though she could barely see him through the windshield, the familiar ominous feeling hung in the air.

On impulse, instead of going to her own car, she turned down the walk toward the man, moving as fast as her bad leg would allow. In response, the man started the car, backed up rapidly and dangerously, turned around, and sped down the street. Squinting, she tried to see the license plate, but the car was too far away. She wasn't imagining it! He was stalking her! *Why? Who is he?* She was shaking so badly, she wondered if she could make it back to the car. When she finally reached it, she leaned against the door, exhausted, breathing as though she had run a mile.

She sat behind the wheel, trying to calm down. She should have memorized his front license plate instead of trying to get a look at his face. By the time the shaking had stopped and her heart slowed to a more normal rate, she knew what she had to do. Go see Syrus—the man she suspected. *But he drives an old blue pickup,* she remembered. "Well, he may have another car," she said aloud, not able to quiet her suspicions.

It took twenty minutes to drive back to Hartner and Hart. She parked as close to the back entrance as she could and then tried to run as she had several times before. The injured muscles refused to respond. Tears of frustration blurred her vision. "Someday!" she promised herself out loud. "Someday I'll be able to run again."

In the elevator, Casey chastised herself. She had forgotten to look for Syrus' pickup. Coming up here right now would be useless if he wasn't in his office. Then she remembered that Syrus had told her to meet a young man, Brad Barker, newly hired by the company to work on the advertising team. What had surprised Casey was Syrus suggesting to the company that Brad might help carry her photo equipment and at the same time provide her with a measure of security.

Reaching Vicky's desk, she hid her lingering anxiety. "Is the man of mystery in?"

"Yes," Vicky nodded, smiling. "Just barely walked in. Hurried past like he was going to a fire."

Syrus' door was partially closed, so she knocked. Hearing a muffled, "Come in," she entered.

He didn't look up, so she sat down and waited, studying him intently. She noticed with relief that he wasn't wearing a suit. But he looked rumpled, and his hair was more out of place than usual.

Syrus looked up. "Oh, it's you. Why are you looking at me like that? Do I have egg on my chin?"

"You look a little disheveled this morning."

"So tell me something I don't know. It's been a difficult morning."

"Do you own a black car?" she demanded.

Syrus' brows rose. "What's going on, Casey? First, you call

me messy and then ask me a question like a top sergeant."

"I'm not in any mood to be diplomatic."

"I'm not in the mood to answer you, even if it were proper for you to interrogate me," he replied, his eyes steely.

For what seemed like an eternity to Casey, they glared at each other. Then she looked down and drew a long shuddering breath. "It's rather inane of me, I know, to ask if it was you I saw watching me from a black car this morning."

"What happened?"

"If it was you, I don't need to tell you!" She got up, tried unsuccessfully to move about, and then sat down. Syrus' silence made her uneasy and talkative. "All right. This is what happened." She related the frightening incident. All the while, she tried to discern anything suspicious in his expression. "It looks like a man is stalking me."

Syrus' expression didn't change. He simply laced his long fingers together, thinking. "Three times is beyond coincidence. Have you told anyone else but me about these incidents?"

Casey felt a ripple of relief that he was now taking her seriously. "No. I don't have any friends, remember? And I don't want to worry my father. He's gone through too much already because of me." As if to herself, she added, "Maybe I should tell the FBI, but then maybe not. Surely it can't have anything to do with my case. It's probably some kook who's seen my picture in the papers." She knew she was rambling, but she wanted to provoke some reaction from Syrus, who remained silent, an impassive expression on his face. "I don't know what the stalking laws are here. I could go to the police and find out."

"That's a good idea. You might also tell them you think you're being stalked. Unless you feel they'd be skeptical because of your impending indictment."

Casey bit her lip in concern.

"Be sure to tell me if you see this man again," he said calmly. "Have you met Brad yet?"

"Not yet. I will before I leave."

"Take him with you to the photo shoots. He's good with lighting and composition. Besides, you'll feel safer."

"All right," Casey said quietly, her suspicion concerning Syrus mitigated somewhat. She arose and moved to the door.

As she put her hand on the knob, she heard Syrus say, "Wait."

She turned. "Yes?"

"I don't think you should tell anyone in the office about the incidents. Brad is the only one who knows. But I suggest you not even mention it to Vicky. We don't want rumors flying around Hartner and Hart."

"What kind of rumors?"

"Rumors that you're delusional. Remember, the newspapers reported Nick saying that about you."

"Oh, thanks, Syrus, that's all I needed today." She went out and slammed the door.

Syrus stared at the door and then picked up the phone and dialed. "I don't think Casey will be telling anyone about this morning."

Outside Syrus' office, Casey felt like screaming. Her nerves were frayed. She wanted to run away and never come back to Hartner and Hart. Finding a chair at an empty desk, she sat down and breathed deeply a few times, reasoning with herself that all she needed was some lunch and she would feel better. First, however, she had to meet Brad Barker and suggest he go with her tomorrow. Even that looked unnerving right now. She put her elbows on the desk and covered her face, wishing she could go home, go to bed, pull the covers over her head, and sleep—a sleep without nightmares—for days and days. A hand on her shoulder startled her.

"Are you all right, Casey?"

Casey looked up into Vicky's face. "Oh yes. I'm fine. Thanks, Vic. I'm just tired. It will take a while before I get my strength completely back." Forcing herself to brighten, she added, "Every day, I feel a little stronger."

"Good. You've gone through a lot. I think you're brave to

come back to work so soon."

Casey stood up. "Not bravery, boredom." She smiled at Vicky. "Thanks for being concerned. It helps. Now, point out Brad Barker to me."

"He's that blond guy four desks back, near the aisle."

"Thanks."

The young man looked up as she approached. He stood up. "You're Casey Carter."

"Yes. You're Brad?"

"Yes ma'am. I'm glad to meet you. Sy told me I'm supposed to help you for a few days."

Casey quickly perused the young man. He didn't look a day over twenty-two. His hair was light blond and cut so short, it wouldn't lay nicely. A stocky build and only a couple of inches taller than herself, he wore tan cotton pants and a blue shirt, which matched his eyes. His broad face had a scrubbed look, giving him a wholesome appearance. In addition, he had an aura of determination about him. However, it was his wide, contagious smile that won her over.

"Yes, you are," she replied. "And I'll be very grateful to have it. Even though it's Saturday tomorrow, I have an appointment at one o'clock to shoot in east Phoenix and an appointment at 3:30 near there. Does that work for you?"

"It sure does," he replied eagerly. "I've heard about your talent, and I'm anxious to watch you work, learn from you."

Casey was surprised and pleased. "And maybe I can learn from you." She smiled. "If the shots don't turn out as I envision them, I may retake them in my studio using rear projection. I won't need you for that, but tomorrow meet me at 12:15 behind that gray block building next door."

"I'll be there," he stated firmly.

This gave Casey's body a shot of adrenalin. She felt stronger, more resilient, and less nervous as she walked toward the elevator. With Brad along on her shoots, she wouldn't feel so vulnerable.

Chapter Eleven

Gentleness in a man is strength.

Casey slept late Sunday morning. She awoke and stretched, not feeling as rested as the clock indicated she should feel. She lay there thinking about the nightmare that had jolted her from sleep sometime in the middle of the night. It had seemed so real that she recalled it clearly. A dark-haired man was chasing her. Whenever she found an avenue of escape, it proved to be a dead end. Just as he was about to grab her, several men pulled her to safety, but they turned out to be working for the dark-haired man. She woke up screaming. She felt terribly defenseless, especially since she had changed her mind about going to the local police. She grimaced in thought. *The police would probably mark it down as the product of an over-active imagination or call me delusional.*

As the nightmare receded from her consciousness, daylight brought a more positive and upbeat frame of mind. Having Brad along yesterday on her shoots may have discouraged the stalker or made him lose interest. At least, that was the way she felt this morning and was determined to continue to feel that way tomorrow and the next day. This thought gave her the energy to move out of bed, shower, and get dressed. It was a beautiful Sunday morning and she was going to take advantage of it.

Sundays were lonelier for Jacob. He had been taught by his

parents that it was God's day—a day of rest, a day to renew oneself spiritually, but not keeping himself physically and mentally busy gave him too much time to think. The phone burst the silence.

The caller ID revealed Casey's name. "How did you know I needed to talk to you?" he asked.

"I guess because I needed to talk to you," she replied. "I called to see if I could come over and make dinner for you."

"Sounds great! I'll help you."

"Should we invite Nan to eat with us? We need to talk more about the plan and how we're going to put it into action."

The suggestion to invite Nan gave his spirits a boost, but he had hoped that by some kind quirk of fate Casey had changed her mind about going ahead with her plan. "You haven't changed your mind yet?"

"Yet? You expect me to eventually?"

"I was hoping."

Casey laughed. "I love you, Dad. I'll be right over. Call Nan."

Nan arrived wearing another unique outfit. Casey smiled as she studied it.

"Are you going to invite me in?" Nan asked.

"Not until you tell me what you're wearing."

Nan laughed. "I'm afraid I'm a clothes freak who is never quite in style. I've had this for years, but taking care of my husband was so labor intensive I couldn't wear anything but pants or jeans. Well, anyway, what I have on is called a batik skirt set. It's all cotton."

Casey was intrigued. The long cotton jacket had loose sleeves just below the elbow and was tied together just below the bustline, revealing a scoop-necked blouse underneath. The jacket and the long skirt had interesting white squiggly designs with a slight cast of light purple. The whole outfit together looked bluish-purple. "That's a good color on you, Nan. Come in. You're inspiring me. Since my accident, I haven't been able to wear what I used to so I've lost interest in clothes."

Entering, Nan replied, "You're beautiful in anything you wear. But it will lift your spirits if you start dressing as you did before."

"You're probably right. Come on into the kitchen. Dad and I are about through preparing dinner.

"It smells good. I don't like to cook only for myself. I was just going to have a sandwich. This is a treat."

Nan was relieved to see that the kitchen was more inviting than the front room. The cabinets were ivory cream. In the middle was a long oval island of sage green, topped with light, shiny granite. Three tall wrought iron bar chairs, covered in cream leather, stood on one side of the island.

Jacob had on an apron and a ridiculous cook's hat. He was stirring something.

Nan's face creased in silent amusement. "Well, if you don't look professional, Jake."

He turned and grinned. "Actually, I wore the hat for you— just for effect. Casey bought it for me as a joke, since I've done most of the cooking in our household."

"Ah, a man that can cook! And I thought you cooking hamburgers up at the cabin was just a fluke."

"Sit down on one of the bar chairs, Nan," Casey said. "All I have to do is set our plates and silverware out. We're eating in here."

Nan perched on one of the chairs and watched father and daughter finishing the last-minute details.

"Actually," Jacob said, as he placed bowls of spaghetti and spaghetti sauce on the island, "we didn't know if we could throw a meal together. Since we're both living alone now, we've let our cupboards get bare."

"Oh, but Dad's spaghetti sauce is something to die for, Nan. He could be a world-renowned chef."

"Flattery won't get more meals out of me, Casey. I think it's about time I retired."

"Aw, Dad," she complained as she got a green salad out of the refrigerator and placed it on the island, "I'm a working girl again and I don't even have time to grocery shop."

"You mean you hate to grocery shop."

"Well, whatever."

Jacob grinned at Nan. "See, among other things, my daughter tries to outmaneuver me."

The three felt comfortable eating together, visiting and making small talk, something Nan hadn't been able to enjoy for years.

Gathering in the family room after cleaning up the kitchen, Jacob announced, "I tentatively hired a detective last night over the phone."

"You have? Even though you don't agree with my sinister plot, you certainly move too fast for the flies to land. Thank you."

"I wish I could say you're welcome," he muttered grimly. "The detective's name is Monty Mosier. I've used him before to help me locate people who have stolen property from the apartments or skipped out on their rent. He's good."

"I don't think one person can do it all, Dad."

"When I gave Monty an idea of what you wanted to do and why, he told me he had an assistant he used all the time. His name is Herman Snardly, but he likes to go by 'Snard.'" Jacob smiled. "From what Monty told me about him, the name fits. He used to be a petty thief. He can pick locks, open safes, and so forth. He's a master of disguise—a multitalented guy. Monty assured me that he's totally reformed. An ex-thief with many skills."

Casey and Nan listened with their mouths open.

"Of course, I'll have to meet this Snard and make sure for myself that he's honest and trustworthy, the kind of person who can pull this off." Jacob looked at his daughter questioningly. "Well?"

"The last person I would have thought of is an ex-thief, Dad, but the more I think about it, who would be better at sneaking around?"

Nan laughed. "Sounds like the perfect guy."

"Okay then, I'll have Monty bring Snard to my office so I can meet him. I have a project of my own for them to work on. Then if I'm satisfied that I can trust Snard, I'll work through Monty so Snard won't know who's behind it."

"But, Dad, *I* would like to work with Snard. I think I can explain it to him better than you."

"No, Casey. I don't want to take a chance that Russ Eden could find out that you're behind it. You can coach me carefully and I'll deliver the message to Monty in detail. I trust Monty and he'll see to it that Snard understands what we want done."

Casey wanted to protest once more, but her father's expression stopped her. "Okay, Dad."

"I have a request, Jake," Nan interjected.

"Oh? What?"

"I know Casey is sure that Russ is as Tiffany says, but I'd like to look into the man's eyes. Could you ask Monty to arrange for me to be around for the first episode?"

Jacob frowned in concern. "I don't think that's a good idea, Nan."

"Please, Jake. Monty can see to it that Snard and I don't meet. I think you'll feel better if I confirm what Casey says about Russ. You see, I've had some experience. I have a dear friend who was severely abused. I knew her husband."

Jacob stared at the floor, his brows furrowed, trying to put his concerns aside. He looked up into Nan's gray eyes and felt a little bit of the shell around his heart crumble away. "All right, but only if I can be sure that Russ Eden can't possibly know who you are."

"I'll make sure he won't. Now—how about letting *me* meet

Monty and give him our ideas."

Rubbing his chin in thought, Jacob nodded. "Okay. I'm sure you can put it over to Monty better than I can. I'll meet with Monty and Snard, and if I feel all right about Snard, I'll arrange for Monty to meet you at my office."

"Good!" Casey exclaimed. "Now, let's make a list of ideas to give 'sneaky Snardly.'"

Nan laughed and they began writing each one down.

Jacob listened to their ideas again, hearing new ones added and others discarded. He shook his head. "No *man* could possibly come up with this kind of waggery."

"Waggery?" Nan's eyebrows peaked. "I'm not sure what that means, but it sounds like it fits the situation well."

The two women laughed. They went on until they ran out of inspiration. The phone rang. Jacob stood. "Excuse me, ladies, I think it's one of my managers again. I think I've got to evict some tenants. It's getting harder and harder to find good tenants any more. I'll take the call in my study."

When Jacob left, Nan was curious. "Your father made his money with apartment buildings?"

"Only partly. He owns office buildings, a couple of strip malls, and other things."

"Oh."

"Actually, Dad went to law school, specialized in corporate law, and then went to work for a big company. By the time I was in first grade, he realized that my mother wasn't going to be home very much to take care of me, so he began investing here and there. When he had enough income from his properties that he didn't have to work full-time, he quit his job. This gave him the freedom to be here when I got home from school."

"Why wasn't your mother home?"

Casey briefly explained.

"Your mother was Sil Jacobson?" she asked in awe.

"Yes."

"I went to quite a few of her productions in the Phoenix

area before she became famous. I loved her voice."

"Thank you. She had a rare talent and Dad knew he couldn't ask her to stay home. Besides, I think he knew that even if he begged, she wouldn't. She loved the stage; she loved performing."

Nan was silent for a few moments. "I'm sorry you didn't have a mother around very much. I know how that feels. My mother died when I was two and my grandmother raised me. She was great, but not even a grandmother can take the place of a mother. I longed to know her."

"I'm sorry."

"But I'll have to say, I admire your father. How many fathers would do what he did?"

"He did much more than what I've told you. He went to parent-teacher conferences, took me to dance classes, went to my recitals, took me to piano lessons, and saw to it that I practiced. He taught me to play tennis. We hiked the hills of Sedona together. I could go on and on."

Nan was contemplative. *I wonder if Silvia Jacobson realized what she had as a husband, and as the father of her child?*

"What is it, Nan?"

"I don't think I've heard of such an unselfish man. My grandfather was a giving man, but I doubt he could have done what your father did."

"What about your husband, Nan?"

"He was ill much of our married life. He didn't have much of a chance to give or to live up to his potential." Not wanting to go into it further, she changed the subject. "Casey, your dad told me about the accident. I don't understand. If the car was on fire, why was just your right leg burned and cut and not the rest of your body?"

"I don't know. The police questioned me over and over. But I have no memory of what happened after we started down the hill. Apparently the car hit the trees at an angle that broke the window, causing shards of glass to hit my leg. All I know is by the time the rescuers got to me and smothered the flames with their jackets, I had second-degree burns from my thigh down close to my ankle. There were a few spots that were third-degree, but thankfully only a few."

Nan shivered. "How did you manage in the burn center?"

Casey suddenly felt emotional. "I couldn't have made it without my dad. He was there every day, all day, and it seemed like most of the nights. He played my favorite CDs softly while reading Psalms and poetry to me. I don't know how his voice didn't give out. Sometimes, he'd break down and cry. But he went on."

When Jacob returned, he found both Casey and Nan wiping away tears. "What's the matter with you two conspirators? You're not feeling sad for the sorry nincompoop you're going to victimize?"

They both laughed. "Hardly," Casey replied.

"Did you get your problems solved, Jake?"

"Not yet. I'm tempted to sell all my apartment buildings. Renters can be a real pain, especially when they take off in the middle of the night and leave the place trashed."

"That's dreadful. I can see why you need Monty now and then." Nan picked up her purse and stood. "I think I'll leave so you two can spend some time together. Thank you for the delicious dinner. Let me know if and when I can meet Monty."

"I will. I'll walk you to your car," he offered again.

"Thank you. I'll see you, Casey."

Jacob and Nan walked slowly toward her car. Nan stopped and turned to admire Jacob's house once more. It was a large, peach-colored rambler with a peach tile roof. A peaked gable rose high above the entrance, and five large windows and three small ones added symmetry to the front. In the center of the circular driveway five small palm trees stood stately amidst a rock garden surrounded by green lawn.

"I love the outside of your home, Jake."

He smiled. "What about the inside?"

"I love the painting in the entryway."

He laughed. "Yes, Silvia had interesting taste, didn't she?"

"I would say so."

When they reached the car, it was Nan who leaned against the door. She looked up into Jacob's warm brown eyes, which at the moment appeared anything but haunted. Her heart kindled as she thought of the sacrifices he had made in order to "mother" Casey. Her gaze traveled over his face and she felt herself tremble. A startling thought flashed through her mind. *Am I falling for this man? No! It can't be. It's just admiration. It's too soon after Chet's death.* Besides, it was always the other way around. Men fell in love with her. In college, she'd had several proposals, but the right man hadn't come along.

Jacob smiled. "I think I've lost you to some far-away place, Nan."

"Yes. It was far away." She moved away from the car and he opened the door for her.

"Thanks for coming and helping us out. Just having you as support is invaluable to me. You'll be well-paid."

"Paid?" Nan was incensed and her voice reflected it. "I'm not doing this for money. I will not accept pay for helping two friends."

Jacob knew he had insulted her. "But you deserve it," he said, laughing. "Who else could be as kooky as my daughter?"

Disarmed, Nan laughed with him. "Thanks for the compliment . . . I think. Well, go in and visit with your kooky daughter. You're quite a pair and you're quite a father, Jake. I'll see you." She turned the key and he reluctantly closed the door. As she drove away, she saw through her side mirror that he watched her until she was out of sight.

Chapter Twelve

*The untuned string of hope quivers with
notes of distrust and fear, but once tuned
its beauty is heard bright and clear.*

Monday morning Casey began developing the pictures she had taken on Saturday. Studying them, she found that one of the shots hadn't turned out as well as she wanted. Quickly leaving the darkroom, she called the models and the home owner and made another appointment for that afternoon. Then she called Brad and enlisted his help and company. Her comfort level directly increased when she thought of Brad going along. Last Saturday, she noticed Brad looking around and watching carefully while they drove to their destination, and again as they parked, and when they prepared to leave. It had given her a feeling of safety. Also having Brad's upbeat personality along cheered her, and as a bonus he carried the equipment to and from the car. She felt helpless enough just coping with her weak leg, but carrying equipment made her feel more so.

Since the reshoot wasn't until this afternoon, she decided to take advantage of her free morning and try to find a path she once hiked at South Mountain Park before the accident. She couldn't remember the name, but it was exceptionally scenic and she wanted to videotape it for her project. Picking up her video camera, she locked the studio door and got into her van. She looked around as Brad had done, and then a thought struck her.

This was an impromptu trip. How could the stalker know

about it? *Wait. How would he know any of my schedules?* He would have to watch her building and follow her when she left. This thought was more frightening. He could push his way into her studio and no one would know!

She felt her heart race and every muscle tighten. Living with Nick had turned her into a fearful, quaking human being. "No," she contradicted herself. "It actually has made me a stronger person. It was the nightmare of the accident that has left me fearful." Saying a prayer that she could conquer the fear, she calmly looked around her parking lot, as well as Hartner and Hart's lot. She didn't see anything out of the ordinary, only Syrus' old blue truck sticking out like a sore thumb. She smiled.

Driving south on the Pima Freeway she became conscious of a small tan Toyota behind her. It seemed to speed up or slow down in cadence with her car. Had she seen that when she left the office? It seemed that she had, but then maybe she hadn't. She had been watching for a black car. Still, she had to make sure. Taking the off-ramp, she drove a couple of blocks. The tan car slowly followed. Quickly making a U-turn in the middle of the street, she sped toward the oncoming car. As she passed, she saw that it was Brad! She pulled over, slammed on her brakes, and waited for him to turn around. He parked behind her. They got out of their respective cars simultaneously.

She made an effort to keep her control, not wanting to vent her irritation on him. "What are you doing, Brad?"

"I'm doing what Sy told me to do." He grinned. "You're one sharp gal. How come you caught on I was following you?"

"I'm asking the questions, Brad. Why did he tell you to follow me on my own time?"

Brad's brows shot up. "You'll have to ask him. I'm just following instructions."

"You know more than you're telling me. What's up?" Gazing directly into his eyes, she watched for a flicker. It came.

The smile that appeared so easily on Brad's face was

suddenly missing. "Believe me, I'd rather be photographing or putting together clever layouts for ads, but for right now, I've been told to follow you because of a possible stalker. If you want to complain, complain to Sy."

"I'm going to do that. Right now." She turned abruptly, got into her van, and sped off. Glancing in the mirror, she saw that Brad was still following her. "Something isn't right here," she muttered, feeling a distinct feeling of unease.

Casey waited restlessly for Syrus. He was meeting with someone and not available. Brad had come in after her. Refusing to look in her direction, he busied himself at his desk. At last, the man left and she went to Syrus' partially open door. She knocked but didn't wait for an invitation.

Syrus looked up, surprised.

"Yes, you should be surprised."

His faced closed. "Why?"

"You know why."

"Give me a clue, Casey. I'm very busy this morning."

"Why did you instruct Brad to follow me on my own time?"

As usual, when he chose, Syrus' face revealed no reaction to Casey's agitation. She waited for an answer, but it didn't come.

"Don't tell me that Hartner and Hart is paying Brad to protect me every time I get in the car and go for a jaunt."

A caustic smile tipped his lips. "Don't feel so sure of yourself, Casey. Since the man has followed you twice on Hartner and Hart's time, they feel somewhat responsible."

"Why?"

"You've heard of litigation haven't you, Casey?"

"They think I might sue them if I'm attacked on my own time?"

"Put yourself in their shoes. Under the circumstances

would you feel responsible?"

"No."

"You're naive."

"Why didn't you tell me you were going to have Brad follow me?"

"Didn't think it was necessary. I underestimated your suspicious nature."

"Careful might be another adjective you could have used. After all, a man appears to be stalking me."

"Do you want me to ask them to have Brad quit protecting you? I'm sure he'd be happier doing what he loves best, working on ads."

Casey was silent. "I don't know. Having him with me Saturday made me feel safe, but today, he made me feel uneasy."

"Did that come from him or inside you?"

Casey got up as if to go. Instead, she gripped the back of the chair. "I've never been one to be fearful until . . ." She rubbed her brows, feeling close to tears of frustration. "How well do you know Brad?"

"Well . . . I believe I know him well enough. I'm a pretty good judge of character and he seems like an honest young man."

She wanted to retort, *If I trusted you completely, I could trust your trust.* Instead, she said. "All right. Let the big bosses protect their backsides."

Syrus grinned. "And yours?"

There was no answering smile on her face. "In effect, our backsides are all one and the same. Aren't they?" She pivoted on the heel of her good leg and left.

Jacob looked across his desk at Monty Mosier. As always an unlit cigar hung from his lips. He had on his usual attire—a rumpled brown sports coat over a knit shirt and jeans.

Monty grinned. "Okay, tell me about this weird job of yours."

Jacob scowled. "I doubt that you'll ever have another one like it." He told him first about Russ Eden's abusiveness.

Monty's face turned hard. "I know all about that. My sister barely escaped with her life from an abusive husband."

Jacob nodded with understanding. "Then you might find some satisfaction doing this job." Jacob launched into the unorthodox assignment and watched Monty's brows arch higher in amazement.

"How did you ever come up with all that stuff?"

"Two women came up with it. I'll have you meet one tomorrow."

"That figures. It had to be women. The only thing I could think of was shoving my knuckles into his face."

"Same here. Now, I'd like to meet Snardly."

"He's waiting out in your reception room. I'll bring him in."

Monty returned with a medium-height, nondescript man, the kind no one would notice or the kind someone would easily forget if they saw him. *Perfect*, Jacob thought. He reached for Herman Snardly's hand and found his grip hard and quick. In fact every movement he made was quick—from his hand running through his mousy brown hair to his impatient fingers tapping the back of his hand. He seemed poised and ready for action.

After looking into Snardly's eyes and asking him a few questions, Jacob felt that Monty's confidence in him was well-founded.

One week later, Casey, her father, and Nan were seated together in Jacob's family room for the purpose of making last-minute plans for "Project Russ," as Casey called it. The week had been uneventful. The stalker hadn't appeared and Casey was beginning to relax, hoping he had been frightened off or gotten discouraged.

Nan told Casey of her meeting with Monty and his eagerness to take on the job. Then they both asked Jacob to describe Herman Snardly. His description of Snardly gave them confidence that he could pull it off.

Together, the three studied the report Monty had delivered to Jacob at his office that morning. Casey was distressed to see that one of the places Russ Eden had gone in the middle of the day was to a motel with another woman. Another place was an out-of-the-way restaurant with a woman other than Tiffany. He spent one afternoon on the golf course, and later that night he and Tiffany had dinner at the country club with three other couples.

"Russ' friends, no doubt," Casey said.

They quickly looked through the rest of his comings and goings. "I have enough to start with. I'll give Monty a call and sic Snard onto our target."

"Poor Russ," Nan said, smiling.

"I would love to see his reactions," Casey said. "Is Monty going to tell you about them?"

"You bet," Jacob replied firmly. "I have to know in order to watch for dangerous signals."

"Good," Casey said, relishing the whole thing, a devilish grin on her face.

Jacob just shook his head, his worry lines showing.

"Loosen up, Jake," Nan teased, "we deserve to have some fun out of this."

Chapter Thirteen

Faults are thick when love is thin.
—Anonymous

Russ Eden preened in front of the mirror like a peacock. He had just purchased the olive brown Hart Schaffner & Marx suit and noticed, as he had in the department store, that it brought out the green in his eyes and enhanced his dark hair. He wanted to look the part at the meetings.

Fred Reisner, the president of the company, had flown in from New York and had scheduled a meeting with his staff this morning. Later this evening at the Sheraton Hotel Fred had arranged to have a meeting with all the managers and their staff from each of the western offices. He and Fred would be the main speakers at both meetings.

Tiffany watched Russ with resentment. She had counted his suits. This was number thirteen. Masking her feelings, she smiled and admired him. "You look handsome, Russ."

"Yeah?" he questioned, pleased. Then his eyes locked on hers through the mirror. "I guess I could trust that compliment if you could keep yourself looking nicer. I think you've put on a couple of pounds."

"No I haven't, Russ, it's just that some of the clothes I have are out of style."

"You're in denial about your weight—as usual, Tiffany. And are the clothes out of style? Or is it that your taste in clothes needs to improve?"

Tiffany had been to the library as Casey had suggested. She knew some of the ways to respond, but at the moment, fear impeded her intentions. "Do you want breakfast this morning, or just coffee and toast?" she quickly asked.

His voice rose. "Did I ask you a question, Tiff?"

"I'll try to improve my taste, Russ."

He smirked. "And how are you going to manage that on your own?"

"Do you want me to go to a style consultant?"

"We can't afford one! Just use your brains, if you have any." He roughly shoved her aside with one of his arms as he passed her on the way to the kitchen. Nervously, she followed him.

"I see the toast isn't made. I'll get coffee at the office. I told you my staff and I are having a meeting at ten o'clock with Fred Reisner. I was hoping for a little more sustenance this morning."

"You need to tell me, Russ. Some mornings you want breakfast and other times you don't."

He turned to face her. She saw the anger building up inside him. She remembered one of the things she had read about re-directing someone's anger. "Oh dear," she said looking at her watch. "I'm almost late for work."

He glanced at his own watch. "Damn! Is it that late? Thanks to you, I'm running behind! Remember, I won't be home until late. I have a meeting tonight."

Tiffany didn't know how to answer. He hadn't told her and if she stated that fact, he would call her absent-minded. If she nodded and acted as if he had told her, he would storm on about breakfast or something. She simply kept quiet.

Even though time was short, Russ continued, "Too bad wives aren't invited. But then again, maybe it's just as well. You'll look better when you lose a few pounds. A couple of those female managers would put you to shame."

Tiffany seethed inside. She hadn't gained a pound. If any-thing, she had lost. Her stomach had been giving her trouble lately. She watched him run to the door leading to the garage. "Good luck on your speech," she said. He responded by slam-ming the door. Her heart was still pounding as the sound of squealing tires reached her ears.

On the way to the office, Russ ruminated on the suggestion Fred made last night that he have Norm Wadley say a few words this morning too. Norm was the assistant office manager. His own duties were to oversee Norm and visit the regional offices as needed. He had to admit that Norm was efficient and good with personnel, but he was just a pain in the behind to him.

Russ didn't know quite how to explain what bothered him about Norm except in one area. Norm always seemed to be watching him. He squirmed in his seat at the thought of the questions Norm regularly asked, *How long will you be at lunch? I need to know because I have to go over something with you. Man, I'd like your position. Three-hour lunches are my style.* He would say it in a joking, offhanded way, but it rankled Russ. He would have liked to smash his face—or better yet—fire him. If it were up to Russ, Norm would be gone before he could blink his prying eyes.

Arriving at the large building where Global Investments took up the entire sixth floor, Russ quickly parked and locked his car. He should have been there earlier. As he rushed into the building, a couple of men walking and talking together bumped into him as he entered, blocking his way for a moment. Irritated that they were unaware of their rudeness, he swore under his breath and ran to the elevator.

Norm had just gathered the staff into the conference room when Russ walked in. "Hey, boss," Norm stated facetiously, "you look like you just walked out of Saks Fifth Avenue. Always the impeccably dressed executive. Fred should be impressed."

"And you?" Russ queried.

"And I look like I just walked out of a thrift store?"

"I recognize that suit. I gave it to the thrift store last week. Good taste, Norm, good taste."

The staff laughed and so did Norm. Russ smiled, feeling smug.

A blonde woman with a prominent overbite pushed a cart of doughnuts, sweet rolls, napkins, coffee, tea, and juice into the conference room, placing it all carefully on the long credenza.

Fred Reisner walked in, greeting and shaking hands with everyone; his voice as always was friendly and warm. He was medium height. His full, dark hair framed a wide face. His diacritical brown eyes and large nose gave his face an intimidating look—until he smiled, which he often did. Everyone liked Fred and felt comfortable around him. After he shook the last hand, he said, "How about we go to the food bar and let our lovely hostess serve us. After we've finished, we'll start the meeting."

Everyone milled around, visiting while eating and drinking their coffee or juice. As the seats filled up Fred nodded to Russ, letting him know he was in charge of the agenda.

Russ smiled confidently, got up, moved to the head of the table, and buttoned his coat. Then in his self-assured way, pacing his words carefully, he thanked Fred for being there, expressed his division's need for Fred's help and leadership, and spoke of their great desire to make the company grow. As he always did when he talked, he used his hands.

After about two minutes, he became aware of strange expressions on the faces of his staff and a bemused expression on Norm's. Always his best in front of an audience, Russ found himself feeling uncharacteristically nervous. Something was wrong. He looked questioningly at Norm who stared pointedly at his right coat sleeve while pointing to his own. Finally getting the message, Russ looked at his sleeve intently. Though he had been able to keep talking until then, he turned speechless with shock and embarrassment. The underside of his sleeve was covered with something yellow and slimy looking. "How in the . . . how did that get on there?" he asked, trying to sound light.

Norm cleared his throat and tried to lighten up the situation. "Hey, Russ, it looks like you stuck your sleeve in egg yolk this morning."

The staff nervously stifled their amusement, but Fred Reisner laughed out loud.

Russ felt the blood rush to his face. "Didn't eat breakfast, Norm," he quipped, forcing a smile. "Must have brushed up against something somewhere. Excuse me, I better go clean it off. Before I do, though," he said, trying to regain his composure, "Norm, come on up and give your report while I'm gone."

The staff clapped for Norm as Russ rushed out, bursting with anger. The blonde server followed with her empty cart.

"May I be of some help, sir? Could I help you clean that off?"

"What? Who are you?"

"I'm the doughnut girl."

"Oh. Uh, I don't know what in the hell this is. Where could I have gotten this on me?" he asked, staring at his sleeve, still in disbelief. He touched it gingerly, "It's something sticky, like glue! Where could it have come from?"

"May I help you, sir?" she asked again.

"Could you get this off me?"

"I'll try." She pulled on it and a strip of rubbery slime came off. "It didn't even leave a stain. Imagine that," she said.

Russ looked at the woman for the first time. His eyes were drawn to her brassy blonde hair and disgusting overbite. He couldn't stand imperfection in women. It repelled him.

"Why are you looking at me like that?" she asked.

"Don't touch me. I don't want your help."

Looking hurt, she whined, "I was just trying to help." She turned her cart and quickly moved down the hall.

"Disgusting girl!" he muttered under his breath. Striding quickly to the employee's restroom, he began pulling the sickening stuff off and throwing it into the waste container. Studying the sleeve of his newest suit, he saw no evidence of a stain of any kind. He frowned. "How's that possible, with that slime?"

Russ studied himself in the mirror. Though an impeccable reflection stared back at him, his face flushed red again as he thought of the embarrassing episode. Trying to put it behind him, he left the restroom and entered the conference room, holding his head high with a confidence he didn't feel. He slipped into his seat and waited until Norm finished speaking. Acting as if nothing had happened, he got up, gave his speech, and gave Fred a complimentary introduction.

The meeting room at the Sheraton was full of round tables covered with white tablecloths, set for dinner. A crew of waiters moved in and out among the visiting managers, bringing the first course. Everyone took that as a cue to find a seat at one of the tables.

When the meal was over and the dessert dishes removed, coffee was served. This was Fred Reisner's cue. He strode to the podium and greeted all the office managers. His agenda was to have each manager speak five minutes, after which Russ would give his speech. Fred would be the last speaker.

Russ listened to the managers and knew which ones were full of bull and which ones exaggerated their progress. He was edgy and bored waiting for his turn to speak, hoping to impress Reisner and at the same time incite enthusiasm in the managers. If they produced more profits in the coming year, it would reflect well on him and help him in more ways than anyone in the company knew.

As the last manager finished, Russ heard Fred introduce him with pleasing adjectives. He stood and wound around the tables toward the podium. Suddenly hearing chuckles, then laughter, Russ looked around, wondering what in the world would be causing the annoying distraction. The closer he got to the three-foot platform where the podium stood, the greater the laughter. When he went up the two steps onto the dais, the laughter increased. Looking down at his suit, his sleeves, he saw nothing amiss. Standing in front of the podium, holding up his hands to quiet the group, he forced a grin and spoke through the mike. "Okay, let me in on the fun."

This brought on a more raucous burst of laughter. He glanced nervously over at Reisner and saw that his face was crimson with anger. Russ shrugged his shoulders and held out his arms questioningly at Reisner, who pointed to something behind him. Turning and looking on both sides of himself, Russ could see nothing.

Finally, Fred got up and lifted up the long piece of toilet paper that hung from underneath his coat so Russ could see it. He stared at it in disbelief. Shocked and confused, he felt frozen, unable to move. Finally he looked at Fred. "How could that have gotten there?" he whispered.

"Those things happen sometimes, Russ," he whispered back. "Sorry. Excuse yourself and go into the restroom and take care of it."

Russ felt the heat of anger rise in his face. "Someone has played a practical joke on me!" he hissed in rage.

"I doubt that," Reisner said. "Go on, and I'll fill in for you until you return. Leave by the door behind us."

His face hot with humiliation, Russ gathered the offending paper into a wad, turned, and left as quickly as he could. Out in the hall, he dropped the wadded toilet paper and took off his coat. Horrified, he saw that it had been stuck onto the underside of his coat with a wide piece of sticky tape.

"It was a practical joke!" *More than that*, he thought, *a vengeful act*. "Whoever did this, I'll not only fire him on the spot, but I'll destroy him!" he muttered, his chest heaving. *How can I go back in there?* He had never been able to deal with any kind of humiliation—and this was the worst. The door swung open and Fred Reisner entered the hall.

Relieved, Russ showed him how someone had taped the toilet paper to his coat.

"Well I'll be damned. Who in the company would do such a thing?" He studied the paper. "This isn't toilet paper. It looks like it, but it's much stronger. It had to be, to keep from tearing when you sat down at the table to eat. Come with me, Russ, and I'll tell the group what I think has happened here and we'll go from there."

"Thanks. I don't know if I could have gone back in there under the circumstances."

Back on the dais, Fred stood at the podium and related the facts. A murmur went through the group. "Who did this?" Heads swiveled around, glancing nervously at each other, wondering. As expected, no one accepted responsibility. "If I find out who pulled this deplorable stunt he or they will be fired immediately. This kind of thing is beneath the dignity of the company. I regret you all laughed at it. Now, let's forget what happened for the moment because I'm going to ask Russ if he'll be a good sport and go on with his speech."

Chapter Fourteen

The door to the human heart can
only be opened from the inside.
—Anonymous

Casey watched her dad pace restlessly around the room while they waited for Nan. He had called her an hour ago and asked her to come over. Was he anxious only because he wanted to tell them the results of their project or was he also eager to see Nan?

Hearing the chimes, Jacob rushed to the front door. Instead of Nan, he saw a tall, homely blonde woman standing before him, smiling over protruding upper teeth.

"Hello," he said politely. "May I help you?"

"You don't recognize me?" the woman asked in a high nasal twang.

"No. I'm sorry."

The woman laughed. "Good," she said in a normal voice.

Jacob did a double take. For a moment he was speechless. "Nan?" he asked.

"Yes, it's me."

He stepped aside for her to enter and shook his head in confusion. "Casey's waiting in the family room for us."

Casey's brows rose in surprise as she waited for an introduction.

Nan pulled off the wig and took out the teeth. "Hi," she said, grinning like a Cheshire cat.

"Nan!" Casey exclaimed. "Why—?"

"Guess."

Casey's eyes widened in sudden understanding. "You were

involved with Project Russ in some way. Tell us!"

Nan laughed. "You're right, I was. Ol' Snard did a good job this morning. I was there to watch it happen and see the aftermath."

Jacob shook his head in consternation. "Monty told me about it, but he didn't tell me about you."

"I told him not to, that I'd tell you," she said, stuffing the wig and teeth into a large straw purse. She sat down, noting the contrast between Casey's eagerness and Jacob's concern. "Jacob, don't worry. So far, all went well." She told them about the incident, the staff's reactions, and most importantly Russ' reaction.

Casey clapped her hands in glee. "Good! Good! I would love to have been there to see his face."

"Disguised as the blonde doughnut girl, I got to see how our target handled it in public and then saw his real reaction . . . up close."

"Tell us," Casey said, sitting on the edge of her seat. She followed Nan's gaze to her father and was puzzled to see his solemn expression. "Dad, don't you get any satisfaction from that?"

"As a matter of fact, I don't. I felt for the guy."

"Why?" Casey asked, incredulous.

"All we have is Tiffany's word that he's abusive." He talked directly at Casey. "You and I know how devastating it is for people to believe lies."

"Maybe I can help you, Jake," Nan said. "As I told you, the reason I wanted to be around for the first incident was so I could see Russ for myself, to look into his eyes. I followed him out the door with my empty cart and offered to help clean off his sleeve. At first he hardly noticed me. I pulled off a piece of the gummy yellowish slime and remarked in amazement that it hadn't even left a stain. It was then he looked at me."

She shivered. "I saw such coldness, such malevolence in his eyes, that I actually felt a jolt of fear. His reaction was also mixed with undisguised revulsion at my appearance. I pretended to be hurt and walked away."

The room was heavy with silence as Jacob and Casey absorbed the disturbing information. Then Casey added quietly, "Dad, Tiffany told me Russ couldn't stand anything less than perfection in her appearance and that he was always repulsed by unattractive and poorly dressed women. Of course, no one can be perfect, so he constantly criticizes Tiffany. As if he were perfect himself," she added bitterly, reflecting upon her own past experiences with Nick.

"That's reprehensible," Jacob remarked. "Monty called me about half an hour ago. I think I'll enjoy telling you what happened tonight."

"Tonight? Another one?" Casey reveled in the thought.

Jacob nodded and then told the toilet paper incident with relish. He allowed himself to chuckle over it while Casey and Nan laughed so hard, tears ran down their cheeks.

"Oh, how that does my heart good!" exclaimed Casey.

"Mine too," Nan said.

"Snard is doing a good job, Dad. The sticky stuff didn't harm the suit."

"Yes. I complimented Monty on that, and told him to continue to be careful in that area."

"When does Monty intend to do the next bit of mischief?" Casey asked.

"He isn't sure, but he'll inform me as soon as possible."

"I'm anxious to hear Russ' version through Tiffany."

Jacob's business phone rang in his office. "Excuse me, I have to take that."

Nan watched him stride out of the room. She liked the way he moved, the way he carried himself. The admiration on Nan's face was not lost on Casey.

"It's so nice you and your father have each other," she murmured.

"You didn't have children, Nan?"

"No. I always wanted a big family. But even before there were any signs of illness in Chet, I couldn't get pregnant. After tests were made, we learned that Chet was sterile." Her eyes pooled with tears. Quickly looking down to hide her emotions, she aimlessly picked up an attractive loose-leaf binder from the coffee table.

Casey watched Nan, thinking. *How sad. She would have been a wonderful mother.*

"What is this?" Nan asked, surprised, turning to the first page. What *are* these . . . cartoons?"

"When I was young, that's the way Dad taught me things he thought I should know. He drew cartoon characters with dialogue."

"Is it all right if I look at it?"

"Certainly."

Nan's eyes widened in surprise. "He's quite an artist." She turned page after page. Stopping at one page to read the dialogue, she was amused by the message. She read aloud the dialogue of two silly looking characters. One said, *"We must be flexible or we might break."*

"Yeah?" the other one said. "I don't believe you."

"Okay, give me a hard shove and I'll show you."

The doubting character did so. The challenger fell backward in a roll and jumped back onto his feet. "See how flexible I am?"

"I'm flexible too," the one who shoved said.

"No you're not, you're rigid."

"All right, shove me and see."

Mr. Flexible shoved him hard. He fell backward and broke in two.

Nan chuckled. "What did you learn from that?"

"Dad taught me that life is hard and if we refuse to roll with the punches and get back on our feet we'll break. When we're rigid it means we don't adjust to change, that we aren't humble enough to learn how. When we don't we'll suffer more. Something like that. This is just one of the volumes he made for me. I was in high school when he created this one. I was going through some difficult times with girls I thought were friends, among other things."

"Hey, you two, what have I missed while I was away?" Jacob asked, grinning, as he entered.

"You missed the story of Mr. Rigid and Mr. Flexible," Nan said.

His face went blank, and then he saw the binder in her hand. "Oh." He smiled. "My feeble efforts to teach my daughter."

She smiled at Casey. "I think you've succeeded admirably. And what little I've seen of this booklet is fascinating."

"You think so?" he asked, surprised. He couldn't help but remember that Silvia thought they were silly.

"Yes I do. I'd like to look through them all some time."

"Oh, they're not much to see. Do you want a bowl of ice cream, a sundae, or a banana split?"

Nan looked over at Casey. "I'd better go."

"No. We three need to celebrate our success today with a banana split," Casey insisted.

"By all means," Jacob reiterated, his warm eyes gazing into hers. "We want you to stay. After all, my visit with you was shortened by the phone call."

Nan's heart ricocheted. "All right," she managed to state in a matter-of-fact tone. "I think I'd like a banana split."

One hour later, Casey watched her dad escort Nan to her car. She frowned. It seemed to her that Nan was looking at her dad in a way that had more meaning than mere friendship. It worried her. *Is she falling for him?* she asked herself. She would feel responsible if Nan got hurt. She'd had enough pain in her life. It was obvious that her dad was attracted to Nan and enjoyed her company, but would he let it go further? She paced impatiently around the room. *Why is Dad taking so long? What are they talking about?*

Finally, she heard the front door open and close. The minute her dad entered the family room she asked him what he and Nan found to talk about.

He looked at her curiously. "Why do you want to know?"

She shrugged her shoulders. "Just do, that's all."

"For one thing, I thanked her again. I told her that your

spirits were brighter and that I wasn't quite as worried about you."

"Oh? Well yes, you're right. Project Russ has been therapeutic, and has helped take my mind off my own worries. But more than anything, I hope it will help Tiffany."

"I'm glad. But I wish I knew what it's going to do to help her."

"We'll simply have to be patient and wait and see. Uh, Dad, I want to ask you a question before I go."

"All right," he said, sitting down across from her. "What is it?"

"How do you feel about Nan?"

The surprise on his face told her she was right. Marriage was the furthest thing from his mind. "What are you getting at, Casey?"

"Would you like to date her?"

"That would be leading her on. Our relationship can't go past friendship. Why are you asking this?"

"Because I think she may be starting to feel something more than friendship for you."

"That's ridiculous."

"Dad, you have no idea how attractive you are and how wonderful you are. Nan can see all that."

He smiled. "Why thank you, Casey. I think, however, you're a little prejudiced. It has been a long time since I felt attractive—and certainly never wonderful. Don't worry. If Nan feels something, she'll soon realize it's only because she's been lonely for years. She didn't get to experience a normal, satisfying marriage for most of her married life. She'd feel that way about any nice man she became acquainted with right now. I'm certain she's aware that she's at a vulnerable point in her life."

Casey got up. "I can't believe you, Dad! For one who's been so wise all my life and given me such good advice, you're totally naive when it comes to yourself and women." She walked over to her dad, bent down, and kissed him. "Good night. I'm not saying another word—for now, that is." She grinned.

Russ relaxed somewhat. In fact, in spite of his humiliation, he felt he had given one of his best speeches. When he sat down, Reisner whispered to him. "Great job, but I need to talk with you after the meeting."

Russ dreaded it. He wanted to get out of there as quickly as possible, but he had to mingle among the managers, glad-handing them and talking with them as if nothing had happened. The one advantage to all this was he could study their faces, their eyes, to see if any one of them was the guilty party. No one flinched, no one seemed uneasy.

His first thought was that it was Norm Wadley, but Norm was already sitting at a table near the front when he entered. His mind flitted from person to person and then to his wife. He didn't trust Tiffany. He could sense a slight difference in her lately. He couldn't quite figure out what the difference was, but it was bothering him!

Finally, everyone left for their hotel rooms or for home. The only ones left in the hall were Russ, Reisner, and the cleaning crew.

Pulling aside a couple of chairs, Fred offered him a seat and took a deep breath. "The evening was successful, but I'm very concerned about those embarrassing incidents—not the incidents in and of themselves, but *why* someone would want to do those things to you. There has to be a reason. Do you get along with all the managers?"

"Yes I do. I feel I have a good relationship with each one of them."

Fred nodded. "In visiting many of them, I found that to be the case. How about your staff?"

"I believe I have an equally good relationship with all of them. The only one I'm concerned about is Norm Wadley. I don't know if he's jealous of me, bucking for my job, or what."

"Why do you say that?"

"Well, sometimes, I don't come in early. I write to the

managers on my computer at home where I won't be disturbed. Other times I go meet with special clients for an extended business lunch. I don't think it's Wadley's place to needle me about my comings and goings, but he has an annoying penchant for doing so." The moment he had expressed these feelings, Russ regretted it. *What's the matter with me? I'm usually more careful about over explaining myself, more discreet!*

Fred mused on his remarks for what seemed an overly long time. "I see. Well, I think we had better call it a night." He shook hands with Russ and told him he would see him in six months and to keep up the good work.

Unsettled by Reisner's questions and his lack of reaction to what he'd told him about Norm, Russ released his frustration on the gas pedal, speeding toward home. Whipping into his driveway, he jammed his finger on the garage door opener and pulled into the garage. Still mortified and angry over his humiliation, he strode into the house to find Tiffany. Only one small lamp was on in the family room. He found the bedroom dark. Switching on the light awoke Tiffany. *Or so she wants me to believe,* he thought.

Tiffany blinked, looking a little disoriented. "How did you do today?" she asked hoarsely.

"Where were you today? I called your office and you weren't there. They said you called in sick. I don't believe it." His voice rose. "Where were you?"

"Russ, I didn't even go to the office or anywhere. I think I have the flu or something. I've been throwing up all day."

"I don't believe you."

"Wh—why?"

"I think you had something to do with what happened to me today."

Tiffany pushed herself to a sitting position, confused and fearful. "What happened?"

His voice low with rancor, he told her in detail the humiliating experiences.

She was in shock. "How could those things have happened?

How terrible for you."

He sat down on her side of the bed and grabbed her shoulders so tightly she winced. "Answer me, where were you?"

Tiffany jerked herself away, unable to hide the anger. "I was right here in bed!"

Glaring at her, he noticed that her face was flushed. He felt her forehead. "You're burning up with fever." He recoiled from her.

"I know."

He shoved her back against the headboard and strode out of the room. He went into the bathroom and washed his hands. It had been a mistake to touch her. What if he caught something?

Entering the garage, he pulled out his car keys, which also held a key to her car, turned the ignition switch, and checked the odometer. It was exactly the same as it had been last night. She hadn't been anywhere—at least not in *her* car. At last he had to concede that Tiffany was innocent of anything that had happened to him this morning and this evening. Besides, he couldn't see how she could have pulled it off without him spotting her. And why would he think she would do it in the first place? He wanted desperately to blame someone. The first frisson of fear went through him.

Chapter Fifteen

Sometimes tears make rainbows.

The next day after a sandwich and a drink at a fast food place, Casey headed out to South Mountain to search for the path she was intending to look for when Brad unintentionally disrupted her morning. Having nothing pressing to do this afternoon, she wanted to use as much time as her leg would allow.

She reasoned that since the stalker knew she was aware of him maybe he wouldn't bother her for a while, perhaps permanently.

It was a beautiful day. The overbearing summer heat was still a few weeks away and the traffic was amazingly sparse. She turned onto South Central, which led her directly into South Mountain. The pale yellow flowers of catclaws and pink-white flowers of buckwheat bloomed prolifically along the roadside. Rolling down the window, she breathed in the fragrance as she carefully watched for the trailhead that might lead to the path.

She glanced into the rearview mirror and noticed she wasn't the only one wanting to enjoy the desert spring. A car was driving close behind. She moved over, making room for the car to pass, but it stayed behind. *Maybe the person is only looking at the scenery*, she thought. She increased her speed. The car behind kept pace as it too sped up. It was then that she noticed it was a *black* car and that the driver was a man! Fear nearly strangled her for a moment—then it turned to anger. "How dare he infringe upon my life!"

"Where's Brad when I need him?" No sooner had she said it, than a tan car some distance back came into view. Tentative relief rushed through her. She hadn't seen it before because of the curving road. She hoped with all her heart it was Brad. There was one way to find out. She stopped suddenly. So did the black car. So did the tan one. "It is Brad!" she exclaimed with relief.

She assessed the situation quickly and made a decision, hoping Brad would get her message. She maneuvered her car until it straddled the two-lane road, leaving no room for the black car to pass. Watching carefully, she saw the tan car moving slowly toward the black one. The stranger whipped his car around and drove in the other direction. The license plate was unreadable. Brad quickly straddled the road as she had done, backing up cars behind him. The black car went off the road, bumping over the foliage and dirt, and then drove back up on the road and sped off. Brad followed him, but a billowing cloud of dust hid the black car for a few minutes. Driving as fast as she could, Casey followed.

The chase carried them out of the park to Baseline Road where the black car led them to Interstate 10 going north. Turning east on Highway 60, the Superstition Freeway, the car headed toward Apache Junction at a high rate of speed. The black car was much more powerful than Brad's small one and was soon out of sight. Casey followed Brad, who led her back to Scottsdale and Hartner and Hart's parking lot.

Casey felt like crying she was so angry, and the emotion left her shaky.

Brad got out and ran over to her. "You all right?" he asked, concerned.

She nodded. "Thanks for being there. I don't know if he's the same man or not, but the car looks like it and he certainly acted like it."

"I got close enough to see both the front and back license plates. They were both smudged with mud," Brad stated grimly.

"But his car was clean and shiny, no mud on it. It had to have been put on there to hide the numbers!" Casey pounded the steering wheel in frustration. "I was foolish to think I scared him off when I caught him the other day."

"Let's go in and talk with Sy about it."

"Why? What can he do?"

Brad shrugged his shoulders. "I don't know. All I know, is I have to report to him. Why don't you come along?"

The last thing she wanted to do was meet with Syrus. "I don't have the strength, Brad."

"I'll help you. Come on," he insisted.

"All right, just for you. Not for me." She held back the impulse to tell Brad about her suspicions of Syrus. Casey hung heavily onto Brad's strong arm until they reached Syrus' door. Brad knocked.

"Come in," Syrus said. Surprised to see the two of them together, he looked from one to the other, his eyes lingering on Casey. "What's up?"

Casey sat down and Brad reported what had happened.

"Why were you out there, Casey? You didn't have a job to do for the agency."

"That's my business. My personal life is my own."

"It's Hartner and Hart's too when they pay someone to keep you safe," he stated sharply.

"I didn't ask them to."

"We've discussed this before, Casey. Let it go." He turned to Brad. "Did you get the license plate?"

"No. It was smudged with mud though the car was clean."

"Did you see the face of the driver, Casey?"

"Enough to see that it was a man."

Syrus tapped the desk, thinking. "Would you consider not going off into the wilderness alone for a while, Casey?"

One hand covering her eyes, the other one clenched, Casey muttered something.

"What?" Syrus asked.

She looked up. Tears of frustration were glistening in her

eyes. "I said, I'd like to punch that guy out. I'm tired of him frightening me! I'm tired of him ruining everything I try to do! I want my life back!"

"Do you want to call the police?"

"No. I want to go home." She got up, muttered a thanks to Brad, and left.

Despondent, Casey drove into her driveway and into the garage. She didn't want to be home. She wanted to be hiking the paths of South Mountain. Moving painfully into her kitchen, she sat down at the kitchen table and cried. She had never been an emotional person, but here she was, turning into a blubbering baby. If only she could go to her dad. But what could he do, except worry himself to death?

There was one thing she could do. She reached for the phone and dialed one of the numbers she knew well—the FBI man, Robert Welles. She doubted the FBI would do anything about it because it probably didn't have anything to do with her case. As far as she was concerned she had no case. Nevertheless, it made her feel better to do something. After a few minutes she was put through to Mr. Welles. She wanted to scream at him, demand to know why they hadn't solved whatever angle of her case they were working on, but instead she only reported this latest incident. He in turn thanked her for telling him and told her to be careful. She hung up the phone and muttered, "Gee thanks, Mr. Welles. That was helpful."

She decided to put on her swimming suit, get into the soothing water, and do her therapy early. "Maybe the sunshine will lift my spirits."

The phone, shattering the silence, startled her. She answered it quickly.

"Casey," came a muted voice. "It's Tiffany."

"Tiffany! I'm so glad to hear from you. What's up?"

"I don't know. Apparently some practical jokes have been

played on Russ and he thought that somehow I was responsible. When he came home, he wouldn't believe that I had been home sick all day. I heard him go out into the garage. He always checks on my mileage to find out if I've gone somewhere he doesn't think I should go. It took that to make him believe me."

Casey let out a silent sigh of relief. "What happened to him?" she asked anxious to hear Tiffany's version.

"The worst things in the world. They played on his vanity, his pride." She told Casey what Russ had told her.

"Amazing. How was Russ this morning?"

"Edgy and nervous, certain someone in the company is out to get him."

"Stay out of his way. Did you go to the library and read some of those books I suggested?"

"I did. They really helped me know that I wasn't the only one this has happened to. Also they gave me courage. I tried one of the ideas yesterday morning. I managed to redirect his anger. He got a little flustered and stormed out of the house and left for work."

"Good! Keep it up. Please keep me informed about everything, Tiff. Promise me. It's very important that you do."

"I promise, Casey. Thanks for your help and friendship."

The call had eased Casey's worries over Tiffany. It also confirmed that the pranks were having their desired effect.

Feeling relaxed after the swim, therapy, and shower, Casey was wondering what she could find in her bare refrigerator and cupboards for dinner when the phone rang again. Quickly answering it, she heard a familiar voice.

"Casey, this is Betty." When there was only silence, she added. "You know, your neighbor, Betty Middleton."

"Oh, Betty! I'm sorry, my mind was on a friend. How are you?"

"I'm fine, how are you, dear?"

"I'm doing better each day."

"Good. I called to see if you'd like to come over for dinner tonight."

Casey was surprised but pleased. She needed company tonight. "I'd love to, Betty. I'd ask what I could bring, but I haven't been grocery shopping in a couple of weeks."

"Oh my, no. You don't need to bring anything. Would 5:30 be all right with you?"

"It would be perfect, Betty . . . and thank you."

Casey smiled. She liked Betty because she was always the same—cheerful and warm. She was also looking forward to a home-cooked meal. She ate a lot of fast foods and her own meals were almost always thrown together at the last minute, without much thought or advance planning.

Having something to look forward to, Casey got the energy to clean house and do the laundry. When it was time to get ready, she went to her closet. She was tired of wearing her full silky pants. She picked out a long blue A-line cotton skirt and a blouse with tiny pink and blue flowers. The skirt was one she'd had for years and was long enough to cover her leg to the ankle. Its fullness made it comfortable to wear. The last time she noticed, the trend was long straight skirts, which would rub against her scars. Slipping on some white sandals, she added a little makeup. Wearing something different lifted her spirits, even if it was only for herself.

Locking the front door, she walked over to Betty's. Before she could push the bell, the door opened. Betty's round face was beaming. She was a short, trim woman with the most beautiful white hair Casey had ever seen. Her blue eyes were large and expressive. She had been a widow for five years and her children and grandchildren took good care of her. They came to see her often and she noticed they frequently took her places.

"You look lovely, Casey. Come on in."

"Thank you. Mm, something smells good. I'm starving."

"I hope so, I've cooked enough. Come into the kitchen and sit down while I finish."

"Can I help you with anything?" Casey asked, following her in.

"No. It's all done except a little more thickening in the gravy."

Grateful to sit and watch, Casey saw that the table was set with three places. "You're having someone else to dinner, Betty?"

"Yes. My grandson, Craig. You remember. I told you about him."

Casey frantically tried to recall, but before she had to admit she had forgotten, Betty continued.

"He's that handsome thirty-three-year-old bachelor grandson of mine that I'm worried about. You know the one that looks like the movie star, Tyrone Power. He has a good job, makes good money, but he isn't married. His mother and I are frustrated that he isn't looking for a wife like he should be."

Casey's heart sank. The last thing she wanted to be involved in was Betty's matchmaking. She remembered the conversation now. Betty had mentioned that she would like her grandson to meet her. Determined to be gracious about it all, Casey said, "I wish I could introduce him to someone, but most of my friends are married."

"That's the problem he's finding. He says they're usually married, divorced, or weird."

The doorbell rang. "Oh, there he is. You stay right there and rest and I'll bring him in."

Casey could hear Betty's enthusiastic greeting, and his more muted one. They entered the kitchen and Betty said, "Craig, I want you to meet my sweet next-door neighbor, Casey Carter."

The look on Craig's face told Casey that he was as surprised as she was at the prospect of having another guest.

"Well . . . this is a nice surprise," he said, smiling and shaking her hand.

"It's nice to meet you, Craig. Your grandmother has been telling me about you and how you look like Tyrone Power."

His face flushed. "Grandma! You're impossible. Besides, no one today even knows who he was."

"I do," stated Casey, grinning. "I like old movies." Privately, Casey didn't like Tyrone Power's looks. He was too much of a pretty boy. Aloud she stated sincerely, "But I find you much better looking than Tyrone."

Betty was pleased at Casey's candidness. She nodded and smiled. "I agree."

Craig laughed. "Hey, thanks."

Dinner tasted so good to Casey, she overate. Betty had gone to the trouble to prepare fried chicken, mashed potatoes, and gravy. On top of it all, she had made a blueberry pie.

Their conversation was pleasant and relaxed. Casey found out that Craig was an executive of a software company and that he lived in Phoenix in his own townhouse. He asked her about herself and was apparently one of the few who didn't know about her situation. He was intrigued that she was a photographer presently doing assignments for Hartner and Hart.

"I've always wanted to delve into photography myself but never got around to it."

"It's fun. You should try it."

"I might one of these days. I'm curious. Why are you living in a senior citizen community?" he asked, the corners of his blue eyes crinkling with amusement. "With the exception of my grandma here, you look like a beautiful pink rose blooming in a garden of withered flowers."

Casey acknowledged the compliment with a slight smile and a tilt of the head. "I live here because I feel safe."

He was puzzled. "Safe from what?"

"Safe from standing out like a sore thumb."

"I'm sorry. I don't understand."

"I was in an accident and my right leg was hurt. I limp." Then she laughed. "So do a lot of my neighbors."

He chuckled. "I guess that's reason enough to live here. But let me clue you in, you'd stand out anywhere but not like a sore thumb."

"I take it that's a compliment?"

"You bet. How about going out with me sometime soon?"

Why did he have to ask me in front of Betty? she thought miserably. She wasn't ready to date. "Uh, I don't know how soon it can be. Right now I'm in the middle of some projects that are taking a lot of time and thought."

"Well, let me think," he replied. "You do have to eat don't you?"

Casey could see she wasn't going to get out of it gracefully. She nodded slightly.

"Taking you to dinner after work should help. You wouldn't have to cook. You can go home anytime, right after dinner if you need to."

She glanced at Betty, who was beaming with pleasure. *How dear of Betty,* she thought. *She knows my history and it doesn't bother her.* "All right, Craig. That would be nice. Call me sometime."

"How about tomorrow night?"

"I'm expecting a family friend to visit Dad and me," she said, hoping her dad would have some more news.

"All right, Saturday."

An idea came to Casey. "On second thought, even if the friend comes over, I don't have to be there all evening; she can visit with my father. Let's go ahead and make it Friday. But I'm not sure where and what time. I won't know the details until the last minute. Is that all right with you?"

"It sure is," he said, pulling a couple of cards from his wallet and taking a pen from his shirt pocket. "Give me your phone number." He wrote it down and tucked the card in his pocket. Handing her the other one, he said, "Here's my phone number in case you need to reach me before I call you."

"Thank you. Now, how about you and I cleaning up the kitchen, Craig?" Casey suggested.

Betty protested, but she was made to sit down and watch

and listen, which she did, thoroughly pleased that her grandson was attracted to Casey and seemed to be enjoying himself.

Chapter Sixteen

Fortune does not change men.
It only unmasks them.
—Anonymous.

By the second day the flu had abated, and Tiffany felt she could drag herself back to work. When she stepped out of the closet, she saw Russ getting out of bed.

"Would you like some breakfast, Russ?"

He jumped. "Don't sneak up on me that way."

"I didn't mean to. Do you want breakfast this morning?"

"No. I couldn't eat a thing. I'm still burning over the other day. When I learn who did this, they'll wish they'd never been born."

Not wanting to hear any more, Tiffany quickly left the room. In the kitchen she nervously poured herself a bowl of cereal, made a piece of toast, and forced herself to eat.

She returned to the bedroom and saw that Russ had shaved and dressed. She watched him pick up his hand mirror and examine his suit in the back and study it in the front. "Look carefully, Tiffany. I don't have anything on this suit, do I?"

"No, not a thing. You look handsome and well-dressed, as always. I can't imagine the practical jokes will continue after what Fred said."

"What do you know about it?" he lashed out.

Seething inside at his vindictiveness, she merely said, "I guess not a thing. Excuse me. I'm leaving for work early. I have some catching up to do."

"I've changed my mind. I want a cup of coffee and a piece of toast."

She wanted to yell at him to get it himself, but she dashed into the kitchen and toasted some bread and poured him coffee just as he entered.

"I said I didn't want anything to eat. What's the matter with you?"

This contradictory pattern of Russ' ordinarily was crazy-making, to her, but the knowledge she had gained from the books helped her recognize it for what it was. "Of course you did. What a fool I am," she said imitating Bianca's manner of speaking in *The Taming of the Shrew.*

Russ was used to her desperately trying to explain herself and was momentarily taken aback. "Are you being smart-mouthed with me?"

"No. I was serious," she replied, looking as childlike as possible. "What time will you be home tonight?"

"I don't know," he answered impatiently.

"I have to go now so I can catch up at work." She went over to kiss him good-bye.

"Don't!" he said pushing her away. "You may still have that bug. I don't want to get the flu."

Relieved, Tiffany smiled as sincerely as she could. "All right. See you tonight. Have a good day."

He stared after her, suspicion beginning to fester. "Something's different about her."

Arriving at the parking lot of Global Investments, Russ looked around. No one was anywhere near his car. He got out, pressed the lock button on the keyless entry, and walked carefully toward the building, nervously looking behind him, walking a few feet more, and then looking on each side of him until he reached the entrance. Two men passed him as he entered, but the hall was clear after that. He breathed a sigh of relief, feeling more certain all the time that the jokes played on him were the work of one of the managers. It could be one of those two he'd had to chew out for their negligence and poor judgment. Somehow he'd find out who.

Norm Wadley had driven up almost at the same time as Russ. He'd had to run to the office supply store to get something for the office. Remaining in his car a moment, he noticed as always that Russ kept privileged hours. He was always late in the morning and spent hours away from the office. He wished he could tell Reisner what precious little work he did for his big salary. But then that would appear self-serving. He knew he didn't look the part of an executive like Russ, tall and handsome. He was short and stocky with thinning blond hair. But he had something Russ didn't—the company's interest at heart.

As these thoughts were buzzing around in his head, Norm had observed Russ' strange, almost erratic behavior. It was obvious he was still nervous over the practical jokes played on him. "Couldn't happen to a more deserving guy," he muttered, smiling. He didn't like Russ Eden and he couldn't figure out why exactly. He seemed well-intentioned, confident, and capable. He was either a very sincere man or an incredibly clever one, and he couldn't decide which.

He waited until Russ went in the building before he got out of his car. When he entered the office, he found it all astir. "What's going on?" he asked.

Russ turned around. "This is what's going on!" he yelled, pointing to his face.

Norm stared at him, shocked at the sight. Russ' face looked as if someone had blown soot in his face. One side of it was all black, covering his ear and neck.

"Where were *you* when I came in?" he asked suspiciously.

Norm cocked his head in disbelief. "You suspect I did that?"

"Well, someone did and you weren't here when I arrived."

"I just came from the office supply place. I wasn't anywhere near you, Russ. Besides, why would I do that? What could I gain from it?" He threw up his hands and walked away.

Russ stormed into the restroom and took a paper towel, wet it, put soap on it, and scrubbed. Only a small bit came off. "I can't believe this!" Rinsing off the soap, he pulled out his cell phone and called Tiffany's workplace and asked for her.

"I'm sorry, Mr. Eden, but she isn't at her desk right now."

"Where is she?" he asked suspiciously.

"She and two others are in Mr. Bowen's office going over some accounts. Shall I have her call you?"

"No." He hung up. He couldn't wait. *I know,* he thought, *I'll call Sheila.* They had their standing appointment for lunch today, after which they would go to their usual hotel. *We'll meet now instead and she can help me get this off!* He dialed her number and heard her sultry voice answer. "Sheila, we have to meet now. I need your help."

"Why?"

"Don't ask why," he said, trying his best to keep his voice calm. "Do you have some of that cream, you know that cleans makeup off?"

"You mean cleansing cream?"

"Yeah, that's it. Bring some with you. It's very important."

"All right, Russ," she answered, puzzled.

"Call and book us a room at the Phoenician on Camelback Road as usual and we'll order room service for lunch. Call me the moment you've booked the room. I'm leaving now and I'll be waiting in my car until I hear from you. I'll go in the side door we use sometimes. It's always locked, so let me in. I can't let anyone see me and don't ask me why. You'll know when you see me."

"All right, Russ. I'll do it right away."

Leaving the restroom, he told his secretary he was going home to try and clean his face. "Soap and water won't take it off. Maybe my wife's cleansing cream will do it." With effort, he put on a smile.

Standing uneasily by the hotel's side door, Sheila waited for Russ. Finally, she saw him walking toward the door, his hand over one side of his face. Opening the door for him, he entered. "Take me to the room, quick."

She led him down the hall to a room on the first floor, unlocked the door, and let him enter first. Putting a Do Not Disturb sign on the door, she shut and locked it. When she turned and saw Russ' face, she gasped. "What's on your face?"

"I have no idea. But it won't come off with soap and water. That's why I asked you to bring the cleansing cream."

"Oh. Come into the bathroom and we'll try it." Opening her purse, she pulled it out. "You'd better take your coat and shirt off. It's on your neck too, she said, examining him. "At least it didn't get on your shirt." She watched him disrobe. "How did you get that on you?"

"I didn't!" he yelled.

"Don't yell at me, Russ."

"I'm sorry. I'm just a little edgy. I had some practical jokes pulled on me the day before yesterday during an important meeting and so I watched very carefully when I walked into the building this morning. When I entered the office, every-one did a double take. I have no idea how it got on me. Wait a minute. There were two men coming down the hall, and as we passed through the double doors at the same time, I felt a poof of air on my face. I thought it was the air coming from opening the doors. One of them could have blown something on me. But how? They passed by so quickly."

"But why would anyone do such a thing?" she said, rubbing the cleansing cream all over the soot-colored black on his face, neck, and ear. "We'd better let it stay on for a few minutes before I rub it off. Why don't you sit down and relax, Russ."

"All right," he said, letting out a heavy breath. "But it's a little hard to relax under the circumstances."

Sheila washed the cream off her hands, smiling. He called her for help, not that simpering wife of his. She remembered when Russ first entered the dining room of the country club. All the single women and some of the married ones stared at him. Did he look at any of them? No. When he saw her, he came straight over to her and asked if he could share the table.

She looked at herself in the mirror and saw the image of a slim blonde with perfect features. She was well aware of her beauty, but being wealthy on top of that had its drawbacks. Her first two husbands had married her for her money. Russ Eden, on the other hand, was well off from what he had told her rather offhandedly, and from what she had found out. His salary was in the six figures. And the way he talked about his wife, she was sure it wouldn't be long before he left Tiffany and married her.

Russ waited impatiently for the stuff on his face to do the job. His cell phone rang. Supposing it was someone from the office, he answered it. He paled when he heard that distinctive male voice he knew so well.

"I've left you e-mails twice now and haven't had an answer. I haven't received a report from you this week. What's up?" the voice said in a low, calculating tone. "Where have you been? What have you been doing?"

How could he have forgotten? *Of course. It's been these hell-ish pranks.* Having been instructed not to use names, neither addressed each other. "A meeting with Fred Reisner and the managers this week has kept me busy, also some difficulties at the office."

The silence on the other end sent fear through Russ.

"You mean you didn't have even a *moment* to look at your e-mail and report?"

"I'm sorry. It won't happen again. I'll take care of it this afternoon."

"I think that would be a very good idea," the voice said slowly, emphasizing each word. "I want that erased off your computer. Your wife didn't look at it did she?"

"No. I keep my office locked at all times." Russ heard a click and knew he had hung up. He started shaking. He had always been on top of things until these damnable episodes. Taking a few deep breaths, he got up and went into the bathroom where Sheila was repairing her makeup. "I think it's time to wipe off this grease."

Sheila took some tissues and wiped. "It's coming off, Russ."

When she was through, he looked into the mirror. "It's left my skin gray. Put some more on."

The next time Sheila wiped it with a warm washcloth. A little more came off. "It's mostly gone, Russ, just a tinge is left."

Russ frowned, grabbed the washcloth and scrubbed with soap and water hoping that would finish it. Rinsing and wiping his face, ear and neck, he saw a slight stain of gray still there. "I'll be damned! What in the hell is that stuff!" Swallowing his anger, he said, "I've got to go, Sheila. We'll have to see each other next week. That call reminded me of something very important I have to do."

"But, Russ," she said softly, moving close to him, "I've been looking forward to this all week."

"I have too, baby," he said, caressing her cheek. "I wish I could stay."

"Oh, all right. Call me soon, okay?"

"Soon, baby, soon."

Chapter Seventeen

Stiff-neckedness prevents one from looking heavenward, from bowing in prayer, from turning side to side, from learning from others.

Casey, dressed in a pair of pale blue silk pants with a white sateen tee underneath a filmy long-sleeved blue shirt, arrived at the restaurant promptly at six. Her dad had offered to take her and Nan out to eat as a change of routine when he reported Snard's latest escapade. Nan drove up almost at the same time. They both got out and complimented each other's clothing and laughed.

They entered together. The hostess led them to the table where Jacob was waiting.

He stood and smiled. "Wow! What a pair of beauties."

A simultaneous "thank you" greeted his ears.

Nan's heartbeat quickened as she studied Jacob. He was dressed in black pants and a gray sport coat with a black high-necked T-shirt underneath. "You look like you stepped right out of *GQ*, Jake."

He looked puzzled. "What's *GQ*?"

Nan and Casey laughed. "Never mind," Nan said. "It's best you remain in the dark."

"Well, shall we hear the report before we order or after we eat?" Jacob asked.

"Let's hear it before," Casey suggested. "Then we can relax while we eat."

"That's all right with me. How about you, Nan?"

"Either way is fine with me. I just appreciate not having to cook for myself tonight."

"Our friends did it again. However, I don't know how it affected Russ. They couldn't witness it since his reaction, whatever it was, would have been at the Global Investment offices."

Her voice eager, Casey asked, "Since Snard has been doing his own version of some of our ideas, I'm curious to hear what he did this time."

Jacob told them in a lowered voice what Monty had told him. "They waited in the hall of Russ' workplace. When they saw Russ drive up and park in his usual spot, they watched him. They said he looked as nervous as a bird pecking in the grass, looking up and around every other second. As he neared the entrance, our pair pretended to be engaged in conversation, arriving at the doors the moment he did. Snard shot black powder on Russ' cheek as they passed."

Casey and Nan laughed.

"The interesting thing is," Jacob said, "Monty told me that though the black powder is harmless, it's hard to get off. No matter how our victim tries, a slight stain will remain and has to wear off gradually. Not enough that it's that noticeable, but it will be to a man like Russ."

Casey clapped her hands. "If that had happened to Nick after the other two incidents, he would be close to going nuts. Tiffany will probably call me. She has already called me about the other two incidents. Her face clouded. "We've got to watch very carefully from now on. If Russ reacts like I think he will, maybe we'll have to talk Tiffany into going somewhere safe."

Jacob's brows furrowed in concern. "That's what has worried me from the beginning."

"But, Dad, in the long run we'll be helping Tiffany. Let's just pray for her safety. Haven't you taught me that all my life?"

"Yes, but we do have to use our good sense. And I hope to heaven we have."

"Let's think where we could have her go for a few days just

in case," Casey said, buying time until Craig arrived. She had called him and told him where to pick her up.

They batted ideas around. Jacob vetoed two ideas: staying with Casey, or staying with Nan.

"I don't want either one of you to be in danger," Jacob whispered adamantly. Just then he noticed a young man walking toward them.

"Hello, Casey," the young man said.

"Oh hi, Craig. Dad, I want you to meet Betty Middleton's grandson, Craig."

"Oh. Good to meet you," he said, shaking the young man's hand.

"Thank you, sir. It's nice to meet you."

"Craig," Casey said, "I'd like you to meet our friend, Nan Hunter."

Craig shook hands with Nan, smiled, and nodded.

Casey stood. "Well, shall we go, Craig?" She smiled at her dad's shocked expression. "I forgot to tell you that Craig asked me out to dinner. I told him to meet me here."

"Oh?" he said, looking suspiciously at his daughter. "Well, in that case how about you two joining us for dinner?"

"No thanks, Dad. We'd like to get acquainted."

"All right then, have a good time."

"You too, Dad. Bye, Nan."

Jacob and Nan watched them leave and then looked at each other, at a loss for words.

"What just happened here?" Nan asked.

"I think Casey has set us up."

Nan laughed. "Are you uncomfortable with it?" Before he could protest, she said, "I'm not really hungry, Jake. In fact, I feel a little tired."

Jacob eyed her skeptically. "You won't feel tired when you get some food into you."

Relieved that Jacob hadn't taken the proffered way out, she responded warmly. "Thank you. You may be right."

On the way to the restaurant, Casey confessed. "You see, Craig, my mother died about five years ago and Dad doesn't want to marry again, but he's too young and vibrant to go on through life alone. I'm simply nudging him in the right direction."

"Not only is my grandmother a matchmaker, you are too, I see," he said smiling.

"I never thought I would be a matchmaker for my dad. He's such a wonderful man. I didn't think there could possibly be a woman good enough for him. I guess that tells you how much I think of Nan."

He nodded. "It certainly does."

"I kind of had to pull a fast one to get them to go out together tonight."

"That's obvious. I'm glad I could help." He turned to her and smiled.

Casey's heart started working double-time. His dark hair and sensitive blue eyes under thick dark brows did remind her of Tyrone Power. However, he had a larger and more distinctive nose and fuller lips, which easily spread into a smile, wider and warmer than that of the late Mr. Power.

She couldn't help but compare Nick's looks to Craig's. Nick had an . . . it was difficult for her to put into words. Then it came to her. Nick had an animal magnetism about him. It was exciting because it seemed so masculine. Now, she saw it for what it was—selfishness and evil. She shivered at how she had allowed herself to be fooled. Craig's looks were just as handsome, but his attractiveness came from a healthy, natural masculinity.

"Are you cold?" Craig asked.

"No. I'm just feeling a little uneasy. This is my first date since my husband was killed a little over three years ago."

"Three years! How did you dodge all the guys for that long?"

A heavy feeling came over Casey. Craig didn't know about the months she spent in and out of the hospital or any of the scandal connected to her. Apparently all Betty told him was that her husband had died in an accident and she got hurt. *Dear, kind Betty*, she thought. Casey knew she had to tell Craig tonight and get it over with. If it didn't bother him and he still wanted to date her, she would be thrilled. She had to admit she was attracted to him. If all the scandal troubled him, she needed to find out now.

Casey was silent for so long he repeated his question.

"Craig, after dinner I need to tell you some things. Your sweet grandmother is a dear friend, but she didn't warn you. So I have to."

He sobered. "That sounds foreboding."

"Well, for now let's just enjoy ourselves."

"I'm for that," he announced cheerfully, certain that it couldn't be as serious as it sounded.

After dinner, Jacob suggested he follow Nan home so he would know where she lived. On the way, Nan reflected on how comfortable she and Jake had been with each other tonight. A far different experience than when they first ate together at the cabin. They shared concerns in their own private lives and joked about themselves and their foibles.

When they arrived at Nan's condo, Nan drove up behind the garage and Jacob parked beside her, got out, and opened the door for her.

"So this is your place."

"Yes. It's small, but it was perfect for us during Chet's illness. Would you like to come in?"

"I would, very much, but I forgot to bring my cell phone and I told one of my managers to call me if another problem came up with the same tenants." Jacob paused, not wanting the evening to end. "I know—I could drive you back to my place for a while. When you're ready to go home, I'll bring my cell phone with me."

"I'd like that. There's something I want to see."

"Oh?" he questioned, leading her over to his car and seating her.

"And what is it you want to see?" he asked, backing out.

"I'll tell you when we get there."

"Now you've got me curious."

Arriving at his home, Jacob drove around the circular driveway and parked directly in front of the entrance. Opening the door for Nan, he took her hand and helped her out.

His hand sent a jolt of pleasure through Nan. Immediately, she reproved herself. _I'm letting my emotions run away with me._

They were silent as they entered the house. Nan felt a sliver of excitement at being alone with Jake, but she shook it off.

Standing in the family room, Jacob shrugged his shoulders and held out his hands, "Well, I'm curious, what is it you want to see?"

"I want to see some more of the comic books you made for Casey."

"Aw," he said passing it off. "You don't want to see those. Let's watch a movie. I've got a lot of good videos and DVDs."

"I do too. I want to see those books and your artwork."

He studied her, bemused. "I'm flattered you want to see them, Nan, but they were meant only for Casey's eyes, and later maybe her children's." Nan's expression told him that he had sounded abrupt. He told her the truth. "The fact is, I'm embarrassed to let anyone else see them."

"Why?"

"Oh, I don't know. I've never had art lessons. Besides, they open me up, and I'm not sure I'm ready for that right now."

She gave him a small, mysterious smile. "After what we've gone through with each other in such a short time, you're not comfortable about me finding out what a great guy you are?"

"Oh sure, that's the reason," he said, his face turning grim. "I'm such a great guy that my daughter marries a—"

"Jake," Nan interrupted gently.

"What?" he asked, unsettled by the soft, coaxing expression in her eyes.

Nan just smiled.

"I'd rather not show them to you."

"Please," she begged, a coy smile on her face.

"Nan, what's got into you?"

She shrugged her shoulders. "Please, Jake."

"Oh, all right." He stepped over to a cupboard underneath a bookcase and pulled out several and handed them to her. "Go ahead and look through them while I watch the football game."

"I want you to look at them with me. I may need you to explain some of them to me."

"They're self-explanatory."

"Come on, Jake," she said, patting a place beside her on the couch.

Her gray eyes were warm and intimate, making him feel clumsy and tongue-tied. His legs seemed to have a will of their own. He sat beside her.

"Thank you, Jake."

He threw her a sideways glance in response. She put the pile on the coffee table, picked one up, and began turning the pages. She laughed. "You say you haven't had art lessons?"

He nodded.

"That's hard to believe. These are so clever, so funny."

Jacob squirmed. He wasn't used to this kind of admiration from a woman other than his mother. As Nan paged through the book, she smiled at some, her eyes misted at others, amazed at the lessons so clearly and cleverly portrayed that a child of any age could understand.

"These took a lot of time and thought, Jake. How did you find the time, working and being both a mother and father to Casey?"

"How did you know that I had to be both?"

"Because Casey told me. I recognized the name Sil Jacobson. I'd been to several of her performances here in Arizona before she went to New York. She had a marvelous voice. It just came out naturally for Casey to tell me that her mother wasn't home very much."

"I see."

"You didn't answer my question. How did you find the time to do all this with everything else you had to do?"

"I just made time. I think we find time for what we really want to do, don't you?"

"Under most circumstances, yes."

"I'm sorry. I imagine your situation left you with no time for what you wanted to do."

"Well, I think I could have read more, studied more in between the chores, but I think I was more emotionally worn out than physically. I'm ashamed to admit I wound up mindlessly watching TV with Chet more often than I should have."

"Sometimes we have to do things to survive emotionally, Nan. I know I did. Don't be too hard on yourself."

She nodded her thanks and turned the next page. The title was, "Stiff-Neckedness is Pride." Jacob had drawn a silly look-ing long-necked character, his chin slightly tilted up, staring straight ahead.

The next page continued, "A Humble Person Is Not Stiff-Necked." Jacob had drawn another long-necked character with a mobile neck in three different stances. Under each, the printed words said, *A humble person will look to heaven for guid-ance. A humble person will bow his head in prayer and listen to the answer. A humble person will turn to the right or the left and learn from others around him, his family, his friends, and his neighbors.*

Nan was silent for some time before she spoke. Her voice was low with emotion. "How profound, Jake. I've read about stiff-neckedness in the Bible, but I never gave it much thought. You ought to consider getting these published so other chil-dren can benefit by them."

"That's very generous of you, Nan. You've given me hope

that maybe I did do something right. I've spent a lot of time doubting myself, wondering what kind of a father I've been to Casey, for her to marry the kind of man she did."

Following an enjoyable meal and conversation that covered topics of mutual interest, Casey quietly and briefly as possible told Craig about the accident and the notoriety surrounding it. When she was through, all he said was, "Let's go." They had been silent on the drive back to the restaurant where Casey left her car. Casey was numb, not knowing what he was thinking or feeling.

He parked and turned to her, took her hand, and kissed it. "Thank you for telling me. I can't imagine anyone believing anything bad about you, Casey. Surely the truth will come out eventually. I'm just glad you're rid of that guy. You're one of the fortunate ones. Some women are terrified to leave their abusive husbands."

Casey was relieved to hear his positive reaction.

"Are you busy tomorrow night?" he asked

"No."

"Would you like to go with me to a Music by Moonlight concert?"

"I'd love to. I've heard of it, but I've never been."

"It's held at El Pedregal Festival Marketplace at the Boulders on the way to Cave Creek. We'll throw a blanket on the ground and listen to the concert and drink tall, icy drinks."

"Sounds like pure therapy. I need something like that."

"Great! I'll pick you up at your house at seven."

Chapter Eighteen

The closed winter of loneliness gives way to the open heart of spring.

Saturday was the first day of May and the Arizona heat hadn't yet settled heavily upon its inhabitants. Jacob had barely stepped out the back door of the kitchen when the phone rang. He ran back inside and grabbed it, hoping it was Casey. He wanted to talk with her about this Craig. Instead it was Nan's voice he heard.

"Nan. This is a surprise. I thought it might be Casey. I fully intended to quiz her about that boy she went out with."

"I'd like to ask a few questions myself. But he did look like a nice young man, didn't he?"

"He did, but then so did—" He stopped in midsentence. "No. Nick never did look like a nice young man to me."

"Really? You must have good instincts then, Jake."

"I guess so. It was Silvia who got sucked in."

"Did I interrupt you at something? Your 'hello' was a little breathless."

"I was just on my way out to do yard work before it gets too hot. My yard men don't trim, and they don't get all the weeds."

"I love yard work," she stated wistfully. "My condo here has very little yard, but it's taken care of by the association."

"If you love it so much, come over and help me." Even as he suggested it, he wished he hadn't. Nan had been on his mind when he went to bed last night and the minute he woke up. He wanted to be with her, but it would be leading her on.

Realizing Nan hadn't replied, he added, "It's all right if you don't want to come. Don't be afraid to say so."

"Well, actually I called to invite you to dinner, but if I come over and help you with the yard work, I . . ." Her mind was racing. "I know. I'll do some quick grocery shopping then come over and do yard work with you until it's time to fix dinner."

In spite of his good intentions Jacob's pulse accelerated at the thought of spending the day and evening with her. "Sounds like a winner, Nan. Come on over." When he hung up, he was torn. What was he doing anyway? His feelings for Nan seemed to have catapulted. Was it because she had been so appreciative of him last night? Was he that hungry for a woman's admiration? He paced around the kitchen, thinking. No it hadn't just come on last night. He admitted he had been fighting his attraction to her from the beginning.

He had an impulse to call Casey and chew her out for the little deception she pulled last night that threw them alone together. Instead, he started outside to work off his confusion when the phone rang again.

It was one of his apartment managers wanting some advice. Thirty-five minutes later he headed outside again.

He had been in the yard only a few minutes when Nan's soft voice greeted him. He shot to his feet. "Hey," he said, thinking how beautiful she looked in the jeans and red T-shirt, her dark hair falling in one braid down her back. She had a pair of work gloves in her hand.

"Have gloves, will work," she said, smiling up at Jake. Her heart quickened as she observed how good-looking Jake was in jeans and a T-shirt.

They gazed at each other, neither able to speak. It was as if an electric current flowed between them, holding them fast. Impulsively, Jacob took her in his arms and pulled her against him, his face against hers. She felt so good in his arms, tears stung his eyes. "Oh, Nan, Nan. I don't know what's happening to me," he half whispered. "I don't want to hurt you. I can't marry again."

Pulling away and looking up into his face, Nan saw traces of tears. "Why not?"

He was taken aback by the blunt question. "I don't know"

"Maybe I can help you understand why. I've read that men who've been unhappily married don't want to remarry. Is that your situation?"

"How did you know?"

"I didn't," she replied softly. "A man needs a wife who gives nurturing care and support on a daily basis. From what Casey told me, you really didn't have that. I suspect that for many years you were full of needs that weren't met. Why would a man trust marriage after that?"

"Holy mackerel, Nan, I can't pull weeds now. You've just put a kink in all my plans."

A shadow of a smile on her lips, she responded. "I'm game for whatever you want to do. If you want to pull weeds, we will. If you want to sit down on the lawn and talk, we'll do that."

She looked up at him with eyes that were deep, cloudy pools. He felt as though he were falling into them. He backed away. He couldn't think when she was so close. "Do *you* want to marry again after your difficult experience?"

Nan hadn't expected that question. She looked down. "Actually, I think my experience has made me *hungry* for a normal marriage, where each can serve the other." She looked up. "But even so, I'm not sure I'm ready for it."

"You understand then?"

"Yes. I understand, but . . ." She couldn't say the rest.

"But what?"

"I'm confused because I . . . I've met the most wonderful man."

Jacob was shocked. *Already? Was it the man he saw her with in the restaurant?* He could only stare at her in dismay and then mumble, "And . . . who's that?"

She smiled that beautiful, warm smile. "You, of course, Jake."

He shook his head in a stupor. "Me? I thought it might be that man you were with at the . . . me?"

Nan laughed. "Part of your appeal, Jake, is that you aren't aware of it."

"Where's that Nan I met in Sedona who was so fearful?"

She shrugged her shoulders and shook her head. "I don't know. All of a sudden she disappeared. I think maybe it's because of you."

"Me?"

"Yes. You seem to bring out the best in me. I feel braver and more confident about going on without Chet."

"Let's sit down on the porch bench," he replied huskily. Matching action to words, he sat and patted a place beside him.

"Good." She smiled. "That's exactly what I was hoping you'd say."

Jake, who had suddenly turned a little nervous, could only muster a weak half-smile.

"Don't be nervous, Jake." She smiled. "There aren't any monsters in your closet."

He laughed. "Where did that come from?"

"From a children's book. I have bunches of them. I've collected them through all the years I've yearned for children."

That did it. Jake moved closer to her, put his arm around her, and kissed her on the forehead. "I'm so sorry you didn't have children. You would have made a wonderful mother." Tears stung his eyes. Blinking them away rapidly, he wondered why he was feeling emotional today.

"Thank you, Jake," she murmured, laying her head on his shoulder. Contentment flowed through her like a pure mountain stream spreading out through melting snow.

They sat together like that for some time, silent with their own thoughts.

Then, in the tenderest voice she had ever heard, Jake said, "You can have grandchildren, Nan."

Tears sprang to her eyes and before she could stop them,

sobs came from deep inside. She sat up and covered her face. It felt as though all the tears she had held back for years decided to come at that moment and she could do nothing about it.

Jake's comforting arm pulled her close and she heard him say, "That-a-girl, let it all out."

A while later she felt Jake put a tissue in her hand. She wiped her eyes and blew her nose. "I don't know where all those tears came from," she said in an unsteady voice.

"Because you've been holding them in all these years while you took care of Chet."

"I guess so, but why now ... oh yes, the grandchildren." Her tear-stained eyes gazing into his, she exclaimed, "I *can* have grandchildren! I've never thought of that possibility. Why?"

"Maybe because you thought you might not ever marry again."

"Yes. Of course. But I may not, Jake, maybe I won't." The tears started all over again.

"Yes you will, Nan," he said through her sobs. "You have too much to offer a man. When you're ready, they'll be standing in line." A pang of jealously shot through him just thinking about Nan with other men. *What's the matter with me? Haven't I decided that marrying again was not an option for me?*

Nan's tears dried up. Wiping her eyes and cheeks, she smiled. "Thanks for letting me cry on your shoulder. I haven't had anyone since Gram died. And you're right, I *will* probably marry again. Dating sounds foreign to me, as it probably does to you, Jake. I've been trying to decide whether to go out with a couple of men I've been putting off, but," she said, straightening her shoulders with determination, "I believe you've just given me the push I needed to go out with them."

Jake frowned. "Where did these guys come from so soon? How did you meet them?"

Nan smiled. "That sounds a little like an interrogation."

"You can't be too careful these days, Nan," he said tersely.

"The few friends I've kept in touch with keep trying to set

me up. And I trust these friends, so you don't have to worry about me."

Jacob got up and paced the porch. Nan watched him curiously.

"Why the big frown, Jake? Why the restlessness?"

He stopped in front of her, pulled her up, and held her tightly in his arms. "I don't want you to date other men. You're going to marry me and we'll *both* have grandchildren when Casey marries again." The words just came out. He hadn't planned it, they just came. Part of him was shocked, but mainly, pure happiness flowed through him, healing his lonely heart.

Nan looked up into his face. "Wh-what did you say?"

"I spoke too soon. I mean, will you marry me, Nan?"

"What a fool I am," she said, trying to squirm out of his arms. "You're just feeling sorry for me, Jake."

"No." He felt a hard knot in his chest. "I'm feeling sorry for myself, sorry that I didn't meet you long ago. I realize that I love you, Nan. From the moment I met you, I began to heal and I didn't recognize it until last night."

"You . . . really do love me, Jake?" she asked, dubious.

"I do, with all my heart. Will you marry me?"

She gazed into his eyes and saw in them the love he expressed. Her breathing turned shallow and rapid. She didn't want to turn him down for fear he wouldn't ask again, but still she couldn't help but doubt his feelings. "We haven't known each other very long. Are you sure, Jake?"

"Yes, I'm sure. I'm shocked myself, Nan. I've tried to be levelheaded about my growing attraction to you, but I'm afraid it's impossible." He gazed into her wide, incredulous eyes, suddenly afraid she didn't feel as he did. "You haven't answered me."

She hadn't doubted her own feelings for Jake; rather, she had tried to squelch them. To let herself freely feel now and believe he loved her was difficult. "I need a little time, Jake."

"How long?" he asked.

"I . . . don't know."

Their eyes locked. Then Jacob's eyes slid down to her beautiful lips—lips which he had found enticing from the moment he noticed them on the cabin porch. Slowly he bent down and gently touched them with his. A sudden, searing emotion coursed through him, leaving him almost weak. He pulled her close and kissed her ardently.

In each other's arms, years of loneliness fell away. It felt so right—as if they had known each other eons before, in another time and place, and had at last come home. Their lips met again and again, sweeping them away into that all-encompassing magic—the sweet passion of the heart.

Breathless, they gazed at each other in awe, scarcely believing what they had just experienced. Jacob took Nan's face in his hands. "How long before you can answer me?"

Jake's kisses had broken down her tenuous restraint, her doubts. "Not long. How about now?"

Jacob's face brightened, and then slowly his brows creased with concern. "Only answer now if it's 'yes.'"

"Yes."

"Yes?" Jacob questioned. "You'll marry me?"

She nodded and smiled. "Yes. I love you too, Jake."

Jacob groaned and pulled her close. "Incredible," he whispered in her ear. Then with unaccustomed impulsiveness, he said, "There's no reason we can't be married right away is there?"

"I can't think of one," she replied softly.

Releasing her, he exploded with excitement. "Let's go down to the jewelry store right now and buy an engagement ring."

"Oh, Jake, let's do." Suddenly a look of concern came across her face. "You know, we're acting like a couple of impulsive teenagers. Besides, we're hardly dressed to go shopping for a ring."

He laughed. "I know. Isn't it great?"

"But we really haven't known each other all that long."

Jacob sobered. "I prayed about us last night, Nan, and the warmest feeling of peace came over me. I didn't quite understand what it meant until now."

"I've been praying about us longer than that, Jake. Our relationship, though awkward at first, felt right."

"It did?"

"Yes. And I didn't understand that, either."

"Well, shall we go down and get a ring?" he asked, looking as eager as a young boy about to go on his first camping trip.

"Dressed like this?"

"Dressed like this," he stated decisively.

"Let's go!" she exclaimed.

Casey had just gotten out of the shower when the phone rang. It was her dad. "Oh hi, Dad. What's up?"

"What are you doing tonight?"

"Craig has asked me to go to a Music by Moonlight concert tonight."

"How late will it last?"

"I don't know. Why?"

"Because after Craig takes you home, could you come over for a few minutes?"

"It might be late, Dad. Wouldn't tomorrow be better?"

"No. I don't care how late it is. Come over, will you?"

"What's this all about?"

"I want to show you something."

"Hm, you have me curious. I'll see you when I see you then."

"Have fun tonight, Casey."

"Thanks, Dad."

The evening was pleasantly cool. The moon shone brightly and the beautiful symphony filled the air, soothing Casey's battered emotions. Craig seemed to be enjoying it as much as she was. As the evening wore on, Craig put his arm around her and she laid her head on his shoulder. They had become acquainted easily and comfortably.

After it was over, he took her hand as they walked to the car. It all felt so natural to Casey and she looked forward to more dates with him. They visited on the way home, and when Craig parked in front of her condo, he didn't seem to be in a hurry to take her in.

Looking at her watch, Casey saw that it was eleven o'clock. She couldn't keep her dad up any later.

"I'd like to invite you in, Craig, but Dad called and asked me to go over to his house after our date."

"It's a little late isn't it?"

"I told him it might be. He said to come anyway. He wants to show me something. I can't figure out why it can't wait until tomorrow, but he said it couldn't."

"All right, I'll take you in."

On the doorstep Craig said, "What are you doing Monday night?"

"Nothing that I know of."

"Why don't we go swimming here at the condos and then barbeque some hamburgers for us and Grandma?"

"Sounds fun. Let's. I'll make a dessert."

"Great."

Suddenly Casey realized the last thing she wanted to do was go swimming. Her leg would be in full view in a swimming suit.

"What's the matter, Casey?"

"Well uh, I don't feel very comfortable in a swimming suit. You know, showing my . . . my injured leg."

"Don't worry about that. You'll look beautiful to everyone but yourself."

Still, Casey felt uneasy.

"You have to get over being self-conscious sometime. It might as well be with me."

She hesitated. "All right. What time?"

"Shall we say six o'clock? We can swim an hour and then cook the burgers."

"Okay. See you then."

Driving over to her dad's, Casey smiled, grateful that Craig made her feel so relaxed about her leg. Shortly, a frown erased the smile. "But he has no idea how bad my leg looks," she muttered. She took a deep breath and decided that a guy seeing her in a bathing suit had to happen eventually, and it might as well happen with Betty's grandson—someone with whom she felt comfortable.

Arriving at her dad's, she saw the porch light was on. He was definitely waiting for her. She got out, went to the door, and turned the knob. It was unlocked so she walked right in. Entering the family room, she was surprised to see Nan there, because her car wasn't. She was sitting on the couch with her dad. They were both dressed casually in jeans.

"Well, hi. I didn't expect you to be here, Nan."

Her dad and Nan stood up and walked over to her. They were smiling and looking happier than she had seen either one of them.

"What is it, you two? Something's afoot."

Nan held out her left hand. Casey saw a beautiful, glistening diamond ring! She looked at the two of them astounded, certain it couldn't mean what it indicated.

"We're engaged to be married, Casey," her dad said, his eyes shining.

"You're what?"

"We're engaged!" Nan exclaimed exuberantly.

"You . . . you can't be. You have only known each other —"

"Nevertheless, we love each other and want to get married right away, Case."

"Dad!"

She looked from one to the other, shocked. "You're acting

like a couple of irresponsible high school kids. This is way too soon."

They both laughed and hugged her. "We are at that, Casey," her dad agreed. "But thanks to your deceptive little arrangement last night, you hurried it along."

"Please, Dad and Nan, I can't even congratulate you until you sit down and tell me step by step how this happened."

"We'd love to," Nan said. "Wouldn't we, Jake?"

"You bet. You begin, Nan, and I'll fill in my side of it."

Nan began with the events at the cabins, the awkward moments, the current that seemed to run underneath. She told all the details she knew Casey would want to hear.

Then her dad told the rest.

Before long Casey was blinking back tears. "I'm so happy for you two."

Their eyes were luminous with moisture. "Thank you, Casey," her dad said.

"Yes, my dear," Nan added, "thank you for supporting us in this rather sudden decision." Impulsively Jacob and Nan moved into each other's arms.

Chapter Nineteen

Taking for granted our blessings is human; repenting for it is divine.

Casey was busy most of the day Monday doing a couple of shoots on location and then returning to the studio to develop the film. The best of these she printed. Now and again as she worked, a twinge of excitement fluttered in her breast when she thought of Craig.

She arrived home just in time to make a chocolate cake for the barbeque. Putting on one of her favorite CDs, she busied herself putting the ingredients together. After the cake was baked and cooled, she found herself glancing frequently at the clock as she iced it. The closer it got to six o'clock the more nervous she became. She was acutely conscious that every minute was bringing her closer to the time she was looking forward to and at the same time dreading.

Before the accident she had never given much thought to her appearance in a bathing suit. She knew she was attractive, had a good figure, and was athletic. She was also aware of all the admiring looks that came in her direction.

This was no longer true. Now she was disfigured. Much of her leg bore horrible, discolored puckering scars that ran from just above her ankle to her thigh. Every eye, like a magnet, would always be drawn to the sight.

Where once she felt confident in her ability to move gracefully, all she knew now was self-consciousness, awkwardness, and pain.

Can I do this? she thought in panic. *How will Craig react?*

What will I see in his eyes?

She shook her head. This kind of thinking wasn't getting her anywhere. It had to come sometime. "And at least," she said, wryly, "nobody can accuse me of being provocative." Putting on her best swimming suit and her one long cover-up, she slipped on flip-flops.

When the bell rang, she grabbed a towel and the cake and went to the door.

Craig smiled. "Hi, beautiful. That cake looks good," he said, taking it from her. "Shall we go?"

She nodded and smiled, noting that he looked handsome in the Hawaiian print shirt, which covered his swimming suit, leaving his nicely shaped masculine legs bare beneath.

They went next door to Betty's, left the cake, and the three of them walked up to the pool. Betty was the first one to take off her cover-up and shoes. Leaving them and her towel on a chair, she smiled at her grandson.

"Need some help, Grandma?" Craig asked, placing his shirt and towel on another chair.

"I could use a little getting in."

"While they were going down the steps of the lower end, Casey quickly took of her cover-up and stepped in before Craig could see her. Relieved that she could put off the "unveiling" a while longer, she joined Craig and Betty in a water game.

The hour went by quickly. "I'm starving," Craig said. "How about you two?"

"That's the best workout I've had in a while, Craig," Betty said. "I feel like I could eat three hamburgers."

Craig laughed. "Yeah. We'll see." He helped his grandmother out, and then held out his hand to Casey. She took it, for her leg was tired and it was difficult getting out.

When she took the last step, her leg was in full view. Before Craig could mask it, the horror on his face was unmistakable. A flood of emotions and memories swirled around inside Casey like pieces of a puzzle that didn't fit. She had seen revulsion on Nick's face whenever he saw a deformed person, when he saw women whose bodies weren't beautiful and well-shaped. When she had seen her own burned and cut leg for the first time, still half in shock, she screamed inside, *Nick will be repulsed by my leg!* Then she remembered some faraway voice telling her that Nick had been killed in the accident—yet he seemed to hover around her like a heavy dark vapor in her head, behind her eyes.

Though shocked and starkly ill at ease, Craig noted Casey's withdrawal. "Casey? Did you hear me? I said I didn't know your leg was so severely injured. Grandma didn't tell me." He seemed to be trying to find words to hide his feelings. "I'm . . . I'm sorry. You must have gone through a lot of pain. Here's your towel. Dry off."

"Thank you," she mumbled, quickly doing so. Then slipping on the cover-up and flip-flops, she glanced at Betty, whose face was one of concern. *For Craig or for me?* she wondered. "I'm ready, let's go get those burgers cooked," she said as brightly as she could, forcing a smile.

Through the rest of the evening, though not obvious to Betty, Craig was different with her. He was just as witty and outwardly warm, but Casey knew that he was putting up a good front for all their sakes. It was obvious that Craig needed a woman he could be proud of in every way. She hadn't recognized it, but his pride probably demanded that a girlfriend or wife reflect well on him. It was now apparent that Craig had thought her injury was only temporary.

Disappointed, she knew he would never ask her out again. She simply didn't measure up physically. That's why he was thirty-three and still unmarried. He was looking for the perfect woman. He would find at least an approximation of her eventually because she felt he sincerely wanted marriage. His adjustments would come later as he came to learn that whoever he married would be an imperfect human being. Since Craig was a nice man and basically kind, he would somehow make do without perfection in his wife.

In college, she had known many men like Craig and she

could easily spot them because her dad was the opposite, and her ideal. It had only been coincidence that the woman her dad fell for and married was beautiful.

In spite of being able to recognize pride in so many men, why hadn't she recognized the sick pride in Nick? It had been ego-crushing that she had made such a stupid and terrible mistake.

To ease the discomfort on both their parts, Casey suggested that Betty come with them while Craig walked her home. She hugged Betty, thanked Craig, and then said good night.

Once inside the house, she caved in. Listlessly, she took off her swimming suit and got into the shower.

In her nightgown, she sat down and turned on the television, trying to take her mind off the memory of Craig's face. Tears blurred her vision. Facing it as she never had before, she knew that it was possible she would never marry again, that there might not be a man alive who could face her deformed and scarred leg. She had been fearful of getting married again, and insecure about her judgment until she met Craig. He had given her hope. If a nice man like him couldn't take looking at her leg, what man could? Her chest began to heave with anguish, and then wrenching sobs racked her body.

Some time later, long after the sobs subsided, her exhaustion led her thoughts elsewhere. How she had taken for granted her physical strength, her strong and healthy body. How she had taken for granted, as if it were her due, her foot dexterity, her ability to move quickly as she became a champion tennis player. How she had taken for granted her ability to dance, and to hike the hills with her father.

"Forgive me, dear God, for being so ungrateful for what I had," she murmured.

Chapter Twenty

He who listens with his heart gains understanding.

Casey couldn't make herself go to work the next morning. The wounds of the previous evening were still too raw. She had begun to like Craig more than she had realized and at the moment she couldn't face anyone. Except Belle. She needed to see Belle. Picking up the phone, she hoped she had an opening today.

Later, sitting in Belle's office, Casey felt a little self-conscious, not quite sure why she had come. By nature she was a private person, and by circumstance had become more so. Now here she was, running to Belle like a hurt child.

"What happened, Casey?"

"How did you know something happened?"

"Because you're down in the dumps. You weren't like this last time."

"I guess I just need to cry on someone's shoulder and I don't want it to be my dad's. I don't want to ruin his happiness."

Belle's brows rose questioningly. "His happiness?"

"He just got engaged."

Belled clapped her hands and a smile spread across her face. "Wonderful! I was worried about him. I didn't think he would ever marry again."

"He was determined not to, but the loveliest woman came into his life, a woman I think is good enough for him."

"That's quite a compliment to her. I know how close you and your dad are. Okay, now what happened, Casey?"

Casey thought about it a moment, let out a long painful sigh, and told Belle the story.

"That was a rough experience, Casey. What did you learn from it?"

Casey replied without hesitation. "That many men are egotistical and need their manly pride stroked in unhealthy ways. Like Craig, they need to sport a beautiful, unflawed girl on their arm. It lets them bask in reflected glory and other men's envy."

Belle nodded.

Casey covered her face. "I can't believe it." She looked up, totally distraught. "That's the way Nick was! What's the matter with me, Belle? Didn't I learn anything?"

"Nothing's wrong with you. Craig isn't like Nick. He's basically a nice guy. He just has that one unhealthy need—one he's probably not even aware of. When he gets married, he's going to have to live with imperfection—his wife losing her figure when she's pregnant and maybe keeping on a few unwanted pounds afterward and so on."

"*If* he gets married."

"Yes, that's the danger for him, but I suspect if he's as nice as you say, he will eventually."

"I think you're right. He's not selfish. He's just a little vain."

"Nevertheless, when a nice guy like Craig turns out to be prideful in an area that's very sensitive to you now—physical imperfection, it's damaging to your already fragile ego."

"Thank you for understanding, Belle. It's more validating than you know."

"When Mr. Right comes along, he isn't going to mind your leg, only that it's painful for *you* physically and emotionally."

"I don't believe there is a Mr. Right."

"And you didn't believe there was a woman good enough for your dad."

Casey bit her lip in thought. "That's true. I guess there's another aspect too. If there's a Mr. Right, I may have to date.

It makes sense that every man who isn't Mr. Right may react to my leg simply because he *isn't* the man for me. Not because he's egotistical."

Belled nodded. "Good thought. Now, since you've broken the ice and have begun to date, please continue."

"I'll try. I'll work on myself."

"Good! Whether it feels like it or not, you've been very successful in your life. And you'll continue to be successful. Remember what I said a minute ago about Mr. Right."

Belle got up, went over to the bookcase and selected a book. "When you can, Casey, you ought to buy this book and read it. It will help your fears. It's called *The Gift of Fear*, by Gavin de Becker." She opened it up and read a quote from the book: "'In my life and work, I've seen the darkest parts of the human soul. (At least I hope they are the darkest.) That has helped me to see more clearly the brightness of the human spirit. Feeling the sting of violence myself has helped me feel more keenly the hand of human kindness.'"

"What a wonderful way to look at life."

Belle closed book. "I'm sure you've already unconsciously experienced this and will continue to do so because you're a fighter. You're determined to have a good life."

After the session Casey went home. Though feeling unburdened and hopeful, the memory of Craig's rejection still hurt.

Russ leaned back in the chair provided by the shop. He closed his eyes. It was always relaxing to have a manicure. He was proud of his hands. Women always told him how attractive and masculine they were. Marcie's touch was more soothing than that of any other manicurist he had used. While his fingers were in the warm water, Marcie massaged each one.

"Marcie," a woman's voice broke into his peace.

"Yes?"

"I told the woman on the phone that you were busy, but she

was insistent and promised not to keep you."

"Oh, all right. Relax, Mr. Eden, and leave your fingers in the water. I'll be right back."

Russ nodded, irritated, but his eyes remained closed. He hadn't slept well lately. He was edgy as hell. The gray on his face was almost gone, but his anger wasn't.

He heard Marcie come back and sit down. A stifled scream jarred his frayed nerves. He shot to his feet, glaring at Marcie. "Why scare me like that? What's the matter with you?"

She stared up at him unable to say anything, only point to his dripping hands, her own hand shaking. He looked down. It took a moment to see where she was pointing and when he did, he blinked in disbelief, turning his hands over and back. His fingers were a hideous and sickening shade of green! The water was clear and soapy when he had last looked. Now it was green! "What is that you put on my fingers?" he said, trying to keeping calm.

"I . . . I didn't put it there. It wasn't there when I left. Did you see anyone put anything in it?" she asked.

Russ paled. *Not again!* he thought. "Wash it off, quick!" He sat down and waited while she got a basin of soap and water and tried to get it off. It stubbornly remained. "Get a brush and scrub!" he suggested more vehemently than he knew he should have.

She did. It still remained.

"Try some cleansing cream," he said with barely controlled patience.

"All right, Mr. Eden," Marcie said, clearly distressed while she wiped his hands dry. Going to the shelf and picking up a product the shop sold, she opened it and rubbed it all over his hands. "Let's let it stay on for a few minutes."

He asked to speak to the manager. Marcie looked over at the manager, who was already nervously standing by, watching and waiting to see what she could do.

"I'm Ginger, the manager, sir."

"How do you suppose this happened?"

"I have no idea. This has never happened in our shop before."

"Who called Marcie on the phone?"

"I answered the phone. It was a woman and I assumed it was a customer for Marcie."

"Who was it, Marcie?" he asked.

"Sir," Ginger interrupted. "Why these questions? It's normal that we get calls from our customers."

Russ' animosity toward the woman boiled up inside him. Soon his self-restraint would be at the breaking point. With great difficulty he put on his most charming smile. "I'm aware of that, Ginger. I'm just trying to help you solve this problem."

Ginger relented. "Who was it, Marcie?"

"I don't know. Someone was on the line, I could tell. I kept saying hello. Then a muffled voice said something. I told the person to speak up. The voice said something indistinguishable and went on and on. Then suddenly I heard the dial tone. When I came back the green was on Mr. Eden's fingers."

Ginger shook her head. She turned to the row of operators, who had been watching the highly irregular proceedings, while at the same time trying to also give their attention to the customers. "Did any of you do this?"

All but one shook their heads. The one, highly incensed at the accusatory question, refused to respond.

Ginger, beside herself with embarrassment, addressed everyone in the shop. "Did anyone here see anything or anyone suspicious?"

One customer spoke up hesitantly. "I saw an odd-looking woman leave rather quickly. I assumed she was a customer. But I didn't see her do anything, nor did I get a good look at her."

"I'm so sorry, Mr. Eden," Ginger said. "Though Marcie was about through with your manicure, you won't be charged. Now, let's wipe off the cleansing cream," she said, taking over. Distressed, she found it made very little difference.

Like a dam holding back a rising tide of water, Russ held in his riotous emotions and said evenly, "Try the soap and water again."

Ginger did so and then rinsed his hands. "Whatever it is, it isn't coming off. I'm sorry, Mr. Eden. I don't know how, but someone besides the operators and patrons did this and I certainly wish I knew who."

Russ stood up and forced a smile. "I do too." *Good PR at all times* scrolled through his head over and over. He pulled out a bill, leaving a large tip for Marcie.

"Oh no, we can't accept your money, Mr. Eden."

"Why not?" An edge of sarcasm crept into his voice. "Apparently this is not your fault." He turned and quickly walked out, his chest so full of rage he felt as though he might blow up any moment.

When he was out of view of the salon, he looked around, moved cautiously to his car, and then nervously looked behind him. He had just managed to get around to the driver's door, when a policeman stepped over and planted a ticket on his windshield.

Russ snapped. All the pent up fury burst out. "Hey!" he yelled, glaring into the face of the officer. "I'm here, don't you dare give me that ticket!"

"Don't yell at me, mister, the parking meter is red. You're getting a ticket."

"B–but I'm h–here, don't you see?" He stammered as all reason left him. "Look at my fingers. Someone's trying to get me."

The policeman stared at his fingers. "Why are they green?"

"I didn't do it, someone in there did it!" he said, pointing to the salon two doors away. "I told you someone is trying to get me. I need your protection."

The policeman stared at the wild-eyed man and then shoved him against the car. "Turn around and put your hands up on the car."

"No, officer, no!" he exclaimed, fear eating at his insides. "I haven't done anything! Someone else is doing it!"

"I said, turn around and put your hands on the car!"

Russ' hands kept flailing wildly while he repeated over and over, "Someone is out to get me!"

"Put your hands behind you," ordered the policeman.

Still unable to control himself, Russ continued jerking from side to side as though looking for someone, his hands moving about erratically. The policeman, unable to grab his hands, pulled out his radio. "I need backup." He indicated his location as he pulled out his gun and pointed it at Russ.

Russ stared at it in shock. "L . . . look, officer, I . . . I'm an executive of Global Investments. I'm a law-abiding citizen. I'm innocent. S-someone's out to get me!"

"I don't care if you're the president of the United States and a terrorist is out to get you. Put your hands up."

A siren wailed as another police car screeched to a halt beside them. The newcomer jumped out and helped his colleague handcuff the man with curious green fingers.

Hearing the police siren, Ginger stepped out onto the sidewalk and watched in shock as a policeman cuffed one of her best customers, shoved him into a police car, and drove off.

The parking meter policeman then called for a tow truck to remove the car.

At the station, Russ had to go through the humiliation of taking the breath test. "I told you I wasn't drunk," he said, trying to keep his voice even.

"You're still going to be booked for resisting arrest," the policeman said.

Russ panicked. "Can I call my lawyer?"

"In a few minutes."

The shock of being brought handcuffed to the police station had scared Russ so badly, he was, by effort of sheer will, finally able to regain his composure. An idea came to him. Norm! He'd call Norm. He would vouch for him. *Wait*, he thought, *Norm could be behind all these pranks!* He didn't trust Norm, or anyone else at the office, but he didn't have any other choice.

When at last he was allowed a phone call, he contacted Norm, asking him to come down to the police station and vouch for him.

When Norm internalized what Russ was saying, that he had actually been taken handcuffed down to the police station, he smiled. He would have liked to leave him there, but he told Russ he would be right down.

While Russ waited, handcuffed and humiliated, fear now dominated his whole being. He had been trained never to lose control. It had been drummed into him night and day by the "five" who were, in actuality, his ultimate employers. It wasn't Gobal Investments that was making him a wealthy man but rather the special financial services he performed for this shadowy five-member group known to him only as the "Pentad." These men knew virtually everything about him, things he thought no one but himself knew.

That the services he rendered to this group were illegal didn't bother him at all, but the controls they imposed on his life were almost draconian. They controlled how he talked, how he dressed, how he spoke. Appearances—which had always been crucial to him—were deemed a necessity to them as a cover for their activities.

A shaft of fear sucked the breath out of him. *They can't learn about this incident.* They had instilled into him a dread of the consequences if their actions were found out, if *they* should be found out. These consequences had never been spelled out, leaving it to his imagination to conjure up that thing which he feared most of all.

He feverishly thought back over his conduct the last few days, satisfying himself that he had handled everything reasonably well considering the things that had happened. He hadn't lost control of himself, at least not complete control. Control was everything to him and to the Pentad.

Norm entered the police station and looked around. Russ tried to get his attention but found it impossible with his hands cuffed behind him. Norm said something to a person at a desk, and then a policeman took him over to Russ.

"How did this come about, officer?" Norm asked, puzzled.

The policeman told him the details.

"May I talk with Mr. Eden?"

"Go ahead," the policeman said.

"What happened, Russ?" Russ turned around and showed him green, cuffed hands.

"What's that green stuff on your fingers?"

Russ, calmly and evenly, as though nothing were unusual, explained what had happened.

"Sir," Norm said, turning to the policeman, "I believe I can explain why Mr. Eden lost it for a moment. I think maybe any one of us would have." He then briefly related the practical jokes that had been played on Mr. Eden. The policeman laughed, especially at the toilet paper prank.

"I know, on the surface, it may seem humorous to you, sir, but put yourself in Mr. Eden's shoes. He was at that meeting to instill confidence and enthusiasm in the office managers. I think that prank went beyond a practical joke, don't you?"

Reluctantly, the policeman agreed with him. Norm continued. "We don't know who's doing this. Is it possible you could help us out here?"

"We'd have to have some hard evidence before we could do anything."

"Under the circumstances, would you consider releasing Mr. Eden? He's an upstanding citizen of Phoenix, and the company he works for, Global Investments, is an asset to the city. It's completely out of character for Mr. Eden to react to an officer as he did. I'm certain he won't do it again."

After conferring with some others, the policeman unlocked the cuffs and with a warning allowed him to leave. "Oh, by the way, Mr. Eden, your car has been towed away. Here's the address. For a fee you can get it out—and see to it that you pay the ticket you got at the parking meter."

When they got into Norm's car, Russ said, "Thanks, Norm.

I won't forget this. You did a great job of convincing the policeman. Would you mind driving me to the tow station?"

Norm nodded.

While they were driving, Norm was silent. It unnerved
Russ. "What is it, Norm?"

"I'm concerned now about these so-called pranks. They're
going too far. We're going to have to keep our eyes open and
watch."

Russ' anxiety ratcheted down a notch. *Now I'll have another
pair of eyes to watch my back.*

Chapter Twenty-One

*The energy required for . . . honesty is
far less than the energy required for
secretiveness.*
—M. Scott Peck, M.D.

*B*elle Levine had just finished another session with Casey,
but this time it was at her own behest—with no charge
to Jake. It was actually a favor to her. She needed to ask Casey
a few more questions before she could complete the research
for a paper which would be presented at the annual convention
of the American Psychology Association. She hoped it would
then be published in their professional journal. After working
with Casey a couple of times, Belle was delighted. Her case
was just the one Belle needed to give added proof to the premise of one segment of her research for a paper entitled "The
Father's Role in a Daughter's Ability to Recognize an Abusive
Relationship in Marriage."

Having read extensively on the subject of the role of fathers
in the home, Belle began her own in-depth research. Her clini-
cal studies yielded impressive statistics and generalizations,
but they gave her too few actual cases where the father was
in the home, let alone active in the family in a positive way.
Casey's experience was the most dramatic example she had
encountered and it added just what she needed to complete the
research and her paper.

Casey's story, added to the others she had uncovered, made
Belle certain that her studies could be an important tool
for marriage counselors. They could impress upon couples
the importance of an active father in the home—how his

influence helped their daughters choose the right kind of mate in the first place, and in the second place helped them to quickly recognize abuse if it happens.

"Thank you, Casey," she said at the end of the interview. "It appears that your father's involvement in your life made it possible for you to see Nick's abusive ways quickly, and gave you the courage and desire to do something about it."

"I certainly know that I had Dad's example."

"It's more than that, Casey. Your father was equipped to prepare you to function in the outside environment." Belle picked up a paper from the coffee table. "Let me read to you what one well-known authority, Karl Zinsmeister, said. 'Studies show that fathers have a special role to play in building a child's self-respect."

"Interesting," Casey said.

Belle was silent, letting her absorb it, appreciate it.

At length Casey murmured, "I didn't realize . . . totally. That makes me even more grateful for my dad. May I copy that quote so I can read it to him?"

"You bet. Here's a pencil and paper."

When Casey was finished, a look of pain crossed her face. "But what does a mother offer a child? I didn't really have a mother—just a 'friend' who visited once in a while."

"From experience, from my studies, and also from the same authority, it seems that mothers take a dominant role in preparing children to live within their families—present and future. But from what you've told me, Casey, your father went beyond fatherhood and took upon himself the task of teaching you what your mother should have taught you. With those advantages and with your unusual character traits, you've been able to not only survive but also to live a successful and useful life—whether it feels like it or not—and you'll continue to do so."

"I hope so. The child who has both a loving mother and father seems to be getting pretty rare—if my friends are any example." Casey paused, her eyes deep in thought. "But I suspect anyone can choose to have a good life, no matter what their circumstances were, growing up."

"And," Belle added, "hopefully women can choose for themselves to do whatever is necessary to make their life good within marriage no matter the circumstances. If that isn't possible, then they must learn what to do to be safe. And that's very difficult in most cases. To paraphrase Gavin de Becker, being abused by the man you love sets up two instincts that should never compete: the instinct to stay in a secure environment, and the instinct to flee a dangerous environment." Belle's face reflected deep concern. "Many victims don't have the energy or strength to flee because of that conflict."

Casey rubbed her temples. "It's all so sad. From your experience, Belle, how often does an abuser agree to get help and then reform?"

"It's rare, but it does happen. There are men who are very unhappy over their actions and are so remorseful at hurting their wives, they admit they need help, seek help, and eventually change."

"It seems there's a fine line between that kind of man and the man who will only get worse or become so violent he'll kill. How can a woman distinguish that fine line?"

"That's very difficult. After all my counseling, you'd think I'd know. Though every case is very much alike, there are subtle differences in each one. Low-level or subtle verbal abuse isn't always recognized as abuse by a spouse. When the verbal abuse escalates to vicious and cruel, sometimes it just remains that way in a marriage and doesn't become violent. In other marriages, the vicious and cruel verbal abuse turns violent. I suppose there's one way a spouse can find out—the same way you decided Nick might turn violent—study and pray."

Casey leisurely swam in the pool; the bright, warm sun mellowed her spirits. Her thoughts were on what Belle had told her about fathers. She shuddered when she thought of the kind of father Nick would have been if they'd had a child or two. *Why is it when I'm thinking happy thoughts, the memory of Nick always intrudes?* She fervently hoped that when the case was finally closed, she would be able to put all thoughts about him and their marriage so far out of her mind, they would only be a dim and distant memory.

Making herself do the therapy exercises, she got out and headed to the condo for a shower. As she entered, she heard the phone ring.

"Casey," came her dad's welcome voice. "I called you at work, I called your cell phone and it was off, so I decided you had gone home early."

"Belle called and wanted to see me today. Since I didn't have any urgent assignments, I came home after visiting with her."

"Are the sessions helping?"

"Definitely."

"Great! I called to tell you that I have some news. Monty reported to me today. Nan is fixing dinner for us tonight. We'll be eating at six. Are you busy with that young man or can you come for dinner?"

"No. I'll be there," she said, feeling grateful to Nan.

Jacob had given Nan a key so she could start dinner any-time. Coming home earlier than usual, he saw Nan's car parked in front. His heart quickened with anticipation. He drove into the garage and entered the hall. The smell of dinner cooking greeted his nose—a comforting experience that had been rare in his married life until Casey got older.

He saw Nan checking on something in the oven. She was dressed in jeans and the lilac shirt she had been wearing when he first saw her.

Hearing his footsteps, she turned and smiled at him, and

then turned back to her task of poking a fork into the scalloped potatoes. Closing the oven door, she straightened up. He came up behind her, slid his arms around her waist, and kissed her neck. She let out a squeal of delight. The expression in Jacob's eyes melted her, but doubts were beginning to creep in. "Hi," she said softly.

"Hi yourself. Something smells wonderful. It's great coming home to the smells of dinner cooking."

"I'd hoped for that, Jake." She averted her eyes a moment, not wanting him to see the anxiety that seemed to come and go.

"What is it, Nan?"

Can I tell him that for some illogical reason I doubt the love I see in his eyes? No. "It's nothing, Jake."

Jacob crooked his finger under her chin. "Let's not keep secrets between us, Nan." He led her over to the bar stools. "Let's sit down. We need to discuss something important before we go any further in our relationship. My daughter hid most of the fear and pain she was going through during her marriage. If she hadn't, would the accident have happened? I've asked myself this over and over. But one thing is clear to me. I don't ever want any more family secrets to destroy the unity of our family again.

"There's such a thing as family privacy," Jacob continued, "which shouldn't be invaded. But in my mind the definition of family secrets is everyone knowing the problems, but no one daring to say anything about them. Many times it's just out of ignorance, fear, misguided loyalty, or misguided love that we make these mistakes. The only one who can point out to us the right path or the reason for these mistakes is the Lord himself. And I've found out through experience that he usually guides us through each other."

Tears welled up in Nan's gray eyes. "You're so right, Jake. I've had such guilty feelings, such sorrow over my grandmother. I asked her to come and live with me and Chet because she was alone and getting a little frail with age. She was hesitant to come because she knew I had my hands full taking care of Chet. She didn't want to be a burden. I assured her she would only be a help. She came and for a while, all was well. It was a wonderful companionship for me since Chet was unable to give me that."

Jacob took hold of one of her hands and held it comfortingly. She smiled. "After about three months, Chet began to feel that I was neglecting him because I was spending too much time with Grandma. In reality I wasn't. His disease had begun to weaken him more and in his fear and despondency he felt he needed my every thought, my every moment. Grandma saw it, I knew it, but we didn't come right out and openly discuss it with each other. I was afraid if I did that I would be disloyal to Chet. Under those limiting circumstances I did my best to ease Grandma's mind, but apparently I didn't. Without my knowledge Grandma found an assisted-living place, and told me she was moving there. Nothing I could say would convince her to stay. She had the money, but it was devastating to me because getting away from Chet to see her would be terribly difficult. Only six months after she had moved she just quit eating and died." Nan drew her hand away from Jacob and quietly sobbed.

Jacob pulled her off the stool and held her in his arms until her sobs subsided. Then he spoke quietly. "The real tragedy of it was that both you and your grandmother knew and saw the situation as it was, but neither confided in each other, neither asking the other's advice or help for each other or Chet. You were both suffering silently. It was a family secret that all three of you knew about. In reality it wasn't a secret, just as Casey's problems in her marriage were obvious to me and her grandparents, yet she refused to burden us, or to be more accurate, refused to seek our help. And we were careful not to interfere too much."

Nan looked up into Jacob's understanding face. "Maybe nothing could have been changed for you and Casey or me and Grandma, but if Grandma and I hadn't tried to push the problem under the rug, or if we had only communicated and asked for help, at least it would have alleviated my terrible guilt and some of my grief."

"Exactly, Nan. Now, tell me what's bothering you."

How can I tell him anything but the truth now? she thought. "It has been so many years since I've had real companionship. Our love, Jake, yours and mine, has come about so fast it feels . . . ephemeral somehow. As though it might evaporate into the shadows. I'm not sure I can really explain it. It seems woven with fragile gossamer threads and it scares me."

"All you need, my beautiful biligaana, is confirmation." He bent down and kissed her long and passionately. "How's that?" he asked, his voice husky with emotion. "That certainly validates it to me."

"That helped tremendously," she murmured, slightly breathless. "How about once more to make sure?"

He grinned. "You bet!"

Seated in the dining room, the three of them were finishing Nan's delicious meal of scalloped potatoes, spicy chicken wings, and a green salad.

Casey sighed. "It already feels like we're a family."

"You couldn't have said anything kinder to me, Casey," Nan said, smiling at the young woman who would soon be her step-daughter. The thoughts of having a daughter thrilled Nan to the deepest core of her being.

Jacob had been watching Casey since she had arrived. Something wasn't right with her. When they finished eating and had cleaned up, he said, "Let's go sit down where it's more comfortable."

Jacob and Nan sat on the couch and held hands.

Casey smiled at the sight. "You can't imagine what a load you've taken off my mind, Nan, by taking Dad off my shoulders."

"Gee thanks!" exclaimed her dad, laughing.

"You're more than welcome, Dad."

"Well, speaking of burdens, Case, what burden are you carrying right now?"

"What?" she asked, surprised.

"Something's wrong. What is it?" Just as she was about to open her mouth, he held up his hand. "Stop. Don't say 'nothing.' Nan and I have just been having the same conversation you and I have had several times—you know about family secrets. Tell us, please."

Casey looked over at Nan. "See what I have to put up with? I'm warning you, he has an eagle eye. I never could get away with anything."

"Quit avoiding my question, Casey."

"It isn't important, Dad. You and I have already gone over this. There's no need of worrying you with it."

Jacob looked over at Nan, "See what *I* have to put up with?"

"I see two people who love each other dearly and want to protect each other—maybe too much," Nan said. "Tell us, Casey. You have me now to help your dad carry the burden. He's not alone anymore."

The tears, still too close, threatened to come at Nan's last remark. "Thank you, Nan. That's more comforting than you know. Well, Dad, the thing we talked about has happened. Craig, his grandmother, and I went swimming together. The 'unveiling' of my leg didn't have a good effect on Craig. He seemed repulsed when he saw it. Right then I knew he'd never ask me out again. I didn't realize I liked him as much as I did, so I'm just feeling a little let down."

Pain pierced old familiar places still not healed, rendering Jacob mute.

Nan spoke softly. "Let down? That's putting it rather mildly, isn't it?"

Casey looked down and nodded, blinking back tears.

"May I see your leg, Casey?"

Slowly, Casey lifted up her silk pant leg.

Nan got up and went over to look at it closely. Her heart lurched and her eyes filled with tears. She bent down and put her arms around her and kissed her cheek. When Nan was able to contain her emotions, she straightened up and went back to her place beside Jacob. "This makes me want to hear the delicious news of our poor beleaguered Russ Eden, Jake," she said grimly, wishing with all her heart that it were Nick Carter.

Casey's face brightened. "Oh, yes, Dad, let's hear it."

Nan and Casey's laughter escalated as Jacob told them in detail what the clever and sneaky Snard had pulled on their victim this time, the end result causing the usually cool and collected Russ Eden to lose control with the police.

Casey's fist hit the arm of the chair. "Yes! The episodes are having the exact effect I've hoped they would." She sobered, biting her lip as she contemplated the results. "But I think we should hold off for a little while until I talk with Tiffany. I need to know how she is, how Russ is acting around her and how he's treating her."

"I definitely agree, Casey," her dad said. "I'll keep Monty on the job, watching Russ, but inform him to hold off doing anything more until we give him the go-ahead."

Chapter Twenty-Two

*Human relationships never
sail on smooth seas.*

Tiffany answered her desk phone. "Oh, hi, Casey. I was going to call you today."

"Can you talk now?"

"Yes. No one is around. What's up?"

"That's what I want to ask you. How is everything with you, with Russ, with you and Russ—all of it."

"Strange things are still happening to Russ. Someone is really out to embarrass him or something. He's become so paranoid, he's getting absentminded."

Just as I'd hoped, Casey thought. "Has he been all right with *you* while this is happening?"

"He suspected me again after the last weird thing, of course, but after checking he found out it was impossible for me to have done it. It's a little unbelievable, but he hardly pays any attention to me lately. All he does is call and check up on the people at work, and everyone he knows, to see if he can catch anyone in a lie. When we go out, he constantly looks around and behind himself and asked me to do so too. It's rather humorous, because now he knows how I feel when I go out for fear he's following me. I hope whoever is doing these things continues, because I've been getting less of his unwanted attention. He doesn't seem able to do anything but worry about who's doing these things and how it makes him look."

"Tiff, would you consider taking off work and staying

somewhere else if he starts acting too weird? He might become dangerous to you. I'll find a place for you if you'll consider it."

"Thank you, Casey. I think that might be a good idea. Even though he hasn't been as abusive lately, he still frightens me. I'll start making preparations at work for a spontaneous vacation of sorts."

"Good. Let me know if he turns on you in any way, won't you?"

"I will, Casey. I would never dare do this if you weren't behind me."

Casey made an important decision. She decided to consciously open herself up to dating. But along with that decision came another, more difficult one—to test the men in the beginning and never let herself be hurt as she had been with Craig.

All week she had been in and out of Hartner and Hart, and as she had promised herself, she made the effort to smile and talk with a couple of male employees who had tried to get acquainted with her. Since she had been far from encouraging before, she was surprised that they both had responded positively. Though not interested in either one, she felt she owed it to herself to get to know them if they chose to ask her out.

Today she felt her shoulders tense up at the prospect of dating and she felt edgy as she headed for Syrus' office with an envelope full of pictures. *Why let thoughts of dating put a damper on my spirits?* she asked herself. Things were going well. Her father was happy. She was no longer hurt over Craig, and it appeared that maybe they might be able to help Tiffany.

Syrus' door was open. He was assiduously studying something, and as usual an unruly strand of dark hair fell over his forehead. "Excuse me, Syrus," she said from the doorway.

He looked up, startled. Carefully turning over the material he had been studying, he smiled.

"Ah the ever-prepared Miss Casey. Come on in and have a seat."

"I just wanted to deliver these to you. I don't need to take your time."

"Please be seated, but before you do, would you close the door?"

Casey sighed. She wasn't in the mood to spar with Syrus today. Nevertheless, she did as he asked.

He studied her with his intense charcoal-brown eyes. "You look better today. Not so tired."

She was surprised at his intuitiveness. "You're observant. That's something only my dad would notice." She smiled.

"Your dad. I'd like to meet him sometime."

"Why?" she asked bluntly.

He leaned back in his chair and a lazy smile eased itself upon his face. "I'm interested in people and what makes them tick. From what I've heard, your dad has been very involved in your life."

"Who told you that?"

He thought a minute. "Actually, I think I read it in the newspaper, about your dad sitting at your bedside day after day in the hospital. One of the more favorable reports I believe."

"Did you want to talk to me about something, Syrus?" she asked, an impatient edge to her voice.

"I wanted to ask if you called the police about a possible stalker?"

"No. I only reported it to the FBI."

"And what did they say?"

"They told me to be careful," she said with disdain. "How helpful was that?"

Syrus didn't respond.

Casey let out an impatient breath. "That's why I wonder if anything is being done to close my case."

"When was the last time you heard from them?"

"They don't call me and inform me of anything. They just want me to inform them. Between you and me I think the police and the FBI are down at their respective offices playing tiddlywinks."

Syrus blinked a couple of times. "Tiddlywinks?"

"Yeah, you know that silly little game grandmothers used to play when they were little girls? My grandmother saved her game and we played it together a lot. It's fun. You should play it sometime instead of worrying about what your bosses think about me."

Syrus' emotions hovered between amusement and frustration. "As I've warned you before, if you want contract work from Hartner and Hart, you'll stop acting so contemptuous about their efforts to protect you."

Casey stood up angrily. "Protect themselves from a lawsuit you mean. Could I have the names of the man or men who are suspicious of my part in the accident?"

"What do you think?"

"I think I'll go up and see Mr. Hart and ask him!"

Syrus' brows rose in mock surprise. "Go ahead. Good luck."

"What do you mean, good luck?"

"You figure it out."

Casey turned and stormed out, slamming the door.

Angry at her insolence, Syrus stood up and tapped his fingers on the desk impatiently, trying to decide how to handle the situation. That was absolutely the last time she would slam the door. Never had he dealt with anyone like Casey Carter. If it were up to him, he would . . . Not quite sure what he would do, he didn't finish the thought. Instead, he moved around the desk to the door. He opened it and was about to follow her and call her back into his office to discuss the door slamming when he saw her stop at Grady Carlson's desk. Grady, one of his advertising specialists, was all smiles and eagerness. He could see that he was offering her a chair. Casey accepted and sat, her back to Syrus. By the expression on Grady's face, Syrus could tell Casey was putting on the charm. Annoyed, he shut the door, waited for about eight minutes, and then opened it just in time to see Casey walking away. Syrus moved quickly toward her, but she disappeared into the hall. The elevator was already closing when he reached it. He waited for another one and headed down, anger still churning inside him. No matter how he admired the girl's fortitude, her spunk, she had to respect his position!

Casey was out the door when his elevator opened. He followed her out to the parking lot, his long strides catching up to her.

"Casey! Stop."

Startled, she turned and looked up at him. "What are you doing out here?"

He noted her flushed face and the pools of moisture at the corners of her eyes and hesitated; nevertheless, he reprimanded her. "I followed you out to tell you that I strongly suggest you don't slam the door on me like that. Ever."

She blinked several times, trying to register what he was saying. Finally, she mouthed an "oh." Her large blue eyes were direct, as usual. "I did slam the door, didn't I?" she said in a soft voice.

Momentarily flustered at her sudden change of attitude, Syrus soon collected himself. "Yes. As a matter of fact you did," he replied coolly.

"I'm sorry. I don't know why, Syrus, but you seem to . . . uh, nettle me at every turn."

"So it would seem. I'm warning you, Casey. No more overt acts of incivility."

Her mouth ajar, she watched as his long legs carried him rapidly to the entrance of the building, where he disappeared.

Chapter Twenty-Three

*Getting to know another human being
takes effort, patience, and love.*

Sitting in his office at work, Russ smiled as he thought of how well he had handled the green-hands affair at the office all week. Here it was Thursday, seven days later. The green was finally wearing off. When he told Norm how he intended to handle it at work, suggesting that he not say otherwise, Norm had just shrugged his shoulders. His excuse for wearing gloves was that he had developed a rash from touching a poisonous plant and the gloves protected the medication. The staff bought it.

Yet, there was a nagging fear inside over his loss of control with the police. But how would the Pentad find out? As long as he performed, they didn't check up on him—at least that's what they said. One thing was certain, he had to condition himself against any possible prank in the future, that no matter what it might turn out to be, he would not lose control. His life had been acting the part, putting on the facade people liked and expected to see. Hadn't he held himself in when he wanted to bat Tiffany around? Wasn't he smart enough, composed enough to realize he could control his wife with words? Words didn't send a woman to the police. Words didn't leave evidence.

He leaned back in his chair, thinking of what the head of the Pentad had said. *Very few men are as clever as you are. We know you well. We know what you're really like inside. We've watched you carefully. You come over as intelligent, composed, and credible at all times and under all circumstances. Your words come out like polished stones. On top of that, you have a quick wit that only a very smart man could have. All these qualities draw people to you, flattering them, giving them confidence in you and themselves. Remember, appearance is everything. It doesn't matter what you do in your private life as long as you retain the positive perception people have of you. If you lose that you'll be terminated.* That last word had been invested with something that made him more afraid than he had ever been. Fear wormed its way through his insides as he remembered.

Nervously, he spoke out loud. "It doesn't matter what the employees of the salon think of me." All that mattered is that he and Norm had explained it satisfactorily to the police. Once again, he convinced himself that in every other instance he had done rather well. The only exception was Norm. He was the only person he hadn't been able to win over. Resentment twisted inside him.

Focusing his mind on something more pleasant, Russ decided to reward himself for the very successful services performed for the Pentad today. Tomorrow he would meet with Sheila for lunch, but his reward today was something else—something he relished doing. In fact it had turned into kind of a hobby. He chuckled.

A tight knot in the pit of Casey's stomach came back with a vengeance when she entered Hartner and Hart the next day, remembering Grady Carlson's reaction when she lifted her pant leg the day before. He had asked her for a date and as she had promised herself ahead of time, she sat down by his desk and tested him at once. She managed to keep her cool when it looked as if he was about to pass out at the sight. She smiled and asked if he still wanted to take her out. He muttered, "Sure." But she gave him an out. "Thank you, Grady, but I'm busy that night. I'm sorry." When he didn't pursue it further, she smiled and said, "See you around."

Grady was in his thirties, reasonably good-looking, and not married. All the single women at work had tried to interest him, but he seemed oblivious to everyone except her. He had come on to her, but she hadn't been ready until now. Casey knew that he wouldn't ask her out again. This would be no great loss to her, but what was so devastating was knowing that this would probably be the reaction of all men who might ask her out.

She wouldn't be here today if Syrus hadn't had Vicky call her and tell her to come over and discuss the pictures she had delivered yesterday. In doing so, she would have to pass right by Grady's desk. The elevator opened and she stepped out into the hall. Taking a deep breath, she put on a smile.

"Hi, Grady," she said, cheerfully.

He gave her a quick nod and a smile. Holding her head high with a confidence she didn't feel, she limped on past him toward Vicky's desk. Though she could hear the hum of typing, copying, shuffling papers, all the comforting everyday noises at Hartner and Hart that were familiar to her, still she couldn't feel as calm as she tried to appear.

"Hi, Vick, is Sy free?"

"He's always as free as he wants to be," she said, grinning.

This made Casey laugh for some reason. "Yes, he's different, isn't he?"

"That's an understatement," Vicky whispered, "but he makes life interesting around here anyway."

"He makes my life . . . you know I can't think of quite the right adjective yet," Casey whispered back.

She walked on, hearing Vicky snicker behind her. *Now I know the right word—bumpier. He makes my life bumpier. He seems to know which button to push to set me off. Does he makes life more interesting?* she asked herself. She stopped in front of Syrus' door, trying to decide, and then nodded her head and admitted that, in fact, he did. As unsettling as it was to talk with him, she realized that deep down she looked forward to coming to his office. "Kind of like a love-hate thing," she muttered under her breath.

"Are you talking to yourself, Casey?" Syrus asked, grinning, "Or me?"

Surprised, she didn't realize Syrus' door was open. "As a matter of fact I was talking to myself about you."

"Oh? Dare I ask what you were saying about me?"

"You dare, of course, but my lips are sealed. You wanted to see me about the pictures?"

"Yes. Wheel your chair around and let's go over them."

Casey was surprised that Syrus was so cheerful after his anger had sent him out into the parking lot the day before to chastise her. *Why do I slam doors like that, anyway?* He had already put up with a lot from her. No matter how he provoked her, she had no right to talk to the head graphic designer the way she did. She shuddered at the thoughts of her brassiness. What was it about Syrus that brought this out in her? Was it distrust because of her past? Was it because he was tall and had dark hair like the stalker? She rubbed her brow with consternation.

When she had positioned her chair and sat, she noticed that Syrus was intently studying her.

"Why the grim expression, Casey?" Syrus asked.

"Why do you scrutinize me all the time?"

"Scrutinize you *all* the time?"

"Well, much of the time. Are you trying to decide whether or not I'm guilty of causing the accident?"

"Didn't I tell you I believe you?"

"Yes. So why do you study me?"

"I do that, do I?"

Casey sighed in exasperation. "You know you do. Why?"

"If I do," he began, a twinkle in his eyes, "maybe it's because you're nice to look at."

"Never mind. I knew I couldn't get a straight answer."

The twinkle left and Syrus gazed at her for so long she squirmed. "You're doing it again, Syrus."

"I was wondering why you were upset yesterday when I stopped you in the parking lot."

"How do you know I was upset?"

"It was obvious."

She would rather die than tell Syrus Tucker of Grady Carlson's reaction to her leg.

"You expect a straight answer from me when you won't give me one?"

"I have a job to do, Casey."

"So do I. So let's go over the pictures.

Casey disconsolately walked back to her studio. Syrus had been different when they went over the pictures. He had been solemn and businesslike. She couldn't keep up with his unpredictability "What's up with him, I wonder? Will I ever know the man?" She shrugged her shoulders. As she was about to turn off the alleyway toward the entrance of her studio, she saw a beat-up red car parked nearby. A man with a visor cap and dark glasses was watching her with his window down. He opened the car door and stepped out.

Casey moved as fast as her leg would carry her. Looking back at him, she noted that he only ambled toward her. Quickly unlocking the door, she entered and locked it, her heart pounding so heavily she could scarcely breathe. The man knocked on the door.

"Who is it, please?" she asked nervously. She didn't allow anyone here except models.

There was no answer, just another series of knocks. Quickly, she pulled out her cell phone and dialed Syrus. When he answered she blurted out, "Where's Brad? There's a man banging on my door and I'm scared."

"He should be around. I'll be right there. Don't open the door!"

Casey went to the window. She couldn't see the man outside the door, but the knocking was getting louder. It wasn't long before she saw Syrus running across the parking lot in her direction. The noise stopped. She saw the man run to his car and drive off so fast he almost hit the wall. She could see Syrus trying to memorize the license number.

"Casey!" Syrus yelled through the door.

Casey opened it. She never thought she would be so glad to see Syrus as she was at that moment. "Come in," she said breathlessly.

"Have a seat," she said pointing to two folding chairs. "The man wouldn't answer when I asked who he was. He just kept pounding on the door."

Syrus' face was grim. "Give me a piece of paper so I can write down that license number before I forget it. I'll have Brad take it to the police to check it out." He wrote the number down then looked at her. "Was he the same man, Casey?"

"I don't know. He certainly wasn't as subtle. This car was ready for the junk heap, and this man wore a cap and dark glasses."

"Was he familiar to you?"

"I never got a good look at the man who followed me before and I was too frightened to get a good look at this one. All I could concentrate on was trying to get this leg of mine to move faster . . . wait. He was tall like the first man, and I could see dark hair on his neck. Now that I think about it, he could have caught me, because I can't run. It was strange; he just ambled toward me and then after I got in, pounded on the door. I think he was just trying to frighten me. But why?"

Syrus shook his head, his brows hovering over his eyes, thinking.

"If it's the same man, he's clever enough to change cars this time. But maybe I have more than one stalker," she added. "If you'll excuse me, I think I'll call the FBI man and report this to him."

Syrus waited and listened with interest. When she disconnected, he asked, "Are you all right?"

"Yes. Shaken up, but all right. Thanks for coming so fast."

"You're welcome," he replied distractedly. He stood up and restlessly began pacing.

Casey watched him, wondering if she finally trusted him now. She still wasn't sure.

"What worries me, Casey, is that if it's the same man, he's getting bolder. You're going to have to be even more careful."

"You know, Syrus, I'm feeling surprisingly calm."

"You are?" he asked, surprised.

"Yes. At the moment you're carrying my problem." She grinned. "Or as Dad used to say, my hot potato."

"It's not amusing, Casey. This is serious."

"Really?"

"You know what?"

"What?"

"You're about to drive me up the flagpole!"

Casey laughed. "I'd like to see that."

He ran his hand through his obstinate hair. "Do you have plans tonight?"

"No. Why?"

"I saw Grady talking to you yesterday. Just wondered."

"Grady asked me out, but I was busy that night. I'm afraid he's too satisfied with his life to put forth much effort," she hedged. Then added, eyeing him pointedly, "It seems there are a lot of men out there just like him."

"Me, for instance?"

"If the shoe fits."

"Well, for your information, the shoe does not fit." Syrus looked at his watch. "It's almost five. Let me take you out to dinner."

"Are you trying to prove something to me?"

"Now what would I want to prove?"

"That you aren't like Grady."

"Well, that's obvious. I'm a lot more handsome."

Her face alight with laughter, she got up and walked around Syrus, looking him up and down. "Well, you do have more unruly hair, anyway. You're not as buff as he is. More like Ichabod Crane, I'd say. But your eyes . . . ah, your eyes."

Syrus, his thumbs in his jean pockets, looked amused. "My eyes, you say. What about my eyes?"

"They're scary."

"See, I told you I was more handsome than Grady."

Casey, giddy over her recent fright, found a chair and doubled over with laughter. Syrus grinned and waited. When she was through, he said, "I'll follow you home, and then I'll take you to dinner."

"If it's business, no. I'm in no mood to be cross-examined. So what is it, business or social?"

Syrus scratched his head. "I think it's social."

"What about Hartner and Hart? Do they allow their executives to fraternize with the help?"

"I've been told to keep an eye on you. Tonight I think I'll keep both on you, both scary eyes."

Casey laughed helplessly. "All right," she managed to say as she grabbed her purse. "I'm ready. Shall we?"

Following Syrus' instructions, Casey waited in her car as he walked to his truck. Soon he came cruising down the alley. "All right," he said through the window. "You go ahead and I'll follow right behind you."

"Okay. I don't think anyone would dare follow me with that formidable blue masterpiece behind me."

Syrus grinned. "Of course not. See you."

Casey led him out of the alleyway and headed toward her house.

When they arrived, she drove into the garage and Syrus waited in front. In less than a minute, Casey waved him into the house. He got out, his long strides meeting her at the door.

"Come on in. I just want to wash my hands and brush my teeth."

"Do you have an extra toothbrush?"

"I do." She left and came back. "Here, it's almost new." He

raised his brows. She grinned. "It's brand-new." She led him to the guest bath.

They came out at the same time. "This isn't exactly where I thought you'd live, Casey."

"My dad didn't think so either. It draws mostly senior citizens."

"Why did you choose a senior citizen community?"

"Because most of them don't walk any better than I do."

Syrus laughed. It was a deep, infectious laugh Casey hadn't heard before.

"You should laugh more often, Syrus."

"You don't help me in that regard. If you were just a little more malleable and easier to direct—"

"I do everything I'm directed to do when it comes to photography and assignments. Why should I take any other directions?"

Syrus' demeanor changed dramatically, darkly displeased.

"Sorry. I really like your smile better, Syrus—much better than your glower. Do you think you can smile more?"

"Come on," he said, fighting back a smile while he opened the front door. "Do you have any preferences? Since I'm fairly new in town—"

"You know, I think I kinda like Rosarita's," Casey said, stepping out.

His face lit up. "And to think you thought is was a dump. I practically had to drag you out of the truck when I first took you there."

"See how teachable I am?"

Syrus sounded like he was about to choke.

On the way, Casey decided to try and find out as much as she could about the mysterious Syrus Tucker—catch him off guard. In spite of the sparks and acerbity, the longer she knew him, the more curious she became.

When they arrived, Syrus offered his hand to help her out. She decided to take it and surprise him. It did and she laughed.

"All right, let me in on the joke," he said opening the door to Rosarita's.

She just gave him a small, mysterious smile.

Rosarita's face lit up when she saw Syrus. "Mr. Tucker, I see you have your favorite blonde with you today."

"I do for a fact, Rosarita. We want a booth at the back."

They immediately ordered their favorites without looking at the menu, and then Casey asked, "How many blondes do you bring here?"

"Dozens."

"And you told Rosarita that I'm your favorite?"

"Of course."

"Then why don't you treat me like I'm your favorite?" she asked, her eyes twinkling.

"If you deserved it, I would."

She gazed into his smiling eyes. "So you're quite a lady's man?"

"What?" he asked, puzzled.

"You know, those dozens of blondes."

He looked askance at her.

"Have you ever been engaged?"

"No."

"Ever been married?"

"No. Why all the personal questions?"

"If you can ask them, why can't I?"

"I guess you can. I doubt I can stop you."

"How old are you?"

"Why do you want to know?"

"Just curious."

"I'm thirty-four."

"Wow. And never been engaged or married. That's terrible, Syrus. There are a lot of single women out there who would love to marry a man of your caliber."

Syrus' face turned a deeper color. "That's enough, Casey."

"Oh, you can give, but you can't take, huh?"

The waitress placed their food before them.

"Eat and quit asking questions. That's *my* job."

She looked up and saw a teasing light in his eyes. "All right," she complied. "I'm hungry so I'll give you a reprieve . . . for a while." They ate in silence. Then, after Casey had satisfied some of her hunger, she continued her quest to know the real Syrus. "Did you go to school to study graphic design?"

"No. I graduated from college with a couple of majors and then got a master's degree. I studied graphic design on my own. When you have a master's, it's easier to get a job, period."

"Have you always done graphic design?"

"No. I'm kind of a jack-of-all-trades, so to speak. I've done a lot of things."

"Such as?"

"I've punched cows, raised thoroughbred horses, worked on oil rigs, thrown papers, shoveled manure, plucked chickens in a processing plant . . ."

" But most of those things you did when you were younger, right?"

"You didn't specify an age."

"No I didn't. But it sounds like you were an industrious young man. What have you done since you got your master's?"

"Too many things."

"Such as."

"I see you're on a mission, Casey."

"I am. I want to know more about you."

"Why?"

"Because I'm tired of wondering about you. Vicky calls you 'the man of mystery.' I'm tired of working for a mystery man."

Syrus laughed. "I had no idea you were curious about me. You always seem so all-fired anxious to get out of my office every time you come."

"Well, of course. You interrogate me."

"That's my job. Finding out more about *me* isn't yours."

Sparks flew from Casey's eyes. "Didn't you say that tonight

was social, not business? The purpose of socializing is to get acquainted isn't it?"

"Whew! Okay, but may I finish my dinner before I answer any more questions?"

Casey begrudgingly nodded and silently finished hers. Though stuffed to the brim, she ordered a dessert to prolong the meal.

"You eat a lot for one so small. I guess I'll have dessert too."

"Now, while we're waiting for dessert, tell me what you did after you got your master's."

"I managed a bar, played professional basketball for a while, managed a hotel, was a headwaiter, traveled different places—but not necessarily in that order."

Casey was shocked. "What did you get your degrees in?"

"Languages and international economics."

Syrus smiled at Casey's wide-eyed incredulity. "What's the matter? Shocked?"

"A little. You certainly didn't use your education with all those jobs."

"Oh, but it takes brains to be a bartender and a waiter."

Casey shook her head. She knew Syrus was teasing her, but he was even more puzzling to her than before she questioned him. "Well, it doesn't sound like you can stay at one job very long."

"Nope. I get bored easily. My mother says I'm too adventuresome."

"Does that mean you won't be a graphics designer at Hartner and Hart very long?"

Syrus shrugged. "That remains to be seen."

"Does Hartner and Hart know your history?"

"Some of it."

Casey let out a disgusted breath, took a couple of bites of dessert, and shoved it aside. "Well, all I've got to say, Syrus Tucker, is that it doesn't sound like you have much ambition."

Syrus threw back his head and laughed.

Casey frowned at him, puzzled. "What's so funny?"

"I guess you don't think the man of mystery is so mysterious after all—maybe even a little boring?"

Scrutinizing him slyly, Casey's eyes turned suspicious. "Ha! You're wrong. You're even more of an enigma than before, and hardly boring." Her brows furrowed over suspicious eyes. "You know . . . somehow, I don't think you're telling me everything." The surprise on Syrus' face made her laugh.

He held a straight face. "If you want to know more, go out with me every night."

"All right."

Syrus' brows shot up in surprise. She could almost see him gulp in consternation.

Casey laughed. "I called your bluff, didn't I? You really are a confirmed bachelor. No thanks to going out every night. You'd only tell me what you wanted me to know, anyway."

Syrus' gaze pinned her with an intensity she hadn't seen before.

Casey fidgeted. "Why are you looking at me like that?"

"As I told you in your studio, the shoe doesn't fit. Let's go. I have some work to do at the office."

"And I'm exhausted."

Syrus laughed and Casey threw him a scathing glance.

Chapter Twenty-Four

*Man is a coward, plain and simple. He loves
life too much. He fears others too much.*
—Jack Henry Abbott

The mystery of who was out to get him had been on Russ' mind night and day. All morning he sat in his office chewing on it, still unable to successfully direct his suspicions in anyone's direction. A thought came to him. Rejecting it at first, it returned, looming larger and larger in his mind until he was so agitated and restless he couldn't stay in the office another moment.

He decided to go home for lunch, where he could think more clearly, as well as go through Tiffany's things. She was never home at this hour. Her work was too far away to go home mid-day.

While driving, the idea began to escalate until he was perspiring. He wheeled into the driveway and into the garage around back and shut off the motor.

Throwing his coat onto the family room couch, he loosened his tie and headed for the bedroom to begin his search. The moment he stepped in, he saw Tiffany huddled up on the bed, a blanket over her.

Angry that she had ruined his plan, his voice rose. "What are you doing here at this time of day, Tiffany?"

Tiffany's eyes blinked open, surprised to see her husband standing over her. "I had to come home. I was having severe cramps. I took something and I guess I fell asleep."

Russ glowered at her and then turned and paced a moment. *What can I do now?* he thought, annoyed beyond all reason.

Then he knew. Why not just come right out with it? He would be able to tell by her reaction whether his suspicion had any merit.

"What are you doing home, Russ?"

"I forgot something," he lied. "As long as you're here, Tiffany, I'd like to talk with you about the things that have been happening to me."

Fear skittered through Tiffany. She could always tell by his demeanor when trouble was ahead and today he looked dark and frightening. He had never struck her, but she knew it would happen one day. She sat up and leaned against a pillow, clutching the blanket. "All right. Maybe together we'll think of something we haven't before."

Clever, he thought, *either that or she's totally innocent*. He sat down on the bed. "Remember when the newspapers carried the story about your friend, what's her name?"

Tiffany's fear escalated. "You mean Casey Jacobson?"

"Yes. You told me you two were close friends at one time. But that isn't the name they used in the paper."

"She married a man named Nick Carter. Why are you asking about her?"

"I was wondering if you told her anything about us when you went to lunch together."

Tiffany paled. "How did you know about that?"

"I followed you, that's how."

"How did you know it was Casey?"

"I parked a few cars down from yours and when you came out, I saw her. She looked like the picture in the paper, even though her hair was short. When I saw her limp, I knew for sure it was your friend who got hurt in the accident."

Tiffany's mind raced. All three times she had looked at every car in the parking area. She had been sure his wasn't there. "Why . . . why would you distrust me so much that you would follow me?"

"The big question is, why didn't you tell me about your luncheon date?"

"I simply forgot."

"Didn't I ask you to tell me when you see your friends? I tell you when I see mine."

"Do you? All of them?"

Ignoring her question, he continued attacking her. "How many times have you had lunch with your friend Casey?"

"Three. But I haven't seen her in weeks. We both decided that for a while we were too busy to have lunch together."

Suspicion ate at his insides. "Three! I only knew about one. Since you've hidden the fact that you've had lunch with her, I'm wondering what you told her about us."

"Just the usual. We just got caught up. We mostly talked about her situation, her burned leg, and the fact that her case isn't closed yet and so on."

"What's the usual, Tiffany?"

"I took a picture of you and me together to show her my handsome husband, told her how long we'd been married, where I work, what you do for a living—the usual questions women ask each other."

"It just hit me this morning, Tiff, that you've been different since that luncheon date."

"I have?" she asked, opening her eyes wide, looking as innocent as she could. "How could having lunch with an old friend make me different?"

"You tell me, Tiffany," he stated, his eyes slits of distrust.

"How do you mean different?"

"Maybe less uh, or more . . . never mind, I can't describe it."

"Isn't it you who's different?" she asked, trying to redirect him with questions.

"Of course I'm different. I'm shocked and angry over the things that have been done to me! And I'm wondering if your friend Casey has had anything to do with them."

"Casey?" Tiffany's mouth dropped open, incredulous. "Russ, she's crippled! She barely has enough energy to go back to work. How could she possibly do those things, and even if she could, why would she want to embarrass her best friend's husband?"

He could tell that Tiffany was genuinely shocked at the suggestion and wasn't hiding anything. Still, his suspicion was not totally quelled.

The weekend droned by monotonously for Casey. When she returned to work the following Monday, the first thing she did was go up to Syrus' office to see if he had a job for her but found him gone. Vicky told her that he had taken off a few days to go up to his ranch in Colorado. She was surprised at how disappointed she felt. It was probably because she'd had such a boring weekend.

When Syrus had brought her home from Rosarita's, Casey had been totally nonplussed. What had she really found out about him? His replies were too concise, which made him seem a little guarded, and this certainly hadn't helped her trust him. It only aroused her curiosity. Though still shocked at some of his answers, she found herself smiling at his sense of humor. And, begrudgingly, she was impressed that he had minimized his accomplishments.

On the way home, he had told her about his ranch, which apparently was more of a hobby than a serious business. He had become animated when he talked about it, and this proved to be an interesting insight into the man.

With Syrus gone, her work decreased, so she found time on her hands to work on her own project. She bought some things with which to protect herself: Mace, a fake gun, and a piercing whistle. Gathering up her cameras, she placed them in her backpack and went to her car, nervously looking around. Hoping Brad was on the job, she headed back to South Mountain Park.

Chapter Twenty-Five

In ourselves our safety must be sought.
By our own hand it must be wrought.
—William Wadsworth

Since the day they became engaged, Jacob and Nan had been inseparable. She cooked dinner for him, he took her out, they went for walks. Tonight they were sitting on the back porch together enjoying the evening. His arm was around her shoulders, holding her close.

A couple of times Nan had mentioned setting a marriage date; Jacob hadn't responded but would tactfully change the subject. She had waited for him to suggest a date, but he hadn't. In the first place, she had been surprised he was able to commit himself so soon, especially since he hadn't wanted to marry again, but now she was concerned. They were older, they each had been married before, and in her mind a long engagement was not a good idea.

"Jacob," Nan began hesitantly, "when do you think we should be married?"

"Well . . . I've been wondering where we should live." He looked at her. "I don't think you would want to live here."

"I wouldn't mind at all. There isn't much of a feeling of Silvia here, more of you and Casey. The only thing is, her taste in decorating isn't my taste."

"You really wouldn't mind living here?"

"No. Really."

"Good. This has been Casey's home for many years. I'll tell you what, you can gut the place and redecorate."

"I can? Wonderful. I'd love that, Jake. But you didn't answer my question about when you feel we should get married."

Jacob stared straight ahead. "I think we had better wait until Project Russ is over with and settled."

"I agree. I want to be able to concentrate only on us. I don't know how Casey feels, but I think we shouldn't have more than two more tricks pulled on Russ. If those don't accomplish what we want, maybe we should call it quits."

"I agree wholeheartedly, Nan. We'll talk it over with Casey."

"I hope by then the guy will be so unraveled Tiffany can escape the marriage safely . It shouldn't take more than two or three weeks for Monty and Snard to finish. After they're through, approximately when do you think we should be married?" Nan knew she was pushing Jacob, but she had to find out now if he could really go through with it.

Jacob removed his arm from around her, got up, took a couple of steps, and stared out at his backyard. Without turning, he said, "I want to get married tomorrow!" He burst out, still not looking at her, "At times I don't feel I can wait another minute." Slowly, he turned to her. "But we've only known each other a month. How about six months from now?"

"Are you serious, Jake?"

His eyes troubled, he nodded. "I am."

"I thought it was too good to be true that you could change your mind so quickly after five years of building up a resistance to remarrying."

He sat down beside her and took her hand in his. "I love you, Nan. I want to be with you every minute, so I don't understand why I . . ." He couldn't go on.

"Do you feel fear?"

His troubled eyes pleaded with her to understand. "Maybe that's it, but it's even more than that. There's something that's bothering me, holding me back, and I can't figure out what it is. My mother used to say quite often that men aren't good at introspection. And I'm afraid it's true."

"How do I know you won't still feel the same way in six

months? How do I know that by then you'll have figured out what's bothering you?"

"You don't, I guess."

Nan pulled off her engagement ring. "Here, Jake, consider us unengaged as of this moment."

"No, Nan, no, please—"

"It will be better this way. Really. You need more time. How much, neither of us knows. In fact, we need time apart for a few days. I'll come over only when we're working on Casey's project."

Jacob pulled her to him and muttered desperately. "Nan, don't do this."

Nan, still holding the ring, put her arms around his neck and lingeringly kissed his wonderful lips. Then she smiled at him, hiding the ache and the fear inside. "It's all right, Jake. Let's give this a try. Maybe you can figure out what's troubling you if you have some time alone to really think." She shoved the ring into his hand and stood up. "Please take me home."

All week Casey continued to have a delightful time scouring the different trails on South Mountain, taking pictures for her files. She hiked the Alta Trail, the Mormon Trail, and the Holbert Trail. No one followed her, not even Brad, as far as she knew anyway, and she felt a freedom and exhilaration that had long been missing from her life. Her leg even felt stronger.

Early Saturday morning she resumed her search. Reaching South Mountain Park, she entered on San Juan Road and drove to the Bajada Trail, parking on the nearest trailhead. She took only her digital camera this time because the added weight of the backpack made her tire more quickly, deciding that if she found something to videotape for her project she'd go back to the car and exchange cameras. There were a number of cars parked at the trailhead, so she knew she'd have company. She put the Mace in her pocket and headed for the trail.

Having found a number of beautiful sights to photograph, she took her time and ended up hiking farther than she ever had. As the day grew hotter the hikers thinned out and her gait slowed. She turned around and headed back. Finally reaching the trailhead, she found only her car and one other left. Limping tiredly toward her car she heard a movement behind her. She glanced over her shoulder and saw a man peering through a mesquite tree only a few yards away. Chills prickled her skin and she realized this was the closest she had ever been to her stalker.

Shakily, her hand reached into her pocket and carefully pulled out the Mace. Her heart pounded so hard she could scarcely breathe. "Hello," she said, trying to sound friendly.

He didn't respond.

"Who are you?"

He didn't say anything, didn't move. Nor did she. "Are you following me?" she called out angrily.

She heard a guttural laugh. Then, as in her worst nightmare, fear pinned her to the spot. Her breathing erratic, she said a quick prayer, and at last she was able to move—inching slowly toward her car, watching him as she did so.

He jumped out from behind the tree, smiling. A canvas hat hid his eyes and a mustache and beard covered his face.

Though consumed with fear, adrenaline coursed through her, giving her strength. "What do you want?" she asked coolly.

A grimace of a smile on his face, he took slow, deliberate steps toward her. Engulfed in waves of panic, she stopped, waiting for him to get closer. When he got close enough, her hand flew up and sprayed his face and eyes. He yelped, grabbed his face, and danced around in pain while she quickly snapped a couple of pictures of him. Then moving as rapidly as she could, she reached the car faster than she thought possible. Unlocking it, she got in, locked it, turned the key, and whirled out of the trailhead onto the road. Watching through the back window, she saw him run after her. Frantically she shoved the pedal to the floor, leaving him far behind. He finally disappeared as she recklessly turned the bend. It was then she saw the welcome sight of Brad's tan car coming toward her. They both stopped and he got out.

Rolling down her window, Casey breathlessly told him what happened.

Grimly, he nodded. "I'm going after him."

"No, Brad!" she yelled, fearful for him. Ignoring her, he ran to his car and drove past her. She pulled off the road a little and waited, leaving the motor running. There was no way she would leave without knowing Brad was safe.

Lowering the windows so she could hear an approaching car, she watched through her side and back windows. She desperately wished she were physically able to help Brad. *I could have before the accident,* she thought bitterly. She listened to every sound, but all she heard was the screech of a prairie falcon, the almost indistinct scuttle of a lizard through the brush, and a bee buzzing over a desert flower.

Opening the door, she stepped out and looked down the road. All she saw move were the wings of a hummingbird as its long beak, in staccato movements, sucked out the nectar from the purple blossom of a desert beardtongue. She sat back down, closed the door, and waited.

Though it had been only twenty minutes, it seemed like hours before she saw Brad's car come down the road. He pulled up behind her and got out.

"I couldn't find any sign of the man anywhere."

"I'm just relieved you're all right, Brad. It was frightening. He would have hurt me, I'm sure, if I hadn't sprayed Mace in his face."

"You know I have to report this to Sy, don't you?"

She nodded. "So? My life has to go on, Brad."

He shook his head. Instead of his usual smile, he gave her a look of concern. Silently he returned to his car. He followed her all the way back to her house and then turned around and left.

The phone was ringing when she walked in. She was relieved to hear her father's comforting voice. "Dad, it's nice to hear from you." *More than you know*, she thought. "What's up?" she asked, trying to sound calm.

"Nan and I have discussed it and we think we ought to inform Monty to have Snardly execute only two more incidents. We're hoping they'll unravel Russ enough for Tiffany to get out. Anyway, whether they will or not, we're concerned about going on with it any further."

"You know, Dad, I'm feeling the same way. Go ahead and tell Monty."

She put the phone in its stand. The control she had exerted during the terrible suspense of waiting for Brad, and the rigid restraint that drove her all the way home wilted as suddenly as a flower in the desert heat. The full impact of the danger she had been in—the terror of it—besieged her fragile emotions. Every muscle in her body began shaking, bringing painful tremors and spasms to her injuries.

Monday morning, Casey received a call at her studio from Syrus, asking her to come over to his office. Since he always had Vicky call, it meant only one thing—he was upset over Brad's report. She had been expecting a summons to his office and wasn't in any mood to defend her actions. Locking her studio, she started toward the offices muttering, "It's my life, isn't? Hartner and Hart can't dictate to me!"

Entering the third floor, she wasn't even aware when she passed Grady's desk. His reaction to her leg was no longer important. Giving Vicky a smile as she passed her, she stepped into Syrus' office, shutting the door knowing he would want privacy. She stood before him defiantly.

Syrus leaned back in his chair. His brows lowering over his dark gaze, he spoke quietly. "Sit down please."

She did so, waiting for the explosion.

None came, only a quiet threat. "You're on probation with Hartner and Hart."

She spoke just as quietly. "What am I supposed to do with my free time, Syrus? Twiddle my thumbs?"

"Isn't that better than getting hurt or worse?"

"The man was the one who got hurt," she said, smiling.

Syrus leaned toward her, his eyes shooting daggers. "Don't be smug, Casey. That won't happen again. He'll come from behind next time."

Casey had already thought of that, but she wasn't about to acknowledge it to Syrus.

"I'll try to be more careful," she replied in a bored tone of voice.

"With that attitude, you're about to have a lot of time on your hands."

She stared back into his smoldering eyes, stubbornly unmoved. "Fine. You're one moody man, Syrus Tucker. You take me out to dinner and act charming and affable, then I come to your office and you crack the whip like a lion tamer." She stood up and moved toward the door.

He shot to his feet and around the desk, over to her. He gripped her arm tightly, his jaw working furiously. "And why do you think I crack the whip?"

She shrugged.

"It's all I can do to keep from shaking you. You're supposed to be a grown woman, but you're still acting like an irresponsible child."

"You know, I'm tired of hearing that. I hardly think that's a professional remark coming from someone who has the position you do. I think I'll report you."

Syrus dropped his hand, looked up, and rolled his eyes in frustration, his fists clenched. Glaring down at her, he said, "Please do. Maybe they'll fire me because I can't do two full-time jobs—head graphics designer and bodyguard!"

Something inside Casey jarred her. There seemed to be an expression of desperation in Syrus' eyes. *Maybe he really cares, beyond just doing his job well.* She wanted to reach out and comfort him, reassure him that she would try to be more careful, try to make his job easier, but her stubborn nature prevailed.

"You're excused, Mrs. Carter."

She looked up at him, her eyes emitting sparks. "I told you never to call me that again."

"Then change your name back to Jacobson," he said with a smile that didn't reach his eyes.

"I can't. The case isn't closed."

"As I said, you're excused, Mrs. Carter."

Infuriated, Casey opened the door, stepped out, and slammed it.

Furiously, Syrus opened it and saw Casey standing there, her eyes wide and her hand over her mouth.

"Oops," she said in a small voice. "Sorry. I forgot."

Surprised at her sudden and humorous remorse, Syrus successfully squelched a smile, but not his sense of helplessness at trying to handle this difficult girl. In spite of it, and though he fought it from the beginning, he looked forward to being with her. Her strength, her depth, and her vulnerability brought out a deep yearning inside him for a different kind of life, and at the same time awakened an awareness of his emptiness, which was filled when he was in her presence.

Chapter Twenty-Six

*Fear has a different face for those
who inflict fear on others.*
—Anonymous

Early Tuesday morning, an unexpected call came from Fred Reisner, asking Russ to pick him up at the airport at noon. Feeling edgy, Russ wondered why he was back so soon. Just before he left for the airport, he took his new ivory Cadillac SRX to be washed and detailed. Driving a classy car had always been important to Russ. In his mind it spoke of success and, he reasoned, it looked good for the company. Purchasing the car had given him the lift he needed and had taken his thoughts off the constant fear that had been plaguing him lately. He smiled as he drove it to the airport. The Cadillac SRX had both style and power, and all the amenities.

When he picked Fred up at curbside, Fred whistled. "Some nice vehicle you have here. I've looked at this very one. Do you like it?"

Russ couldn't have been more pleased. "I just got it, but so far it rides great. Would you like to drive?"

"No thanks, maybe later."

"What are you here for, Fred?" Russ asked as he wheeled out into the driving lane.

"At the last minute, I decided to visit family in California and then visit a few offices out there."

"Oh? And how did you find them?"

"Great. The managers seemed to be doing well."

"Good. How about lunch at the country club?"

"Sounds good. I decided to take a layover here because I

want to pass on a couple of suggestions the managers gave me."

"I'm willing to listen to any suggestion to improve the operation," Russ replied, his voice smooth as polished granite.

It had been over a week since Nan had broken the engagement and Jacob still hadn't resolved the underlying disquiet inside him. At least fifteen times he had picked up the phone to call Nan and plead for her to go out with him, be with him while he tried to solve his problem. But he put the phone down each time, trying to think of what was best for her. He knew what was best for him—her calming presence.

"I can't lose her!" he exclaimed aloud. "What is the matter with me?"

He paced his downtown office. He couldn't keep his mind off her, day or night. *I know, I'll pretend it's over, gone, then set a date to get married,* he thought. *It has to resolve itself eventually.* But could he fool Nan? *No. It would be impossible. She's too intuitive.*

She had already doubted his love and he had to reassure her.

He had prayed for introspection, the elusive quality his mother said men usually lacked. The only thing he could come up with was his unhappy marriage, but somehow that wasn't the problem, though something told him that his unease was connected to it in some way.

His anguish and loneliness was totally unlike the loneliness he felt when Silvia was away. He sat down at his desk, covered his face, and groaned. "I can't lose her. I want to be able to give her my whole heart, give her what Chet couldn't. Dear God, help me to conquer this before it's too late."

Reisner spent two hours with Russ at lunch and Russ was beginning to feel at ease with his boss for the first time since the humiliating episodes. Reisner seemed to have forgotten them. Since Fred's plane was due to leave in two hours, they left the club and amiably chatted on the way out to the car. Russ pulled out his key, pushed the remote, and unlocked both doors. Fred headed to the passenger side and Russ to the driver's side. Before they reached it, Russ stopped and stared at the car. "This isn't my car, Fred," he said.

"I heard it unlock for you."

"It did unlock, didn't it," Russ said, staring at it in confusion. "But how can this be my car? You saw the condition it was in when I picked you up at the airport." Certain it wasn't his, he tried the door. It opened. In the backseat he saw his briefcase. He realized with horror that it *was* his car.

Just then a golf buddy passed by. "Hey, Russ, that the new car you told me about?" He chuckled. "Where have you been with it? Out in the barnyard?"

I've got to restrain myself, he thought wildly. With great effort, he grinned at his friend, "It sure looks like it, doesn't it?"

The man nodded and laughed as he walked on.

"It does look like manure, doesn't it?" Russ asked, trying to keep the fury out of his voice. He felt he would burst with rage.

Fred frowned, studying it as he walked around to the passenger's side. "Do you have an enemy or two, Russ?" he asked, concerned.

"Not that I know of," Russ replied, feeling totally humiliated. "Do you think the stuff will come off?" he asked, inspecting the SUV, finding that it was covered all the way around with what looked like excrement.

"I don't know, Russ. But we've got to get to the airport. Worry about it later."

Russ' hand shook as he put the key in the ignition.

Fred noticed. "I think I'd like to drive to the airport, Russ. How about it?"

"Sure." He got out immediately and they exchanged places. "I thought you'd want to drive it anyway before you left."

During the drive, Fred extolled the virtues of the vehicle, asking him questions, aware of how upset Russ was, completely baffled about the incident himself. Just before they reached the airport Fred said, "I'm worried about these pranks, Russ. Find out who's doing them. It doesn't look good for the company to have one of their executives targeted like this."

"I will, Fred. You can be assured of that," he said, a little more venomously than he meant to.

"Take it easy, Russ. Be careful how you handle it."

"Oh, I will, Fred. I will. I don't want anything I do to reflect poorly on the company."

As he let Fred off at the curb, he thanked him for the visit and drove off, heading straight for his own garage. No way was he taking this to a car wash and be humiliated any more. He gripped the wheel and pressed the pedal. He was so full of blinding rage he didn't hear the siren behind him. It finally registered. "No. No!" he yelled as he slowed down and pulled over.

The policeman bent over. "Did you know you were going a hundred miles an hour?"

"I was?" Russ asked, unable to comprehend.

"Yes. May I see your driver's license?"

"Officer, I was racing to get home to get that damn stuff off my car. It may be eating the finish off!" he bellowed.

"I said, give me your driver's license."

"My driver's license?" he asked. "Oh, yes." He pulled it out and gave it to the policeman, his chest heaving.

When the procedure was over and the officer handed him the ticket, he pulled out carefully, and drove the speed limit all the way home, his hands tight on the wheel, his knuckles white. He was grateful that he lived in an area where the homes had garages behind the house. He braked to a stop and ran inside to change into work clothes.

Back out, he grabbed a hose, turned the water on full blast, and then squirted the car. Nothing came off. He tried again and again. Finally, he dropped the hose and went over to the green stuff and gingerly touched it. It was rubbery! It felt like the same stuff that had been put on his suit. He pulled on it and a strip came off. Fearfully, he studied the finish of the car. It hadn't hurt it. Relieved, he began pulling it off, but the stuff only came off in thin strips. It would take all afternoon!

He was still at it when Tiffany drove in at five-thirty. She stopped, staring at the scene before her. The hose was running, water was covering the driveway, and Russ was pulling something off his new car.

She got out nervously. Something was dreadfully wrong. "What is it, Russ?"

"Can't you see? Are you blind? Someone put crap all over my car while it was parked at the country club. Fred Reisner was with me. He saw it all."

"Fred was in town?"

"Didn't I just say so? Look at this."

Tiffany walked over and touched it. "What is it?"

"It's the same thing someone put on my suit coat, only a different color—a color made to look like horse manure!"

"Why?"

His eyes were wild and frightening. "Why? How would I know? What a stupid question."

"Who would want to do this to you?"

He stepped over to her menacingly. "That's what I want to know. Have any ideas?"

"Do you want me to help you get the stuff off?"

"No! I don't want you to touch my car."

"All right, I'll go start dinner." She quickly turned and walked through the water to the faucet, turned it off, and went into the house through the garage, shaking and fearful.

Casey developed the pictures she had taken Saturday,

anxious to see the man who had threatened to attack her. She studied the two pictures, and since he was bending over clutching his face, there wasn't much to see. Disappointed, she put them aside and left the dark room.

Her cell phone rang.

"Casey," her dad said, "Monty just reported another incident. I can tell you about it on the phone if you'd like."

"On the phone? Dad, I want us to meet together as we always have. That's part of the fun. I'm always free. I'll be over after dinner, unless Nan has offered to cook for us again."

"No, she hasn't. Come after dinner."

When the called ended, Casey frowned. Her dad didn't seem the same. *Something's wrong*, she thought.

Chapter Twenty-Seven

The ability to learn from others, no matter their age or station in life, requires humility.

Nan was dreading going over to Jake's. It had been terribly difficult to break the engagement. She hoped it would give Jake a wake-up call. But as time passed, she felt desolate and heartbroken. It had been eight days and he hadn't called once.

It had taken her until yesterday to finally realize that a relationship with Jake was not going to work. He had tried, but he was too set in his thinking and in his feelings about remarrying. She had cried more tears over Jake than she had over Chet's death. Her heart felt like it was being torn to pieces.

Today she realized she deserved a man who wanted to get married. If she were to remarry she needed a man who would love and cherish her with his whole heart, holding nothing back. Jake could have given her the kind of love she yearned for if only he'd had a happy marriage. Since that wasn't the case, her life had to go on without him.

Slipping on a blue scoop-necked denim dress with dolman sleeves and a generous cut skirt, along with her silver concho belt around her waist and silver earrings to match, she studied herself in the mirror, wishing she didn't want to look nice for Jake.

Shortly after Casey arrived at her father's, Nan arrived.

Jacob's heart was heavy with conflicting emotions as he greeted her at the door. It intensified when they entered the family room and he witnessed Casey's affection for her.

"Nan! It's good to see you."

Nan returned Casey's embrace and swallowed the lump in her throat. "It's good to see you too, Casey. I almost don't want our meetings to end," she whispered in her ear. Then looking at Jacob, she mustered her enthusiasm, "Well, let's hear the latest."

Casey's brows twisted in confusion when she saw that Nan didn't sit on the couch.

Pain clutched at Jacob's heart as he sat on the empty couch. He took a deep breath and cleared his throat. "Before I tell you the latest episode, I need to relate what Monty told me. He said from watching Russ, it was obvious that Russ was very proud of his car. He recently bought a Cadillac SRX and in the short time he's had it, he has taken it to an elite car wash and had it detailed twice. Monty said that it seemed to him that a fancy, expensive car was extremely important to Russ' image."

"I'm sure it is!" Casey stated emphatically. "It was to Nick. From what I've read, many abusers hide their insecurity behind their egoism and elitism."

Jacob nodded his agreement as he thought of Nick and then continued. "Apparently an executive from Russ' company was in town again and provided a good opportunity for Snard to do what he had been planning next. However, he said it was the trickiest to do because it was in the parking lot of the country club where people were coming and going.

Monty sat in a car nearby helping Snard watch for people who might notice what he was doing.

When he was through, he sat with Monty to watch the effect their efforts had on Russ. Jacob then explained what Snard had done to Russ' new car and then described Russ' expression of horror when he first saw it.

Casey clapped her hands. "Perfect! That would have sent Nick into a rage. His cars were his babies."

"That was certainly obvious to me, Casey," Jacob said and then continued. "I was concerned at first. I thought the stuff would cause damage to the finish of the car, but Monty assured me it wouldn't. However, it will take Russ a long time to get it off because it only comes off in thin strips."

"Even better!" Casey declared, smiling. "When are they going to do the next thing?"

"They plan to do it this week sometime. They'll let us know. They've done a good job for us. They deserve good pay."

"Dad," Casey began, "I need to know right away when they intend to do the next one. When I know, I'm going to suggest to Tiffany that she find a good excuse to go out of town."

"Good," Nan said, nervously wringing her hands.

It was then that Casey noticed her ringless left hand. "Nan, you aren't wearing your engagement ring."

She saw Nan glance uneasily at her father. "What's happened?"

"I broke our engagement, Casey. I'm sorry."

Casey's brows drew together in distress. "Why?"

Nan stood up. "I have to leave now. I'll let your father tell you."

Casey stood. "I'll walk you to your car, Nan, and you can tell me your side of the story first." She glanced at her father and saw misery written all over his face.

"All right. I'll see you, Jake." He simply nodded, unable to speak.

As they closed the front door behind them, Casey said, "Tell me everything, Nan."

They walked slowly to the car.

"Your father has been having a difficult time making himself set a date for our marriage. I pressed it and found out that he simply couldn't commit to a date. I'm not quite sure why. Apparently, he has built up a wall around himself, a wall stronger than he realized or he wouldn't have asked me to marry him. It wasn't till I pressed him that he realized something was bothering him. Please, Casey, don't worry about it. He loves me, but he's feeling relieved. Don't stress him over this."

Casey hugged Nan. "Thank you for telling me. I'll see you sometime this week. Good night."

Nan watched Casey walk toward the front door, determination in her straightened shoulders. "Please, Casey," Nan yelled, "don't push him. We can't marry." Turning and waving, Casey entered the house, leaving Nan in a state of concern.

Casey found her father pacing the family room when she entered. "All right, Dad, tell me your side of it."

Jacob sat down, placed his elbows on his knees, clasped his hands, and pressed them into his forehead. "Casey, I didn't break the engagement."

"Did Nan have a legitimate reason to break it?"

Despondently, he nodded. "I guess she did."

"Do you love Nan?"

"More than I thought I could love a woman again."

"Then why did you allow her to break the engagement?"

"I don't know why, but I couldn't make myself set a date. She had the right to give the ring back."

"Do you want to marry her?"

"Very much."

"Then why—"

"I don't know. Maybe it's fear, maybe I haven't dealt with issues I should have, I don't know."

"What are you going to do about it?"

"I wish I knew."

Casey's words were edged with desperation. "You've got to do *something*, Dad."

Jacob's voice rose. "Drop it, Casey!" Instantly he folded with regret. "I'm sorry, honey. I didn't mean to get angry."

"I know you didn't, Dad." Tears flooded her eyes. "I just wish you'd put the energy that you put into your work toward your own happiness."

Swallowing back emotion over losing Nan, Jacob got up and went over to his daughter and held out his arms. "Thank you for caring, sweetheart." Casey stood up and threw her arms around her father's waist, her wet cheek pressed against his chest. Father and daughter remained that way until their emotions subsided.

Chapter Twenty-Eight

Caring too much what people think cripples.

While getting dressed, Tiffany covertly watched Russ dress for work. He had been up most of the night cleaning his car, strip by strip. His bloodshot eyes darted around every little while, as if he were trying to think what he had to do next. His hand shook as he tried to knot his tie. She pretended not to notice. Anxious to leave his presence, she asked if he wanted any breakfast.

"What?" He couldn't seem to focus.

"Do you want breakfast?"

"Uh, no. I think I'll get a cup of coffee at work," he muttered. He began frantically searching for his car keys. "Where are my car keys?" he asked, eyeing her with suspicion.

"Did you leave them in the car?"

"No! I never do that."

"But anyone might forget if they wanted to hurry and get that gunk off their car."

He shoved her aside and went out into the garage. She heard him start the car and back out, relieved she had been right and he had gone.

Worry over Tiffany began to form in Casey's mind early Thursday morning and increased as the minutes ticked by. Promptly at nine o'clock she called her at work.

"I'm so glad you called, Casey," Tiffany said, her voice

breathless with anxiety. She briefly filled Casey in on all the more recent things that had been happening to Russ.

"I wonder who could be doing those things," Casey said.

"I don't know, but I'm really scared, Casey. I'm afraid Russ is losing control. Though he hardly knows I'm around lately, I'm planning to take your advice and get away. I called my mother. I told her for the first time that Russ is abusive and she's eager to help me. She's been ill so she's going to call tonight and ask Russ if I can come and help her through her illness. And, Casey, I can hardly believe it, but my father has stopped drinking and he too wants me to come."

The tight knot of worry eased inside Casey. "I'm happy for you, Tiff. When will you be leaving?" she asked, trying not to sound anxious.

"I've already called and reserved a flight for Saturday morning."

"Why not leave Friday?" Casey asked, knowing another episode was coming.

"I tried, but I couldn't get a flight at a decent hour."

"Would you please call me from your mother's when you get there? Maybe I had better have her phone number so I can call you if I need to."

"I'll call you, but here's her phone number."

"Be careful, Tiffany. I'm afraid I won't rest easy until you're on the plane and home."

"Thank you for being there for me, Casey. If you hadn't cared enough to push me, I don't know where I'd be today. I don't know when I would have admitted to myself that Russ was abusing me."

Driving to work on Friday morning, Russ frowned over the call he had received the night before from Tiffany's mother. At first, he was resentful that she would expect Tiffany to come out and help her, and then he decided that it would be a good time to have Tiffany out of the way for a while. He would have more freedom to come and go without questions. He could do what he had to do.

Since the car incident Tuesday, he had been trying to get back his equilibrium, and today he felt a little better, more in command. He prided himself that he had been able to put on a facade of normalcy at work. No one could tell how he was really feeling. He joked with the women and was businesslike with Norm.

Russ kept working steadily until noon. He stood up and stretched. Smiling, he thought of his Friday routine—lunch with Sheila, sleek blonde Sheila, after which they would check into a hotel for a couple of hours.

He left his office and stopped at Jeannie's desk. "I have a business lunch and some research to do after that. I'll be gone for several hours."

"All right, Mr. Eden."

They arrived at their usual meeting place, the Phoenician on Camelback Road. She always went in first and registered under a different name. Today, because of his uneasiness, he had asked her to order a meal brought up to the room.

Russ entered the lobby, and as usual sat down and paged through a magazine. After Sheila registered, she walked by him, surreptitiously whispered the room number, and then went up by herself. While waiting the usual twenty minutes before going up, he looked around nervously. He still wasn't himself. Taking a deep breath, he tried to immerse himself in the magazine.

"Excuse me sir," a voice behind him said.

Russ looked up, startled. He saw a homely looking hotel maid. "Wh-what? What do you want?" he asked impatiently.

"I believe you have something in your hair."

He blinked as if not comprehending, and then his hand flew

up to his head, feeling around. On both sides of his head near the top, it felt like two sticky lumps!

"I believe it's gum, sir," the maid said. "Move your hands and hold still please, I can get them out for you."

Stunned, he dropped his hands. He felt her doing something and by the time he could react, she was through. His hands shot up to his head. In utter disbelief, he realized the stupid airhead had cut them both out with scissors, leaving behind two large holes.

He jumped up, bursting with fury. "You stupid retard," he hissed at her back as she scurried away. "You left—"

Before he could say another word, she was out of the lobby, disappearing down the hall. He didn't dare go to the manager and complain. He didn't want to call attention to himself; he was married and an executive of Global Investments. Besides, he had two bald spots on his head. Like a searing fire, rage spread through his brain, his chest, his gut, through every muscle, every nerve, turning him into a bomb about to explode. It took every bit of will he had left to contain it long enough to cover both sides of his head and dash to the elevators.

Getting out on the second floor, he ran down the hall to the room and pounded on the door.

Sheila opened it and stepped back in shock at his red, distorted face. "Russ! What's the matter?"

He slammed the door shut and turned around, pointing to his hair. "That's what's the matter!"

Sheila sucked in a sharp breath. "How terrible! Those weren't there when I left you."

"I know!"

"B—but how . . . how—"

"I don't know! It happened so fast, I didn't realize what she was doing! A maid came up behind me and told me that I had something in my hair. I reached up and found two big wads of gum. I didn't feel anyone touching my hair! How could it have happened?" His eyes were so wide they almost bulged. He tried to shake his head—instead it only swayed, appearing punch-drunk. "How . . . how could someone have put gum in my hair?"

Frightened at the look in his eyes, at his actions, Sheila repeated dumbly, "Wads of gum?"

"Yes! Wads of gum!" he yelled.

Sheila backed away. She had never seen the suave, cool-headed Russ in this state.

"Wait a minute." His eyes darted back and forth. "I remember. A man stumbled over my feet and mumbled an apology. It must have happened then. There had to be two of them! One to distract me by stumbling over my feet while the other put gum in my hair!"

"You think someone put them there on purpose?" Sheila asked in disbelief.

"Of course, you stupid girl!"

"Russ, why are talking to me that way?" she whimpered.

He stared at her with an expression of contempt. "How could you think it was an accident!"

Not sure whether his look of malice was directed at her, she hesitantly asked, "Well, uh, why did you let the maid *cut* them out?"

"I didn't *let* her! It happened so fast I didn't know what she was doing!"

Sheila began to back away from him, not knowing what he might do.

"Do you have a mirror in your purse?" he asked, ignoring her reaction.

"Yes." She went over, picked it up, fished around for a few seconds, and handed the mirror to him.

He went into the bathroom and Sheila cautiously followed. Turning his back to the large mirror and holding the smaller one in front of him, he saw that the chunks of hair had been cut clear to the scalp! He let out a howl that could have been heard through the next three rooms.

"It's hideous," Sheila said in a whisper. "I can't imagine someone being that careless."

"Careless? That's hardly how I'd describe it. Revenge, that's what it is! And you call it careless?"

The venom in Russ' voice and the hate in his eyes heightened her fear. She tried to leave the bathroom, but Russ roughly shoved her, causing her to fall against the marble counter. Sheila grabbed her side in pain, shaking. Russ had never acted like this before. He was always the epitome of smoothness and charm, always calm and composed. Holding her side a moment, she knew she had to get out of there.

Slowly she edged herself out of the bathroom, picked up her purse, and moved toward the door, holding her breath. Russ didn't notice. He was still looking at the back of his hair through her mirror, muttering and rubbing the bare spots. "What am I going to do? What am I going to do? Someone has just ruined my hair! I'm ruined!"

Sheila had just unlocked the door and turned the knob when Russ stepped out and saw her.

"Where are you going!"

"I have to go, Russ," she muttered. She quickly opened the door and closed it before he could react, avoiding the threat she knew was on his lips. She ran down the hall, looking behind her every little while until she reached the elevator. It had been her lot to marry two violent men and she was terrified.

Russ glared at the door, spewing venom at the woman who had slammed it in his face. "No woman walks out on me and gets away with it!" he yelled. Benumbed yet frantic, he knew he had to get out of the hotel without being seen. The thought of someone seeing his hair paralyzed him for a moment. At last able to move, he went to the door, opened it, and peeked out. No one was in the hall. Stepping out cautiously, he moved quickly to the elevator, entered it, and pushed the button to the first floor. When the doors opened to the lobby someone was waiting to go up. He was paralyzed until he realized someone standing in front of him couldn't see the back of his head. He stepped out of the elevator, shoving his back against the wall. Looking around, he decided to go out the side entrance. He'd done that many times. Moving like a crab, the back of his head scraping the wall, he finally reached the exit. Once outside he assessed the situation. People were walking to their cars, others were getting out and going into the hotel.

Now his problem was twofold. He had to try to get to his car without anyone seeing the back of his head; equally important, he had to watch for someone who might be waiting to destroy him.

Anyone watching Russ as he moved erratically from the hotel to his car would have wondered if perhaps some strange disease of limbs or mind afflicted him, or if perhaps he were a demented ballet dancer who felt a compulsion to practice in a hotel parking lot. His head swiveled from side to side like that of a sailor lost in a trackless ocean, searching desperately for land. At times his steps were mincing, then long, with a sudden hopping dance sideways, facing first one direction then another, and the whole pageant was interspersed with occasional clumsy pirouettes.

When at last he managed to reach his car he let out a shuddering breath of relief. Backing out onto the street, he drove toward home as fast as he dared, his chest heaving with rage, fear, and humiliation.

The thoughts of leaving Russ had filled Tiffany with such fear she decided to change her ticket to Friday night late, even though she had to transfer several times to get to her destination. She had gone home early Thursday afternoon, packed, and placed her suitcases in the trunk so that she could leave for the airport directly from work and wait until the plane left.

She had called her mother and told her the change of plans. She was grateful that her parents had recently moved. Russ would have a harder time finding her. She had even asked her mother to call from some place he couldn't trace.

Before she left work Friday afternoon, she called Casey,

who sounded so relieved, it only added to Tiffany's nervousness.

At her studio, Casey idly picked up the picture she had taken of the man who had threatened her at South Mountain. "Maybe I should have this enlarged and give it and the negative to the FBI." Since she didn't have the sophisticated equipment necessary to both enlarge and enhance the picture, she decided to take it to a special lab. It was now late Friday afternoon. If she took it in right away she could pick it up Saturday morning.

On the way to the photo lab, her cell phone rang. Hoping it was from Nan or her Dad, she answered it.

"Casey," her dad said, "Monty has just filled me in on the latest and last episode. It's very important that I talk with you and Nan tonight, but you'll both have come to my office. I have to stay here tonight and do some things that can't wait. Is our usual seven o'clock all right with you?"

"Yes. Is Nan going to be there?"

"Yes."

"I'm glad this is the last, Dad."

"You'll feel even more so when you hear what I have to tell you."

"Uh-oh," she murmured, feeling more anxious already. "Let's hope it tips the scales in Tiffany's favor. See you tonight."

Tiffany, realizing she had forgotten a couple of things she wanted to take with her, drove back home after work. As the garage door opened, she was shocked and frightened to see that Russ was already home. She was about to back out and leave, but knowing he might have heard the garage door open, she decided to fake it somehow. Breathing in and out deeply to calm her racing heart, she left the garage door open and got out. Putting on as serene an expression as she possibly could, she entered the house. She could hear some movement, then a thud, then some movement. Fearfully, she walked through the main part of the kitchen and looked into the family room.

She gasped. Russ was storming around the room, banging his fists against the wall, the table, and anything he could find. "Russ?" He didn't hear her. "Russ?"

He turned to her. "It's about time you got home! Where have you been?"

"Russ it's only four. I usually get home at 5:30."

Russ looked at his watch. "Oh."

Trying to hold her voice steady, she asked, "Why are *you* home early?"

"Look!" he yelled, pointing to the back of his head. "See for yourself!"

Tiffany went over to him and tried to see. Sit down, Russ, I can't see it. You're too tall."

He planted himself on a footstool and Tiffany saw the two gaping bare places. "What . . . what happened to your hair?"

"What does it look like?"

"Russ, be calm and tell me."

He rubbed his brow and stared at the floor as if he were trying to think.

"I was sitting in the lobby of the Phoenician hotel when —"

"What were you doing there?" Tiffany asked suspiciously.

Russ looked at her, his face blank. "What? Uh . . . a business lunch. Don't interrupt me!" His wretched tale came tumbling out of his mouth in a torrent.

"Gum? I don't understand, Russ."

He shot to his feet and glared at her. "Do you think I do?"

"I wasn't there, I don't know."

He started pacing. His eyes glazed over, thinking. *Appearances! Appearances are the most important!* The voice seemed to roll through his head over and over till he felt like killing someone. He stopped and gazed wildly at his wife. "What am I going to do? What am I going to do?"

"Let me think, Russ. I know your hair is one of your nicest assets, so you don't want to shave your head, do you?"

"Shave my head?" he asked, incredulous. "That would look terrible!" Fear engulfed him at the thought. "I've got to think of something else. But what?"

How was she going to leave for the airport? Her mind flitted from one thing to the other, desperately trying to think of something. An idea came. "Why don't I go down to the department store and buy several kinds of hats for you to try on, the kind that would look all right to wear at the office."

He stared at her, blinked a few times as if it wasn't sinking in, and then his face brightened slightly. "You may just have come up with the right thing to do."

"Let's measure your head, Russ," she said. Going to the kitchen, she opened a drawer and retrieved a tape measure. He sat down and she measured. Picking up her purse, she said, "I'll be back as soon as I can, but remember, it's rush hour and I may have to go to more than one department store."

"All right, but hurry," he whined.

"I will," she replied, deciding the things she came for were unimportant. She had to get away from him as quickly as possible.

With Tiffany gone, Russ panicked. He prowled the room clutching his knuckles. He desperately needed something to calm his nerves, but the Pentad had warned him not to drink more than one small glass of liquor at any time. *Always being in control is one of the most important facets of appearance.* The infernal voice in his head drummed on and on, *Control . . . appearance . . . control . . . appearance.* Whose voice was it? It was his own! He went to the liquor cabinet. "I need something . . . to help me calm down." Pulling out a bottle, he opened it and gulped a swallow. He sat down on the couch and took another swig. "Calm . . . just a little relief."

It was a somber threesome who sat together in Jacob's office. Jacob sat at his desk with the other two facing him. The strain between Jacob and Nan was apparent and this dampened Casey's spirit. She had hoped they could patch things up before they met again.

"This last episode," Jacob began, "is going to hurt Russ Eden's ego for some time. Monty relished telling me every detail, so in turn I'll try to do the same for you." He did just that and then told them how it was accomplished in the hotel lobby, and how Russ reacted.

Casey and Nan reveled in the story. After all, this was one of the tricks they themselves had thought up and to have it done so cleverly by Snard, dressed up like a hotel maid, was hilarious to them.

"If you think that was funny," he said, "you both should have seen Monty actually imitate Russ out in the parking lot."

"Well, Dad . . . *you* imitate Monty."

"Hey, I'm not the actor Monty is. I'll try to tell you."

"All right, tell us; then show us."

"Apparently Russ' ego was so hammered he was on the ragged edge, fearful that someone in the parking lot would see his hair, and he also appeared to be terrified that someone would sneak up behind him and do him in."

Casey's eyes, blazing with eagerness, implored her dad. "Come on, Dad, you were always a ham for me growing up, remember?"

"But I didn't have an audience," he said, looking at Nan.

"I'm not an audience, Jake. I'm just Casey's conniving, plotting conspirator."

Jacob smiled. "All right. I'll get up and make a fool of myself for you." Scooting back, he stood up, pushed the chair inside the desk for more room, and imitated Monty's performance.

Casey and Nan's laughter turned hysterical, and soon they were wiping away tears. Jacob sat down and laughed with them. The laughter released the mounting tension generated by the questionable project, especially since this was the last of the episodes.

Casey was the first to speak. "If this had happened to Nick on top of everything else, I'm sure it would have pushed him over the edge. He would have been as fearful and skittish as a cat, and act every bit the blithering idiot Russ did. Now, I have some very good news. Tiffany will be leaving to go back East tonight. She had her mother call and ask Russ if she could come out for a short while and care for her while she was ill. He was resentful, but he said yes." Casey frowned. "He must have an ulterior motive to have allowed it. Nevertheless, she'll be out of his reach."

Jacob let out a huge breath of relief. "I can't tell you how glad I am to hear that, Casey. I know I've said this several times before, but I've felt responsible for Tiffany's safety."

"Yes, it is a relief to know that Tiffany's leaving," Nan said.

"Well, Dad," Casey said, getting up and going around the desk to hug him. "You did a great job for us and for Tiffany. Thank you."

He nodded and smiled.

Casey went to the door. "I've got to go. I'll see you both later." She left quickly, hoping Nan would stay a minute.

Nan got up. "I have to go too. You've been a good sport tonight," she said, smiling at his imitation of Monty.

"Would you stay a little while, Nan?" he asked, moving around the desk to where she was standing.

"Why?"

"I need your company."

"Chet needed my company too."

"Your company or your attention and service?"

"It doesn't really matter. I do have to go."

"Please, Nan, I've missed you. I've gone through twelve days of hell."

"Oh? If you had called and told me that a couple of days

after I returned your ring, I would have responded. Now we have nothing to talk about." She gazed into his troubled eyes. "Do we?"

"I have something to say. Will you listen?"

"I don't think there's anything you can say that will make a difference. When you didn't call, I was brokenhearted. Then I realized something. If I ever remarry it will be to someone who wants to get married, who wants me with all his heart, holding nothing back."

She turned to leave, but Jacob gripped her arm. "Do you suppose someone will come along who doesn't have some hang-ups?"

"Probably not. If no one comes along without the 'fear of marriage hang-up,' I'll remain single. Please let go of me, Jake."

"No. Not until I say a few things. Even though we're still relatively young, Nan, at our age who could either one of us meet that hasn't had trials, who wasn't a little set in their ways, not to mention who would likely have a number of children to complicate things?"

"You're right, Jake. So maybe neither one of us should expect to remarry."

Fear sliced through Jacob's heart. He wasn't making any headway. He hadn't expected such cold resistance. He let go of her arm and she turned to go. He spoke to her back. "I went to see a therapist this week. I'm trying to break down this . . . whatever it is that's holding me back." He noted that Nan had stopped, but her back remained to him. His hopes rose. "She told me that I needed to learn to trust again. I'm not sure the problem is trust, but something's in the way. Please, Nan, help me—and I promise you that if we get married, I'll love and cherish you because . . ." his voice broke, "because I already do. I want to love and cherish you the rest of your life—but only when I'm trustworthy."

The silence that followed seemed to echo through all the hollow, vacant places in their souls, leaving only the rhythm of heartbeats, the cadence of existing, not living—the void ahead for them without each other.

Nan slowly turned around; her heart felt compressed in a vise. Her lips trembled with words held back, words she didn't know how to say. Instead, she said, "I gave my heart to Chet. But after his death, I've doubted that any man was capable of loving me the way I could love him—until I met you. I know that you loved Silvia deeply, but she gave her heart to the opera. I know how painful that must have been for you because I experienced the same kind of pain in a small measure and in a different way. After he became incapacitated, Chet's heart was too bruised to be able to love me as he did in the beginning. He was ill for so long I even began to wonder if he ever loved me like I loved him." She paused.

They remained standing apart. Jacob had listened intently, hoping for words that would give him the permission to close the gulf.

"I'm glad you're seeking help, Jake. I hope you can conquer your problem. In the meantime, I'm going on with my life."

Jacob started to protest, but Nan held up her hands. "Jacob, I love you. But I'm determined to make a good life for myself without you."

Jacob's eyes, deep and searching, pleaded with hers while they stood apart—both afraid to move toward each other, neither having the courage to move away.

At length, Jacob spoke. "I don't think I can overcome my problem without your help, Nan."

"I can't help you, Jake. You're the only one who can do it. But *if* I tried to help you, could you promise me that you could overcome it?"

Jacob ran his hand through his hair, his brows furrowing. He wanted to lie and tell her yes. Instead, he replied almost inaudibly, "I wish I could promise that. How I want to promise that, but . . . I'm not sure at this point."

"That isn't enough for me, Jake. During our time apart, I've come to believe I deserve better."

"I know you do, Nan." He wanted to tell her how much he meant it, how wonderful she was, but what would it accomplish? "It's difficult to believe that we love each other and are standing on opposite sides of this terrible impasse."

"It seems we've come full circle to the way we were up at the cabin, having made no progress at all—except for the painful realization that we love each other and still have to say goodbye. Good night, Jake," she said, opening the door.

Jacob moved toward her.

"Please, Jake, don't walk me out. It's hard enough to leave you as it is."

Chapter Twenty-Nine

How much more grievous are the consequences
of our anger than the acts which arouse it.
—Marcus Aurelius

Saturday morning, Casey got up early, did her water therapy, and then showered and ate breakfast. During all of it she thought of Tiffany's call from her parents' house last night, telling her what happened to Russ' hair and that she had managed to get to the airport safely. Tiffany related how protected and loved her parents made her feel when they greeted her. This morning, as she thought of Tiffany's call and all the events leading up to it, she wept. They had been successful and her prayers had been answered.

She needed to call her Dad and Nan and tell them the good news. She felt overwhelmingly grateful when she thought of the part they had played in rescuing Tiffany. She simply couldn't have done it alone.

While in this emotional state, she couldn't shake the feeling that she should look closer at the picture of the man who had tried to attack her. At nine o'clock she got into her car and left for the photo lab to get the enlargement.

Russ Eden awoke at seven thirty with the sun shining in his face. He sat up suddenly and then grabbed his head. It hurt like fury. "What happened?" His dazed mind groped for answers. He saw that he was fully clothed; then he saw the empty liquor bottle lying on the floor. He sat there, his mind foggy. Finally, he stood up carefully and walked into the kitchen to find Tiffany. Not finding her, he went into the bedroom and saw the bed made but no Tiffany. "She must have gone to work," he muttered as he went into the kitchen for a cup of coffee. He sat down on a bar stool, still fuzzy, and then he remembered with horrifying clarity.

"My hair!" His hands flew up to his head. "It wasn't a nightmare, it's real!"

He stared into space, thinking, trying to remember. "Yes, Tiffany went to the department store to buy me a hat. Where is it? I need to wear it to work … Wait a minute. It's Saturday," he said, feeling great relief. "So where's Tiffany?" he muttered. "She usually sleeps late on Saturday." He got up quickly, grabbed his head in pain, and went back into the bedroom. He opened her closet door and saw that quite a few clothes had been taken out. He looked for her luggage and found it gone. Oh yes, he remembered now. *She had a flight out to go help her mother. But that was this afternoon. I'm sure of it!* Suspicion began to gnaw at his insides. *She didn't buy me a hat, she didn't leave me a note telling me anything . . . nothing about the hat, nothing about leaving early!*

He went into the kitchen and looked up her mother's phone number and called. The number had been disconnected. He started shaking with fury. "No woman ever leaves me and gets away with it!" Yelling only hurt his head more. He needed some coffee. "My nerves are shot," he moaned.

Moving around carefully, he finally got the coffee made. He sat down gingerly and sipped his coffee until he finished the first cup. Then he poured another and drank it. Feeling a little better, he headed for the shower, trying to think what to do next.

When he got out, he was like a man possessed—his mind focused only on one thing, his glazed eyes seeing only that one thing. He calmly shaved and then threw on jeans and a knit shirt; he knew where he was going to get some answers. Combing his luxurious dark hair, noticing how nice it looked from the front, rage filled him again. Grabbing his canvas hat and dark glasses, he went to the garage, got into his car, and drove off.

from the front, rage filled him again. Grabbing his canvas hat and dark glasses, he went to the garage, got into his car, and drove off.

Casey paid the photographer and pulled out the enlargement. She studied it closely. The man was standing so that she could see only the left side of him. His hands were covering his bearded face. She studied his one arm, *and* then her eyes slid down to his jeans, then to his hiking shoes. Was it the same man who had banged on her studio door? The others were clean shaven. Were there two men, or was there only one who disguised himself?

Looking at him from the top again, she noticed his left hand, the one she could see. He was moving, so both pictures were not completely clear, but one was a little better, so she studied that one. Was there something on his hand? "Do you have a magnifying glass," she asked the photographer.

"Sure. Here it is, ma'am."

"Thank you." She looked at his hand and saw what looked like a small scar. She frowned and handed the glass back to the man. "Thanks."

Getting into her car, she had a nagging feeling that there was a clue in the picture, but what was it? She drove toward home, thinking and feeling uneasy, but soon told herself it was simply because she had been looking at the man who had frightened her so terribly.

When she arrived at the garage, she waited in front of it, not opening the door, about to change her mind, go to her Dad's to find out if he and Nan had resolved anything, and tell them the good news about Tiffany. Deciding to go later, she pushed the garage door opener, drove in, and then pushed it to close. It closed partway and then went up again.

She pushed it again, and once more it closed partway and then went back up. She rolled down the window and looked out to see if something was blocking it, when a man wearing a canvas hat and dark glasses appeared.

She let out a small scream. "Who are you?"

"Where's Tiffany?" he asked in a deep, somewhat guttural but angry voice.

"Tiffany?" Casey's heart almost stopped. "Are . . . are you her husband, Russ?" she asked, her eyes probing his face.

"Yeah, I am. Where is she?"

Knowing his unbalanced state, Casey could scarcely breathe. "Why would you come here to ask *me?*"

"Because Tiffany can't hide anything from me. I followed her when she went to lunch with you."

Fear almost choking her, she forced her voice to sound calm, "Russ, I don't know where Tiffany is. I haven't seen her in weeks."

"I don't believe you. Where is she?" he asked again, still in the same guttural, gravelly voice. Russ began moving slowly toward Casey's open window.

Something clicked in Casey's mind. *That voice sounds familiar. Where have I heard it?* "How would I know where she is?"

Putting his right hand on the seat back, the fingers of his left hand wrapping around the steering wheel, Russ leaned in, his face in hers.

Casey stared at Russ' hand still wrapped around the steering wheel. Something was familiar. *It was a small scar!* She had seen a scar in the pictures she had developed. Her breathing grew shallow. *Is Russ the man who attacked me in the desert?*

"Get out. We're going into the house."

Her mind raced frantically. Swiftly she put the key in the ignition and turned it, while her left hand started rolling up the window.

With lightening speed, Russ grabbed her left hand and at the same time reached for the car keys, turning them off. "You're not going anywhere. Get out!"

Casey's heart plummeted. "Russ, why are you doing this? I can't help you find Tiffany."

"I said, get out!"

"All right," she gasped. Opening the door, she shoved it against him as hard as she could. He fell against the shelves, striking his head. She tried to run to the open garage door, screaming, "Help! Help!"

He grabbed her arm, but she shook free from the dazed man. While moving around the car, she pulled over a small ladder into his path, tripping him. As he was trying to stay upright, she reached the door to the house, stepped in and almost slammed it shut. Throwing his weight against the door just before it closed, he sent Casey flying backwards onto the floor.

He hovered over her menacingly. "You can't hurt me and get away with it. Do you hear?" he asked, pulling her roughly to her feet and painfully gripping her arm. "Move!"

Her heart pounding in her ears, she moved numbly from the kitchen into the small connecting family room.

"Sit down!" He shoved her onto the couch.

"Russ," she managed to gasp out, trying to placate him. "Tiffany showed me your picture. She was so proud of you. Surely, she'll call you soon and let you know where she is."

A grimace of a smile came across his face. "She did, did she? If she was so happy, why did you and she plot to ruin me?"

Could Russ have found out that I was behind the pranks? she frantically asked herself. *There's no way. Or is there?* Her fear mounted. "What are you talking about, Russ? Please, let's talk about it reasonably!"

"Reasonably? I've read the papers about you. You're a kook. You killed your husband," he stated in a gravelly tone.

"That's not true. Besides what does my accident have to do with finding Tiffany?"

"Tiffany? I don't care about Tiffany," he stated with antipathy.

Casey could scarcely catch her breath. *He must know I'm responsible for everything!* Her voice came out barely audible. "Then why are you here asking about her?"

An ugly chuckle came from deep down in his throat. "Lift up your pant leg. I want to see that burned leg of yours."

"Wh . . . why?"

His face twisted with anger. "I said lift up your pant leg!"

Desperately trying not to let him know how frightened she was, she took a deep breath and as calmly as she could, lifted her pant leg only part way.

"Lift it higher!"

Fearfully wondering where this was leading, she did as he asked. Russ removed his dark glasses and studied her leg up and down. A harsh, ugly laugh erupted from his throat. "It's even more ghastly than I thought it would be."

Casey was shocked at his cruelty and looked up into his eyes, free of dark glasses for the first time. She was startled— then terrified. Those were *Nick's* eyes! She would never forget those malevolent eyes as long as she lived! Then something came into her consciousness. It was the change in Russ' voice from guttural and gravely to normal. She could never forget that voice! *Nick's voice! But it can't be!* she screamed in her head. *It can't be! Nick is dead!* Her heart beat against her rib cage so violently she could scarcely take in a breath. She stared at his arms. Of course. They were familiar too. *They're Nick's arms! How can that be? He died in the fire. They found his body!* Finally, she realized he had been watching her closely, a self-satisfied smile on his face.

"It's nice to know you haven't forgotten me, Casey."

"N—Nick?" she stammered.

"Yes, it's me, Nick."

"No! Nick died in the fire!"

"I planned the accident. I wouldn't let myself die. I'm too clever, Casey."

Her breathing was erratic; her words came out in a voiceless whisper. "Why . . . why did you want to kill me?"

"You should have known you could never get away from me. No woman leaves me! That's what you were planning to do wasn't it?"

The fear she felt when she thought he was Russ had turned into a terror of such magnitude, she began hyperventilating. The room whirled, and everything went black. Someone was shaking her and a voice far off was yelling at her.

"Wake up, Casey! I'm not letting you off that easy. I want you awake when I kill you." He yanked her to a sitting position and pulled a gun from his pocket.

Casey numbly stared at the gun. It didn't seem real. She was just reliving the nightmare.

Nick Carter was furious. "What's the matter with you, Casey? Wake up! Where's the strong-willed Casey? The independent Casey?" A derisive laugh erupted from his throat. "She's shaking! Like a frightened little rabbit. That's what she is, a scared rabbit!"

Casey blinked. It was real. Nick was alive, and he was right there in front of her! And he was going to succeed in killing her this time!

He smiled. "That's better. I want you totally aware when—"

Dear God, help me! Casey prayed. The panic receded slightly and her breathing became calmer and so did her voice. "That's the gun they couldn't find in the ashes."

"Smart girl."

"How are you going to get away with killing me this time, Nick?"

His smile was diabolical. "Maybe you're going to commit suicide with it."

Casey's mind raced. At one time she had wanted to disable Nick emotionally, and they had succeeded in disabling him as Russ. A thought came to her. Somehow she'd take advantage of that now. She smiled seductively. "Why would I want to do that when I'm with such a handsome man?"

The remark startled him. "What are you talking like that for?"

"I was always attracted to you, Nick. You know that."

The smile left his face.

"Are you attracted to my new face?" he yelled.

"It's your charismatic eyes and voice I'm attracted to. I could grow used to your new handsome face."

For a moment Nick forgot what he was going to say and looked pleased; then he looked confused. "Wait a minute. You're not going to manipulate me. It's your fault my face got burned! You shoved the container of gasoline toward me and the flames from your pants shot up into my face. It hurt like hell and you're going to pay for it!" His anger shortly subsided into satisfaction. "However, *my* burns were first degree with only patches of second degree." His smile was ugly. "You were supposed to die, Casey. You found out too much. I left that envelope on the table remember?"

"I didn't have time to even look at the papers I pulled out of that envelope. You returned too quickly. You went through all that for nothing."

One of Nick's eyes twitched at the thought, almost believing her for a fraction of a second. "No I didn't, because I don't believe you! Anyway, you were getting out of hand, Casey. I couldn't control you. You would have tried to leave me, so I'm going to kill you now and make it look like suicide."

Terror rose up in her throat, but she kept praying. "You won't get away with it, Nick."

"Oh yes I will. Now with your fingerprints on the gun, the gun they didn't find, they'll know you murdered your husband."

"You're probably right, Nick. You were always clever, but would you answer some questions first?" she asked.

"What questions?"

"Have you been following me? Stalking me?"

A smile slid over his face. "Yeah. Did it scare you?"

"Yes, it did." *No wonder I had such an ominous feeling!* she thought. To buy time, she asked him about each incident.

He admitted to all of them.

"And there were other times you didn't know about. It became one of my hobbies. I had a great time. I rented the black car—even the red junk heap I was in behind your studio. I scared you when I banged on the door, didn't I?"

"Yes, Nick, you scared me. Does that make you happy?"

"It sure does." Then his face changed and his eyes burned into hers. "But, Casey, you still intrigue me. I haven't been able to get you out of my system. Your friend Tiffany is insipid compared to you."

"Why did you marry her then?"

"Because I needed a wife for appearances and she's beautiful. But you know," his eyes glazed over, "now that I think about it—your short hair is disgusting, and your leg is gross. It's going to be easier to kill you this time."

She saw his finger tighten on the trigger. Her heart stopped, and then just as suddenly, her mind cleared. "Wait! Your fingerprints are all over the gun. You're not wearing gloves. And here I thought you were always so sharp and mentally aware at all times. You're losing it, Nick."

"What? I . . ." His eyes darted around. "Gloves? I'll wipe my fingerprints off and place the gun in your hand." He raised his hand and pointed the gun to Casey's head. "Turn your head," he said shoving it to one side with the gun.

"But, Nick, that's my left side," she said calmly. "I'm right handed. You're not thinking. You're flipping out big time."

"Stop saying that!" he yelled. "I'm in perfect control!"

"No you're not, Nick. Where's your cool composure? If only people could see you now—making careless mistakes, yelling."

"Shut up! Do you hear me?"

"Your perfect image is gone, Nick. People will know that it was all an illusion—that you're one big fake, a big liar." Casey watched Nick's face turn red with rage, but she kept on, counting on his impaired state of mind to give her an advantage. "People will learn that underneath that impeccable appearance, there's only a shaking, fearful coward of a man who is only brave enough to hurt women."

"Shut your mouth! I'll show you who's composed and in

control. Turn your head the other way!"

From the corner of her eye Casey saw a form rush across the room. The gun flew out of Nick's hand. Someone had a stranglehold around his neck. Other men entered, holding guns on him.

"Wh—What's this?" croaked Nick, the whites of his eyes giving him a crazed look.

Before Casey knew what was happening, someone was pulling her up from the couch and holding her tightly against him. "It's all right, Casey, it's all over. You're safe now."

She couldn't see who it was but the voice was familiar. "Syrus?"

"Yes," he said, "it's all over."

She pulled away from him. "Wh—What are *you* doing here?" she gasped, her heart still drumming painfully against her chest.

"I work for the FBI."

Casey's head rocked back and forth in shock and confusion.

"The FBI? No one knew about me!" shrieked Nick.

"Tape that man's mouth shut!" Syrus ordered. "Take him into the kitchen area and keep him there until I tell you differently."

All the reserve Casey's prayers had given her disappeared and she began breathing rapidly. "Nick isn't dead, Nick is alive." Her voice rose almost to hysteria. "That's Nick! Nick's alive!" She shook violently and began hyperventilating.

Syrus, still holding her, helped her stay on her feet. "Breathe deeply, Casey. Breathe deeply."

She tried. The short rapid breaths gradually became slower and then deeper. Syrus continued to hold her tightly until the dizziness left, until she became more stable.

Jacob suddenly appeared. "Casey! Casey, you're all right." He grabbed her and hugged her, tears of relief brimming in his eyes.

"Dad! Why are you here . . . I mean, how did you know?"

"The FBI called me and told me to get here quickly." Fear lingered on his face. "But they wouldn't let me inside until they were sure that Russ Eden had been captured," he said, glancing at the bound man. "I was terrified for your safety, Casey."

Casey, still confused by Syrus' arrival just in time to save her life, stared at him with incredulous eyes. "Did you call Dad?"

"I had one of my men call him."

Syrus held out his hand to Jacob. "I'm Syrus Avery Rothman, alias Syrus Tucker. I'm very glad to meet you, sir."

"You're Syrus Tucker? Casey's boss?"

"I *acted* as Casey's boss," he said, looking at Casey and smiling, "or should I say whipping boy?"

All Casey could do was stare up at him, her eyes wide, her mouth open, still shaking inside and out.

"Mr. Jacobson," said Syrus, pointing to the connecting kitchen area, "I'd like to introduce you to Russ Eden."

Jacob, still holding onto his daughter, moved over to him and studied him, saw his malevolent eyes, his hate. He felt Casey tremble.

"Take off his hat, Dad, and let's look at the damage."

Nick squirmed spasmodically.

"Turn him around," Jacob said to the men holding him. When they did so, Jacob lifted his hat. Jacob and Casey stared at the grievous sight.

"He did a good job, Case," Jacob said quietly.

"He did, didn't he? But, Dad, look carefully," she said, her anxiety level rising. Do you see blond roots?"

"Blond roots?"

Nick's breathing turned into heavy snorting.

Syrus looked at Casey, stupefied. "You're responsible for that?"

Casey, holding on to her dad for support, nodded, waiting for a reprimand.

Instead, Syrus said, "Turn him back around, boys. Mr. Jacobson, I want you to meet Nick Carter, alias Russ Eden."

"Nick Carter?" Jacob stared disbelievingly at the wild-eyed man. "It can't be. Nick is dead! Besides, it doesn't look like him."

Casey let go of her father and leaned against a counter for support. "Dad, he's had plastic surgery because his face got burned. And he dyed his hair dark brown."

Furious grunts issued from Nick's throat. Syrus grabbed his shirt, his eyes spewing lightning, his voice menacing. "Shut up. Don't make another sound, don't even swallow."

Nick's eyes were slits of hate.

"Did you hear me?" he asked, grabbing his shirt again.

Nick's head bobbed up and down, the whites of his eyes framing his irises.

Jacob studied him intently. "Nick?"

The cuffed and taped man refused to respond.

Syrus gave him a shake. "Answer him."

Nick quickly wobbled his head up and down.

"Nick Carter?" Jacob asked again, still in a state of shock.

Again, Nick nodded, his eyes darting with panic.

Jacob's breathing became heavier and heavier. "You caused the accident."

Nick's chin lifted, his eyes full of hatred.

Syrus grabbed his jaw, his fingers digging into his cheeks. "Don't ever look at Mr. Jacobson like that again. Do—you—understand?" Nick shook convulsively. "Answer everything he asks you or I might look the other way and let Mr. Jacobson's knuckles do the job next time."

"You caused the accident." Jacob repeated. Nick's eyes turned glassy and gave a slight nod. "You intended to *kill* her?"

There was a slight hesitancy, but he nodded.

Jacob's eyes impaled him. "You caused her leg to be horribly burned and slashed and broken?"

Nick's eyes darted around. His whole body twitched, his head jerked.

Jacob's eyes didn't leave Nick's face. His fists clenching, his jaw rippling, he began trembling with anger and a pent-up desire for vengeance. The air was electric during the long and tense silence. The only sound was the choking, rasping breathing coming from Nick's throat. Finally, closing his eyes to the sight of the pitiful man, Jacob pressed his fists hard against his brow. His trembling shoulders began to shake convulsively as his chest heaved spasmodically. Gradually, little by little, muscle by muscle, Jacob went limp. His hands fell to his sides, his shoulders slumped, and his head dropped to his chest.

Casey threw her arms around her father's waist.

Jacob enfolded his daughter in his arms and for a few moments they clung to each other, trembling.

Syrus watched father and daughter, grateful that he could be a part of apprehending the man who had hurt them both.

At length, Jacob reached for Syrus' hand, holding it in both his. "How can I ever thank you for saving my daughter's life?"

Syrus smiled. "There's no need to, sir. She's one amazing girl. She handled this man well. We overheard how she got him to confess."

He stepped over to Nick and smiled. "Nick, ol' boy, you thought *you* were in control? Casey was the one in control all along. You're not man enough to handle a woman like her." A guttural noise from Nick's throat protested. "By the way, you're under arrest for murder and two counts of attempted murder, as well as a laundry list of other crimes." Then Syrus read him his rights.

Nick's head jerked backward, his breathing heavy.

Casey gasped and stared at Nick. "Murder?" Her face paled. She turned to Syrus. "Oh yes," she said almost in a whisper, "the remains of the body that was found."

Nick grunted ferociously.

Syrus' face leaned close to Nick's. "I said shut up." Syrus went to the back door and held it open for the SWAT team. "Take him out, boys." Shutting the door behind them, he returned to Jacob and Casey. "I need to meet with you both," he said to Jacob. "When will be a good time?"

"Anytime. We have a lot of questions we need answered." Jacob replied. "As soon as possible. Tonight?"

"Tonight at seven o'clock will be just right for me. Where would you like it to be, Mr. Jacobson?"

"Is my home all right?"

"Yes it is."

"Let me give you my address."

"I know where you live. I've followed Casey there several times."

"You have?" Casey asked, still numb with shock. "In—uh—your blue truck?"

Syrus smiled. "No, in a nondescript FBI car."

"I knew something was suspicious about you."

Syrus nodded. "Yes, you knew."

"Casey," Jacob said, "you're going home with me." She didn't resist.

As the three of them started out, Casey's leg buckled and Syrus caught her and lifted her into his arms. He could feel the spasms in her leg, the trembling of her body as he carried her to her father's car.

Chapter Thirty

*The cost of victory is never
counted, only suffered.*

Jacob drove into his garage and walked around the car to carry Casey in.

"I can walk in myself, Dad," Casey insisted.

"You probably can, honey, but let me carry you this once. You let Mr. Rothman carry you." He smiled.

"I didn't have a choice. He caught me as I started to fall. I'm all right now. I'll hang onto your arm."

"All right." He held out his arm. When she took hold, he could feel the weight of her body as she struggled to walk. Together they made their way out of the garage and into the kitchen. "You've done amazingly well, Casey. I'm feeling totally wasted and shaken up."

The memory of his terror choked Jacob. Silently, he led his daughter to the couch in the family room, propped her up with pillows, and rested her legs upon it. "Can I get you anything to eat or drink?"

"No thanks. I couldn't swallow a thing. Oh, Dad . . . Dad, can you believe it? That Russ Eden was . . . is Nick?"

Jacob shook his head. Casey trembled. "He . . . he tried to kill me again." She covered her face and sobbed. Jacob knelt beside her and held her in his arms. It was some time later before either could speak.

Casey's sobs eased into silent tears. "Dad, it was so pathetic. Even though Nick was bound and gagged, he was still arrogant, but even his arrogance and anger couldn't hide what was left of him after his facade was stripped away. It left him naked for all to see what he really was—a weak, fearful, cowering man." Her chest heaved with dry spastic sobs, and then her whole body, from her shoulders to her toes, quivered.

Jacob became concerned. "I know, honey. It was terrible to see, but try to let go and relax. Let's be grateful he's in the hands of the FBI and won't be able to hurt anyone again."

Casey silently nodded and gradually, the quivering of her muscles lessened until at last she lay quiet.

Encouraging her to lie flat, Jacob put a small throw blanket over her legs. He knelt beside her, placing a comforting hand upon her arm. She closed her eyes. In the safety of her father's presence, she soon fell into forgetful asleep.

Jacob sat in a chair and watched her. Then choking back emotion, he bowed his head and thanked God for saving his daughter's life.

Casey's nap was short but effective. Jacob took her home and waited while she packed a small bag so she could stay with him over the weekend. Casey was grateful she didn't have to be alone. She was still trembling inside over the frightening and unbelievable events which led to Nick's resurrection.

Back at her father's house, still in shock, Casey moved slowly and methodically about in her old room, unpacking her bag and trying to absorb the events of the last several hours. She undressed and took a warm bath, trying to loosen the tight muscles in her neck and shoulders.

In his office, Jacob was making plans. He dialed Nan's number, hoping she was home. Relieved, he heard her warm hello.

"Nan, this is Jake."

"Yes, Jake. Is something wrong?"

Surprised he asked, "Why do you ask that?"

"There was something in your voice."

"You're amazing, Nan. Everything is all right but something very frightening has happened. Casey was almost killed." He heard Nan gasp. "I would like you to come over tonight. They've arrested Russ Eden and an FBI man is coming over to answer our questions. You need to be here."

"Of course I do! I'm part of it all."

"Thank you. Come over around 5:30. The man from the FBI is coming over at seven."

After her long soothing bath, Casey put a yellow A-line batiste skirt that reached her ankles and a boat-necked, cap-sleeved blouse to match. Then she slipped on white sandals. She looked into the mirror with her swollen eyes. There was no sparkle, nothing. "I'm a sight."

Going over to her bed, she pulled a pillow out and curled up around it to rest and think. Before a thought could enter her mind she was asleep again.

Jake's heart bolted when he heard the doorbell chimes at five-thirty. He opened the door to a somber-looking Nan. He gave her an encouraging smile. "Hey, all's well now, Nan. Don't worry." He took from her hands a ceramic pot full of something warm that smelled wonderful.

"I don't know if you and Casey have eaten, but I brought some vegetable soup for you now or tomorrow."

"That sounds great. We haven't even thought of food."

Nan followed him into the kitchen.

Jacob set the soup down on the bar. "Let's eat here."

"By all means. Let's make it easy."

"Hello, Nan," Casey said as she entered the kitchen. "Something smells good."

Nan noticed the lack of vibrancy in Casey's voice. She went over to her and put her arms around her. "Casey, oh Casey." She looked into her face. "I don't know what happened, but your dad said you could have been killed."

Casey nodded, giving her a feeble but reassuring smile. "But I was saved by things happening in what can only be described as an amazing way. I think someone was looking after me—us."

"I'm so grateful. I desperately want to hear what happened, but you and your dad had better eat first."

Huddled together in the family room, Casey, feeling stronger after the nourishing soup, faced her dad and Nan, who tonight were sitting on the couch together. In a subdued voice, she began relating the events from the beginning, telling them for the first time about the stalker.

"A stalker?" Jacob asked. "Casey! Why didn't you tell me about this?

"There was no need, Dad. I kept the FBI informed. If they couldn't do anything, what could you have done?" She related each incident, ending with the last frightening one when she sprayed Mace into his face and took his picture. Unable to make herself look at her Dad's face, she only looked at Nan. "I had the pictures developed and blown up, which revealed something on his hand. I felt it was important but didn't know why."

Since her dad hadn't as yet heard it all either, Casey began relating all the events in sequence, starting with the garage door not closing. She saw Nan's shocked expression and her dad's tortured one. And in the retelling of it, the fear became more than a memory to Casey and she had to stop and catch her breath. "I saw on Russ' hand what I saw in the picture. A scar. It was then I knew he was the one who had been stalking me and I was scared that he had somehow found out we were behind all the pranks that had been bedeviling him."

Casey continued, telling Nan about the chase into the kitchen and the events that followed. "In my fright, it took me a long time to remember that emotionally Russ had been compromised and that I could use it against him." Then Casey disclosed the most shocking news of all.

Nan was dazed. "Russ is . . . is Nick Carter?" she asked. "How can that be? You mean all those times we were wishing it was Nick we were doing those things to, it really was? That Russ Eden *was* Nick Carter?" She had to repeat it to believe it. In her anxiety, she had taken hold of Jacob's arm. All through Casey's account, she had clung to him, reacting with muffled sounds of fear. "Thank goodness you're safe!" she cried.

Casey told her in touching detail about her father's reaction when he learned that Russ was Nick. Soon, Nan covered her face, her shoulders shaking. Jacob took this opportunity to put his arm around her and hold her close, realizing how much he truly loved this remarkable woman.

Casey watched and waited, feeling emotionally spent. When Nan had gained her composure, Casey continued. "Here's another surprise, Nan. The man I worked with, in effect, my boss at Hartner and Hart, was a man named Syrus Tucker. I don't know why, but from the moment he began working there, we butted heads. I'm afraid I've given him a hard time, and he's been pretty rough on me. Well—it turns out, he really isn't the graphics director. He works for the FBI. He came into the house with the men who grabbed Nick. He was the one who pulled me up off the couch, held me so tightly I could hardly breathe, and told me it was all right—that I was safe."

Nan shook her head in confusion. "I don't understand. The FBI man acted as a Hartner and Hart graphics director?"

"Yes, and he was awfully good at it. Syrus is the one who's coming over here tonight to answer our questions. His real name is Syrus Avery Rothman."

Nan had noticed how weary Casey's voice was as she related the events and explained everything, but when she talked about Syrus, her voice sounded more vibrant. "This is all so strange and unbelievable," Nan responded.

"Yes, it is," Jacob agreed. "We hope to understand it better when Mr. Rothman arrives."

Nan got up and moved around and then crouched in front of Casey. "How do you feel, having been able to play all those pranks on the man who was so cruel to you and hurt you so horribly?"

"I've been surprised at myself. As I think about it, I should really enjoy it, gloat over it, feel great elation over it. But, Nan, our pranks really did unbalance him. He wasn't the same Nick who was always so smooth, calm, and composed in public. What we did actually sent him over the edge. I just feel numb. I can't absorb it all. When Nick was bound and gagged, I should have felt pity for him, but I was still afraid. Then the fear turned to disgust over his angry and defiant eyes, his piti-ful snorting and grunting."

"Did you see his hair?"

"Yes. I made sure that Dad took off Nick's hat. It really did look dreadful. But, Nan, it was . . . it was pathetic. He was pathetic. All I can think of now is how tragic it is that Nick chose to use his talents in such evil ways. He had so many gifts that could have made him a leader in anything he chose to do. He drew people to him. He had charisma . . . he was witty and smart. But without the ability to love or even feel for others, it didn't mean anything. I can't gloat over what we did to him. It seems like I should have had at least a momentary feeling of triumph, but I didn't." Her face looked troubled. "And even with the tragedy of it, I can't feel pity for him. Maybe someday I'll be able to, and maybe—"

The doorbell chimed. "You know Mr. Rothman, Casey, why don't you answer it?" her father suggested.

"No, Dad. I don't want to."

"All right." Jacob got up and left the room. He opened the door to the tall, dark-haired man whom he had met earlier. "Come in, Mr. Rothman."

"Thank you, sir."

Syrus held out his hand to shake Jacob's. "Again, I can't tell you what a pleasure it is to meet Casey's father. She's a most unusual young woman."

Jacob smiled. "Thank you. That she is. Come in."

They entered the family room and Jacob said, "Nan, I'd like you to meet Mr. Syrus Rothman."

"Please, everyone call me Sy or Syrus."

"All right, Syrus," Jacob said. "I would like you to meet Nan Hunter."

Nan got up and went to him, holding out her hand, shaking it with enthusiasm. "I'm so glad to meet the man who saved Casey's life."

"Thanks, but she had a big hand in saving herself. Now, I'm sure you have a few questions to ask me."

"Have a seat, Syrus," Jacob said.

"Thanks." The chair he sat in faced the couch and the other chair in the conversational grouping, making it easy to converse.

Casey stared at this man who now seemed like a stranger. He was wearing a charcoal black suit, white shirt, and a conservative tie. "Why the suit, Syrus?" she asked. "You've never worn one at the office."

Jacob was surprised at his daughter's blunt question.

Syrus smiled. "I wear this under duress. I'm in FBI Special Operations. I'm required to wear one, unless I'm on special assignment." He winked at Casey "Like, uh . . . head graphics man at Hartner and Hart."

"But . . . but," stammered Casey, trying to reconcile these two different personalities, "I don't understand. How could you have been so good in that position?"

"I'm sorry, Casey, that's a question you'll have to ask my superior. He's flying into Phoenix for the case and he'll meet with you. He knows you'll have some questions that I'm uncomfortable answering. His name is Robert Welles, the man you've had to keep informed of what was happening."

He looked deep into Casey's direct blue eyes. "The first thing I want to say is there never was an actual indictment hanging over your head. It had to appear that way for reasons I'll explain to you shortly. You're free. You have your life back."

He smiled, his eyes still holding hers.

Casey's head shook slightly, the expression on her face was one of incredulity. "Really? There *never* was a real indictment?"

"No."

"Why then," Jacob asked angrily, "did they have to put her through all that for so long?"

"I can understand your anger, Mr. Jacobson, but keeping it a secret meant capturing a powerful syndicate that used people like Nick to launder huge sums of money and who didn't stop at murder. Yours and your daughter's suffering wasn't in vain, I assure you. It may have saved many lives."

"At the moment, that means nothing to me. You have a lot of explaining to do, Mr. Rothman," Jacob replied coldly.

"That's why I'm here, to tell you what I can, and my superior, Robert Welles, will explain the rest."

Casey let out an audible sigh. "It's so difficult to take all this in, and"—she gazed into space—"that it was Nick, it was *always* Nick." She shivered. "I wonder if I'll ever be able to quit looking over my shoulder."

"Knowing you, Casey, you will. What questions would you like answered? I'll answer all I can. I'll let you know as we go along which ones I can't answer."

"I was aware of being stalked at least six times. Nick admitted that he was the stalker—but was it you on any of those occasions, Syrus?" she asked pointedly.

"Only the second time. I was following the man who was following you."

"I thought so," she replied smugly.

"Yes. You caught me. You've been hard to fool, Casey. Nick confessed he couldn't get you out of his system. Apparently one of the reasons he stalked you is that he's obsessed with you, but in spite of it—or perhaps because of it—he intended to kill you. Alive, you were a constant reminder of his failure."

Every muscle in Casey's body stiffened as the frightening scene flashed through her mind. "How did you happen to show up at my house when you did?"

"We were following him. My men reported his erratic behavior at the hotel so I had extra surveillance watch his house, taking shifts all night. And of course, the next morning we followed him toward your house. We were momentarily held up by a stalled car and traffic jam, so we didn't see your struggle with him in the garage. He told us about it. We got there in time to see him push himself into the house."

"Is Brad Barker an employee of Hartner and Hart?"

"No. Brad is an FBI agent."

Casey's face mirrored her feelings. "Why would Hartner and Hart go along with this?"

"I'll let Mr. Welles answer that one."

"Were the executives of Hartner and Hart really wondering if I was guilty, Syrus? Was my job really on the line, as you said?"

"No to both questions. The man I referred to as 'my boss' is one of the FBI agents who was suspicious of your part in the accident. I simply let you think it was someone in Hartner and Hart because you were so difficult. Our number one job was to keep you safe. I would have told you almost anything that I thought was necessary to accomplish that."

"No wonder you asked me all those questions."

"Yes. You were so sharp I had to think fast on quite a few occasions to keep you from getting more suspicious of me than you already were."

Casey looked at him darkly. "Who's the real Syrus? The unpredictable man who kept me off balance at Hartner and Hart or the one here tonight who is completely businesslike and official?"

Syrus looked down.

Casey could almost hear the wheels turning in his head.

When he looked up, his eyes unsettled her.

"Would you really like to know, Casey?"

"Yes. I would."

"I'm on official business here tonight. I'd like to talk with you some more, when I'm off duty."

Casey flushed. His words said one thing, his look implied another. She found herself tongue-tied, unable to reply.

Jacob unwittingly came to her rescue. "I'm grateful to you for saving my daughter's life, Syrus," he said, his voice rising, "but I'm still seething over the hell the Bureau allowed her to go through for three years. Why were you suspicious enough to tell us an indictment was hanging over Casey?"

Casey found her voice. "And where did the body come from that they found after the accident? There was no one else in the car but Nick and me."

"The body was lying on the floor in back. Evidence suggests that it was covered by a blanket. In the confusion and fear it's understandable that you wouldn't have noticed. Especially with Nick waving a gun at you."

Casey shivered. "This is much worse than I thought."

"To answer your question, Mr. Jacobson, there were several things about the accident that were contradictory and made us suspicious. First, the men coming from the opposite direction said there were two people in the front seat. Nick didn't plan on witnesses showing up. Secondly, there was no gun, yet the corpse had a bullet hole in the right temple. If Casey had killed her husband while driving the car and while he was sitting in the passenger seat, the bullet would have entered his left temple. So how did he get a bullet hole in the *right* temple, and how did the corpse wind up in the back? And as I said, we couldn't find a gun in what was left of the car, nor anywhere in the vicinity. If Casey had killed him at home there would have been blood stains somewhere that no amount of scrubbing could conceal."

"What about dental records?" asked Jacob.

"Good point," answered Syrus. "One of the first things we did was to try and confirm whether or not the body was Nick's. We searched for his dental records. Unfortunately, Casey had already told us that as far as she knew, Nick hadn't been to a dentist since they'd been married. If he did visit a dentist, for example to have his teeth cleaned, he probably used a different name and paid cash. Yet this corpse had a mouthful of dental work, some of it very recent. It didn't make sense that Nick would hide from Casey that he went to the dentist.

"Nick obviously didn't want us to locate the dentist who had done the work. But in case we did, he covered his bases. So he thought. When we finally did locate the dentist who had done dental work on a man named Nick Carter, we found that the teeth matched those of the remains. Nick had counted on that to establish his death, but for some reason he hadn't counted on the memories of the dentist and his staff. Their description of the man didn't match the picture we had of Nick."

"Do you know who this man was?" asked Jacob.

"It took awhile, but we were finally able to identify him. Nick probably picked out someone who resembled him superficially and offered to pay his dental bill if he'd use the name Nick Carter."

Casey trembled. "Why did he kill him?"

"That's obvious isn't it? He wanted the authorities to think it was him so he could disappear. As I explained, Nick had been laundering large sums of money gained illegally by this international syndicate. The bank was the perfect place to do this. The syndicate always had contingency plans in case a problem occurred. For example, Nick would appear to die or just simply disappear, only to resurface somewhere else under a new identity."

"I still don't understand why he tried to kill me the first time."

"In his disturbed state, Nick told us everything this afternoon. He couldn't get it out of his head that you hadn't found out what he was involved in when he accidentally left that manila envelope on the hall table. And because he couldn't control you, he knew you wouldn't have gone with him when he had to disappear. The plan for him to disappear was already in place, but he simply couldn't leave you, Casey. He was so obsessed with you that in his mind, if he couldn't have you, no one could. In the end, this was the thing that really tripped him up. If he had just disappeared, gone to another part of the country, he would, in all probability, still be free."

Casey frowned in confusion. "But if the plan was to have him go to some other area of the country, why did the syndicate allow him to live in Phoenix, where there was a chance, no matter how remote, that he might give himself away?"

"Same answer—this obsession of his. He wanted to be near you, watch you, and apparently, while he was at it, scare you and make you suffer. He told the syndicate that since you didn't die as planned, he needed time to get rid of you in a way that wouldn't seem suspicious. Also, he had built up a lot of good contacts locally that would take time to replace in some other location."

"It's so hard to imagine that kind of obsession and hate simply because he couldn't control me. What I want to know is how Nick caused the car to be so quickly engulfed in flames. I have no memory of what happened after we went over the hill."

"He had gasoline in a plastic container that he put by his feet next to the door. You were probably too frightened to notice. He told us that he had driven to that very spot ahead of time, probably during those two days he was gone. He planned it all very carefully. There were several large trees a little way off the highway that he had counted on to stop the car, giving him time to escape, and leaving you on fire and the car set to explode.

"Just before you arrived at the spot, he unlocked and partially opened his door, loosened the cap on the gas container, and then grabbed the wheel, sending it careening down the slope. When the car came to a halt at the trees, you were terribly hurt and in shock. He threw gasoline on the floor and on your leg, but just as he struck a match, you lashed out, knocking the container toward him, saturating one side of his shirt and face. When the gas ignited, the left side of his face and hair caught fire. He rolled out of the car and down the hill, finally putting out the fire, but his face and shoulder were now pretty badly burned. Not as seriously as yours, Casey, but he already intended to change his appearance with plastic surgery."

The three of them listened, aghast at such an unbeliev- ably dangerous stunt. "How did he get home, burned like that, without raising suspicion?" Jacob asked.

"Previous to the kidnapping, he'd rented a car near the Scottsdale airport, using forged identification. He then drove up into the mountains to locate the place where he was going to stage the accident. He parked that car just off of a side road, hitchhiked back to Scottsdale, and called a cab to take him to where he'd parked his own car.

"After the accident he managed to slide down the hill and stumble, unobserved by those occupied with saving Casey, to this rental car. He was suffering a lot of pain from the burns, but he'd planned ahead. In case he was injured, he had some painkillers on hand in the glove compartment, which would serve until he got back to Scottsdale. Disguising himself with a hat and dark glasses, he left the car in the car rental lot and walked to the airport. The syndicate had a private jet waiting to take him to an out-of-state medical facility that did work for them. After the burns healed, they did plastic surgery to change his features. When his face healed, the syndicate had obtained a new identity for him."

"Nick was one of the syndicate's more valuable men. It was the syndicate who found out that Global Investments in Phoe- nix would shortly be looking for a replacement for a retiring executive and with their powerful connections had him apply for the job once his face had healed."

"Is Global Investments involved with this syndicate?" Casey asked.

"No. No more than Arizona Central Bank. The syndicate always uses individuals in various institutions who are in a position to handle the incoming and transfer of large sums of money without arousing suspicion. Money and power is what it's all about."

"I can scarcely believe that my daughter married a man who was part of a criminal organization. How long has Nick been involved with them?"

"Since about a year after he married Casey."

"How did you find out Nick was one of the syndicate's more valuable men?" Jacob asked.

"That's a question for Mr. Welles."

"How did you get the position at Hartner and Hart?" Casey probed.

"That's another question for Mr. Welles, Casey. Now, may I ask you a question?"

"I still have a dozen for you, Syrus, but go ahead."

"Since you knew about Nick's hair, do you know anything about the other strange things that have been happening to him? He's sure you do. In fact, he thinks you're behind them all, since you wanted to look at his hair."

"What things are you talking about, Mr. Tucker—uh—Rothman?" she asked in her most innocent voice.

Syrus' brows hovered menacingly. "May I remind you, Casey, you're talking to an FBI agent, not Syrus Tucker."

Jacob and Nan glanced at each other questioningly.

"Promise I won't get into trouble with the FBI?" she asked saucily.

"You're about to get into trouble with this part of the FBI if you don't answer."

Casey laughed. "At least I got you off your official high horse for a moment."

A smile twitched at Syrus' lips. "I'm waiting, Casey."

Casey sighed and turned serious. She told him as briefly as she could about her friend, Tiffany, Russ Eden's wife, and her fears for her. She told him about talking her father into hiring a detective and his assistant to play on Russ' narcissistic paranoia. "This was something I was fantasizing about doing to Nick. I hoped it would disarm Russ to the extent Tiffany could get away from him. Russ sounded so much like Nick. Of course he *was* Nick, but many abusers have the same patterns, so I wouldn't have suspected, even if I had known he was alive. Did the agents know about the toilet paper incident?"

"There's more?" Syrus asked, incredulous.

She first told him about the slime on Russ' suit coat when he went up to give a speech in front of his staff and his boss. Then she related the toilet paper stunt.

Syrus chuckled through both stories. A look of amazement on his face, he said, "Even if it were legal for the FBI, we never would have thought of doing any of those things. And, I might add, the police would consider it harassment."

Jacob nodded. "I knew that, and unwillingly condoned it." He smiled. "You're right. Only women could think of things like that. Casey and Nan here came up with some ideas. Then my detective and his assistant carried them out in their own fashion. I didn't want to go along with it in the first place because I felt Russ could be dangerous, but in the end I changed my mind. Casey felt so strongly that it might help her friend."

"Apparently, it did help her friend." His gazed shifted to Casey. "Well, Casey, I believe you also helped to save your own life by doing all those things. Nick Carter was one of the sharpest men the syndicate had, yet when it came to you, he seemed to lose all perspective. His first attempt on your life was poorly executed. But the second time was actually sloppy, done in a fit of crazed emotion. He left both your garage door and back door open. He never would have done that under normal circumstances; he was too thorough.

"My men saw the green hands and the hair stunt, but they couldn't understand what was happening. At the same time, they were wary about interfering or getting involved. In our undercover work, we covertly questioned people who knew Nick as Russ. They said that when these things started happening, he wasn't the same man, that he began acting strange, that at times he'd ramble about this and that, not making sense."

"You say that these pranks helped to save Casey's life?" Jacob asked, wanting more assurance.

"Yes, they did, Mr. Jacobson. Nick Carter was cool, calculating, and constantly on guard. If the image he'd created for himself hadn't been completely compromised, he wouldn't have been so careless about leaving the garage and back door open. Pulling those pranks on him shook him up to the point he couldn't think clearly."

Jacob looked over at his daughter. Dumbfounded, he repeated, "Casey, you not only saved Tiffany's life, but you helped to save your own." Then he turned to Nan. "And if it hadn't been for your help, Nan, Casey couldn't have gone through with it."

An emotional Nan could only nod in acknowledgment.

Syrus turned to Casey and his gaze locked on hers. She squirmed. His eyes seemed to look right through her.

"I would like to make a couple of things clear, Casey," he said. "First, Nick was planning to kill you someday, but your pranks sent him after you sooner and in a crazed state of mind—which *did* help save your life, but on the other hand, it was very dangerous. I wouldn't recommend any woman try that kind of thing with her husband. It might drive an abuser to kill when he didn't have any intention of doing so."

"Don't worry, Syrus, I'm not going to advise anyone else to do it. It was nerve-racking enough doing it to the man I thought was Tiffany's husband."

"Good! Are there any more questions?" Syrus asked, looking at each one.

"I have a few," Casey said. "All of them are personal but one. When will the case be officially closed?"

"I can't say because I don't know. But I'll tell you this much, Casey: when it's officially settled, I'll make sure the papers run as much of the story as we can give them. I'll see to it that the FBI gives them enough to clear your name and clear the rumors about your mother."

Tears of gratitude sprang to Casey's eyes.

"Thank you," she murmured. "However, I'm afraid that the majority of people won't be able to reverse what they've made up their minds to believe."

"I know. And I regret that."

Jacob spoke up with a rising edge to his voice, "A newspaper article clearing Casey's name is the least the FBI could do after putting Casey through this for three years."

"I agree, Mr. Jacobson."

A few moments of silence filled the room. Casey broke it with a sigh and a lament. "I assume you won't be working at Hartner and Hart any longer, Syrus."

"That's right."

"Who'll take your place?"

"The man I replaced temporarily, Dean Waukman. He was given a paid leave of absence by the company. Hartner and Hart has been very cooperative with the FBI."

Casey shook her head in amazement. "And I was about to go tell the executives off—all because of what you kept insinuating, Syrus." Then she remembered another question. "You said that someone in the FBI was suspicious of me?"

"There were those in the FBI who were still suspicious of your part in the accident. It was their job." Syrus looked around the room. "Are there any more questions I can answer?" The three were silent, so he stood. "Well, I'd better be leaving. I'll call you, Casey, and let you know when Mr. Welles can meet with you."

Jacob got up and shook hands with Syrus. "Again, I can't begin to thank you enough for saving my daughter's life."

"It was my job, Mr. Jacobson, there's no need for thanks. Besides," he smiled at Casey, "I think it was a joint effort. Casey unknowingly helped me."

"There *is* need for thanks," Casey contradicted. "It seems to me, Syrus, you went the extra mile."

A slow grin stole across his face. "You're the one who made me run the extra mile. You taxed my patience to the nth degree, but—the pleasure was all mine. Well, good night to all of you. It has been a privilege to meet you, Mr. Jacobson and you also, Ms. Hunter."

"I'll walk you to the door, Syrus," Casey offered.

"Thank you."

They stood at the door looking at each other, both in different roles now. "I don't know what to think, Syrus, what to feel about you. You put on such a good act, I don't know who the real Syrus is."

"Is it important for you to know?" he asked, his eyes inquisitive.

"After what you put me through, I deserve to know," she retorted.

Syrus laughed. "Back to the old Casey, I see. I too deserve something for what you put *me* through."

"Oh? And what could I possibly give *you?*"

Syrus' dark eyes gazed into hers for a moment, and then he smiled. "When my duties here are over, I'll call you. Good night, Casey. It's been quite an experience getting acquainted with you—and dealing with you." He opened the door and exited quickly. Casey watched him walk down the driveway and was suddenly aware of how broad his shoulders looked in the suit, how purposeful and masculine his stride was. She felt bewildered.

The shock of everything still lingering, she slowly went back in to talk with her dad and Nan.

After the three of them discussed the fearful and astonishing events of the day and the information imparted by Syrus, Casey excused herself. "After two naps, I'm still a little shaky and exhausted, so I'm going to go to bed." She hugged her dad and then Nan.

"You do that, honey. You've been through a lot today," Jacob said. "To put it mildly."

When Casey reached her room, she went over to the bed and wearily sat down, wondering how long before she and her father would be able to completely comprehend and come to terms with all that had happened.

"Tiffany!" It simply exploded from her mouth. How could she have been so thoughtless? She needed to inform her of the shocking facts. After all, they did involve *her*. It was late back east, but she had to talk to her tonight.

Tiffany's hello sounded breathy and fearful.

"Tiffany, it's Casey."

"I know. I saw your I.D. You wouldn't call so late if something weren't wrong. What is it?"

"Everything isn't all right with Russ, but you're safe and I'm safe."

"What do you mean?" she asked fearfully.

"You'll know when you hear the story. Dad and I are still in a state of shock that won't wear off for some time."

"I'm almost afraid to ask what happened."

Casey placed some pillows at her back and rested on the bed. She began the story at the point where Russ appeared in the garage, ending with the FBI knocking the gun out of Russ' hand. Intermittently, she heard Tiffany gasp or cry out. Then Casey hit her with the blockbuster. "Get prepared, Tiffany—you were married to my husband, Nick Carter. Russ Eden is an alias."

The silence was fraught with disbelief. "But Nick is dead!"

She told her the rest of the story, leaving out Nick's involvement with the crime syndicate, afraid it would jeopardize the case.

"I don't believe it, Casey. I just don't believe it."

"I'm still having trouble believing it myself, Tiff. When I was married to Nick, I told him about my good friend, you, because I wanted to see you. Time after time, he effectively curtailed my seeing you. He did, however, see pictures of you in my album. He thought you were beautiful. I'm afraid that's why he looked you up after he had plastic surgery and changed his identity. I'm sorry."

"Oh, Casey, you have no reason to be sorry."

"I need to tell you something else. I was responsible for all the pranks pulled on Russ."

"You! But how could you—?"

Casey related everything and what she had intended to

accomplish. "The FBI told me that these pranks saved my life because it unbalanced Russ—I mean Nick. They said Nick was so cool and calculating, it wasn't like him to leave both the garage and back door open."

"It did unbalance him. It really did. You saved *my* life, Casey." She heard Tiffany crying.

After Tiffany's tears had subsided, two shocking realizations hit Casey. "Tiffany, you aren't married! Russ—I mean Nick—is a bigamist."

"I'm not married? I'm free? Casey, I'm free!"

"You are, Tiffany. You have nothing to worry about, nothing to fear anymore." Casey paused. "But what a strange turnabout. *I'm* the one who's married. After three years of thinking I was a widow, I now have to get a divorce, of all things."

Jacob and Nan had watched Casey leave the room, her right leg almost dragging. Jacob felt as worn out as Casey looked.

"I think that's my cue to leave also, Jake. Thank you for having me come over and hear about everything. I'm still reeling over Casey's narrow escape, and the shocking news that it was Nick we were victimizing."

"So am I, Nan. I need you to stay for a while. Would you?"

Nan silently weighed his request. She needed to stay a little longer. She had become attached to Casey and hadn't as yet been able to let go of the fear of what *could* have happened to her. "All right, Jake. I'll stay a little while."

"Thank you."

She nodded and scooted to the end of the couch and turned toward him. She had needed to be close to him while hearing the frightening story from Casey and Mr. Rothman, but now she needed space between them.

"What did you think of Syrus Rothman, Jake?"

"I'm a little prejudiced. He saved my daughter's life."

"Did you notice how Casey reacted to him?"

"Yes, and his remarks gave me the impression that she gave him a difficult time." He smiled. "Sounds like Casey. What did *you* think of him?"

"You know he's certainly not a handsome man or even what one would call good-looking, but his face is intriguingly different—he has interesting features. His smile is wonderful, but what struck me is his intelligence, and what appears to be a strength of will."

Jacob considered her assessment. "I would think that a man who worked in FBI Special Operations would have to have those qualities. One thing I'm certain of is I'll always be grateful to him."

Nan's eyes had a faraway look, her mind exploring possibilities Jacob would never think to entertain. She rose. "I think I need to go now, Jake."

Jacob stood also, his eyes pleading. "Don't go just yet."

Nan's heart lurched painfully. She wanted to stay but knew she was still too vulnerable.

"I love you, Nan."

"I love you, too, Jake. I'm so happy Casey is safe—really safe now. You two have suffered enough. Good night." She moved quickly to the front door.

Jacob followed.

Nan didn't look back. She opened the door, stepped out quickly, and shut it behind her. Jacob stared at the closed door, pain clutching at his heart, but he made no move to call her back.

Chapter Thirty-One

Failure is the fertilizer in the field of success.

The next morning Casey awoke to bacon cooking. She looked at her watch and saw that it was eight o'clock. She felt much better. Surprisingly she had slept peacefully and soundly. She put on her house slippers and padded to the kitchen. Her father, busy at the stove, was unaware of her presence. She slipped up behind him and put her arms about his waist.

"Hey, sleepyhead. It's about time you got up."

"Hey, yourself. How long have you been up?"

He smiled. "I've just been out here about twenty-five minutes myself. I think I bombed last night."

"I'm glad you had a good rest too. When I think about it, yesterday seems like a bad dream."

"It's all behind you now, Casey. You have a wonderful life ahead of you."

Casey seriously questioned the "wonderful" part. "It might take me some time to feel safe, to not look over my shoulder, but," she said with a smile and all the enthusiasm she could muster, "life is going to be good for us from now on."

Jacob took the bacon out of the pan, put it on a plate, and then looked into his daughter's face. "I hope you really believe that for yourself, Case."

"We *can* make life good, can't we? You taught me that."

"You're right, we can. You're safe and you're free of the dark cloud we thought was hanging over you. There's so much ahead for you now."

"There is so much ahead for *you*, Dad, if you'll just reach out and take it."

Jacob became very busy getting a plate of pancakes out of the oven. "Breakfast is ready," he said. "Let's eat."

Casey stayed with her dad until Monday night but returned to work on Tuesday. It was the beginning of the last week in May. *The beginning of the summer of my life*, she thought.

As she entered Hartner and Hart, a sinking feeling came over her. Syrus wouldn't be there. Only Mr. Waukman. She smiled at herself. Strangely, it seemed it was going to be more of an adjustment to have it back to status quo than when Syrus first took over. *Maybe the word "adjustment" doesn't quite describe it*, she thought. *More like "withdrawal"?* In many ways Syrus surpassed Mr. Waukman in talent, but Syrus wasn't a real graphics designer. It was all smoke and mirrors. However, her yo-yo relationship with Syrus was real. Even though it was only an affiliation between an FBI agent and his assignment, she had seen glimpses of the man behind the badge.

Stepping out of the elevator, she remembered the first thing she had to do—go to the offices of the executives of Hartner and Hart and thank them for what they had done for her.

Returning from the executive offices, she blew her nose. She had become a little emotional when she thanked the officers. She still felt like crying. *Why? My life is better now. Why am I wanting to hide in a corner and bawl?* She smiled wryly. *Belle would probably call it post-traumatic stress syndrome.* This reminded her that she ought to take Belle out for lunch sometime and tell her everything. For some reason, she thought of Belle as a friend, not just a therapist. Straightening her shoulders, Casey took a deep breath and headed for Mr. Waukman's office.

She stopped at Vicky's desk. "Hi, Vicky."

"Oh, hi, Casey. Did you know that Sy was only taking Mr.

Waukman's place while he took a long vacation?"

"I just heard it."

"I'm going to miss Mr. Syrus Tucker."

"Me too, Vicky. Is Mr. Waukman busy?"

"Go on in. He's free."

It was obvious that Vicky knew nothing about Syrus working for the FBI. Knocking on Mr. Waukman's door, she heard his invitation to come in.

"Well, hello, Casey. How are you?"

"I'm very well, Mr. Waukman. Did you have a nice vacation?"

"I did. My wife and children and I did some traveling and sightseeing."

"How nice for all of you. Do you have some work for me?"

"I'll have some for you tomorrow morning. Nothing today."

Casey's day was free, but oddly, she felt at loose ends, unconnected—an unusual and disconcerting feeling. Retrieving her video camera at the studio, she drove toward South Mountain. None of her recently hiked trails had turned out to be the beautiful path she had once happened upon. Although South Mountain had many trails, she was gradually narrowing the search. There was no one to interfere with her search today; no one would be following her, not even Brad. She smiled at how young and innocent Brad had seemed to be—and yet he was an FBI agent.

May was hotter than usual, and today it was already getting quite warm. Casey had learned to like the heat. It was part of the outdoor world she loved to capture through the lens of a camera. When she turned off onto San Juan Road and neared the place where the man—where Nick—had accosted her, her heart began to race. She looked around nervously. She was surprised at herself. Nick was safely incarcerated. She was safe. She pulled over and stopped, waiting—waiting for what? It wasn't long before she saw a car coming. The doors were locked. She got the spray out of her purse, gripping it tightly.

The car sped by. Soon another one passed. Of course! Sightseers, bird-watchers, and hikers were out. Nevertheless, she felt paralyzed. She couldn't get out of the car. Turning on the key, she wheeled the car around and headed back home, but she changed her mind and decided to go to the library, check out a novel or two, and then look in the paper for musicals or symphonies. She had to keep herself busy until she was able to conquer this irrational fear of being followed.

It was at this moment she thought of Belle. Picking up her cell phone, she called her. A warm voice answered.

"Belle, this is Casey. Am I interrupting a session?"

"No. I have about an hour and a half before my next patient."

"I'm calling because I consider you a friend, not just my therapist."

"That's great to hear, kid. The feeling's mutual."

"I'd like to take you out to lunch today if you have time. Some very shocking and frightening events have occurred. I think you'd like to hear about them."

"I have an appointment for lunch. Is it possible for you to come on over now? I'm anxious to hear what you have to tell me."

"All right. I'll be there as soon I can."

An hour later, after hearing about Casey's "help Tiffany project" and the frightening aftermath, Belle was silent for a while. The seasoned therapist who thought she'd heard everything was literally speechless. At last she said, "That's one amazing story. It seems someone upstairs is looking after you, Casey. Your life was spared once more. Now—you'll heal faster. You have answers you didn't have before." Casey nodded.

Belle continued, "What you did to Russ-Nick was very clever, but like the FBI man said, it was also very dangerous."

"I know," Casey said quietly. "I shiver when I think about it. I'm grateful it was me he turned on instead of Tiffany, but thankfully I survived and Tiffany is free."

"Well, now you can get on with your life, Casey, free of fear."

"I'm not quite free of it yet, but I know it won't be long before I'll be over it."

"It won't, I assure you. You're a fighter."

"Thank you. I hope so. Speaking of answers, Belle, the FBI man, Syrus Rothman, said something that really hit me. He told me the *reason* Nick had to get rid of me. He said, 'Alive, you were a constant reminder of his failure.'"

Belle's brows rose. "That's a very profound insight."

Casey nodded. "I thought so too. I can think of two ways Nick thought he failed. First, he failed to control me. And then when he felt I was planning to leave him, he failed to kill me."

"Exactly. Mr. Rothman has discovered a very important characteristic of abusers. Most don't turn out to be killers, but when a woman finally leaves an abusive husband who isn't a killer, most of the time he can't leave her alone. He keeps hounding her, persecuting her because he can't face his failure to control. He has to win.

"The abusive husband who is unfaithful and dumps his wife has to continually malign her to others, disparage her to others, to justify his actions. He has to appear the 'good guy.' And . . . if his ex-wife attains any success, it's a *rebuke* to him, so he has to continue defaming her indefinitely in order to retain his good image in others' eyes."

"Of course!" Casey said. "That explains why Nick had to poison everyone's mind toward me in case I left him. He couldn't allow anyone to find him in the wrong. I'm sure all this took place before he decided he had to get rid of me. You know, Belle, it doesn't make it any easier to know all this, but it helps to understand why he did those things."

"It does help to understand; then in our mind we can deal with it better."

Casey looked at her watch. "I see it's about time for your patient. I still want to take you out to lunch."

"I'd like that. Call me sometime. And be sure to keep me informed about your father's marriage, and," she smiled, "yours one day."

Casey rolled her eyes. "That'll be the day. Thanks, Belle. I've gained more insight talking with you."

"I have too. I've learned some amazing things today," she exclaimed, smiling. "Thank you for wanting me to know, for taking time out to inform me as a friend."

"Thank you for listening," Casey said, standing up to leave.

Belle gave Casey a hug. "Tell your father hello for me."

The rest of the week moved at a snails' pace for Casey. She completed her assignments for Mr. Waukman and he gave her more. Nevertheless, she felt languid and bored, the boredom turning into impatience. *When is Mr. Welles going to get in touch with us and answer the rest our questions?* She convinced herself that when this was over, all her enthusiasm would return.

At last, Friday morning Syrus called and informed her that Mr. Welles would be in town that night. "If it's all right, Mr. Welles will meet all of you at your father's house tonight at seven thirty."

"It's more than all right, Syrus. I want it over—completely over."

When 7:20 rolled around, Casey, her dad, and Nan were waiting anxiously for Mr. Welles.

When they heard the chimes, her father went to the front door. He returned with a short man around fifty, who looked very trim and fit. He had blond hair and wore gold-rimmed glasses over sharp blue eyes. He smiled readily, but his manner was that of a man with a tight agenda. Casey was glad to see the face behind the voice she had talked to for so long.

After everyone was introduced and seated, Mr. Welles said, "How are you, Casey?"

"I'm still trying to get over the fear of someone following me."

"Judging from the information we have from agent Rothman, you're a very resilient young woman. I don't think it will be long before you'll conquer that fear."

His anger still lingering, Jacob blurted out. "No thanks to the FBI! It seems to me you could have at least saved my daughter the fear of indictment these last three years. I'm sure her leg would have healed faster."

"I can understand your feelings, sir. I have two daughters. Informing people who aren't trained in the Bureau in order to make them feel more comfortable just isn't the policy of the FBI. Many times I wish it was. Your daughter's case was one of those times. Also, experience has shown that such a course may actually increase the danger to that person."

Jacob nodded, only partially mollified. "I appreciate your empathy, Mr. Welles, but it doesn't lessen the regret I feel over Casey having to suffer unnecessarily."

"It's all right, Dad, it's over." She gave him a warm, loving smile.

"What question would you like to ask first, Casey?" Welles asked.

"Can you use your influence to help me obtain a quick divorce?"

Jacob started. "A divorce?" he echoed. "My mind has been so taken up, I didn't remember that you were no longer a widow!"

"I think under the circumstances, we can arrange to get you an annulment—unless you want any of his assets."

"I would rather that Tiffany get those, even though in reality they aren't legally married. Can you arrange for that to happen?"

"We'll certainly try. What's the next question?" he said, looking at Casey and then Jacob.

Jacob asked the next one. "Syrus told us that you've been trying to find a certain syndicate for a long time, but tell us why it took *three* years to resolve the part Casey was involved in."

"Well, for two reasons. First, it took time to discover the identity of the remains. After we did that, we couldn't find Nick. We knew he must have left town and changed his identity, but we had no idea where to start. Secondly, Nick's employer, Arizona Central Bank, contacted us concerning evidence of a dummy company connecting Nick, not only to embezzlement but also to a large money-laundering syndicate. I don't mean to sound blunt or callous, but frankly, at that point we had bigger fish to fry.

"Then we got another break. About a month before Agent Rothman went undercover at Hartner and Hart, someone very credible at the bank corroborated your story, Mr. Jacobson, that Nick was so obsessed with Casey that he didn't want her out of his sight. Turning our attention to this information we felt that maybe Nick, with his new identity and probable plastic surgery, might want to work nearby so he could see her. It was then we assigned Rothman to work at Hartner and Hart to protect Casey, question her, and watch for anyone following her or watching her. And sure enough, Nick couldn't stay away. A man, who we suspected might be Nick, began stalking her."

He turned and addressed Casey. "Later, when you got suspicious of Rothman he had Brad Barker stay close to you. This was before Rothman had him pose as an employee of Hartner and Hart." Robert Welles smiled at Jacob. "You're daughter is a hard one to hoodwink, Mr. Jacobson."

Jacob raised his brows knowingly and nodded.

"In addition to agents Rothman and Barker, we had a couple of others we began using. When one of them saw a man out in the desert hiding behind a tree watching you, Casey, we became suspicious. We had seen this same man follow you. From then on, we caught him following you about fifteen times. After the second time, we had a policeman stop him to say his license plate had expired. Of course the policeman had him show his driver's license with his picture revealing that he was Russ Eden.

"When we checked Eden out we found that the real Russ Eden was deceased. It was a fake identity. This Russ Eden had the same color of eyes as Nick, and was the same height and weight."

"Why would a smart man like Nick, whose need was to control, consent to work with a syndicate, whose nature is to control?" Jacob asked.

"Nick, in collusion with a friend who was a computer guy, had embezzled money from Arizona Central Bank. The syndicate, or the Pentad, as Nick knew them, found out about it and used the threat of exposure to recruit him to their organization. From Nick's point of view, the only downside was the control the Pentad exercised over him. The money they paid him, as both Nick and Russ, over and above what his respective employers were paying him, was making him a wealthy man.

"The syndicate hired only clever, credible men who could put forth the image they needed. Nick Carter filled that bill better than most of the other executives they had under their thumb."

"Thank you for clearing that up for me, Mr. Welles," Jacob said. "But you wouldn't be telling us these things if you hadn't found and arrested the people in the syndicate. Is that right?" Jacob asked.

"You're absolutely right. We had already discovered a number of executives who we suspected were under the control of the Pentad. We hadn't been able to get any hard evidence on them until your daughter here helped us nail Nick. In his frangible state, we were able to plea-bargain with him. He told us the location of the Pentad. Though he knew no names, he described faces. That information plus our own enabled us to move in and arrest the group. It consisted of only five men. They didn't confess, but when we brought the executives in for questioning and told them we had arrested the leaders of the Pentad, they began spilling their guts. They're all in custody for money laundering and murder. There have been other murders."

Jacob's hands clenched into fists. "I can't believe my daughter could be taken in by Nick Carter."

"Believe it, Mr. Jacobson. This guy was good. He wasn't a murderer when your daughter met him. He was simply a very clever man who hid his inadequacies extremely well, including his egotistical and controlling personality. Fortunately, from what Mr. Rothman said, your daughter soon discovered the areas in which Nick was vulnerable. And lucky for all of us, Casey played on his weaknesses and cracked his facade, leaving him fallible and ineffective."

Silence prevailed for a few moments, and then Casey said quietly, "It gives me a strange feeling that you knew so much about Nick, about me, my friends, and my comings and goings, Mr. Welles."

"Remember, Casey, we're the good guys. We needed to know everything about you in order to protect you and to accomplish our greater goal. Do either of you have any more questions?"

"How was Syrus able to step into Mr. Waukman's place and be so good at it?" asked Casey. "He wouldn't answer our questions about that."

Welles chuckled. "The man is brilliant but very modest. We gave him books on ad design and he had read and mastered them in two days. One time, he had to pose as a doctor. He studied the cases he was to be working on and a couple of other medical books. In a week he was ready to be a doctor. He's been a store manager, a bar owner, and many others I can't mention for security reasons. He takes to these assignments like a duck to water.

"Maybe you've heard of the man who was so brilliant at

forging checks that the FBI finally hired him to capture other forgers? Well, I'd say that agent Rothman is even more brilliant. Several times he's threatened to quit the FBI and live a normal life, but we kept enticing him to do just one more job, then one more."

"What would he do to make a living if he didn't work for the FBI?" Jacob asked.

"He could do anything. Or he wouldn't have to do anything. He's mastered the art of investing and is wealthy on his own. He simply keeps working for us out of a sense of duty."

Casey's mouth was ajar during Mr. Welles' explanation. But then, why was she surprised? It was Syrus' eyes. His eyes gave away his brilliance.

"Do any of you have any more questions?"

"Just a request," Jacob said. "I would like my daughter's marriage to Nick Carter annulled as soon as possible."

"We'll get right on it, Mr. Jacobson. After all, not only has she gone through a lot while we were trying to solve the case, she helped us solve it." He stood. "It has been rewarding meeting all of you, but especially the young woman whom I talked with rather often over the phone." He shook Casey's hand heartily and then the others'.

As the three of them walked Mr. Walker to the door, Casey began hesitantly, "For almost two months I've been working with Syrus. I asked him which was the real Syrus, the official one or the one who was so tough on me at work."

Robert Welles threw back his head and laughed. He didn't explain his amusement; he simply asked, "What did he say?"

"He said he'd see me when the case was at the point that he could."

"Then he will. You can count on that. Good night, all of you. It's been a pleasure." Just before leaving, he turned to Casey. "Oh, by the way, if you ever decide you'd like a little excitement in your life again, we'd be glad to make room for you on our team." He smiled at his own joke and was gone before Casey could sputter a reply.

Chapter Thirty-Two

This above all, refuse to be a victim.

—Margaret Atwood

Casey awoke at five o'clock Saturday morning, feeling the urge to try once more to find that elusive path. She was feeling less fearful day by day. Dressing quickly, she went into the kitchen, drank a glass of orange juice, and then made toast and fried an egg.

It was June and Arizona's summer heat was bearing down heavily. She started early to beat the heat, but in case of a longer stay, she filled a water jug to take along.

As she put everything in the van, excitement surged through her. This morning was the first time she *felt* free! It wasn't long after she was married that she began to feel as though she were in bondage. In the hospital she was a prisoner of the bed. Once out of the hospital, the dark cloud of the indictment continued to oppress her. Then—her freedom was seriously curtailed once the stalking occurred. Today was a new day.

She drove with the windows down and let the fresh morning air blow in her face. Entering South Mountain once more by way of San Juan Road, she drove slowly. Most of the desert flowers were no longer blooming, but violet-purple blooms were spectacular among the dense foliage of the ironwood trees. The paloverde trees were covered with showy clusters of bright yellow blossoms. The vestiges of spring lingered. It was a perfect time to videotape.

She drove a short distance, watching carefully. She remembered picking out a marker so she'd recognize the path, but she had forgotten it. Suddenly, she saw a young saguaro with only one small arm beginning to grow. "There it is! That's it!" she squealed. Pulling into the nearest trailhead, she got her video camera and started down the path called the Kiwanis Trail.

The soothing warmth of the bright sun wrapped itself around her like a soft blanket, gently prodding the still sluggish circulation in her scarred leg. A red-tailed hawk swooped low, looking for rodents, and then flew off. Insects moved out of her way, bees buzzed around the blooms.

The path was worn and widened by many hikers and bikers who also found this trail enchanting. She began taping as she walked, every bend more beautiful, framed by blossoming trees. Gradually the trees and foliage thinned out, and the path lost its soothing quality. *It takes trees to make a path beautiful*, she mused, *just as it takes love to make the path of marriage beautiful*. Turning around, she taped the path from the other direction.

Approaching the trailhead where she left her car, she slipped the strap of the case that held the video camera over her shoulder. She stopped short. A shadow of a man was projected from behind a large saguaro. A sudden wave of nausea and fear swept over her. The man was silent, unmoving, waiting. Waiting for her? Nick? Her hand flew to her mouth—too late to stifle the scream that began as a low moan, escalating into a fearful keening sound.

The shadow detached itself, coming around the cactus in her direction. Her vision blurred. Her legs gave way. She sank to her knees. Now the man was upon her, reaching for her.

"Casey! Casey! It's me, don't be afraid."

"Syrus?" she whispered. "Syrus?"

"Here, Casey, let me help you up," he said, gently bringing her to her feet. He pulled her to him, enfolding her in his arms. "Oh, Casey, I'm so sorry. I didn't mean to frighten you. Forgive me."

For a while Casey let herself be held and comforted by his

strong arms. Then suddenly she pushed herself away. "How could you do this to me?" she cried, pounding on his chest. "I thought someone was stalking me again. I was terrified!"

Again his arms went around her, holding her tightly to stop her flailing arms. "It's all right. You're safe. I'm sorry, Casey. I'm sorry."

"What are you doing here anyway?" she asked, blinking back angry tears.

Syrus let her go. "I was going to your home, but as I turned into The Cottages, you were leaving. I couldn't get your attention. If you had looked in your rearview mirror you would have seen me."

"I glanced in the rearview mirror, but I didn't notice it was you. I was so happy to be free for the first time in years . . . then you do this to me," she said with lingering anger.

"I'm sorry. When you didn't see me, I thought I'd follow you and see where you went on your jaunts when Brad followed you. I had no idea I would frighten you, since you knew Nick was behind bars. I saw you start off down this trail with your video camera. I didn't want to disturb you, so I found a place to sit at the side of that big cactus. I guess I lost track. I wasn't watching for you, so your scream gave *me* a bad turn."

Casey covered her face a moment and then looked up at him. "I tried to come out here last Tuesday. A car followed behind, terrifying me. When I moved over, it passed me and went on and I knew I was being absurd. Soon another sight-seer was behind me and it happened all over again. No amount of talking to myself would take away the fear. I had to turn around and leave. Today was the first day I haven't felt frightened—until I saw your shadow behind the saguaro. I guess it's going to take a little time."

"Come on over here with me, Casey," he said, leading her by the arm to a rock, big enough for both to sit. "Let's sit here and talk for a while."

"Okay," she sighed. "That sounds good. I was having such a good time my leg didn't feel tired—until now."

"What were you doing?"

"I saw this beautiful trail once when I was here at South Mountain. Then I forgot where it was and the name of it. The reason I came out here—when Brad followed me—was to try and find it. I was interrupted each time. Today I found it and taped it." Her face lit up. "You ought to see it, Syrus, it's enchanting. Apparently other people feel the same way because the path is rather worn, which is exactly what I need for my videos."

"I know you were videotaping. Is it an assignment?" he asked, puzzled.

Casey explained her project.

"An interesting idea. A thoughtful one, Casey."

She let out a big sigh. "Well, Syrus, as you know, Mr. Welles came over last Friday and answered more of our questions."

"Are you satisfied?"

"I'd say more like—numb. To think you really weren't the head graphics designer but rather an FBI agent is still trying to settle with me. Who are you really, Syrus? I don't know where to fit you in my mind anymore."

Syrus smiled. "I've played so many different roles, I sometimes wonder myself."

"Were you the bona fide Syrus Rothman when you were pushing my buttons, and getting tough with me at work?"

Syrus was silent for a few moments; then a half smile tipped his lips. "Before I answer that, I need to explain something. We've told you the main reasons the FBI assigned me to your case—to protect you and to locate Nick Carter, who we learned wouldn't be able to leave you alone. A third reason was to see if I could pull out of you any memories or clues that would help the case. When the authorities told you an indictment was possible, you resisted being questioned. You're a stubborn girl, Casey. An expert at ferreting out information has found that all the answers lie *within* the individual who experiences the trauma. There are times we can follow a person's intuition until we solve the mystery or until the person recovers memories."

He smiled. "That's why I was so relentless with the questions you said weren't necessary or were inappropriate. I've always found it easy to pull information from an individual's subconscious—until I was assigned to you. I hadn't intended to be so hard on you. It wasn't a role I intended to play—in quite that way, that is. It just happened. You brought it out in me, Casey. I suppose it was the real me—one side of me, anyway. What about you? Was that the real Casey—your feistiness, your recalcitrance, your stubbornness, your insubordination?"

Casey looked down, a sheepish smile on her face. "Now that I know who you really are, I can see that I made your job very difficult. I feel a little chagrined about it. That was a role *I* didn't intend to play. It too just happened. *You* brought it out in *me*. However, I'm afraid it really was me."

He laughed. "I'm surprised Nick didn't choke you."

"That's because I soon learned I couldn't be myself around Nick. I didn't feel safe enough."

"You felt safe enough with me to be the genuine article then? I take that as a compliment."

Casey smiled, thoughtful. "I guess it is." She looked into his eyes and found them soft and mellow. Surprised, she wondered about the change but knew they could shift in a split second. "So you're brilliant enough to be a graphics designer on short notice, to take on the role of a doctor, and many others."

Unused to compliments from Casey, Syrus was self-conscious. "Mr. Welles got a little carried away with his explanation, I see. Don't take him too seriously."

"But I do. I can see it for myself, Syrus. You were more creative than Mr. Waukman. Somehow though, I can't see you as a bar owner." She laughed as she thought about it.

He smiled, his eyes regaining some of their piercing quality as they gazed into hers. "Now that you're rested, how about taking me down that path you put yourself in peril to find?"

"You really want to see it?" she asked, surprised.

"You're darn right I do."

"Are you thirsty?"

"Yes, come to think about it. I hadn't expected a trip to the desert today."

"I've got a jug of water."

"Sounds good. Let's go get a drink before we start. "

Feeling refreshed from the cool liquid, Syrus, pacing his strides to match Casey's, sauntered with her down the path.

"This feels rather odd to me, Syrus—you out here with me. I'm still finding it difficult to reconcile in my mind that you're no longer my boss, so to speak. I don't know what you are."

"A friend."

"A friend?" She sighed. "I've always wanted to share my love of nature with a friend."

"This is a beautiful trail, Casey. What are these blossoming trees?"

Casey guided him along the path, explaining every tree and bush. Between each exposition they silently took in the beauty.

When they came to what Casey considered the end, she said, "The path goes on, but the foliage has thinned out. This is where we turn around."

"Would you like to rest, Casey?"

"No, thank you."

"Then grab an arm," he said. "It will help."

"Thank you," she said, smiling. "It will." When she put her hand in the crook of his bare arm, Casey felt the heat rise from her neck to her face. His arm felt strong and safe—but touching him was disconcerting. She was still unable to fit him nicely into some category—her boss, an FBI agent, a friend?

They were silent until they reached their cars.

"Casey, I want to spend a little more time with you today before I leave."

"Where are you going?"

"I'm not sure. I would say home, but I don't have a home really. I've had to move around so much, stay in hotels and apartments."

"That's sad."

"Do you call your place home?"

Casey frowned. "My first impulse is to say yes, but . . . in reality, I don't have a home either."

"What makes a home, Casey?"

"In the past a home would be where my husband and children lived, but that hope's gone now."

"Why?"

"I'd rather not talk about it."

"Do you have any plans for lunch?"

"Uh, no. Why?"

"Let's head back to your place and we'll discuss it."

"All right."

When they reached the trailhead, Syrus opened her car door and she got in. She sighed. It felt good to sit down behind the wheel.

Driving home, Casey was a bundle of emotions as she thought about Syrus and watched him follow behind. One moment, she didn't know whether she wanted to spend time with him; the next moment, she felt desolate at the thought of him leaving town.

Chapter Thirty-Three

Solving one problem sometimes
presents another.

asey drove into her garage and Syrus parked in front. Soon Casey was at the front door inviting him in. He looked around the bare front room.

"I sold all the furniture Nick and I chose. I couldn't bear to look at it. Come into the family room where I at least have a couch and chair, as you may already be aware. Bare bones really. I haven't had the desire or strength to decorate."

"Doesn't matter. There's a good feeling here."

"There is?" she asked surprised.

He nodded. "It comes from you," he said, seating himself on the couch.

"Uh . . . I don't know how to handle that compliment." She sat across from him in the chair, looking bemused.

Syrus smiled. "Don't handle it, just accept it." He cleared his throat. "I didn't want to leave things as they were; we needed to visit a while before I left."

"You don't know where you're going?"

"Well, first I think I'll visit my parents."

"Where do they live?"

They live in Cambridge, Massachusetts. They're both teaching at Harvard. My father teaches physics, and my mother teaches macro- and microeconomics."

"Wow. What a couple of brains. Do you have siblings?"

"No. My mom couldn't get pregnant early on, so she went back to college and got a doctorate in economics. Then she got pregnant with me. She gave up teaching to raise me. When I left for college, she updated her degree and then got a job at Harvard with my dad."

"How often do you see your parents?"

"As often as I can. Are you hungry, Casey?"

She looked at her watch. "It's lunchtime. Yes, I'm hungry."

"I'd like to take you out to lunch, but . . ." His voice trailed off.

It appeared to Casey that Syrus had suddenly become uncomfortable. "What is it, Syrus?"

He looked down, away from Casey's direct blue eyes. "I feel ill at ease because I'm off the case and you're a married woman."

"Oh. Well, it was a rude awakening to realize I was married instead of a widow."

"It won't be long before Robert Welles will have your marriage annulled. He promised me he'd pull strings to hurry it along."

Casey watched Syrus nervously clasping and unclasping his hands. "Married or not, I think a couple of friends could go to that good Mexican restaurant, Rosarita's, don't you?"

Syrus relaxed and smiled. "Since you put it that way—I definitely think they could."

After they had ordered Syrus seemed more relaxed. He gazed across at Casey and gave her a wide, warm smile. Casey tingled from the warmth of it. Now that she knew who he was, she allowed herself to appreciate what she had only observed before—how his smile lit up his face, and this time, how it gladdened her heart. They weren't at odds any more, even though, in reality, that had only been her perception. She shook her head, thinking how strange it all had been.

"Why are you shaking your head?" Syrus asked, his smile lingering.

"I was just thinking how much more relaxed we are now that I know who you are, that it's all over. The sparks aren't flying between us."

Syrus laughed. "I'm not so sure that's permanent—unless you tell me it is."

Casey looked down and pulled a dubious face. "I wish I could tell you that, but sometimes I can be . . . you know . . ." She left it hanging. She looked up. "Oh, never mind. Let's enjoy the peace while it lasts."

Syrus chuckled. "Hey, I'm all for that."

Rosarita brought their food herself and welcomed them warmly. Casey returned her greeting with enthusiasm, remembering with embarrassment her sarcastic remarks to Syrus about her and the restaurant when he first brought her here.

They ate in silence for a while, with only an occasional "Mmm," from Casey as she enjoyed the food.

During half of the meal, Syrus quizzed her about her "campaign" against Russ Eden. He insisted on knowing the inception and the implementation to the very end. When she was through, she noted a dramatic change in Syrus' mood. She looked at him questioningly and waited for an explanation.

"I admire you for trying to help your friend, Casey, but it was actually very dangerous. Nick Carter is a cruel and unpredictable man. It makes my stomach turn to think how it *could* have turned out."

"Surely you've had more serious life and death situations than mine, Syrus." Casey was surprised at the expression of gravity that came across his face. She held her breath.

"In my opinion, no," he said.

Casey grinned and tried to tease him. "Don't look so somber. I seriously doubt I'll have to inflict that on anyone ever again."

Syrus didn't find her statement amusing in the least.

"Let's share a dessert," she said brightly. "I wasted most of mine last time we were here." She was relieved to see his disconcerting mood leave.

He smiled. "Okay—if you don't hog it."

Casey laughed.

On the doorstep Casey thanked Syrus for lunch and especially for letting her show him her favorite trail.

He smiled. "I enjoyed it. I'm beginning to like the desert." Then he said a quick "Good-bye, good luck," and left.

Casey entered the house and dropped into the chair in her small family room thinking about Syrus and the short time they had spent together today. When Syrus said good-bye, Casey realized it was the end of a rather curious and unsettling association; nevertheless, it was an interesting one. In fact, outside of her father, her association with Syrus Rothman had turned out to be the most important one she had ever experienced. He *saved* her life!

Her mind kept going back to their desert walk and how pleasant it was in spite of the confusion she felt over Syrus' new identity and the drastic change in their relationship. She probably would never see him again and the thought disquieted her. He was such a vital, strong personality; he'd had an impact on her life, and too suddenly their relationship, such as it was, had ended. Moisture gathered in her eyes and soon turned into full-blown tears. Pulling out a tissue, she blew her nose, trying to rationalize her behavior. She decided it was probably brought on by all the trauma she had been through lately.

Getting up and picking out an old romantic video, she put it in, trying to allay the despondency that was rapidly descending upon her.

The next six days crawled by and Casey's enthusiasm hadn't returned as she had expected. In fact, she found herself losing interest in her photography. Each time she went up to Mr. Waukman's office, she couldn't help but wish he were Syrus. It seemed to become more apparent that she missed him as the days went by. Her enthusiasm over her own project had even waned.

Convincing herself that the doldrums would pass, she visited her dad after work on Friday, hoping with all her heart that he had done the only thing that would make him happy.

Ringing the doorbell first, Casey unlocked the front door of her dad's house. She entered and called, but there was no answer. Glancing at her watch, she saw that it was only five. *Maybe he isn't home from work yet*, she thought. Looking out the family room window, she saw him sitting on the patio.

She stepped out. "Hey, Dad, I'm so glad you're here."

His face lit up. "Casey! I've just been thinking about you."

"I've been thinking about you too. Has anything changed between you and Nan?" she asked, sitting down on a patio chair.

"No."

"Have you tried?"

"I can't, Casey." He got up and began pacing back and forth.

"I've failed you, Casey," he blurted out. "You wouldn't have married Nick Carter if I hadn't."

"Why are you bringing that up now? It's all over."

"No, it isn't all over. You still have to deal with that crippled leg and future operations. I know it will improve, but the effects of the injuries will be with you for the rest of your life."

Casey was concerned. Instead of becoming more at peace now that there was no indictment hanging over her—and now that she was safe, he seemed to be more distraught. "Please sit down, Dad. I'm going to read something to you that Belle gave me. There hasn't been just the right moment until now. I have it here in my purse." Jacob sat down and sighed skeptically.

"Belle is doing a research paper for the American Psychology Association. Her premise is—uh—" She opened her purse and pulled out a folded piece of paper. "Here it is. Her title is, 'The Role Fathers Play in Women's Ability to Recognize Abuse in a Relationship or Marriage.' Belle said she had been working on it for some time. She's included some cases which indicate that, but until I came along she didn't have a case history strong enough to serve her premise. My story alone will, she said, have a big effect when her research is published."

Jacob put up both hands as if to fend off any further information on the subject. "Casey, it doesn't matter what she said or what she has discovered, it won't change my sins of omission."

"What? Dad, you've got to open your heart and listen to this—please."

Jacob let out an impatient breath. "Go ahead—since you're determined."

Casey's heart sank. She had never seen her dad like this. She took a deep breath. "All right. This is a quote from her research. 'Studies show that fathers play a special role in building a child's self-respect.'

"Because you played such a vital role in my life, I was able to retain my self-respect, even though Nick tried to destroy it. Because I had self-respect I didn't believe the belittling things he said about me, and eventually I had the courage to make plans to leave him."

Casey scrutinized her father's face, hoping it had sunk in, that it had eased his feelings of guilt. She saw no change whatsoever.

"What did Belle say about a mother's influence?"

"I asked her that. Let me think. . . . She said, from her research, she learned that mothers take a dominant role in preparing children to live within their families—present and future."

"And you didn't have that, Casey," Jacob said bitterly.

"Dad! Belle said that you were so involved in my life that you taught me what my mother should have taught. You were both mother and father to me."

Jacob stood up, rubbed his brow in anxiety, and took a couple of steps away from her, his back to her and spoke quietly and slowly. "That whole statement is a fallacy. A father can't take the place of a mother. A mother can't take the place of a father."

"Dad, remember a couple of my friends who were fatherless through no fault of their mothers?"

"Yes."

"We talked about them at length. Do you remember?" He nodded, his back still to her. "Both their mothers didn't want to work and be away from their children, but they had to. They were both prayerful families and didn't seem to suffer from the effects as much as others we knew about. Remember?"

Jacob turned around and gazed into his daughter's face. "I do remember, Casey. I remember very well. In both cases, there was nothing their mothers could have done to prevent the situations. That's the difference, don't you see?"

"No, Dad, I don't see."

"There was no real communication between your mother and me. That's where I failed you. I should have insisted that we communicate." His voice rose. "I should have made her understand what her responsibility was to this marriage!" The next statement was almost a whisper. "If she couldn't, I should have given her an ultimatum."

Casey was floored. She couldn't find words to refute him. She simply watched him pace back and forth, anger exuding from his expression, from every step and from every movement of his hands.

Finally, Casey said the only thing that came to mind. "Dad, you seem angrier now that I'm safe than when I wasn't."

Jacob stopped in front of her, his face distorted with emotion. "I didn't realize it, but it was *me* I was angry at all along. Nick Carter just got in the way."

Chapter Thirty-Four

Vitality shows not only the ability to
persist, but the ability to start over.
—F. Scott Fitzgerald

*D*uring the week, Casey tried to reach her father on the phone, but he was never home. She tried to catch him at work, but he wasn't there when she called. Finally, she reached him on his cell phone. He had thrown himself into his work with a vengeance. When she wanted to go over and fix dinner for him, he refused, telling her he had to work late.

A loneliness descended upon her unlike anything she had experienced. Her dad wasn't there for her anymore and Tiffany was still out of town. The only one she wanted to talk to was Nan and she was ambivalent about whether she should.

Friday evening, she listlessly opened a can of vegetable soup for supper, wondering if she could get it down. Her appetite was suffering. She knew that she should work harder at eating better. "Maybe tomorrow I'll go to the store and get some vegetables and fruit or something," she murmured aloud.

She had just finished the soup and put the rest in the refrigerator when the doorbell rang. Her heart lifted, hoping it was her dad. Opening the door, she blinked in disbelief. Standing there in jeans and a black knit shirt with a big smile on his face was Syrus. "Syrus! I . . . I never expected to see you again. What are you doing here?"

"I came to see you. Can I take you for a ride in my blue jitney?"

"I, uh . . . guess so. Where are we going?" she asked, still dazed at his sudden appearance.

"Wait and see."

"Just a minute." She went in, grabbed her house keys, and tried to keep up with Syrus' long strides to the pickup.

As they drove off, Casey asked, "Did you see your parents?"

"Yes, I did."

"And how are they?"

"Very well, thank you. How have you been, Casey?" he asked, taking his eyes off the road a moment to study her. "You look like you've lost weight."

"I haven't had much of an appetite."

"Oh? What's the matter?"

"It's your fault, Syrus," she said, a wry expression on her face. "Mr. Waukman is so easy to get along with. He doesn't ruffle my feathers in the least."

Syrus glanced at her, smiling, "And?"

"And I've . . . uh, I don't know, I've been a little down. I suppose it's a letdown from all the stress I've been under. I'm sure I'll soon be back to normal."

"How's your video project coming?"

"I haven't had the desire to work on it for a while."

"And it's my fault you're depressed?"

"Yes," she quipped. "My life was rather dull. I didn't know it until you came along and then left. Now it's dull again."

Syrus laughed. "Was that a compliment or a complaint?"

"I don't really know. Has the Bureau given you another assignment?"

"Not yet. I told them I need a vacation. However, I'm kind of on an errand for Robert Welles today. I've been told to deliver you a message."

"Oh? What?"

"I'll tell you later."

It wasn't until Syrus turned onto Baseline Road that Casey realized where he was going. "Why are you taking me to South Mountain?"

"Isn't that where you like to go?"

"Not lately, no. In fact, I'm not in the mood to go nature walking."

"Where's the Casey who risked her life to do that very thing?"

"I wish I knew," she replied wistfully.

Reaching the park, Syrus drove until he found the trailhead that led them to Casey's favorite path. Parking, he turned off the motor. "Here we are, sprite."

"And why that silly nickname?"

Syrus turned toward her, fingered her short hair. "I have no idea. It just seems to fit you." He got out, went around, and opened her door. "Come on, let's go."

"I told you I'm not interested, Syrus."

"If you don't come, I'll carry you," he threatened, grinning.

"Don't you dare. What's the point of all this anyway? You're just delivering a message."

Syrus held out his hand. "As much as I like this blue relic, I don't want to deliver the message inside it. Please, Casey, come with me."

Through clenched teeth, she said, "All right," but refused his hand.

He led her into the desert a few yards and, with a sweep of his hand, invited her to sit down on the rock they had sat on before.

Casey did so. "As I said before, what's the point of all this?"

"No point really. I've simply begun to like the desert and since you do also, I thought it would be nice to come out and see what it was like on a June evening."

Casey folded her arms. "All right, what's the message?"

"Your marriage has been annulled."

"It has?" she asked, momentarily dazed. Recovering, she added, "I'm surprised. Knowing how long it takes the FBI to do anything, I thought it would be another three years."

"You sound ungrateful, Casey. It took a lot of doing to get it done as fast as they did. They felt they owed it to you."

"I'm sorry. I am grateful, but—as I think about it, they needn't have hurried so fast. I won't be marrying again."

Syrus laughed. "Now that's a joke."

"Why is it a joke?"

"I've noticed the guys at Hartner and Hart standing in line. I'm sure that one of these days someone will come along who'll put up with you."

"Thanks a lot," she retorted. She paused, thinking of her new status. "I find I don't feel any different. But I'll certainly be glad to change my name back to Jacobson."

"That's already been taken care of. You'll just have to put the change of name on all your records, checkbook, and so forth, and sign some papers before a notary."

Casey thought about it a moment, and then her face lit up. "Casey Jacobson. Oh, Syrus! That does sound good. You know, for some reason that lifts something from my shoulders. That part of my life will be as if it had never happened—almost. Though hopefully what I learned from it all will remain, and of course my leg will be a reminder."

"I'm glad that lifted your spirits."

"Thank you for telling me out here in the desert instead of at my little house. It means much more. The desert is more of a home to me than inside those four walls."

"You're welcome. It was for selfish reasons also."

"Oh look, Syrus, there's a black phoebe in that paloverde tree. Sh, listen."

Together they listened and heard its four-syllable song, an ascending *pee-wee* followed by a descending *pee-wee*.

"Nice. Not only are you an expert on desert flora," Syrus said, "but you know birds and their songs. I'm impressed."

"You are? I don't mind saying that it's very flattering to impress a man who's an expert on so many things."

Syrus, seeing the admiration in her eyes, flushed from his neck up. "How about walking down the path again?" he said quickly.

They strolled along, feeling more relaxed with each other. Syrus, because he wasn't alone with a married woman, Casey, because Nick was now out of her life completely. No longer did she have to carry the taint of his name.

Syrus reached for Casey's hand as they walked, but she pulled it away.

"What's the matter?"

"I would rather you didn't hold my hand."

"Why?"

"Because it feels too familiar. I don't know you. Even though I know more about you, you're still an enigma to me."

"How about holding onto my arm then?"

"Thank you," she smiled up at him. "You're quite thoughtful for being such a tough boss."

The corners of his mouth twitched. "Thanks."

"Have you ever seen the desert at sunset?"

"Only from the city."

"Would you like to see it?"

"I sure would."

Returning to the truck after their trek, Syrus put the tail gate down, lifted Casey up, and sat her on the back end.

"Thank you," she responded in surprise.

He went to the cab and came back with a jug of water, cups, and a bag of grapes. "Would you like some?"

"Yes! I'm so thirsty, I could drink from a cactus. And those grapes look really good."

Pleased, Syrus sat beside her and they ate while waiting for the sunset.

"I have all the legal papers for you to sign concerning your annulment and change of name. I forgot to bring them with me. I'll bring them to you Monday night. Are you free?"

"For that I'll make time."

"How about dinner?"

"I'd love it."

Chapter Thirty-Five

Courage does not follow rutted pathways.
—William J. Bennett

Sunday afternoon, Casey went over to her dad's house. *Surely he won't be working today.* Her spirits were up and it felt good. She hoped she could lift her Dad's gloom with the good news Syrus brought her.

As usual, she rang the bell before entering. She was surprised to see her dad, unshaven, lying on the couch watching a football game.

"Well, it looks like you haven't shaved for days, Dad."

Jacob sat up. "Hi, Case, what are you doing here?"

"I've come with some good news."

"Sit down and tell me," he said without enthusiasm.

"You don't sound like you want to hear it."

"I do, Casey. I just have a headache."

"Can I get you some aspirin?"

"I just took some, thanks."

"Dad, Syrus is back in town. He came over to my house, whisked me off to the desert to give me a message from Robert Welles."

"Oh?" Jacob queried, showing a bit more life.

"It's over, Dad. I'm free!" At his questioning look she added, "My marriage has been annulled."

Casey was relieved to see a smile cross his face.

"Am I happy to hear that." He shook his head as if trying to believe it. "They did it unbelievably fast."

"And they also arranged legally for my name to be changed back to Jacobson. I'm Casey Jacobson again—almost. I just have to sign some papers."

Jacob's eyes were moist. Casey hugged him, tears in her own. She had a little of her dad back. "That chapter is closed. It will be as if it had never happened. All my leg will do is remind me of the lessons I've learned from the tragedy, not the tragedy itself."

Jacob held his daughter tightly, overcome with gratitude that she was determined to forget and go on with her life.

Casey looked into her father's face. "Can you do that too, Dad?"

"Do what?"

"Close the chapter?"

"Tell me how I can close the chapter. Wait until you're a parent, Casey, and you'll understand."

"I know I don't understand completely and won't until I'm a mother, but I do think you could put the past behind you and make the best of life ahead."

He got up and walked around, shaking his head. "I can't. My mistakes of the past loom too big. I forgot to say when we last talked that not only did I fail you, I failed your mother."

"What are you talking about?"

"Your mother's parents, as you know, put a high value on excelling in worldly things. The only praise she got was when she excelled in her singing. Since it was rare that she pleased her parents, I was happy for her. I should have tried to help her understand that she was worth much more than that."

"You did! The way you treated Mother told her that."

"She needed much more, Casey. She needed me to *tell* her more often."

"But, Dad, you did in so many ways. If you *had* told her more often, do you really think it would have made a difference? She was raised by parents who gave her the other kind of messages all her life."

"I don't know, Casey, but I should have tried harder."

"But you didn't know that. Don't we have to grow into knowledge?"

He paused. "I guess you're right, yes."

Casey breathed a sigh of relief. At last she seemed to be getting through to her dad. "And just think of all the joy Mother gave to others with her beautiful voice."

"Was it worth abandoning her daughter?"

Casey felt deflated. They were back to square one. "Then she abandoned you too, Dad."

"Of course she did. But at least I had the benefit of parents who were both there for me all my growing-up years. And because of that rearing I knew better. I should have held your mother accountable."

Jacob paced back and forth in front of his distraught daughter. "Casey, it's not a battle, it's a war! We have to fight for the hearts and souls of our children, and we can't do that in the absence of true commitment—first between husband and wife and then to the precious children we bring into this world."

Tears of helplessness flowed down Casey's cheeks. Her dad was right, but how could she convince him that he couldn't have changed her mother?

Jacob saw what he was doing to his daughter. He pulled her up and took her in his arms, rocking her back and forth. "I'm sorry, honey. I'm sorry. I've just been so terrified that you could have lost your life. Because of my blindness, you married a man who abused you and then tried to kill you, and in the process he injured you horribly. Then after we thought he was dead, he stalked you and tried to kill you again." His body shook as they clung together.

The wrenching visit with her father left Casey limp with exhaustion. In spite of all the emotion, they had come to an impasse, one that neither wanted to tackle again. While still there, she secretly searched for Nan's phone number and found it. Making an excuse to leave, she immediately picked up her cell phone in the car as she drove away.

Putting it back down, she wondered if what she was about to do was wise. But who else could she turn to? No one else could help her dad like Nan could. Picking up the phone again, she dialed. Soon she heard Nan's strong, vibrant voice.

"Nan, this is Casey."

"Casey! I'm so glad you called. For some reason I've had you on my mind. How are you?"

"Not good. I need to talk to you," she pleaded. "Could you come over to my house sometime and—"

"Say no more. Are you home?"

"Yes," she said as she drove into her garage.

"I'm on my way there now. What's your address?"

Casey gave it to her.

"I'll be there as soon as I can."

Casey watched anxiously for Nan's arrival. She opened the door as she walked up the sidewalk. "I'm so glad to see you, Nan! Dad won't be very happy about me calling you, but I have no one else to talk to about him."

"It's about your father?" Nan asked warily.

"Don't worry, I'm not trying to get you two together. I feel more hopeless about that than I ever have. I'm terribly worried about *him*."

"I don't know what I can possibly do to help, but run it by me." She looked around the small, empty front room.

"I have a couch and chair in the family room off the kitchen," Casey explained. "As you may guess, decorating isn't my priority right now." Leading Nan, she invited her to be seated.

She smiled. "This is a cute little house."

"It's only a stopgap. It has a swimming pool for me to do my water therapy."

Nan nodded. "Okay, Casey, tell me what's going on."

"Well, never in my life have I seen my father like this— even when Mother died, even when I was badly burned. He seems to have simply given up on life. Oh, he works hard and late, but he won't let me come over and fix him dinner. In fact, he finds excuses when I want to go over."

Nan was bewildered. "That certainly doesn't sound like your father. What do you think is the matter?"

"Instead of being relieved that I'm safe, that Nick is in custody, he's beating himself up for failing me, for failing Mother." She saw Nan's face change from bewilderment to thoughtful.

"Syrus came to see me yesterday with a message from Robert Welles. My marriage has been annulled and my name has legally been changed back to Jacobson."

Nan let out a big sigh. "Oh! What a relief that must be for you, Casey."

"It is. I feel like I have a new start in life. But what concerns me is I went over and told Dad the good news this afternoon, hoping it would make a difference. He was happy about it, but it didn't lift his spirits in the least. In fact, when I went to see him a week ago last Friday, he said something I've never heard him say. He said that all along, his anger was at *himself,* that Nick just got in the way."

"Really?" Nan asked, surprised. After a lengthy silence, she spoke. "I've tried to think what I can possibly do to help and I can't think of a thing."

Tears welled up in Casey's eyes. "I don't know what you can do either, Nan, but will you go over and see him? Try to talk with him?"

Nan bit her lip and looked away from those tearful eyes. Collecting her thoughts, she gazed back into Casey's troubled face. "Casey, pain is something we must bear ourselves. Much of the work of healing is done alone, inside the heart.

"When you were in the hospital trying to heal physically and emotionally, your father was by your side praying for you, giving you love, sympathy, and encouragement, but it was *your* path to walk. No one else could walk it for you. No doubt you prayed constantly for courage and patience to endure, and received spiritual help. But in the end, I've found that healing is a solitary journey."

"But Dad has always faced his pain in solitude."

"Yes, he has. He's faced it, grappled with it, and found solutions, but it sounds like he's going through another dimension of pain he hadn't faced, until now. It's his to carry and deal with, no one can carry it for him—as much as you and I would like to."

Quietly she continued. "Christ, on a much grander scale, bore his suffering alone. There comes a time in each life, I believe, when we must follow his example and prayerfully bear our suffering alone. As someone said, it purifies our hearts, expands our souls, and invites humility."

Casey studied Nan's compassionate face. "It sounds like you're the voice of experience, that you've had more to bear than I realized."

"Hasn't everyone? Trials come to everyone all through life."

"But maybe, just maybe Dad's suffering over my accident and his marriage is over, and this new insight into himself is only the last vestige of it. Maybe he's ready to turn his attention to his own happiness now and he doesn't realize it." She appealed earnestly, "If he is, you're the only one who can help him recognize it."

"From my experience, Casey, women always think they can help a man by telling him, questioning him, and so on. It never works unless the man asks for help. And even then it's precarious. Can you see your dad asking me for help if I went over there?"

"No—but who knows, he may be in a teachable mood when you arrive."

Nan smiled. "I'm glad you're optimistic about it. I wish I could be." She got up and stared out the window, not wanting Casey to see what a difficult thing she had asked of her—what a struggle she was having over it. She desperately wanted to help, but she hadn't been able to help herself yet. She felt weighed down trying to live life without Jake. She wasn't making much headway getting over him and she knew that going to see him would only be a painful setback.

She felt angry at Jake that he was doing this to his daughter. But was she any different? She was only thinking of her own suffering. She took a deep breath, said a quick prayer, and decided to go talk with Jake for Casey's sake. She turned to her. "All right, I'll give it a try. I'll call you or come over tonight after I talk with him and let you know the outcome."

Casey got up, went over to Nan, and hugged her, tears of gratitude filling her eyes. "Oh thank you, Nan. Thank you."

Nan returned the embrace with affection, wishing Casey were her own daughter. She already had come to care for her and knew she could love her as a daughter if just given a chance.

Chapter Thirty-Six

This above all: to thine own self be true,
And it must follow, as the night the day,
Thou canst not then be false to any man.
—William Shakespeare

an rang Jacob's doorbell and waited nervously. She waited and waited. *Maybe he isn't home. Or maybe he's in the backyard.* She rang the bell again—and again.

The door suddenly opened and an impatient, unshaven man glowered at her. "Oh, it's you, Nan. I didn't answer the door because I don't want to see anyone."

Nan couldn't utter a word. All she could do was stare at the stranger before her. He had several days' growth of dark beard covering his face. His eyes were dull and lifeless, bordered underneath by dark circles and above by hooded brows.

"Why are you here?" he asked, his voice flat.

"I came to see how you were."

"Why?"

"May I come in, Jake?"

"I'm not good company, Nan."

"I can see that, but I'd still like to come in. May I?"

He stepped aside for her to enter. He led her into the family room.

She sat in one of the chairs and waited for him to sit, but he remained standing.

"Please sit down, Jake. I only want to talk to you for a minute."

"Why? You broke our engagement." After a fraction of a pause, he added, "And rightly so."

"My visit has nothing to do with us, Jake. Our relationship is over."

"So why are you here?"

"Casey called me, terribly worried about you. She literally begged me to come and see you. I told her I didn't think I could do a thing to help, but after arguing with myself I told her I would at least come over and talk to you."

He glowered and his voice rose. "She shouldn't have called you. As you said, there isn't a thing you can do to help. I think it's best you leave."

"Not until you take off your shirt."

Jake stared at her, stupefied. "What?"

"Take off your shirt. I want to see the bleeding welts on your back where you've been beating yourself up."

"Oh," he mumbled, a twinge of a smile on his face. He sat down and looked at her. "So?"

"So stop."

"It's none of your concern, Nan."

"It is my concern!" she stated angrily. "*You* brought me into your lives. I didn't ask to be brought in. I've come to care for both you and Casey, so it is my concern—whether you like it or not."

"Whew!" he muttered. "I've never seen you angry." He heaved a sigh and stared at the floor. "Okay, what's on your mind?"

"Why is it you think you should be perfect?"

"I'm far from it."

"And that's why you're depressed. Try as you would to be the perfect husband, the perfect father, you found out you're human—like the rest of us mere mortals. You found out that you made mistakes, just like the rest of us. Whoop-de-do!"

He glared at her. "You can twist the knife, I see."

"No, it's you who's twisting the knife, Jake, tearing your heart out with it. And what for? Is it helping Casey get on with her life and be happy? Is it helping you get on with your life?"

Jake stared at the floor, his jaw rippling in silent anger.

"No it isn't," she answered for him. "It's apparent that realizing your mistakes has thrown you into depression. But while you're wallowing in a messy puddle of self-pity, your daughter can't heal from her physical injuries or her emotional wounds." Nan stood up and started to leave, stopping long enough to add one more thing. "I thought you loved your daughter more than that. Good-bye, Jake." She walked quickly toward the front door. Before she reached it, Jake's hand gripped her arm painfully.

"And who do you think you are to make judgments like that?"

"They're not judgments, they're facts—unless you tell me differently."

"You haven't given me a chance to tell you anything," he stated bitterly.

"Then tell me, Jake. I'm all ears."

He grabbed her by the hand and pulled her back into the family room, grasped her upper arms and firmly pushed her into a chair.

Jacob paced a moment and then emptied his soul—everything he had said to Casey and more. When he was through, he sat down on the couch, perspiring and exhausted, having never in his life expressed his inner feelings like that. Chagrined that he felt the need to put himself in a better light with Nan, he waited for a response from her.

Nan smiled. "Feel better now?"

"I just poured out my soul to you, Nan—and you take it lightly?"

"No. I'm flattered you could share that with me. But as I asked before. Are you feeling better now?"

"Well, hell, how do I know!" he exclaimed, getting up and storming around the room.

"Are you hungry?"

"What!"

"Are you hungry?"

Jacob stared at her, trying to comprehend the question. Then to his amazement, all the anger seeped out of him like the air from a punctured balloon. "As a matter of fact I am. I don't think I've remembered to eat for days."

"If you'll go shave off that scraggly beard, I'll take you out for a good, filling meal."

Running a hand through his hair and then over the stubble on his face, he gazed at her for several moments. Slowly, a small devilish smile appeared on his lips, and before she could react, he was pulling her up by the shoulders. "Not before you get the *benefit* of the scraggly beard." He leaned down and kissed her roughly and then tenderly and affectionately. "Thank you," he whispered in her ear. "Wait here. I'll be right back."

Nan watched him leave, her mouth open in astonishment, her heart beating out of control.

Jacob couldn't remember when he had felt so relaxed. He and Nan had finished a steak dinner and were lingering over a piece of apple pie as they bantered back and forth.

Nan pushed her plate aside. "I'm afraid I can't eat another bite. You want to finish my pie?"

"No thanks," he said, finishing his last bite. "I'm full as a tick on a woolly sheep." He gazed into her large gray eyes and after a long pause, he smiled. "Thank you for daring to go into the lion's den tonight and retrieve me."

"You're welcome," she said softly. "I'm still a little astounded that I was able to tame the king of the jungle."

"You did more than that," he said, reaching for one of her hands and holding it in both of his. "You were able to help me begin putting things into perspective." He swallowed hard, his eyes anxious. "I need you, Nan. Can we see each other? I believe I can make some progress now."

Nan gazed at him, trying to discern her feelings. She looked down, fingering a crumb. "You used unfair tactics when you kissed me tonight, Jake."

He grinned. "All's fair in love and war, they say." When Nan didn't smile, he sobered. "You didn't answer my question."

"I don't know, Jake."

Jacob's face turned reflective. "One thing is clear. My problem seems to have had layers—you know, like an onion. The first layer was my unsatisfying marriage. When I successfully peeled that away, I found the second layer was thicker—anger and hate toward Nick Carter. When that layer literally dissipated, I was surprised to see another layer, a third layer, more devastating than the other two—my feeling of being a failure as a husband and as a father. Nan, you helped me to see what it really is, or was—an *obstacle*. That's what has been bothering me all along, what has been holding *us* back." He smiled. "I wonder how long it would have taken me to see it if you hadn't asked me to take off my shirt."

Nan smiled.

Encouraged, he continued. "My failures have been plaguing me for some time, and even though I went over them with Casey and again with you, I didn't see the main problem,—pride that I couldn't be the perfect father and the perfect husband, that no matter how I tried, I still made mistakes, serious mistakes that may have been the cause of my daughter's tragedy—but then—maybe not. I really don't know for sure whether or not she would have married Nick under different circumstances."

Jacob's eyes stared past her, far away. "My mother used to tell me that men were obtuse much of the time. I didn't know what she meant." He focused back on Nan. "I do now. I was painfully aware of my failures, but I still didn't want to really accept my culpability in Casey's situation. I had tried too hard to be both mother and father, priding myself that I could do it. When my anger and hate toward Nick miraculously left me, the fact that I wasn't as successful as I had planned to be as a 'single' parent—realizing that it takes both parents—hit me between the eyes. My pride was bruised. It took you to help me see what was right in my face, in fact what was actually punching me in the nose."

Nan smiled at his choice of words and sighed with relief.

"You believe me then?" he asked hopeful.

"Yes, but I can't help you heal the wounds caused by your mistakes or help you mend your torn pride, Jake. You have to do that yourself."

"No. I don't have to do it myself." Jacob swallowed back acute emotion. "I believe Christ atoned for our sins. Didn't he?"

Nan was so deeply moved she was unable to speak. She could only nod.

"Can we see each other?" he asked, his eyes beseeching hers.

Nan looked away.

Fear knifed through him. "Discovering the cause of my problem is fifty percent of the battle isn't it?"

"Yes, it is, Jake."

"Then, will you let me see you while I fight the rest of the battle?"

Nan's sigh was ragged as she looked away again.

Jacob's chest heaved with fear. All around them people at other tables were eating and laughing, and dishes were clinking as waiters moved about clearing tables, but he heard nothing—only the silence between them.

Finally, Jacob, his voice husky with emotion, spoke. "I'm terrified that I've killed your love after all I've put you through. If I have, I'll go on somehow, but if you feel any vestige of love for me, please, at the risk of sounding like a broken record, let me see you."

Nan's earnest eyes gazed into his. "It would be easier if you had killed my love." A small smile graced her lips and eyes. "My love is pretty tough to kill."

Jacob allowed himself a tentative feeling of hope as he held his breath, waiting for the rest of what Nan had to say.

"I'm a little gun-shy. I gave you my heart completely, Jake. I can't do that again until I'm sure you're really ready to make a commitment." She took in a deep breath. "I think we should spend time together now, for both our sakes, so we can be sure."

Relief rushed across Jacob's features. His throat constricting, he took Nan's hand in his and kissed it. "Thank you, thank you, my beautiful biligaana."

When Jacob looked up, Nan saw him blinking back tears. Her heart swelled with tenderness. "Now—why don't we go over to Casey's and let her see that your spirits are better."

Chapter Thirty-Seven

We find rocks in our packs because they're
standard equipment on hero journeys.
—Dean Black

Monday morning, the world looked considerably brighter to Casey. It was amazing to see the change in her dad when he and Nan came over the night before. From what her dad said, Nan had agreed to see him. She prayed that this time they could make their relationship succeed.

As she was about to leave for the studio, the phone rang.

"Hey, Casey, this is Syrus."

"Oh, hi." The world turned even brighter.

"Can we still get together late this afternoon so you can sign those annulment papers?"

"Yes."

"How about four o'clock? Then how about dinner afterward?"

"Yes to both. Pick me up at home. I'll see you then."

Casey disconnected, smiling. She had something to look forward to. Even if it was only business, it was with Syrus—her fascinating nemesis, and her friend.

On the way to the restaurant, Casey hugged the manila envelope with the precious papers in it, feeling tangible relief. "Thank you, Syrus, for saving my life and then giving it back to me."

"I'm afraid I can't take all the credit. However, I do deserve some of it," He grinned. "After all, I had to hear you complain enough about wanting your life back."

"Yeah, I guess you did. But the FBI deserved a bit of harassing for not letting me in on the truth sooner."

"And I had to take the brunt of your feistiness for the whole Bureau."

"So?"

"So, I think you should make it up to me."

"And how can I do that?"

"Well," he drawled, "I have to be in town for a couple of weeks doing something for the FBI on another case. I'd like to see you while I'm here."

Casey was silent, thinking.

"Is there a problem with that?"

"Well, maybe. I'm not quite sure why you want to see me."

"I'm not sure either." He grinned. "Maybe to do you a favor by letting you see the real Syrus, or maybe it's because I find you interesting to be around."

"The word 'maybe' isn't very flattering, Syrus."

"I don't flatter. I say it like it is. However, I did leave out a couple of maybes."

"All right, I'll see you—since you're requesting it so nicely," she replied with sarcasm.

Syrus chuckled and parked at Rosarita's.

During the meal, Casey asked him what he liked to do for fun, for relaxation when he wasn't working.

"Oh, let me think. I'm afraid I like to do too many things. I like to ride horses, climb mountains, swim, play basketball, you know things like that."

Casey's heart sank. Except for one, they were all things she used to love doing but couldn't anymore.

"What do you like to do, Casey, besides photograph nature?"

"Everything you mentioned but basketball. I used to be a champion tennis player, and I loved to dance."

"I've never played tennis, but I like to dance."

"I'm afraid you won't find my company satisfying, Syrus. I can't do all the physical things you like to do."

"Maybe you won't be able to do them as well, but knowing you, Casey, you'll soon be doing everything physical you want to do."

"I intend to try, of course."

"That a girl. How about tomorrow night we go dancing at this classy place I've learned about?"

"I can't dance, Syrus."

"Sure you can. Slowly, and maybe a little awkwardly, but you can."

"I don't want to."

"Wear a nice dress. I'll even put on a suit and pick you up at six. We'll eat dinner, and then we'll dance. Or dance and then eat dinner—whatever you prefer."

"I don't prefer to dance."

Ignoring her response, he asked, "Would you like some dessert?"

"No thank you."

Syrus walked Casey to her front porch. She quickly unlocked the door, stepped into the house, and slammed the door in Syrus' face. Immediately, she opened it. "Oops. I'm sorry. I seem to be in the habit of doing that. I'm surprised you're still here. If someone slammed the door in my face, I'd be gone." His silent mirth seemed to go on inordinately long.

He said at last, "But you seem to be so remorseful afterward."

"I guess you're still agitating me, Syrus. I do *not* want to go dancing."

"You've made that clear. But humor me. After all, you said I saved your life."

"Oh sure. Put me on a guilt trip."

"Whatever it takes."

Casey let out an exasperated sound. "All right, but you won't enjoy it."

"Oh, but I will. It will be an adventure."

"After all your varied adventures, you refer to dancing with me an adventure? I would call it a hazard."

Syrus laughed. "Are you going to invite me in?"

Still piqued at his insistence at making her do something she definitely did not want to do, she said, "I would, but you see there's no furniture in here."

"I guess I can take a hint. See you tomorrow night. Good night, sprite." She watched his long strides reach his pickup. He turned, waved, and grinned.

She waved back and, in spite of herself, grinned back.

Casey closed the door and went into the bedroom to change into her comfortable nightgown, still feeling disgruntled over Syrus' determination to make a display of her awkwardness. What was it going to accomplish?

Then the real question surfaced. Why did he want to see her while he was here? She couldn't read him. Was it because it was something to keep him busy in the evenings, or did he really want to be with *her?* And how did she feel about him?

Later, she lay in bed with the lights off. She thought of how happy she was to see Syrus and how much she enjoyed being with him. Still, something was giving her a sense of unrest. She tried to understand what it was, but her mind wouldn't focus and soon she drifted off to sleep.

Frustrated, Casey looked through her wardrobe. Everything she owned was out of style. Though she doubted that Syrus was the type of man who would care one way or another, she got in the car and headed for a department store to see if she could find something new that wouldn't rub on her leg. She was delighted to find just what she wanted. Arriving home early enough to rest, she was able to take her time showering and getting ready for the evening.

Despite her dread of dancing, she was excited to put on her new outfit. It was an ankle-length chiffon A-line skirt with large red and black flowers on a white background with an attached white slip. Next she tucked in the white silk blouse. She complimented the ensemble with delicate dangling black earrings. When she put on black heels, she immediately felt the muscles in her leg complain, but since Syrus was so tall she kept them on.

She looked into the mirror at the finished product and was pleased by the image that gazed back at her. The doorbell rang. Quickly spraying on her favorite perfume, she grabbed a clutch purse and went to the door.

Casey smiled at Syrus, knowing how he preferred casual—very casual. "Well, look at you—Mr. Casual, all dressed up in a striking charcoal suit."

He looked pleased. "Thank you, ma'am. And might I add you look—uh—you know, I'm not used to complimenting women. In fact, I'm not used to socializing with them. I'm feeling a little awkward, but here goes." He cleared his throat. "You look beautiful."

"Thank you, Syrus. That was actually quite smooth."

"Thanks." He grinned and held out his arm. "Shall we?"

"Reluctantly, yes."

The Fountain Hills Terrace had an elegant ambience. The plush carpets, soft lights, waiters in tuxedos moving quietly about, and violins playing relaxed Casey. She looked across the table at the still mysterious Syrus Rothman, wanting to understand him, know him better. "This is a lovely place. I've never been here."

His intense gaze softened when he smiled. *As usual, his smile changes his face from interesting to almost handsome,* she thought.

A waiter appeared. "Would you like cocktails?"

"Would you like one, Casey?"

"No thank you."

"We wouldn't care for one, thank you," Syrus said.

After they ordered, they visited, feeling comfortable in each other's presence. Casey found the food delicious. "This is really great. My cupboards are bare and I only had canned vegetable soup last night."

"I'm glad you like it. I think it's great too, even though I get tired of eating out. I can't cook a lick. My mom is worried. She say's I'm too skinny. You know—a little like Ichabod Crane, I believe you said."

Casey laughed. "Maybe I could fatten you up. I'm really quite a good cook. I've had a lot of practice because I had to relieve Dad now and then."

"So . . . do I hear an invitation?"

"No."

"That's all the gratitude I get?"

"I don't know where you're coming from, Syrus, or why you want to take me out, so until I do, you don't get an invitation."

"My mother wants to meet you."

"Why?" It came out more bluntly than Casey intended.

"That's what I asked *her.*"

"And what did she say?"

"She said, 'because I've never seen you so frustrated over a woman.'"

Casey's brows rose in surprise.

Syrus shrugged his shoulders. "You figure it out."

"You know her. I don't."

"I know her, but I don't understand her. Does a man ever understand a woman?"

"My dad is clueless. Nick Carter only cared about himself. Judging by those two, I would say women are puzzling to men."

Syrus nodded vigorously.

By the time they had finished their meal, the orchestra was playing dance music. Syrus shoved his chair back, stood, and held out his hand. "How about it, sprite, may I have this dance?"

"Oh, Syrus. I was hoping you'd changed your mind."

"Nope."

She knew he would accept no if she insisted, but she realized deep down she yearned to try—to see if she possibly could do what once came so easily to her. She sighed and took his hand.

He led her to the dance floor. "It's a slow one, so we'll let your leg guide us." Syrus took her in his arms and held her tightly, hoping to take a little of the weight off her bad leg. He began moving very slowly, too slowly for the beat of the music. Casey followed, a little clumsily, but kept on, using the injured muscles in a way she hadn't since the accident.

Syrus smiled down at her. "You're doing great."

"I used to be dancer," she murmured miserably.

"You still are."

As they continued, she relaxed, allowing her leg to move easier, and she began to believe Syrus.

He pulled her closer, bent his head until his cheek pressed against her forehead. Casey felt a quiver of excitement. The music stirred her almost forgotten hope of true love and romance, carrying her out of the world to a beautiful and magic place where dreams come true. In Syrus' arms she didn't feel the weakness of her leg, nor did she feel the growing strain. The flow of the melody filled her heart, surged through every muscle, and revived all her forgotten and tender aspirations.

Slowly the music ended, thrusting Casey back to reality and to the fiercely protesting muscles of her leg. "I think I need to sit down now, Syrus. My muscles aren't used to dancing and—"

"Of course," he said quickly. "That's to be expected." He held out his arm for her lean on as they walked back to their table.

"Thank you," she said, her voice breathy from the unaccustomed exertion. "Also, I haven't worn high heels since before the accident."

"Why did you wear them tonight?"

"Because you're so tall."

"Oh. Thank you." He smiled. "They made it easier to dance closer."

She sank onto the chair, grateful for the rest, and then slipped off her shoes and sighed.

"It will get easier and easier," Syrus said.

"I'm determined to be able to hike the mountains with my father again."

"Good girl," he said, his eyes warm and admiring. "Then when you can hike, you can dance. Or," he began with a smile in his eyes, "when you can dance, you can hike."

She gave him a grateful smile. Syrus' encouragement and his certainty that she could accomplish these goals gave her hope. Then—like a cork screw—something of a disquieting nature twisted inside her. She rubbed her brows in confusion.

"What is it, Casey?"

"I don't know."

"Why don't I take you home now?"

"Yes. I think I'm ready. Thank you."

Gratefully slipping on her night gown and soft house-slippers, Casey went into the kitchen, put on a CD, and then sat down on the couch, her legs resting on it. Romantic tunes filled the room as she mused over the evening with Syrus.

On the doorstep, Syrus had taken her hands in his and gazed at her. In the moonlight, his dark eyes had an unsettling affect upon her. He thanked her for being a good sport then asked her to go with him the next morning for a tour and lunch on the Dolly Steamboat. He explained they would have to leave early because it would take some time to get to Apache Junction and then the extra fifteen or so miles northeast to Canyon Lake. She had stuttered an acceptance, thanked her, and went in, the uneasy feeling even stronger.

Unconsciously, she gently rubbed the sore and newly used

muscles of her leg. Suddenly, the reason for the uneasy and disquieting feelings that had been troubling her flashed into her mind. Her leg! Of course. For obvious reasons, she hadn't thought of Syrus as a possible suitor, and consequently the promise she had made herself to show her leg right away to any man who asked her out hadn't entered her mind—until now. After her experience with Craig, she had kept that promise and it had been disastrous.

She had a difficult time classifying Syrus as a suitor. If he were, could she show him her leg? She shuddered at the thought that he might react as the others did.

Examining her feelings, she realized that outside her father, she respected and admired Syrus more than any man she had ever known. The thought that he would be repulsed by her leg was so painful she reluctantly decided that after tomorrow she couldn't see him anymore—unless all he wanted was friendship. She would find out tomorrow one way or another. She got up, went to the CD player, turned it off, and returned to the chair. Turning on the television, she tried to get engrossed in a movie.

Chapter Thirty-Eight

All things of enduring worth lie
just beyond the last inch.
—Dean Black

When Syrus picked Casey up early the next morning, the first thing he said was, "How's your leg this morning?"

"A little sore." Her smile was tinged with chagrin. "As much as I hate to admit it, you were right to insist I try dancing. It was actually fun and it gave me hope that I could dance again."

"Good! That's exactly what I hoped it would do."

On the way, Casey was silent, trying to think how she could find out Syrus' reason for taking her out, without sounding presumptuous.

"Hey, you're quiet this morning, sprite. What's up?"

"Don't you have to work during the day?" she asked, changing the subject.

"Most of the time but not today," he grinned. "More important things to do."

"Why do you want to go on the Dolly Steamboat?"

"I've become quite intrigued with Arizona. He picked up a brochure on the seat beside him. "It says here they give the history of the Apache Trail, Canyon Lake, the legend and lore of the Superstition Mountain and the Lost Dutchman mine. It also says they give some information on the flora and fauna of the lower Sonora desert."

"Oh."

"Have you been on the boat?"

"No. It should be interesting," she replied lamely, still confused about his motives.

"Where's your usual enthusiasm, Casey?"

"I am enthused. I love the desert," she said brightly. "I'm glad you're learning to like it."

At last they reached Canyon Lake. The steamboat was a replica of the classic stern-wheeler from America's river boat era. During the ninety-minute tour, cruising the secluded waterways, Syrus listened, intrigued, but Casey was still brooding over her dilemma.

The cruise fed them a lunch of hamburgers and baked beans. Casey tried to put aside her quandary while she and Syrus visited.

"Since you can do about anything, Syrus, where would you like to live?"

"Where would you?"

"I asked you first."

"I think I would be happy anywhere as long as I could travel now and then. I've had to travel a lot in my position and have come to appreciate a great many places."

"Do you think you'll ever marry, Syrus?" The minute it slipped out, she wished she could take it back.

The question took him by surprise. "Why do you ask?"

"Just curious is all. You were the subject of conversation at Hartner and Hart every now and again. Many of the women wondered if you were as you appeared—a confirmed bachelor."

"Well, I'll be," he mused. "Why would they wonder that?"

"Why wouldn't they?"

"Well—to quote Abraham Lincoln when someone called him two-faced, 'Would I be wearing this one if I had another one?'"

Casey doubled over with laughter. Then, with a smile, she wondered what Syrus would say if she told him that the women at work found his face intriguing.

It was apparent that Syrus was completely oblivious of what

she was hinting at so she had no other alternative but to not see him anymore. And this suddenly turned her melancholy.

Syrus scrutinized her. "You seem to be a bundle of moods today, Casey. What's on your mind?"

"What's on yours?"

"I asked you first." He grinned.

"You wouldn't understand if I told you."

"Try me."

Casey decided to go ahead and get it over with. "Well, I guess I've been a little down because I can't spend any more time with you while you're here. I have too much to do."

"That doesn't make sense, Casey. Surely, you're free in the evening."

"No."

His eyes changed into the old familiar expression, piercing and intimidating.

"Don't look at me like that, Syrus. You're not my boss anymore."

"Why aren't you free in the evenings? Are you dating someone?"

"Maybe."

"What kind of an answer is that?"

"It means I don't want to tell you one way or another."

"Why is it I feel you're being recalcitrant with me again?"

"How would I know your feelings?" she retorted flippantly.

Syrus ran a hand through his hair, puzzled. "I just remembered why I'm not married. Women are totally illogical and confusing."

The boat docked and everyone began moving toward the gangplank. Syrus drove down Highway 88 to Apache Junction, west on the Superstition Freeway, and then north on 101 to Scottsdale. During the long drive, Syrus had difficulty engaging Casey in conversation. It turned out to be spotty, desultory, and fitful.

Reaching The Cottages, Syrus parked and walked Casey to

the door. "Can I come in?" he asked in an authoritative tone.

"It think it's best you don't."

"What's going on with you, Casey? I thought we were friends."

"We are. Friends—period."

"Have I indicated anything else?"

"Yes. Last night when we were dancing."

He gazed at her with brooding eyes. His dark brows furrowed in thought for some time before he spoke. "Good-bye, Casey," he said, turning abruptly and striding quickly to his truck.

Casey stepped into the house and locked the door, feeling miserable. She went to the phone and called Nan. When she answered, Casey blurted out, "Help."

"Casey?"

"Yes, it's me, Nan."

"What's the matter?"

"I need some advice or something."

"I'll be right over. I have a date with your father for dinner at six. I'll call him and tell him to pick me up there."

"Thank you, Nan," Casey placed the phone in its stand and looked at her watch. It was 4:30. Time dragged. Restlessly, she went to the front room window and watched for her. Casey sighed with relief when at last she saw Nan coming briskly up the walk. Casey opened the door and hugged her. Soon Nan was sitting in her family room, warm and eager to help.

"What's troubling you, Casey?"

"I don't know. I'm confused about Syrus Rothman and I . . ." She couldn't go on.

"Tell me from the beginning, the middle, or wherever, just tell me what pops into your mind."

It all came out in an emotional outburst—the promise she had made to herself about showing her leg to possible suitors.

She told her about the last two evenings with Syrus and her confusion as to his intentions. "If he just wants to be friends, I won't worry about showing him my leg. If he has other intentions I'll have to."

"Are you afraid of his reaction to your leg?"

"It would be very painful if he reacted to it the way the other two did. I don't want to see him anymore because I don't know whether he just wants friendship or whether he has other intentions. I can't read him." Unexpected tears came. "What shall I do, Nan?"

Nan got up and sat beside her on the couch, hugging her tenderly. She looked into Casey's face. "How do you feel about him?"

"I don't know. All I know is he's the most fascinating man I've ever known."

"Are you falling for him, by any chance?"

"Falling in love with him?" Casey repeated, somewhat taken aback by the thought.

"Yes."

"Our relationship has been interesting to say the least,— but falling for him, I can't imagine that I am. However," she paused, reflecting, "when he held me close while dancing, I got a sensation that was a little startling."

"Are you fighting your feelings perhaps?"

Casey thought about it. "I don't know. Maybe. I don't think he's dated very much. I don't know if he knows how to let me know how he feels. I tried several times in a subtle way to get him to admit something one way or another."

"Men aren't good at subtleties."

"I know, but I'm certainly not going to ask him outright."

"I understand. I've never been able to do that either. I've been a little bolder with your father, but now it's all resting on his shoulders."

"This time I think he'll come through, Nan. You rescued him and I'll always be grateful to you for that. Now—what shall *I* do?"

"Look deep into your heart and pray. If you decide you feel something for Syrus—then be brave and take a chance. This is another time you'll have to walk the path alone. What that chance will bring I can't even guess, but it's up to you alone to find out whether or not you have the courage to take it."

Casey got up and went over to Nan. She leaned over and hugged her, blinking back tears. "Thank you. Just getting it out and talking about it with another woman helps. I don't know whether or not I'll have the courage, but I feel better."

Chapter Thirty-Nine

*Victory is sweet when two hearts
put down the arms of battle.*

very day during the following week, Nan called Casey.
As yet, she hadn't heard from Syrus and didn't know
if he was still in town. Also, she found out that Casey hadn't
made any progress learning how she felt about him. Nan wondered if one of the reasons she was having such a struggle
was because she had quit trusting men in general. And Syrus
certainly wasn't helping by disappearing.

She and Jacob had been seeing each other every minute
possible, all at Jacob's request. Every day he told her he loved
her, needed her, and missed her.

She had observed him carefully and listened to every nuance
of his voice, scrutinized his gestures and body language. Each
day he seemed a little closer to winning the battle.

With his peace came hers, but still she held back, waiting. One day, she asked him, "How will I know when you've
accepted the fact that you weren't the perfect husband and
father you wanted to be—that you've forgiven yourself?"

He replied, smiling, his chestnut eyes warm and compel-
ling, "When I ask you to marry me."

Jacob was taking her to dinner and to a Tchaikovsky symphony tonight. Try as she would, her heart seemed to run
away with her as she got dressed. She felt like a high school
girl with a mad crush.

Seated by Jacob, waiting for the symphony to begin, the evening seemed lustrous to Nan. The lights glimmered. Smiles on peoples faces shone. Clothing rustled softly as people eased toward their seats. There were soft murmurs and occasional laughter. All added brightness to the glorious evening. Then she realized everything was magnified because she finally felt secure in Jacob's love, and especially secure in his desire and commitment to marry.

As the last hauntingly beautiful strains of the symphony were playing, Jacob leaned over and whispered in her ear. "I love you, my beautiful biligaana. Will you *please* marry me?"

Nan's heart catapulted with joy. She turned to him, smiled, and then kissed him on the cheek and whispered back, "Yes."

"You will?"

Unaware of the heads that turned in his direction at his loud declaration, his eyes were fastened only on the beautiful face of the woman beside him.

Nan laughed softly and whispered, "Yes, I will."

Jacob's happiness was so great he kissed her lingeringly, not caring a whit what people thought.

Later, on the steps of Nan's condo, Jacob asked her if they could set a date to be married.

"We can't set a wedding date until Casey is happier."

"What do you mean?" he asked, concerned.

She told him briefly of the struggle Casey was having.

"She went to you and not to me?"

"Yes. I'm sorry."

"Don't be. I'm elated. She needs a mother more right now than she needs a father."

Nan laughed. "Yes, my dearest, even as wonderful a father as you are, you're a bit naive at times. That's why you need me to take care of you."

"Ahhh, to be taken care of by you sounds like heaven to me." Jacob wrapped his arms around her, relief and happiness coursing through him. Some moments later, he lifted her chin and kissed her again and again as if each time was the last he would ever experience—as if his joy might be snatched away at any moment.

Monday evening, three days later, Casey finished her water therapy, showered, and ate a bite of supper. The evening ahead felt so lonely, she decided to go see her dad and Nan, hoping their happiness might rub off on her. She had never felt so despondent in her life—even more despondent than when she saw the burn and gashes on her leg for the first time. As she picked up her car keys and purse the doorbell rang.

It must be Betty, she thought. Betty had noticed her frame of mind and had been solicitous of her lately. She had even brought her a treat one night.

She opened the door and discovered Syrus standing on one foot and then the other, looking very uncomfortable. She was so overwhelmed with relief, she couldn't speak.

"Hi," he said.

"Syrus!" she gulped out. "Where have you been? Since I haven't heard from you, I assumed you left town. Come in."

"The last thing you said was you didn't want to see me anymore," he said, stepping in.

"Oh. That's right. I guess I was a little hasty," she grinned sheepishly, "because I find that I'm very glad to see you."

"You are? I didn't know what to expect." He paused and then blurted out, "The Bureau has given me another assignment."

Casey's heart dropped; nevertheless, she tried to be light. "Oh? Where will it take you?"

"I don't know yet where it will take me."

Casey bristled. "I would rather you hadn't told me you had another assignment if you can't tell me where you'll be going."

"But you asked, Casey."

"Well it's hardly the thing to do, Syrus."

"What is?"

"Come and see me and then go off to some exciting new assignment and leave me wondering where," she stated tartly.

Syrus chuckled. "Ah, the Casey I knew has come out of hiding again."

Ignoring the jibe, she moved to the window and gazed out. "Maybe I'll change jobs, maybe become a detective or something else exciting," she muttered defiantly, glancing at him out of the corner of her eye.

Syrus smiled. "Why don't you go for a ride with me, instead?"

She brightened. "Okay," she said, accompanying him out the door.

Syrus led her to the truck. As she hoisted herself up into the passenger's seat, she asked, "Where are we going?"

"Wait and see."

"Is your job here completely over?"

"Almost. What have you been doing, Casey?"

"Nothing worth talking about."

"You aren't engaged or anything?"

Casey laughed. "That will be the day."

"But you hinted you may have dates this week."

"That isn't exactly what I said, but I didn't have any dates. I scare the guys away."

When Syrus turned south, Casey asked, "Are we going to South Mountain again?"

"Yes. Do you mind?"

"Not this time. I haven't been taking pictures for a while and I've missed getting out."

Some time later, he turned off onto the familiar San Juan Road, drove a distance, and then pulled into the trailhead. "Do I have to beg you to come with me to the rock again or are you going to come willingly?"

She smiled. "I think I'll come willingly."

When they sat down on the rock, Casey remarked, "This rock is becoming quite a monument to us."

"It is to me," Syrus said with all seriousness.

Casey's brows rose. "I didn't know you were sentimental."

"Is that what it is?"

"It sounds like it."

He looked around. "The spring flowers have quit blooming, but I see a desert willow over there with its pinkish blooms."

"Why Syrus, you're beginning to know desert flora."

"I'm finding myself quite enthralled with the desert."

"Look, Syrus, there are five or six butterflies hovering over the willow flowers."

"Yes. I've learned that willow blossoms attract them."

She smiled at him. "It's gratifying to have someone here with me who appreciates all this," she said, spreading her arms wide.

He smiled back. "It's nice to appreciate it with _you._"

"Oh?"

Syrus seemed especially nervous. "That, uh . . . brings me to the new assignment Robert Welles has given me." His piercing dark eyes gazed into hers. "I had to confess to him that I failed in your case."

"What? You didn't fail, Syrus. You saved my life! And you—"

"When an agent becomes emotionally involved with someone when he's on a case, he loses his objectivity. When I knew Nick Carter had taken you into the house, I lost all my perspective as an agent. I was terrified for your safety. I wanted to rush in immediately. I was over the SWAT team, but it was one of my men who had the presence of mind to stop me so we could hear Nick's confession.

"I tried my darnedest not to let my feelings for you get out of control, Casey, but I failed."

Casey gasped. She opened her mouth to respond, but the words wouldn't come.

"I'm thirty-four, Casey. I never dreamed I would be single this long. My job has made it impossible for me to socialize with women, only deal with them in stressful circumstances.

Never once was I tempted to become anything less than objective—until the agency assigned me to you. As I said, Welles has given me another assignment. One more frightening than I've ever been on, one more fraught with danger, one that nearly paralyzes me with fear."

Casey's eyes were large and troubled. "Why are you telling me this?"

Syrus suddenly knelt before her. "Because—I was *instructed* to tell you. My new assignment is to marry you."

Casey blinked. "What did you say?"

Syrus repeated it.

Shocked, she stared at him for what seemed like an eternity to Syrus. Then came the explosion. She shot to her feet. "How dare he give you that assignment!"

Syrus took her hands and pulled her down again. "Because," he began quietly, "Welles knew I wouldn't have had the courage to attempt such a frightening step without an order from the Bureau."

"You're serious?"

"Totally."

"I never would have believed you a coward, Syrus."

"Believe it."

"Are you aware you're on your knees and talking about marriage?"

"Totally."

Wary, she asked, "Is . . . this your way of . . . proposing?"

"No."

"Then what are you doing on your knees talking about marriage?" she demanded.

"Preparing you. Will you marry me?"

The blunt question stilled her for only a moment. "Why?" Her lips pursed. "Because this is an assignment from Robert Welles?"

"No. Because I love you." He paused, searching her face for some encouragement, but he saw only wide, incredulous eyes. He continued, speaking slowly and with all the certainty of his soul. "There's no one who'll love you as I will, Casey."

Syrus anxiously watched her reaction. He was keenly aware of the tears which hovered at the corners of her eyes. He saw fear flit across her face and her struggle for words, but the words he wanted to hear didn't come—only a flustered question.

"Are your knees getting sore?"

"What?" he asked, surprised. "As a matter of fact they are. I'm kneeling on some rocks."

This sent Casey into a burst of laughter, giving her a respite from the nervousness and sudden anxiety.

Syrus grimaced and rubbed each knee but remained kneeling, waiting impatiently for her amusement to subside. "I'm not getting off my knees until you answer me, Casey."

She sobered and the anxiety returned. "I have to talk to my dad." She meant it, but she also had to have time to gather courage to show Syrus her leg.

"Why?"

"Because after choosing a man like Nick Carter, I'm not very confident in my own judgment anymore."

Syrus groaned as he stood up, rubbed his knees, and sat beside her. "Casey, I've just spent two days with your father."

"You have! He never told me."

"I asked him not to."

"Why?"

"I asked him for your hand, that's why."

She blinked in shock. "You did?" He nodded. "Oh. That was thoughtful of you."

"Thanks. But I never got the grilling from the FBI that I got from your dad."

This sent Casey into another bout of laughter. Catching her breath, she said, "Good for Dad." It was then she noticed the sweat dripping from Syrus' forehead and down his temples. Pulling a tissue from her pocket, she reached up and gently wiped his brow and then both temples.

"It's not that hot. Are you all right?"

"No. No assignment in the FBI has ever put the fear into me like this one has."

Casey was both touched and amazed. "The Syrus I knew acted as if he didn't know the word fear."

"The Syrus you knew never had this experience before. I'm terrified of your answer, Casey, but what is it?" he asked desperately.

"I said I have to talk to my dad."

Standing up, he grabbed her hand. "All right, let's go."

"Wait. It's twilight, Syrus. Isn't the desert beautiful?"

"At this moment, I don't know."

Seemingly oblivious to his response, she said, "I love the desert at twilight."

"It's nice. You wanted to see your father, so let's go." He took her hand and urged her toward the truck.

On the way to her father's house, Syrus, still nervous over what might be ahead for him, told Casey what he could about the visit with her father.

Casey's emotional state was one she had never experienced. Trying to analyze it, one thing was clear—her loneliness and her despondency were gone. And she seemed to be suspended in a state of joyous limbo, unable to focus on the why until she saw her father.

Parking in the driveway of the Jacobson home, Syrus went around and helped Casey out, took her hand as they moved toward the front door. Casey rang the doorbell and then turned the knob and found it open. She entered, and Syrus followed her to the room that he had come to know well these past two days.

Jacob and Nan looked up, their faces anxious, curious.

"Hi," Casey said.

"Hi, yourself," Jacob said. "What's up?"

"That's what I want to ask you, Dad. I hear you've been interrogating poor Syrus here."

Jacob laughed, and Syrus smiled nervously.

"I guess I was a little rough on him. As I said, what's up?"

Casey sat down in one of the chairs and Syrus seated himself in the other.

"Dad, as you may know," she began without preamble, "Syrus asked me to marry him."

"And?" her father asked.

"And I don't have any confidence in my judgment since I chose a man like Nick. I can't make a decision without your input." Turning to Syrus, she said, "Maybe you had better go in the other room. You may not want to hear what Dad has to say."

"No way, Casey. I'm staying right here. I gathered the courage to come this far, I'm sticking it out to the end."

"All right, but be prepared." Beseeching her dad with her eyes, she asked, "What do you think of Syrus, Dad?"

"What do you think of him, Casey?"

"Dad! I won't know until you tell me your feelings."

"I'm not going to say until I hear what you think of him."

The subject of the debate squirmed in his seat.

Nan smiled at father and daughter and then gave Syrus a sympathetic smile. He gratefully accepted it and gave her a weak one in return.

"Dad, how can you do this to me?" Casey could see that he wasn't going to budge, so she stared at the floor thinking. "I guess to start with, I think Syrus is brilliant."

Jacob nodded. "Okay, and?" Glancing at Syrus, he saw him run an uneasy hand through his hair.

"Well," Casey began again, not daring to look at Syrus, "he's tough. His eyes are scary. At times they look as though they could shoot lightening. He was constantly provoking me, and in turn I acted in a way you probably wouldn't approve of, Dad." She saw a smile cross her dad's face. "He said I acted like a spoiled brat." Her dad and Nan laughed. "It wasn't that funny to Syrus," she said, glancing sideways at him, only to see a smile on *his* face.

Casey rubbed her brow with her fingers, thinking. Letting her hands fall into her lap, she went on. "I'm amazed at his abilities. I admire and respect him more than any man I've known, except you, Dad."

Her father's expression was unreadable. All he said was, "And?"

She turned to Syrus. "He's hardheaded and bossy." Syrus smiled. Casey's gaze returned to her father. Her voice soft, she added, "He's kind and very thoughtful."

"What are you trying to say, Casey?" Jacob asked.

"I don't know," she said, wanting to scream, *I don't have the courage to show Syrus my leg!* Instead, she said, "Dad, you're not helping me at all."

He smiled tenderly at her. "I'm afraid you're on your own, honey. Nan and I are going out on the patio."

Puzzled at her dad, Casey watched them open the door which led to the patio, close it, and disappear. She looked at Syrus and shrugged. "Well—a lot of help Dad was."

Amused at her reaction, Syrus said, "If it helps, your dad gave me permission to ask for your hand."

Of course! He wouldn't have given Syrus permission if he didn't approve of him. Dad approves of Syrus! Now what was she supposed to do? Time had run out.

"Casey, just because you admire and respect me as you say, and because your dad gave me permission to ask you to marry me, you needn't worry. If you don't have feelings for me, we can date more, be with each other more, and see what happens. If you simply don't *want* to marry me or pursue any kind of relationship, don't let your kind heart make it difficult to tell me."

"Syrus," she began hesitantly, "I can't tell you how I feel about you because . . ."

"Go on, Casey."

"I can't. I'm afraid you don't have the corner on fear, Mr. Rothman."

Syrus' dark eyes studied her, his heart heavy, afraid of what this meant. Suddenly, without knowing why, he knew what he had to do. He got up and knelt before her.

"Let me see your leg, Casey."

Anxiety rippled through her. "Why?"

"Because I want to see what that son of a . . . gun did to you."

"Ooh, I would rather you didn't, Syrus."

"Please, Casey, show me your leg," he repeated gently.

Why do I care if he sees it? she asked herself. *I should be used to men's reactions to it.* Yet she felt paralyzed. Then Nan's words came back to her: "Be brave and take a chance." She took a deep breath to calm her pounding heart. "All right, be my guest." She pulled the loosely fitting pant leg up to her thigh and pressed her lips tightly together, waiting and watching for the usual response.

Syrus swallowed hard as he studied it up and down. Then with both hands gently took hold of her knee, bent down, and kissed it, his head remaining bowed.

Casey felt a drop of moisture on her knee. Stunned, she couldn't move for a moment. Then, with both hands, she lifted his face to hers. His eyes were glistening with tears. "Syrus," she said softly, "what . . . I don't understand."

"I'm sorry, sorry for this, for all the pain you went through and are still going through."

Casey tried to speak, but the words wouldn't come to her quivering lips. At last she was able to murmur, "Thank you, Syrus. This is—uh—astonishing and a little difficult to believe."

"Why?"

"You don't find my leg repulsive?"

"Repulsive? Casey! It's your badge of courage."

"Badge of courage? That's the last thing I expected to hear. I wasn't courageous in the hospital, Syrus, and I certainly wasn't courageous during all that stalking."

He took her face in his hands. "Of course you don't feel courageous, Casey. Only the truly courageous people don't feel they are."

"Really?"

He nodded and smiled, and began gently pulling her pant leg down.

"Wait," Casey said. She stared at the drop of moisture on her knee—*a tear of love?* she thought. Her hands flew to her face to hide the sudden flood of emotion. Her shoulders shook with sobs.

Startled, Syrus asked, "What is it, Casey?"

She couldn't answer. Still kneeling, Syrus put his arms around her and held her until she was able to stop.

Casey pulled a tissue from her pocket, wiped her eyes, and looked into Syrus' face. "You didn't know, Syrus, but I had showed my leg to two men recently and both were repulsed by it. You're the only one who . . ." The tears started all over again.

Syrus took her face in his hands and covered it with kisses, tasting the salt from the tears. "I'm so sorry, Casey."

The tears stopped abruptly. "You shouldn't be sorry, Syrus, these are tears of gratitude and . . ." She paused and gazed at Syrus for so long, he squirmed uneasily, wondering what was next.

"And what?" he asked, holding his breath.

Casey's eyes traveled over his face, stopping at his lips. His eyes had always taken center stage; consequently, she hadn't noticed before how enticing his lips were—the upper lip slightly thinner than the full lower lip. She found herself wishing he would kiss her.

Noticing his nervousness, she knew he couldn't initiate it. Impulsively, she took his face in her hands, leaned over and kissed him. He groaned, his arms reaching for her. She hadn't expected the intoxicating emotions that swelled inside her. It felt as though her heart were on fire. She pulled away, breathless.

His dark eyes smoldering, he sighed heavily. "Thank you. And?"

She looked at him, puzzled.

"I believe there was an 'and' left hanging?"

"Oh. Yes. My tears were ones of gratitude and . . . love. I think I . . . love you."

"Love? You said *love*?"

She nodded, tingling with the realization of it.

"You *think*?"

"I think I've been fighting it for a long time, Syrus. I only consciously acknowledged it today."

"But what kind of love?" he asked, still uncertain.

"The kind that tells me I want to marry you."

"It is?" he asked, his joy still tinged with incredulity.

Syrus stood up, smiled, and rubbed a knee. "It's been a hard day on bony knees."

Casey laughed and then stood and gazed up at him—into those eyes which had so intrigued her. "You really believe there's no one who'll love me as you will?"

"Absolutely," he stated with conviction.

Deeply touched, Casey believed it with all her heart. Then came the unsettling questions—the doubts. She addressed the first one. "But, Syrus, I'll hold you back. Physically I can't do all the things you love to do."

Syrus took her hand, pulled her to the couch, and held both her hands in his. "Casey, all those things take a distant second to being with you. I have no desire to do any of them without you. We'll do them together when you're able, and if by some chance you aren't able, we just won't do them."

She didn't see even a flicker of regret at having to give up any of his passions. "I believe you, but there's something even more important that causes me to hesitate."

"What?" he asked uneasily.

"You're such a brilliant man and apparently an adventuresome one. It just struck me that you might be away from home a lot, either with the Bureau or in any other job you might have. I've seen the effects of both parents not being home with the children. I was one of those children, Syrus."

Syrus smiled with relief. "Is that all? Your father covered that very thoroughly and I assured him just as thoroughly that

I feel as strongly as you both do. Remember, I had a brilliant mother who gave up her career to raise me. She got a lot of criticism from her friends and family, but she didn't waver. And I'm so grateful."

All the doubts gone, Casey allowed herself to give in to the thrill of being in love—a love so much greater than she had felt for Nick. Though she hadn't understood it then, she now realized her love for Nick was limited because Nick himself was unable to return her love—to love in the true sense.

"I'm sure that each of us could find others we could love, Casey, but I know that neither of us will be as happy with anyone else as we will be with each other."

Enthralled by the strength of this conviction and the fervent expression of love in his eyes, Casey melted into the safety of his open arms. "I'm going to have to talk with Mr. Welles," she murmured against his chest.

Syrus pulled back and looked into her face. "Why?"

"I have to thank him for putting you on my case."

"Oh," he said, a big smile creasing his face.

She smiled back and ran a hand through his dark, unruly hair. "I'll always savor those conversations we had, all those times you rankled me, all those times I made it difficult for you."

"You will?" His eyes lit up with amusement. "You could have fooled me."

"We got to know each other in a way we couldn't have otherwise."

"You're so right." He grinned. Her remarks gave him the courage to *initiate* a kiss—a long, tender, and passionate one. Afterward, they looked deeply into each other's eyes, marveling at what painful and frightening events had led them to each other.

"You're the first and only woman I have ever loved, Casey," he admitted, his voice uneven with emotion.

She looked at him with an expression of awe. "To be the only woman loved by such a remarkable and extraordinary man takes my breath away, Syrus." She paused. "At one time, I thought I knew how it felt to be in love, how it felt to be loved, but I didn't. I haven't really experienced either—until now."

Joy radiated from Syrus' smile. He wrapped Casey tightly in his arms, pressing her to his heart.

This is how Jacob and Nan found them when they slipped in from the patio. Jacob cleared his throat.

Casey and Syrus stood and smiled.

"Dad and Nan, I love Syrus. We're going to be married."

Nan rushed to hug Casey, half laughing, half crying.

Jacob gave Syrus a knowing smile and nodded his approval, but his throat constricted when he looked at his daughter. All his prayers for Casey's health and happiness seemed to have been answered at this very moment. He sent up a silent prayer of thanks. He knew without a doubt that Syrus Rothman would make Casey happy and would help her heal emotionally and physically in a way no other man could.

Father and daughter gazed at each other, too full of gratitude and happiness for mere words. Then Casey flew into her dad's outstretched arms.

Author's Note

This is a work of fiction. However, the characters of Nick and Russ are based on real individuals, and, tragically, represent a composite of many men in today's society. Though the actions and personalities of these two characters may seem unbelievable to some, they are, nevertheless, based on well-documented facts and studies.

I have researched many books and sources, but the most valuable facts have come from one particularly courageous young woman. My husband and I have been closely associated with her for more than fifteen years and have learned much from her experience of spousal abuse—verbal and emotional. Credible witnesses testify to what she has suffered and is still suffering. Through her, we have become aware of many other women who have gone through similar experiences.

The only liberty I have taken is in the nature of the wishful thinking of the heroine of the story, who resolves her feelings and her friend's problems with an abusive husband in a very unusual and unconventional way.

But of course, this—above all—is a love story.

About the Author

Alene Redd Roberts was born and raised in the small town of Monticello, Utah. One of her happiest memories as a young child, before she could read, was the daily ritual of sitting on the floor in front of the bookcase looking through books, even loving the smell of them. When she was older, reading a book was like eating candy.

At ten years old, she contracted polio and had to spend a year in the hospital. During those long months, she discovered the joy of communicating her thoughts through her letters. She wrote every day to her family, her friends, her relatives, and anyone else she could think of.

She always had a secret yearning to write, but she never thought she could until her creative writing teacher in college told her she should seriously consider writing. Though thrilled at the professor's confidence in her ability, she decided to table her desire until her children were raised.

She is the author of the popular novel *Gustavia Browne*, published by Cedar Fort. *A Tear of Love* is her eighth published book. "You're never too old to accomplish your dreams!" she says.

Alene graduated from Brigham Young University with a bachelor's degree in drama. Spending time with her husband, Elliott, is her joy. Family, friends, books, nature, and musicals are a few of her passions. She and her husband have five children, nineteen grandchildren, and nine great-grandchildren. They have lived in Arizona and Texas and now reside in Utah.